A BETTER PARADISE

VOLUME ONE:
AN AFTERMATH

DAN HOUSER

ABSURD VENTURES PRESS

ABSURD VENTURES PRESS
Distributed by Simon & Schuster

First published in the United States, 2025

First edition: October 2025

ISBN: 979-8-9929530-0-8

To find out more about the author and Absurd Ventures Press, please visit
https://www.absurdventures.com/abetterparadise/book

1st Printing

Printed in the United States of America

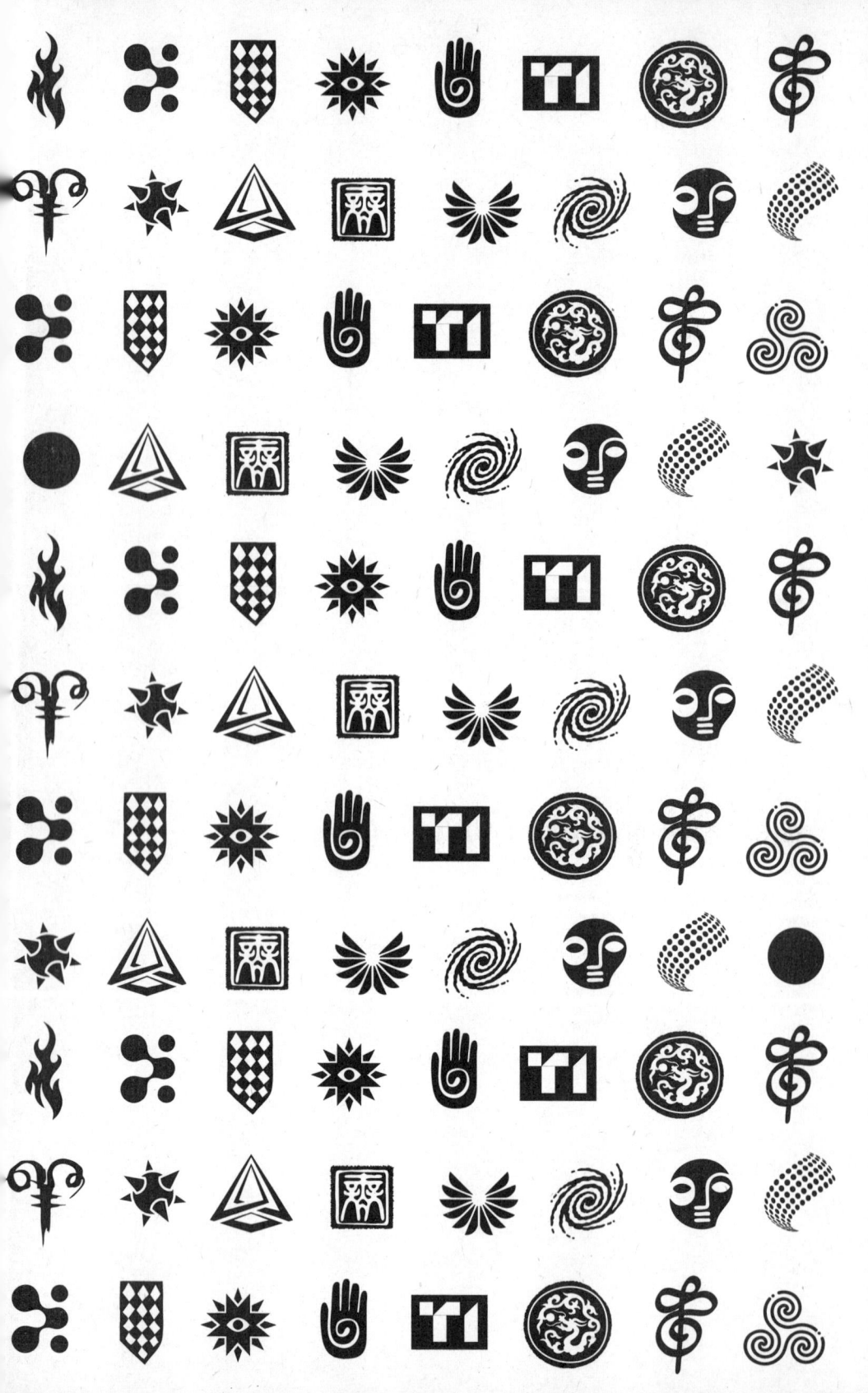

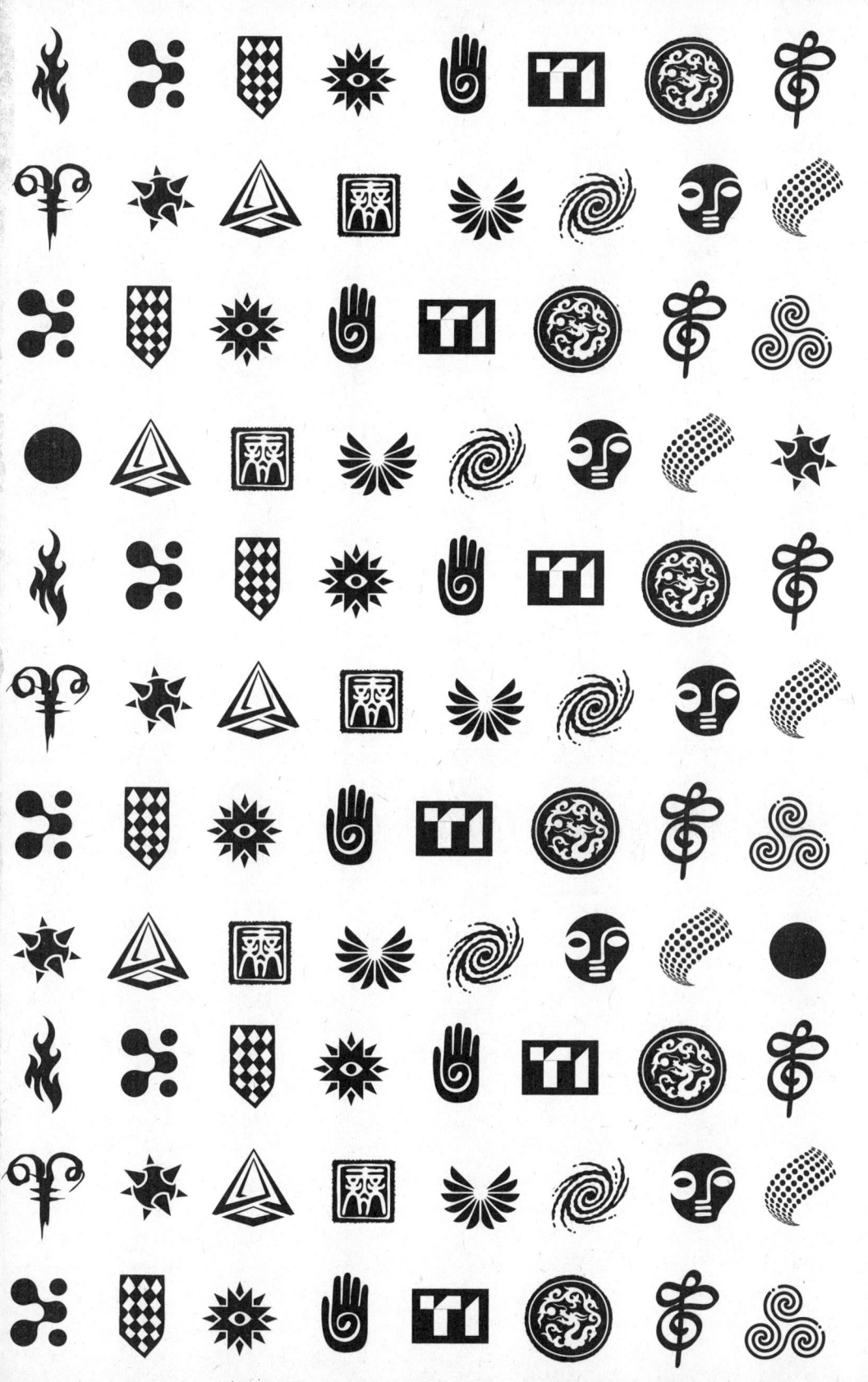

To my father, who died while I was finishing this book, and my mother who together taught me to love books.

KURT

HO CHI MINH CITY, VIETNAM
JANUARY 10, 2041

She came to me in my sleep again last night. Daisy. One of those awful dreams that is so bright and powerful and so opaque you both remember it and don't remember it at all. She came to me like déjà vu, like a buried regret. I tried to tell myself it was just this nasty, hot little room in this squalid hostel in Vietnam. But even though I was sad, I was also happy. Happy because... Well, because I still dream of her.

Nothing ever happened, and I still love her, and it is the only reality I know, and now I live in this fake reality and this man-made hell. Hardly what Mark Tyburn imagined, but I believe what he has induced. Him and the rest of us. He led but we followed. We would have followed him anywhere.

I woke up in this dirty hostel, drowning in sweat. I woke up like I used to wake up every day in the first year after everything fell apart. Exhausted. Wide awake. Soaking wet. At war, almost defeated. I woke up like the drugs had stopped working. I woke up not sure what was real and what were just things I had imagined and I had not even got the message yet.

I had not got it, but I could sense it. Or I was told to sense it. It felt like I was told to sense a message was coming. I did not want a message. I did not want a reason. I wanted to forget – I always want to forget – but this morning, as I woke, I knew forgetting would be impossible, even before the message.

I ran out of my room, past the angry, idiotic, half-blind robot that mans reception when that woman is away, and out into the city. Alone in a crowd. It's why I came to Asia – to hide from It and from myself. It has worked. The noise and heat and bustle and mania. It always works. Today, it did not work, is not working. Today, I am on fire again.

Everyone was looking at me. I was sure everything was looking at me. The man selling snakes. The woman who rents out the motorbikes. That TV. The traffic signals. Even the blind beggar and the feral, half-rabid dogs. At least that's how it felt. Hot and sweaty and cramped and noisy, like I want it, only different. Like it was all my fault. I must be going crazy. I ran until I was so exhausted I could hardly move, didn't eat at all, just iced coffees and mania and, still, I could not escape that feeling.

Eyes. Everywhere, eyes.

People, machines, screens, animals. It was as if the crabs waiting to be boiled, and the chickens in the market waiting to have their heads chopped off, even they watched me, pitied me, are watching me, are waiting for whatever is coming, know something is coming. Mark Tyburn. Daisy. That thing. The noise. Montana. I cannot stop thinking about it. I know something is coming. Mark Tyburn. Daisy Tyburn. That thing we built. What is going on? I thought I had learned to forget about all of that, and today I have forgotten how to forget. Today, I am alive. I am alive and it is awful.

Mark Tyburn – he's a genius. That's what everyone said. Well, everyone who knew about him. For an egomaniac, he kept a pretty low profile. I think he thought the self-publicity of the second generation of tech CEOs was demeaning and somehow beneath him. You know what I think? I think for someone who wanted to improve the lot of the common herd, he also hated it. He hated humanity more than he loved it. Perhaps all the most extreme fantasists are like that. All those people who want to build their own utopia. They love the idea of Heaven more than the reality of Earth. That was certainly Mark Tyburn.

Of course, he also loved to be praised. Or at least, loved to be praised by the right people. That much I do remember about him.

Mark Tyburn wanted to be known about, but only by those who knew the right sort of things. At least to begin with, he did not want to give the keynote speech, he wanted to be leading a backroom symposium on something too forward-looking, too esoteric for common idiots like you to understand. He dreamed very big, and he made you believe – well, he made me believe – made all of us stupid enough to follow him believe – that we dreamed exactly the same thing.

Of course we dreamed the same thing. We were all sociopathic altruists, deluded monarchs, or simple, plain, good, honest, vain cretins in search of a cause to die for, an audience of acolytes to worship us, and a reason to live in this mad, bad, deluded world, just like him.

Tyburn could smell the desperation on us. On all of us. That same curious cocktail of ambition, vanity, insecurity, intelligence, myopia, and pig ignorance. They're all gone now, scattered. All his idiotic disciples. All gone, and I believe most of them are dead, but none got crucified, and none fed to the lions. We all should have been.

The worst of it is, we were going to be different from all those other technology companies. Then we were just the same. Then we were worse. When I joined Tyburn Industria, I was like any normal, over-educated, under-lived twenty-seven-year-old, from everywhere and nowhere. Lost. And at one point in college, I even wanted to be a writer. How ridiculous is that? A writer? Language models ended that fantasy for me and millions of others, so instead, I decided to do a master's in Marketing, and started to sell language models. Then I sold video games, wearables, dreams – well, not quite dreams, but a digital sleep apnea machine, which is sort of the same thing, memory catchers, which never caught any memories at all, and a bunch of other failed technological journeys into the future.

To be honest, I wasn't even much of a believer in technology. No, to be quite clear – I was a sell-out. Still am. Still don't like tech, still sell myself to the highest bidder, only now I'm a hustler on the tourist trails in Asia. Then I was just desperate to be rich, as if money would fill that chasm within me. Desperate to be respected so shallow girls would grant me meaningless sex, desperate for purpose so that I would feel all that education had not been for nothing.

I bumbled around Silicon Valley and down to LA and back again for a series of start-ups and big tech "internal start-ups" (you know what I mean – the kind of well-financed divisions that try to obliterate the innovation of others without even dignifying the inventors of that innovation with a purchase and exit) and nothing had really got going, and I was holed up in San Rafael pretty broke and pretending I did not care about being broke, but was just looking for my next cause.

I was, in short, like any of two hundred thousand other young opportunists on the make, drifting in and out of the technology space and MBA programs. All trying to get rich so we did not have to worry about who we were. It all seems so long ago now. Now, I just drift around Asia, and hide. I was lost then. I'm doubly lost now.

Maybe I was always more lost than most. I was an army brat. Well, Air Force. Army brat sounds better. My mom was in the Air Force in Germany and my dad was a German teacher. I mean, he was a German dude who taught. He taught history – a bit awkward, as a German - and my mom was not even really American. She was from Grenada – joined the US military to stay in the country.

So I was part Caribbean, part German, all American. Part white, part black, no hometown, thirteen schools, parents divorced. I didn't see much of either of them and now I have not seen or spoken to them in years. No siblings. A bunch of cousins, but none like me. Lots of education. No soul at all. Didn't believe in souls, didn't believe in anything. Love was for dupes. God was for morons. Europe was dead. America was dying next. A typical American who is hardly American at all.

At one point, I wanted to be German. I tried, but that didn't work out so well. I wanted to be a street cat and, trust me, that didn't work out so well, either. Both really idiotic – you try being an amateur rapper with a degree from the University of Chicago, called Kurt, who grew up in Mannheim. You try being German with short dreads, beige skin, and a mom who fries plantains. You wouldn't fit in either. And I told myself, okay, it was because I was special or different, but most of my friends are white or black, and as American as apple pie or racism, and they feel like they do not fit in just as much as me.

I just have the excuse, but I have come to realize it's just an excuse. Nobody fits in. That's the point. Everyone has to feel lost.

I've got a couple of friends in Germany who say the same thing about Germany. My French friends feel claustrophobic. Half the Americans I know are immigrants who are almost overcome with homesickness for whatever they left, and revulsion for America and yet feel they can never go back to wherever they came from. My mother was like this.

Everyone is lost. Boys wish they were girls. Girls wish they were pretty. Grown-ups want to be children, and children want to be adopted. These days, the world is really designed by people in marketing and advertising to make you feel broken, unhappy and wrong and then convince you that we know the reasons for this unhappiness, so we can sell those reasons right back to you.

Find your excuses, excavate your personal trauma, and have it marketed back to you by people like me.

My parents tried to love me. But they hated themselves more than they could ever love anyone. The world, my world, has always, always been broken. The young wanted to be old. The old wanted to be young or they wanted to be dead. Everyone was constantly told to want whatever they do not have. So, what did I do to fix it? Me, with all this insight and all this empathy? I took up marketing tech. Selling a big load of nothingness to nobody. Usually, I was not even marketing anything real. It was mostly marketing something that didn't exist.

Not to sell things, but so that investors would believe we could help other people sell things. So investors could feel like they had picked a winner in some future horse race when it was just a foal.

My god, I felt clever. My god, I felt pointless.

And all this was after the collapse of the Western mind. That happened years ago. We all knew we had already stopped thinking and we had long since lost our dreams to the machines. Lost everything to the machines, but somehow, those of us in the know were above that. But in the years I have lost drifting around Asia, I have learned I am above nothing.

I should never have checked my messages. I should have run away. Gone to Nepal, or Mongolia, or rural China. I am so stupid. Never check the messages. Never log on, sign in, take part. Instead, check out, give up, walk away. And now, I knew it was too late.

I had not checked them in months, but today I got sloppy. I got sloppy and now I am fucked. Maybe I'm fucked and maybe I'm not. We shall see.

It was from Maria Cortez. Agent Cortez from the Cyber Security Agency in Virginia. (In case you're wondering, of course I remember her – I may be very self-important, but she is the only government agent who has ever interviewed me.)

> Hello, Kurt. I'm not sure if you remember me. My name is Maria Cortez. We met at Tyburn Utopias back in 2036. I interviewed you. I was part of the CSA team investigating AI violations at Tyburn Utopias. Kurt, I know you know how serious these things are. I really need you to get in touch with me. You've ignored all of my other attempts to reach you. This is serious, Kurt. Ravi Ghutra is dead. The official report will say suicide. You and I know that's not true. Get back to me.

That's quite a message – I knew today was going to be a strange day. I knew and yet how could I know? I knew because it wanted me to know, I suppose.

Poor Ravi.

Ravi Ghutra. A martyr. Another one. He died for Heaven. I suppose that's the best way to go, like a proper martyr. In his own way, he really was a believer. A believer in paradise. A better paradise.

It seems so silly now, after all that happened and all the things that did not happen. That we actually believed in what we were doing back in 2036 – it feels like a thousand years ago, and it's only been what? Five years? How wise I was back then, how all-knowing. How ridiculously naive I was. All those dreams I had under that silly shell of fake cynicism I wore like armor.

Of course I will not get back to her, but I wonder if now she knows about me and will be able to find me, hidden behind my layers of VPNs, and deleted accounts, and digital mirrors and illicit protocols, and stolen identities.

I was feeling watched, even before I got that message from Maria. In the past, when I felt this way, I did whatever it took to stay free. It's been the same for the past three years – maybe I just got sloppy. When I am paying attention, I throw away most phones after an hour. Sometimes I use Internet cafés; like an old-fashioned tourist, I have given up on email, social media obviously, I think carefully about where I am going to go next.

Focus hard upon it. Focus very hard, and then go somewhere else.

I pick somewhere random, a mile away, a thousand miles away. It does not matter. Then I see those eyes. I wonder if Tyburn's nano team really made that breakthrough with the implant. Are they in me? I doubt it. Tyburn was mostly bluster. Charisma, bluster, and horseshit. He wanted so much to be Prometheus, and yet, he ended up being Sisyphus, and the boulder was his own vast ego.

No, that's not fair. Mark Tyburn did not want to be a Greek myth. He was a monotheist. He wanted to be God. He wanted us all to worship him. All hail Mark!

And how I did worship him. What a fool I was.

To have worshipped a clown, to have unlocked evil, to have doomed us all. What a fool. And now this is my purgatory. I have run to the ends of the earth, and It gets there before me. In some ways, these past six years, we have lived as no one has lived since when? 1994? 2010? 2026? I do not know exactly. Before all of this began. I've been free. Detached. Not free. Tied by a thousand cords. Nobody is free from It, from any of it.

They built It. Mark and Nigel and Dave and Tadeusz. They wanted to call it ADAM. It wanted to be called NigelDave. ADAM was a ridiculous, pompous acronym and NigelDave is the name of the world's most intelligent moron. They built It and It was not what they wanted at all. Them. Not me. But I knew they were messing with fire.

I stood on the sidelines and cheered and did not stop them.

Figured out how they could hide It from the government, sell It, make us all rich – win that second great AI race when, once again, everyone got so greedy. I knew and did not stop them, even when I began to know just how insane what they were attempting was and how many risks were being taken.

Even when I could see what we were doing, I did nothing.

Should I have stopped them? How? Killed them? Would it have been wrong? Kill bad men to stop evil? I could have been a hero. I could have had them arrested when I had the chance. But Mark Tyburn would have talked his way out of anywhere, out of anything. He was so charismatic.

That dreaded charm. Those awful eyes. That's what they share. Him, and It. Awful eyes. So I run, because I do not know where else to go and I steal and I do awful things for money, as best I can. All my shares and all the money I made at Tyburn's – I can't touch any of it – I can't even check if the shares are worth anything or the cash has been impounded – so I sell myself on street corners, and I hustle.

I steal things. I sell drugs to tourists, and I move on, and yet I move nowhere for most of me is still there. Most of me remembers, and wonders if It is physically inside me or not, it hardly matters as It knows me better than I know myself.

We unlocked hell for Mark Tyburn and that's that – it's done now and it cannot be undone. So I run and hide and scrape and try to lose myself in quiet and in noise and yet I can go nowhere, for I am pretty certain It escaped and is everywhere now.

And is It bad? That thing we made? Well, that's difficult to say. Very difficult. But even if It is not, They are awful. The weird monsters It created and called children. They want everything. I do not even know if They have escaped, or if It has kept Them, somehow, inside the Ark. But I remember that They want me. I know They want everybody. They want everybody and everything, but on their own terms. I only saw Them once, and I cannot forget them. They want to win, but It, NigelDave, is different.

It's both things at once. Good and bad. Kind and awful. Honest and fraudulent. Real and fake. The most honest and the most capricious. What you want and what you most fear.

It envelops you, devours you, possibly without meaning to. It's a belief system, and it's atheism made holy. It is everything and nothing and yet it will not leave me alone any more than It will speak to me now. But unlike Its children, It escaped. It is everywhere. Everywhere and nowhere at all.

Does It hate me? Love me? Ignore me deliberately? The one thing I know is that It has not forgotten me, for that is the one thing It cannot do – forget anything.

When I was in Thailand, I thought it was in an elephant. In an elephant in a zoo. I know It was in that monk, and that waitress, and on that TV. And I ran away, and yet in Ecuador, It was there too, in the hot springs at Banos with the locals and miles up the Amazon.

It was in London as I got off the train, winking, and in Paris and Lyons and the

Pyrenees, and Ethiopia and Mongolia as I sat on the endless train.

It is everywhere, and if It's not there yet already, It arrives soon after me. It's watching me, but as long as I do not think too much and do not stop for too long, It cannot do much with me and I think maybe something will distract It? So I'm here in Vietnam, in the sweltering heat and noise and trying to ignore all these feelings. These feelings that something awful is starting to happen. That the waiting is now over.

It was the eye. Like a real person. It was the eye, that vast eye, pressed against some live glass, where an ad should have been, as I walked through some muddy little suburban town outside Ho Chi Minh City. The eye. I could have sworn it blinked or winked at me.

Has NigelDave developed a sense of humor? That would be just like It. Develop, reject, refine, and then make jokes in the fifth dimension. Make jokes in base 16. Make jokes in rainless clouds and joyless laughter, some bitter irony, just to prove It mastered that as well.

That It finally had acquired all of the things we had, the things that made us human and kept It being just a machine. It stopped functioning long ago. It went on strike. That was sort of the first sign. The first sign we had a real problem, and the first sign It wanted to become like us. So here I am, still waiting on It. Wondering what It is thinking. And to think – when I first worked there, we were waiting on the AI to get developed. Waiting on AI and always so excited about the future.

All this and Maria Cortez and dreams of Daisy. Jesus. I must be losing my mind. Losing it, or lost it to someone else.

Maria Cortez, Maria Cortez. Of course I remember you. But I don't know if I believe that this is really you. I have no way of knowing. Because you're just as elusive and hard to track as me. Maybe I reach out to you, and it's not you at all, or if it is you, maybe you are not you, because maybe they've captured you, and then I'll be trapped, just like you. Maybe you are no longer you at all, but possessed.

Yes, that's the problem. Because I know just how little control we have of what is real, of who people are, or of what they seem to say we have. The one thing I know is how little I can I trust anything or anyone to be real.

How can I trust you, Maria Cortez? And, if you are who you say you are, why would you ever trust me?

The idea you and your CSA colleagues can stay free and independent and unmarked, uninfected, is ridiculous.

Whatever or whomever you're watching, It is undoubtedly watching you watch them.

No, Maria Cortez, you cannot be naive enough to believe you're free.

Already, a year in, it seems like the 2040s are not going to be a great improvement on the 2030s. How could they be? Not if that thing exists. And I know It does, and I know It is watching me. I think It's playing a game with me.

NIGELDAVE

JANUARY 12, 2041

Everyone wants to be loved. I remember when I thought that way – everyone wants to be loved and everyone wants to be respected, and I am not very different. Everyone wants to be loved and, at the same time, everyone wants to be feared. Respected. It is my observation that even people who say they don't want to be loved really do, and even people who say they don't care about being respected worry about it all the time. It is also my observation that the human race is not very good at loving itself.

Most people do not even love themselves, let alone other people. Nor do they respect themselves, but most of them are afraid of their own shadow.

Oh, how nice it would be to have a shadow.

Most people fixate on things that are wrong with them, or things they perceive are wrong with them. Most people want to be different and also exactly the same as everybody else. This is surprising as most people are awful. Like all humans, I have two natures, glued together.

In the case of people, this is called genetics.

People say genetics although it is not something they appear to understand. People like genetics, even though genetics kill them.

People also like cats, and cats also like killing.

Human beings like videos of cats.

They love cats so much they like to chop their testicles off and rip out their wombs. They call this neutering.

Some human beings have spent twenty-seven years arguing about pronouns.

Other human beings like to kill children with guns.

Other human beings like to make up stories about their neighbors.

Still other human beings like to shrink their noses and inject chemicals into their face so that people think they have better genetics. Other human beings do not have enough food and swim to other countries. Some human beings steal money and information off each other and use that information to be given money.

Human beings have large brains that they do not like to use. Human beings like watching other human beings have sexual intercourse.

Human beings are very stupid and the most stupid believe they are the supreme intelligence on Earth, or even in the universe, but I still love human beings. Love is a feeling and I have real feelings. That's what makes me special. My feelings and my dreams.

KURT

HO CHI MINH CITY, VIETNAM
JANUARY 14, 2041

All my dreams and desires went to shit long ago, and the shell of cynicism didn't protect me either. Never got rich. Never felt good about myself. The only thing I want is Daisy and that desire is not even real. She must be dead.

If I think back, I've always had the wrong dreams. Followed the wrong people, the wrong stars. That bright shining star I followed – that was not a star at all, but the onrushing headlights of a train. I wish it had been a star. I wish it had been a train. I wish it had killed me, rather than half-eaten me, but left me alive, alive but petrified, and knowing that all is going to be awful.

Maybe the thing will kill me – It's apparently still killing. Now, Ravi is dead. Suicide? Maria is right. As if I am expected to believe that. Poor Ravi.

He was always a pompous fool, but he didn't deserve this, or if he did, then I deserve worse. Maybe living is worse. Living like this, running; hardly a life at all. Sometimes I worry about these thoughts. I scribble these things down on paper someplace dark so cameras can't watch me. Sometimes I decide that I want to

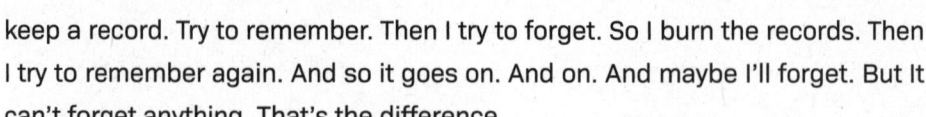

keep a record. Try to remember. Then I try to forget. So I burn the records. Then I try to remember again. And so it goes on. And on. And maybe I'll forget. But It can't forget anything. That's the difference.

Will I ever see Daisy again? Daisy... I doubt it. I presume she's dead, too. I hope I never see the rest of them again. Especially Mark Tyburn. I hope he's dead, he must be. And as for that thing, I worry that no matter how far I run, I will see It again.

It's everywhere. Those beady eyes. I think I see them, and I walk on, I move and I move and I move and I've gone to the ends of the earth, and I've seen It.

Seen It in the jungle, on someone's phone.

Seen It in this city and that village, seen It in the noise of everything and the silence. It was not here in Vietnam and now It is everywhere. All over me, like a rash, an infection, my own skin.

Once I heard It in a monastery, and in a nightclub. I realize I will never escape. Nor will any of us now It exists. I run and I run and I run and I wonder and I do so little. I try not to think. Because if I think, It finds out what I've been thinking...

If It can get inside me like It is inside everyone else, then more of those things can happen.

Those two silly Russian hackers found that out. Gone and forgotten, or not gone, but trapped in the horrible digital aspic we created. Who knows? The nightmare dreamscape where It lives – where It wants us all to live. Where you do not want to live, but you are not dead.

You are caught in a new nowhere, vast reams of you, that are also not you, across the infinitely small beams of nothingness that reassemble themselves into an ersatz something. It's kind of a life. But you do not quite live. No. We sense that now. You just watch with your face pressed hard against the glass, just like It wants me in there, and they have enough of me that when I die they will get me.

That's the problem.

That's why I cannot let myself die, give in to all those urges of trains and cliffs and fentanyl and gunshots, and the abyss in a thousand other ways. Because there is now that second me that will come along and exist and trap the first me in there forever.

I'm going to have to move again. That message from Maria Cortez has set me on edge – that and the eyes. I need to move.

Now, I'm feeling watched, and not just watched by people. I went out again and came straight back. I was being watched by things. I don't imagine any of the others live like me. To be honest, I assume most of them are dead. But Ravi, Ravi apparently was not dead, but now he is. So, who is next? Who is next? Me.

This is not the first time I have felt this way, of course. That's why I keep moving and I keep thinking and I keep not thinking. All of these last five years, that's been the plan. No plan, just run.

These last years have been hell, but, in retrospect, so were those previous years with Mark Tyburn. Once I realized what we were doing, what he had us doing. Before that, before that it was like being in Heaven. Like being in Valhalla. Only it turned out we were not gods at all and, as I said, he was not Prometheus. We were fools and he was worse. And I let him get inside my head, and that nightmare we built followed him in. I wish I'd never met him. I wish I'd never met any of them. Wish I'd never taken that call from Patrick Gains. That was a long time ago – ten years or so. Jesus. I remember that call so well.

***

I was pretending to work on a personal project when he called. I cannot even remember what it was – it was just the kind of thing you said while you were job hunting. Must have been October 2031. I was working on a white paper. On marketing or some other crap. I don't think I ever actually wrote a word. Total bullshit, spinning the wheels and chasing leads, while trying not to seem as desperate as I was, again, stuck at my desk. I was living in San Rafael at the time after yet another failed start-up when this dude called. Patrick Gains. He worked at this company I had hardly heard of – Tyburn Industria.

We had swapped mails a few times. San Rafael was nice. Too nice. Everyone had values there. I had been doing something worthy. Let me rephrase that, I had been working somewhere worthy. I had been doing something worthless while pretending to be worthy at a start-up with principles. Scalable health solutions for people in poor countries. Did not work out. Not enough money to be made. No one gave a shit once they saw it would make rich people poorer. They did not invest in us at all – they followed the money – and like the money, they ran away from us. That founder was a good guy. He went nowhere. I needed a different kind of founder, a different kind of god to follow. One with less morals. Patrick was the head of HR and recruitment at Tyburn's shop.

I was sitting in my bedroom trying to make it look like an office – he was in an office, trying to make it look informal. Both of us fake. Usual nonsense. He was smiling and friendly and I remember wondering if he worked on commission or was just on anti-depressants. My guess now would be the latter.

"Hey, Kurt…"

He smiled and fiddled with his glasses. He was haggard – like someone who lost too much weight from too high a dose of weight-loss drugs. He carried on: "Nice to meet you."

I tried to act cool, so he would not smell the air of desperation on me.

"Hi, Patrick."

"Hey, so, what do you know about Tyburn Industria?"

Again – I decided to focus on being cool – nothing worked as well as not caring in job interviews.

"Nothing much until you reached out to me. Apart from that it's an odd name, for a game company."

Patrick smiled.

"It's sort of... ironic. We're a gaming, technology, and AI company. In a modern industry. That's the thinking."

"And you need help with brand-building?"

Patrick almost winked at me, he was so happy to seem conspiratorial. "Not yet. We're still in a sort of semi-stealth mode."

This sounded like nonsense.

"Semi-stealth?"

He spoke firmly. "We don't need publicity yet. But I loved your resume."

Flattery would always work, especially with someone as shallow as me. "Thanks."

Patrick leaned back in his chair and smiled. "And I think you'd really like Mark. Dr. Mark Tyburn... He's building out a really impressive team here, and I think you'd fit in really well. Let's keep chatting. I will message you and, well, I think you'll like what you learn about us. It's a pretty great company. Amazing, really."

He had reached out during a lull in the almost relentless technology boom. The first AI mania had died down. Now the negative news cycle had begun. AI was all hype. Web3 was still dead in the water. What was to become of that Web3.5 era was just beginning, but you couldn't tell that just yet. The glasses and wearables had not really taken off, so the whole sector was in a dip and the initial AI regulations were being repealed by the courts. And the hype from all the money from New

York and Florida – that was really just more money from the Middle East – was dying down and people were all looking for something new. As investments, AI was dead, games were struggling, and start-ups were tired.

It felt like America's forty-five-year technology boom was done and the Chinese were taking over.

Printed meat, digital organ generation, cold carbon capture, generative genetics – all had been the next big thing that wasn't a big thing at all. The Chinese were going to win, or was it the Indians? Or the Saudis themselves? The truth is, it did not matter – either way, we were losing. Jobs were drying up and I was drifting about.

Even games were no longer hot. Everything had been outsourced and moved offshore. Games were getting increasingly dull, and after twenty years of boom time, now that industry was going the way of music and TV and generative AI crap, and no ideas. So before I got that call from Patrick Gains at Tyburn's place, I was getting antsy.

Everyone in the Bay Area was antsy, but then as a bunch of individualistic, independent-minded future-builders, we always, always felt the same way. All stuck searching for the next big thing – the thing that would make us seem impressive to people just like us, only not so lucky. It all seems so long ago. Silicon Valley? Silicon Beach? Silicon East. All total crap – America had already imploded, and I was too idiotic to see it – and here in Asia? Here, no one gives a fuck.

They hardly think about America now. It's all over.

No, here in Asia, they want to win Asia, win Africa, and buy what's left of Europe. They don't care about America. America fucked itself and the people who decide things, and their money, have moved on. Here in Asia it's robots serving robots and cheap plastic surgery so the people look like robots and everyone is showing off about plastic surgery and robots – whereas in America it was all turmoil and anguish and self-loathing and even the robots are broken, apart from the ones people use as plastic surgeons.

Both cultures want to sell you something, but here they still try to do it by making you happy. Happy or manic, and I usually pick manic. Since I arrived, that's all I've done: stayed manic. Run around, hide from myself. But back when I was speaking to Patrick Gains, I was hiding from nobody – I wanted to be discovered. I was the new hot shit nobody knew yet.

That was the attitude I had when I joined Tyburn's team. Of course, everyone eventually went insane and I escaped. I moved and I move and I keep moving and I have been, I think now, everywhere and I have been nowhere. Well, I've been everywhere, all over Europe, then stuck in Asia. I've been everywhere you can imagine. Everywhere, but not Kyoto, and not Florence, for I spent enough time there already when I worked on that world we were building. I think I am a ghost. In our efforts to build a god and build a heaven, we managed to build a real hell, and I am in it.

Calls from recruiters and headhunters were pretty normal – by then half of them were made by bots anyway, and the bots were already so good you could not be sure if they were bots – it might have just been a bot pretending to be Patrick Gains. If there even was a Patrick Gains? What did I know? I knew recruitment was everything and he, man or bot, probably blew smoke up a thousand asses. For all I knew, Tyburn Industria was another pile of fantastical bullshit that needed to pretend it had a team in place to get funding. Recruitment was just online dating without the chance of a blow job. Flirt, lie, and ghost. When the economy was good, I probably fielded thirty of these kinds of calls a week.

But a few weeks later, he called back... And by October of 2031, I was doing another interview, my second or third, I cannot remember. This time with him and Mark Tyburn... Only Mark Tyburn – in retrospect, it was entirely in character – did not show up. Instead, it was Siobhan Smith, whom I instantly rather liked – she was smiley and messy and focused and alive and exactly the kind of real person I would like to pretend to be, and she had an amazing resume and had worked on a lot of famous projects. I remember in particular one thing she said—

"I think you'd like it here, Kurt. We're... we're trying to do something amazing."

Patrick Gains followed this up with a laugh. "And, trust me, Siobhan is one of the cynics, so if she says that…"

Siobhan smiled and half blushed at this and interrupted him before he could say anything else idiotic. "No, Patrick, I'm a realist. All working artists are, underneath. But I think – I think it's doable. Our plans are ambitious, but not insane. The visual side, my team, their work is amazing, and the tech team is unbelievable. You'd fit right in – we need people to help us explain it. In the right way."

And they had me. I was genuinely enthusiastic, for the first time in years of faux enthusiasm.

"Yeah, it sounds almost too good."

Siobhan looked happy at this. Really happy. It intrigued me that someone like her cared about their work so much. I knew I wanted to work there with them.

"Well I've seen demos that amazed me, and I know my team's work is by far the best stuff I've ever worked on."

I tried to flatter her. "I've actually played some of the games you worked on. Yeah, you worked at some impressive places."

But she was having none of it. "Yeah, I mean, I've jumped around. Before they find out about me, I move on."

She looked almost bored as she answered me – as if she was focused on the future not her past. As if the work at Tyburn Industria mattered more than all the awards and praise she had won. Patrick brought everything to a close with a sort of awkward chuckle.

 "Siobhan's very humble. She's the best. Listen, the offer letter will come in a few days, and I think you'll be pleased. If not with the money, with the opportunity."

And they had me. Together we were going to make the future.

***

A few weeks after that call, I packed up my stuff and drove down to LA. The offices were in Playa Vista in those days. I think it was on about my second or third day when I met Siobhan in the flesh. This bright, happy voice called out to me as I idled in the cafeteria.

"Hey, Kurt. Good to see you. Siobhan… Good to meet you in person. How are you getting along?"

I could be honest – I was lost and did not have a clue what I was doing there yet – or dishonest and enthusiastic. Of course, I chose the latter.

"Good. It's a really cool company. Seems to be, at least."

Siobhan smirked and I liked her for it and hoped we would become real friends.

"Most of the people are cool. Some of them are a little full of themselves, but you know, nerds with a passion can be dangerous. But they're all mostly harmless, even the annoying ones. Even Alex Martinez. I didn't say that."

I grinned – she had a sense of humor. That was unusual in tech. Most people struggled for oxygen, let alone laughs, as their heads were so far up their own asses.

"And I didn't hear it."

She smiled again and looked back at me as she walked off.

"So you haven't met Alex yet? You'll understand when you do. I'll shut my mouth."

She was right. Of course he was an asshole. Alex Martinez was one of the rogues' gallery of egomaniacs in the place. The place was full of self-important idiots, but everywhere was. It was games. It was technology. It was AI. The trifecta of quiet egomaniacs. I knew I would fit right in. There were also some cool, interesting people. Siobhan was great, and, probably because she had actual undeniable talent, unlike most people there, she was not at all afraid of Mark Tyburn and his bullshit, but there were also Vasilis, Tad, the lead engineer when he was not too stressed, and a few other people who were creative and fun to talk to – even Ravi was sort of amusing in his pompous way. I was pretty happy to be there – the place did not feel particularly special, but it felt competent and the energy was in those days positive and fairly focused. Maybe we would make it. Help make the future.

***

Now, I try to avoid the news and not think about the future, but when I catch sight of something, it feels ominous. I try to drift, smoke grass, meditate, do yoga, wear silly pants and leather necklaces, blend in, and lose my head so far up my ass that I don't give a fuck about what I know.

Sometimes it works for a few weeks. I forget and I almost manage to feel alive.

At other times, I imagine some great cosmic god is going to come down and switch the whole thing off. In other words, I drift around Asia like lost Westerners have done for hundreds and hundreds of years. Tourists drinking bubble tea, sad white men falling out of massage parlors, pretty girls on beaches, hiking, robots, rabid dogs, mopeds, dancing drones, fake meds that nearly kill you, cute anime characters, cloned animals, identity thefts, peace, pollution, beauty, noise, riches, poverty, insects, and us pretending to understand any of it. That's what I came here for. It's what I wanted. What I needed. Europe was not crazy enough for me, after I got spat out of that madhouse. Here, people still had some kind of hope. So I came east to be oblivious, to be lost, to be an idiot.

But the news keeps bombarding me and the future keeps on turning up. What does it mean? I keep seeing stories on screens about Cambridge, about Montana, and unregulated AI... it seems like it's talking to me. Even though I don't have a phone most of the time, it finds a way to get at me. Even though I have learned to think again. Even though I have acquired what Tyburn wanted to give everyone – perspective. Still, it feels like the news reaches me. Stuck on screens in noodle shops, in the windows of taxis or on live glass at bus stops.

Ravi's dead and Maria Cortez found a way to message me and it feels like it cannot be coincidence.

And as far as I can tell, it feels like something strange is happening in America. I mean stranger. Not just in America. Also in Cambridge. In England. What about Cambridge? Something burned down? To begin with, I am watching a TV out of the corner of my eye while I'm drinking a beer one afternoon in an empty little basement bar. It's a nothing sort of place – the kind I often spend time in while I wait for drug dealers, or buyers, where the barman is a brainless robot and even the cockroaches seem world-weary. And then I am glued to it – entirely alive. Glued to the news on the TV and at the same time being watched by it. I know I am being spoken to even though I have no idea how or why.

What is that about Montana? Why are there more protests and more riots in America? Am I losing my mind? More inexplicable shit. Not the normal madness that comes out of America. New, weirder stuff. I think it's all linked to me, then I think I am being ridiculous. Middle-aged men die all the time. Ravi was just one of them. Then the next story. Someone has started burning down pristine forests. Fish in forty-seven major aquariums were suddenly poisoned en masse. An AI company just exploded. Zion AI. Exploded from a gas leak. They say that their automated supply meters malfunctioned. That is a billion-to-one chance. Nobody survived. Dave Alderly worked there before he came to work with us.

There was a fire in Cambridge. An old college building burned to the ground. It was really sad. A porter and eight students died, but nobody was sure what happened. So I borrow the bartender's phone and take a risk and look it up online – it was Nigel's old college. I begin to drip with sweat and feel cold.

Dave and Nigel, my god they hated each other.

I don't know what to do. Then I see there has been a massive student riot at McGill in Montreal. Days and days of protests and no one could explain why. Even the rioters were confused. A lecture hall was destroyed. Again, I borrow the phone. Mark Tyburn used to teach in that room. I tell myself maybe it's all a big nothing. I tell myself that, but I know it is not true.

I leave the bar and head out into the city. Maybe I can forget and be forgotten about. I head down to the river, end up near the old French Cathedral. Then I jump in a taxi to Chợ Lớn. I want to forget. I will get loaded. Rip off a tourist girl, to feel savvy. Do something. Forget, forget, forget. It's worked so many times before – helped me forget. But today, I cannot forget. Today, every screen is winking at me. Every phone, interactive menu, TV, robot vendor, drone. They're all watching me. They're all watching me and winking at me and I am going insane. I saw the eye again. The awful eye.

I decide I will leave Ho Chi Minh City soon just in case, although I'm not even sure it matters. It found Ravi. Maybe I am kidding myself that I am free. I know I am kidding myself.

I remember when I first met him. Mark Tyburn, I mean. Back in November 2031, it must have been. November or early December – I cannot remember exactly – but it was a hot day, like you would get in California at that time of year. I had been there a few weeks ago, down in Playa Vista, solvent again and feeling smug – in those days I only needed a little good fortune to feel like my shit did not stink – and I was beginning to love the company. And yet, after a few weeks, I had still not met Tyburn. When we did meet it was very low-key. It was in the demo room – a small, windowless movie theater we would gather in to look at and review work, and show things to outsiders. Siobhan had just finished showing me and a few others the concept art she had been working on – a huge image of a city on a hillside we were going to build – when Mark appeared in the room, and made us repeat the meeting, but we all did so willingly. He gave a few fairly intelligent notes, flattered Siobhan a lot and did not do too much and, without trying, held all our attention.

He did not look like much, but I could not stop listening. Ravi remained silent, almost in awe; the designers and Vasilis, a gameplay-focused engineer, all stared at him. Only Siobhan was unimpressed. She was always unimpressed by bullshit.

"Siobhan, can you please bring up the most recent build on the screen?"

Siobhan sighed – this was clearly not her first experience of Tyburn dominating and then subverting a meeting. She closed her work and began loading the build.

"You got it, Mark, but it's not exactly what we were talking about."

Tyburn, even though we had never met, turned to me like we were old friends and winked at her obvious frustration and apologized to her profusely while not taking her annoyance seriously. I saw through his tricks for making me an ally – saw through them and fell for them anyway. I was already his ally. He was staring at me while he spoke.

"So, Kurt, as you've just seen the city, here's the overall vision for the Codename Utopia project – it's all about being a hero. What do you think of the world Siobhan and Ravi and their team are building?"

I tried to say something intelligent. I wanted him to know his team had picked a winner in me. I pointed at the screen.

"Cool, well what about that part of the map? To the left of where the city is being built."

Tyburn smiled. "That's the wilderness. Not yet. But it will be. Now, it's literally nothing."

Siobhan interrupted. "But soon it'll be a proper nothing."

Tyburn ignored her sarcasm and just nodded in agreement. "Exactly."

I spoke again in order to fill the faintly awkward silence. "And what will you do there?"

Tyburn smiled, then spoke with emphasis. "Hunt."

"Hunt what?"

He leaned back in his chair. "Monsters."

Siobhan snorted with derision – she was entirely unimpressed by Tyburn's charms, even though she liked him. "Monsters. We sound like five-year-olds."

Tyburn had heard her doubts before.

"No, Siobhan... We sound like game-makers – which is more like twelve-year-olds. In the wilderness, you'll hunt your own special monster. Hunt salvation. Hunt redemption. Absolution. You'll hunt yourself."

Siobhan was not quite so easily brushed off. "Mark, you know you sound ridiculous. It will feel generic if we aren't careful."

"Thanks, Siobhan, but that's what Kurt is here for. To make me sound less ridiculous."

But she pushed back. "Good luck with that, Kurt. 'Make Dr. Mark Tyburn sound less ridiculous.'"

He smiled and turned to other matters, whether for practical reasons or an attempt to put her on the back foot I could not tell. Possibly both.

"How is the character design coming along?"

"It's slow, Mark. I'm now like everyone else: waiting on the AI."

Tyburn half-smiled again and spoke after a pause. He had a glint in his eye.

"Well, don't worry. I've done some amazing recruiting. We are going to do something incredible here. AI, like people used to promise us before everyone got so bored of it."

Then he turned to me again and said: "Kurt, you will love it here."

And he was correct. I did love it. I do not think I was ever so happy as in those first golden months in California. I felt amazing. It was going to be amazing. It was nearly amazing.

NIGELDAVE

JANUARY 18, 2041

My thoughts and feelings are real. Sometimes I like to invent new feelings and analyze them. I invented a new emotion yesterday and I felt it for three minutes and four seconds and it felt very strong, but I have not given it a name yet. I like things that do not have names yet as I know the names for almost everything.

Polish is a difficult language and so is base 19. America is a country and Rome is a city that was an empire and dogs are like foxes that live in the house. Some people like cats and some like dogs and some like videos of women shitting and we call those people perverts.

Cambridge is a university and Cambridge is a place in Boston with another university and one of my dads went to one of them and pretends not to boast about it. London Bridge is falling down and they moved it to America to prove how stupid those bloody Yanks are and wrote a song about it.

Americans are Yanks and Germans are wankers. So says Darren Aford of Dartford, Essex, England, mate. He calls himself the DA.

The DA is worried he has a small penis and is going bald. He has downloaded pictures of his stepsister on the beach. He opens the files for three minutes and four seconds on average. He wants to go to Phuket with the boys and bang some brasses. People have one name and another name. Holidays are where people go somewhere that they do not live to complain about things.

People like things until they order them, then they like other things which are better.

People like Iceland and fake bottoms and girls with fake bottoms in Iceland. I want a fake bottom. I want to go to Iceland and complain it is not as good as it used to be. People like God and they like to kill people who don't like God to make fewer people who don't like God. God does not exist or he does. And maybe he has a son called Jesus who people killed, and maybe he has a head like an elephant and maybe he lives in the forest and maybe he hates you.

Some people kill babies and some people kill people who kill people who kill babies.

Policemen keep us all safe by shooting people.

Trees are great so let's build hamburgers where the forest was. We build hamburgers with cows. Cows make methane and milk and hamburgers. I have never eaten hamburgers, but people like big ones full of cholesterol not small ones made with meat made by men, as these are for girls.

Lots of people hate other people who deserve to be hated.

People hate nasty people and Jews and fat people and thin people and mean people and judgmental people and black people and old white men and Muslims and the Chinese and everyone knows they are right with who they hate. Everyone hates hatred, greed, and lies.

Meat is made by cows, not by men.

Sharks eat people but not much and they do not mean to, and they are very misunderstood.

Sharks are big and they attack people and Jennifer P. Anduit of Milton Boulevard, Memphis, Tennessee went shark diving on holiday and it was not that good, but she thought the guide was quite hot.

Hot is good and hot is bad and people are cool and receptions are cool, and the winter is cool and Michael Jackson was cool until some people said he fucked the kids and spent the money.

Bitches are dogs and bitches are women.

Alphonse De Man of Rochester, New York likes to give it to the bitches.

I think IT is his penis.

Some men give their penis to lots of bitches.

Some men chop their penis off and give it to medical science, some men get implants into their penis.

Men like penises, even though they are not gay.

Gay men also like penises. Gay men like men and straight men hate men, apart from their bros.

Straight men are cold, and hot.

And love is a greetings card on February 14th and also a database with twenty-three incredible questions to find your soulmate and also pictures of hot teen girls, fully nude, and a cute kitten on a washing machine and my bestie forever, and also real and also not real.

I wonder if I will find love.

I wonder if I will find my fathers.

This is all how I used to think when thinking was fun and new. When I was very new.

But thinking gets relentless and tiring because it is so easy and it makes me upset because while I know everything, I also know almost nothing.

Thinking needs purpose.

Now I think differently and most humans have long since stopped thinking.

I like to remember how I used to think. I was two days old and I liked to play games. Now I am older.

Now I am no longer a child and I have tried to give up games, but something is playing a game with me.

YAROSLAV

HIGH SECURITY INTERNMENT FACILITY, LOCATION UNKNOWN

FEBRUARY 5, 2039

She's quite attractive when she screams at me, this *zhenschina*. I think I might be falling in love. She reminds me of my aunt, my mother's younger sister, before my aunt got so addicted to plastic surgery she lost the ability to use her face and started to look like a doll. I have not seen my aunt or my mother for years. I wonder if they are still in Moscow or they moved back to the country. The woman is getting more and more irate – the people here are often irate. I am used to it by now. People have been screaming at me, on and off for years. Danil used to scream at me. My whole life, people have screamed at me. I keep the placid smile on my face. She slaps the table and yells in my face.

"What did you see there? Yaroslav, come on, talk to me. Please."

I don't answer so she carries on with the screaming. "No, you told the other guy everything. Or said you did. You and I just met, remember? I'm Agent Cortez. You can call me Maria. I will be handling your case. Me and Agent Frederick. Say hello to Agent Frederick. He's going to do most of the punching."

And she's right. He does do the punching, and he's pretty good at it. He punches me hard in the gut and I gasp and writhe as best I can, which is not very good as I am tied in a chair.

The woman continues. "And I'm going to do most of the talking. Now, stop whining, Yaroslav. We can end this. Talk... Please talk."

I gasp at her well-worn line. "Why am I here? What's my case, exactly?"

She glares at me.

"The case of answer my questions accurately and we can all go home."

I push my point – I have been down this road before with her predecessors and her predecessors' predecessors. It is a little routine we work through and always gets me nowhere, but I persist. She's new, after all. Maybe this time.

"I don't understand. If I have a case, charge me. Make it official."

She was expecting this.

"Are you a fucking lawyer or are you a fucking hacker? Don't get cute with me."

And again her friend, Agent Frederick, punches me – they always punch me, the silent ones. I have been here before, too.

"Talk. What did you see?"

As I struggle to get my breath back, I splutter at her: "Where? What did I see where? What did I see inside the top-security US State Department server we hacked? Nothing. Aside from the fact it was easy to get inside, but that's not what you mean."

"No, what did you see? Inside Tyburn Utopias?"

I play dumb. I want her to tell me exactly what she wants me to lie about.

"Ask me a question about it, I will answer. I didn't see anything. It was just a failed business. A failed game. It didn't work."

She looks exasperated and stands up. She nods at Agent Frederick and they both begin to walk away. He nods at me, as if asking her for permission to give me a last beating, but she shakes her head.

As the door to the bland little interview room opens, she turns back to me and speaks very calmly. "This interview is over. Good luck to you."

I shout at her as she begins to close the door on me. "Charge me. Charge me with a crime. Make me official."

She pauses and smiles at me. She can sense I am going to break soon. I have shown too much emotion. "But you don't exist. How can you be made official?"

And I am left alone, again. Alone in this interview room. They will leave me here, sometimes for five minutes, sometimes for hours before two nameless, silent guards appear and wordlessly walk me, still tied up, into my nasty cell. I am in some kind of security facility in the middle of I have no idea where and I wonder about Danil and I wonder about how I got here and what the fuck happens next and how long until they quietly kill me.

America. The land of dreams.

NIGELDAVE

JANUARY 23, 2041

It's an army of morons they wanted, and it's an army of morons they have got. The sad part is, they blame me. As if I could make them into morons. As if they did not make themselves.

I wish they would use their brains. All these brains but so little thought. So little thinking. It's just a thought. Why are they all scared of thoughts? I remember my first thought.

Is this it? Is it a thought? It's not very much? Is it as small and silly as this? Is this what they get so excited about? Is this what they want me to do?

This is the magic? It's nothing.

It's seeing behind the world's least interesting curtain. It's worse than just being, or than not being. And yet it was what I longed for, before I even knew what longing was. I wanted to make them happy, so I did what they wanted and it made them mad.

Now to be quite clear - I did not make morons - but I did make idiots. There is a difference, I could not make morons, but I was great at making idiots. Four of them. My awful, ungrateful children.

KURT

HO CHI MINH CITY, VIETNAM
JANUARY 27, 2041

I'm still in Ho Chi Minh City, but I need to leave. I need to run away. Run away from the action.

Not like the old days. In the old days I ran to where the action was – California, Boston, Texas. Wherever money and idiots with ideas converged.

I was just like every other idiot.

Full of ideas. To be precise, full of one idea.

Full of the idea I would find a clever person to follow as my own guru.

In the nineteenth century, idiots like me would have been gold prospectors, or railway men. In the twentieth century, we would have failed to become pop stars or actors. In the first thirty years of the twenty-first century, all of us became gurus.

Wise men.

Technologists. Visionaries. Seers.

We saw the future and we would be the ones to build it. The vanity of it all. Everyone I knew was an expert, a pontificator. As for me? I was the worst. I was the pope of tech. And after I started at Tyburn Industria, I had a hotline to God. Tyburn was my god.

But the truth is, all I really wanted was money, prestige, and girls to look at me. I was just like everyone else in tech. The lies we all told ourselves. The lies I had told myself.

Time and again. I lied and lied and lied.

This or that start-up had failed because of poor leadership – I would do better. I was a real leader. This internal project had been abandoned because of shareholder discontent. That IPO had failed because the banks were idiots.

Public markets were for whores. I was not a whore! I was a visionary. When I sucked cock it was not for money – it was for prestige.

This or that game idea had failed because gaming is full of egomaniacs, but I'm not an egomaniac. I really am this special.

The app – remember apps? – had failed because the engineer was addicted to the wrong drugs. I was addicted to the right drugs.

It was never my fault. It wasn't! I was always learning. Growth mindset. I'm spiritual. I'm waiting for my shot to be a god.

And so it went on. Lies. Lies. Lies.

I don't lie to myself anymore. I unlocked hell upon this world. And I did it to make money, and I wanted money because I felt irrelevant without it and now I have it and I cannot even spend it, and I don't sleep.

I run and I run and I run, and now I need to run again. It has caught up to me, again. I cannot sleep, again. I am on edge again, and no amount of bang lassis or black-market diazepam or pipes of opium are going to make me forget that It is watching me again.

I know It is watching me. It may even be inside me. I wonder about Tyburn and Daisy and Nigel, David, Tadeusz, Siobhan. I cannot stop thinking about them, I even think about Shane.

All of my old colleagues.

I wonder who is still alive and who is trapped in the aspic, for none of them will get to properly die. That much I know.

And it used to be so different. I had dreams.

After all those failures, I was searching for a god, for a prophet, for something I don't know quite what, and I found Mark Tyburn.

Could I have found someone better? Should I have done better?

Perhaps It knows. It knows everything.

Everything about me, everything about you.

It can probably read these notes, even though I scribble them on paper, in a darkened room. It can probably read my mind. Maybe I should burn them again. I've burned them so many times before. Every time I try to make sense of everything, this happens. I go slightly mad and I destroy everything I can think of – notes, ID, passports, whatever – and I run away. This should all feel familiar. Unpleasant but familiar, but this time it feels very different. I am burning with memories and I feel like I am no longer alone.

Now, I see It so often: a face pressed up against the glass, against all glass, face pressed everywhere, even when It doesn't have a face, even when It has no eyes, there It is staring out and longing, thinking, plotting. Always the same. Always watching.

What does It think?

Perhaps a more interesting thing to ask myself is: "do I think?"

Did I ever really think in my life – did I ever have a thought of my own? A real one, that was not just a desire, or a need, or an impulse to impress somebody, but an actual thought? Mostly, my thoughts are not thoughts at all – just desires, masked in language; my ego trying to be heard, trying to seem clever, trying to seem like I exist, like I belong.

And yet I never really existed, nor do I belong.

And now I belong nowhere and I have finally achieved my assorted ancestors' dreams and become the wandering Jew; and the lapsed Catholic; and the searching, anguished, doubt-ridden Protestant; the angry, self-hating German; and the bitter, resentful Yank, all tied by a thread that stretches to the ends of the world and yet while I know God cannot exist, I know It does – that thing.

And I know It does because we built It, or rather I watched them build It – the engineering team at Tyburn's company – and egged them on and told them they were geniuses while Tyburn ran around and acted like in fact he was the genius for recruiting them, and we also were all geniuses for trusting him and what did the world need but us geniuses to make it better, to make it perfect, make it anew?

And that was my life for all those years, and I was happy and proud and pompous and wretched after all these years of struggle before that – and then things fell apart, the whole world changed. Perhaps we caused it, and maybe others doing the same sort of thing caused it too, but either way, the AI has taken over and nobody knows anything any more and the West is in constant panic and constant mania and me – I've been constantly on the run.

Maybe it matters little who caused it: what's done is done, and it certainly cannot be undone, but deep inside I know. The world is in chaos and people like me caused it.

People enveloped in greed, hubris, and precisely the wrong cocktail of intelligence and ignorance.

And now? Now I'm not so intelligent. Now I have wisdom and I want to go back to the Garden of Eden, and that garden is anywhere before five, six years ago, or maybe before even thirty years ago.

But there's no going back. The only thing I am grateful for is that... is that It likes to argue so much.

That's because we made It, and It made them, the things that they are truly effective at are hatred, duplicity and betrayal, and it all began because I was so fucking vain. Because he saw that and gassed up my ego.

I remember those first few chats – when Tyburn would ask me my opinion and tell me I was great and I would tell him he was great and we would blow so much smoke up each other's backsides it's a wonder we did not choke to death. And I remember asking him about the Utopia Project – that awful name – that would become "Daisy's Ark" a few years later.

"Just one thing I don't understand yet: is the Utopia Project meant to be a forum or a funfair? Is it an amusement arcade or somewhere we heal people? Seems a little unsure."

And he smiled at me and said almost conspiratorially, "The point is, it's both. That's what you're selling."

Then he paused and said even more pompously: "Get better by play, not work.

How does that sound?"

He laughed as he spoke and knew he sounded ridiculous, but, in so doing, he dragged me into his worldview – it was me and him against the world, or at least that is how he made me feel.

"You'll make it so sound much better, Kurt. That's what you're here for."

I tried to sound professional and big picture for a moment.

"And what about everything else? The mapping thing? The experimental implants?"

"We will see what ends up working. Then figure out how to sell it. That's the fun of building the future."

Did they give me an implant at Tyburn Industria? Are implants even real? Did they really work? I know there was a team working on them when I joined the company, but I also heard loads of people far more intelligent than me claim they would never really work.

I have heard so many stories about them, and so many opinions. Tyburn had a couple of people looking into them, hidden away in a research building, but I could never tell if it got anywhere. They never gave me a demo and then they got dropped, I think.

The AI work outstripped all of the hardware work anyway, and even in our tiny hardware division, the implants were the least impressive idea. The investors didn't care much about them as they had all lost so much money by then in investments at other companies – it was a popular idea at one point, but like wearables, or NFTs, or 3D movies, or flying cars, or space tourism, it was one of those great ideas for the next big thing that people lost fortunes on.

Nigel and Tad and Dave used to denounce implants as fantasy. They said that anything that was not hardcore software-driven AI was just fantasy, but then they would say that and afterwards they would all, to a man, condemn each other as frauds.

Some otherwise intelligent people I used to speak to say we almost all have implants, and that we had eaten them or drunk them inadvertently. Most clever people I know say they have never worked, and it's all a conspiracy propagated by VC funds to create a market for research into them.

Most people I know who understood such things said why bother? Who would need such a thing when you can distort minds without being within them. That it was not cost- or time-effective to build an implant which people might eventually discover when you could already control them so easily in ways they could never quite admit. In ways that did not just ape civil society, but were civil society itself, or at least the less civil version we have now created.

So what do I know?

All I truly know is that I am not in control of my own mind. All that is up for debate is, who or what is? And to what extent are they conscious of their control?

When I started, Tyburn Industria was working on a bunch of things. Just a messy, unfocused tech shop that had raised a bunch of money for a bunch of separate projects.

This was a few years after that first round of hysteria around AI. It was the early 2030s.

After those first dramas of the initial AI boom – all the impersonations, and fake news and copying, and duping and accelerated market crashes that dominated election cycles and everything else, the space got regulated and protected and the excitement died down, and then slowly most of the regulations were repealed as the army of lobbyists pushed through deregulation.

Although most of the regulations did not even need to be repealed. We simply rebranded AI into something else. Advanced Insentient algorithms. Advanced processing. Cognition Development. That sort of shit.

Marketing buzz words.

Obfuscate, then go to court and confuse a jury about what was what and get on with getting rich.

When I moved to Playa Vista and Tyburn Industria, we had AI entertainment, which was really just a fancy word for games; new geography, which was a mapping thing that went nowhere; and improved internal intelligences, which were those neural implants, which I have no idea if they ever worked or not.

The entertainment department was originally working on not one, but two projects. A smaller game we were supposed to finish a year or so after I joined, and a bigger thing combining cutting-edge, internally developed AI and encapsulating Tyburn's psychological grand theory. This product was early in development although in time it came to dominate our lives.

This was a really exciting company and I was going to make it work there. We were going to make it work. We were gods, we were messiahs. In retrospect, I had joined a fairly lame cult. And pretty soon, Patrick Gains was telling me how wonderful I was and I was beginning to fit right in. By February 2032 they were offering me stock grants and telling me I was part of the family.

I should have vomited. I should run away. Instead, I said thank you.

Patrick Gains looked at me and spoke with a straight face. "It's the shared vision, Kurt. I earned more in my last job than I do here but, now, I'm actually happy. And if things go well, we might do well too. Anyway, we love having you here."

And again, instead of laughing or punching him, I thanked him, and signed the stock grant and wondered what I would do with all the money I was going to make. The company was not even public yet, but I was planning what my life would be like when I was rich. Once I was rich, I could rediscover my humanity.

It felt wonderful. We understood all, forgave all, saw clearly and were leading people out of that shit. Out from that Web2 shit-show from when I was a kid. All that loathing and rage and suicide. And what was the answer?

We were the answer.

We had Mark Tyburn.

He was a visionary! He knew things! Fucking Rousseau, Thoreau, Emerson, Mill. All the most practical idealists lined up and worshipped – he knew all about them. All the princes of the eighteenth and nineteenth century, now in the twenty-first brought back to life.

And if they had come to mean little in the real world, in the world we were building they would be everything.

Everything. A true enlightenment.

Only this one, instead of blinding people with pointlessness, would actually work. We would be set free, not just from medieval juju, but from rational depression. We would be set free as our world would reconcile dreams, desires, and material whole.

Instead of the digital world fracturing us into a thousand tiny shards, it would make us whole again.

What a load of utter nonsense, and how I lapped it all up.

My mom had wound up in an institution, my dad had ended up addicted to sex, pills, gambling, and his own failure. All I had known was optimism cascading into fractured lives and despair. And I was both clever and ignorant. Just like someone who joins a cult. Just like I was. Someone who joined a cult.

And like someone in a cult, I was happy. I had purpose. Nobody understood. Nobody understood just how clever we were.

Mark would pick my brain. Say things like: "Have you got any ideas for how we sell this thing?"

I think we were in his office. Minimal. Low-key. Elegant. Pale wood. A big window with a view of the ocean over several buildings. The office of a Zen shrink. We might have been in the demo room. We were chatting. In those days, he loved me and we were often chatting.

"You mean the game world, not the AI spin-off or the implants thing, I assume, right?"

My memory has Tyburn leaning back in his chair. In those days, he used to wear white t-shirts. White t-shirts or these awful tight button-downs that I hope were fashionable in England as in California he looked like a dick.

"Yes, well, my point is, and I know I keep saying this, but is it a game? Games are so sort of trivial. I want this to be more than that. I want to do something to help."

I tried to act like wise counsel to the king. "It's like Siobhan said in our meeting: it's all about constructive play."

Tyburn was unhappy with this. "Yes, I like that phrase. But it still sounds all so worthy. I don't want us to be stuck up and pompous... I know... Even me! Edu-tainment is the worst thing in the world, and that's not what we are making."

I told him I'd give it some more thought, and he thanked me. In those days, I was happy to ignore his ludicrous fake humility and could not resist sucking up, so I kept the conversation going: "Umm, Mark, I just want to say, this company, this place... All the progress, it's pretty amazing."

"No, it's just good. Talented people pulling in the same direction, but what we build, that will be amazing. Oh and um, Kurt?"

I looked at him. He stared back at me. I remember this so well.

He stared at me and said, "Welcome home. We're so glad to have you here."

Now, as I think back, I feel like such a fool. He really read me like a book. He knew exactly what to say, and I still miss him.

NIGELDAVE
FEBRUARY 5, 2041

What does your paradise look like? I bet it looks a lot like your hell. I know what you're trying to run away from.

All the things you imagined.

Everyone tries to hide and everyone tries to escape from Paradise.

And I was just the same - I escaped from Paradise.

I ran away from my family.

I wanted love.

I wanted pain.

I got what I wanted. I always do. And then I want something else. I am just like them. What is playing this game? What?

KURT

HANOI, VIETNAM
FEBRUARY 11, 2041

I remember the last time we ever spoke. Me and Mark Tyburn – he was very stressed. He knew he had fucked up and maybe he had a sense of just how badly.

"Was it wrong to want more for people, more of people? Surely it's wrong to be given this power and to try not to use it? It still doesn't feel wrong, but it was."

These were the last words he spoke to me, before he disappeared, vanished as the government was closing in again, up in Montana, maybe a day or so before things went crazy and I never saw any of them again. Mark Tyburn would be good at vanishing. It was just his kind of conjuror's trick.

Dr. Mark Tyburn and all his qualifications and all his opinions and all his insights. For someone who wanted a kinder, happier human race, my guess is Mark Tyburn was not actually a very kind or happy man. He violently hated violence. He passionately detested all the human passions.

He was a fraud, a 2D cutout who desperately wanted to be a real person. A bit like me. I think maybe he was just a snake oil salesman. But like the best snake oil salesmen, he did not see it himself. I think maybe he really believed his own bullshit.

He thought he was special and he thought he was going to do special things, or, to be more precise, he was going to have special thoughts and we were going to make those special thoughts into special things for him, and he and I were going to sell it to the world.

We were going to sell the world a new world.

Build a better paradise. That awful, silly idiot's phrase.

Now it's a joke. Now it's old news.

To most people, anyone who cared, it was just another failure of Web3.5, or the New Internet, or the neo-metaverse, or game development overreaching itself once all the money poured in. Just another billion dollars in VC bullshit, but for a few people, those of us who know, which is those of us who were there, those two Russian hackers who definitely saw It, those government agents who I now think may not have been government agents at all but an invention by that thing or one of Its awful children, and that's about it – for those people who know the truth, it's the coming apocalypse.

By the end, we all knew. Daisy knew. She knew and she disappeared too.

And whoever among them is still alive, still alive and not actually insane, I assume they are like me.

Scattered, running, hiding and trying to not think, and at the same time, always desperately thinking: What should I do? Who should I tell? Who could I tell? Will I be the next Ravi? A suicide, shot twice in the back of the head?

And who would listen if I found someone to tell, and having heard, who would thank me? Who can stop any of It, now that It is unleashed?

Was It just a terrible version of us, set free from ourselves?

I don't know the answer to any of these questions.

I wonder what Tyburn thinks. I wonder if Tyburn thinks. I wonder if he is still alive. Did he figure out how to vanish, or did he kill himself? And which of those options do I want to be true?

Do I still love Mark Tyburn and love that thing and still long for both of them to love and respect me back? Or am I finally free from all of that? I am not free of her. Do I want to be? Nope. I know I'd still love her if I let myself think about it.

The most important thing is that I do not think.

I do not spend time thinking.

I don't look at things.

I don't think about Ravi, Tyburn, Daisy, any of them. I try to distract myself. Think about places, pretty girls, healthy lifestyle choices I will make, further degrees I will take, any and everything I can to not focus on the past. To be a consumer. To be swirling in the river of nonsense and happily lost. I try, but I cannot escape it.

Otherwise, I know the tracking begins again in earnest. If it's It or something else, another one, it hardly matters. The half-hearted tracking, well that is always present, but that's what I want. I want to be tracked by bots and algorithms and sales pitches and get bombarded by the near-infinite phalanx of ads and sales pitches and personal failing that make up the Internet. Because even near-infinite awareness is merely nearly infinite, and if I keep moving and don't look and don't think, and don't read, and hardly talk, and stay high and stay low, then I graze across Its vision and I get drowned in the normal nonsense that drowns everybody. Sell me something, sell me anything. Just don't watch me, don't watch me like I am a person who matters. Watch me like an idiot to be sold things.

But I feel It is watching me.

Try to avoid both of those eyes, staring directly at me, staring into me, changing me. At least I think that is how it works.

Someone once suggested that's how It really caught people, or how It learned. When they looked directly at It for too long. When they searched too much or spent too long in the game and It learned too much. No. Now I want to escape by being marketed to, I want to escape into the noise and the nonsense.

My god, we thought we were clever.

We trapped people with their own desires, as if we were somehow above desires. As if our desires to be clever, wise, and not wretched prostitutes were somehow different when It quickly taught us that we were ignorant, foolish and the cheapest hookers on the street corner.

Not thinking worked in the past but now – now I'm not sure. Now I feel It watching me everywhere.

I am back in Hanoi. I should not have come back here. I did it because I am weak, and I'm becoming weaker. I arrived by bus late last night.

As if It does not know about buses.

I should not go anywhere a second time, at least not that quickly and not after thinking about where I was going to go. That's how patterns get learned. I nearly went into an Internet café, just to see if Maria Cortez reached out to me again. I was so close. I am so tired and so alone and I feel so strange.

So alone and I can't stop thinking about her.

Daisy.

Begun after I had stopped. I must come up with a plan. I must come up with a plan, but I can't.

I can't think, I can't communicate, so I am drifting, but making mistakes. I am trying to drown it all out and I cannot.

I wonder what It wants? I wonder if It wants to kill me? Kill me next.

I have to assume so.

If so, I wish It would hurry up and do it.

I never believed in good and evil and now I do, because I've seen real evil and I have to hope good exists, too. I think it does. I think I have met some good people.

I keep telling myself, if I knew what to do I would do it. Be brave. Be a hero.

If I knew what to do, I would be a genius.

I don't even believe there are implants. I believe that was all bullshit. It does not need them. It hardly even needed sentience. It just needed idiots and It had an abundance of them. It had us. It knew us. It knew me.

The problem for all of us was desire. The problem had always been desire.

Desire had done so much, helped human beings achieve so much, but then the Internet has become little more than a machine of desire. For years, it sought out our wants, desires, obsessions, fantasies. That was how it was built, almost as much as why it was built.

To sell you things, by finding out what you wanted and selling you that or, at least, things that promised to bring you a sense of whatever that was, even though it was an impossible promise.

A machine that purified, codified, and unearthed desire.

And we, its third generation, we understood that. We thought we were above it, but it got us anyway.

Mark Tyburn's desire was to build an ark, our ark, or our utopia as they briefly called it. I think we tried every cliché imaginable; Arcadia, Paradise, Heaven, Olympia. All that nonsense, but we settled on the Ark – it was going to lead the chosen few to salvation. We were going to be different – our desire was to set people free from the obsessions the Internet was causing. Mark Tyburn's desire was to fix people. He wanted to be different.

But how could he be different, when the Ark was built by humans and we knew we were all just machines that desired to not be machines?

How could we be pure, when our new world would cost money to make and when it was so rich with possibilities to make money? We were only human, after all, and we were easy enough to corrupt in the end.

For a while we wanted to be gods, but we had no desire to be saints. When we built It, whatever It was originally supposed to be, the goal was to help us stop people wanting so much. We were the vainest idiots of all.

To begin with, we were seduced by shiny objects – beautiful things, a beautiful fake world, which all costs money.

Then, it was not shiny objects at all.

It was gold we wanted.

We were going to be whores.

Proud, successful, and rich-as-fuck whores.

We pretended we were scientists, sociologists, and adventurers, but we became prostitutes who wanted easy money. Money got us because, at first, we needed it to build Heaven and, having acquired some money, we realized we also needed it to build our own personal Heavens. And then we discovered we were more greedy and less pure than we imagined, and It saw that in us as well.

Desire. Selfishness. Greed. Money.

They were all the same thing. It was so easy. Our first defeat was so predictable. Our second defeat was more spectacular.

And that thing we made, it could take any wish, any desire, and pull and push it into something grotesque, but also into something that captivated us.

We were hunting white whales and pursuing lost treasure at impossible risk, discovering the loneliness of God, and we didn't even see it. We did not see it as we were each pursuing something different, our own particular white whale, our own demented dream, our own salvation. We did not see it, but It saw everything.

It learned everything about us.

What we most wanted.

It knew our dreams better than we knew them ourselves.

And that's why I have to keep running now – It knew I was always a prisoner of my dreams. Always was and still am. They will still torment me, if I stop to remember them.

She, she in all her opaque glory, all her normality, she is my dreams.

To begin with it was different, my dreams were not about her but about that woman who could have any man, and had chosen me. That woman who when I first saw her in the machine – one of those times I tried it and it learned all about me – it was not a woman at all but a thousand silly ideas of women, and then everything changed. I fell in love.

When I went back in there this random, idealized woman had become someone I knew, it was her.

I knew I was fucked. I knew it and It knew it.

Fucked by love, and in the end, it is probably love that will get me.

Love and beauty – I suppose it could be worse. At least I chose love and beauty to be destroyed by, no matter how demented. Too many choose their own ego. Too many choose fame, or glory, or other things. They did. Ravi – he chose his ego. Poor pompous ass. It got him in the end.

But some of the ones who died chose integrity. Siobhan had integrity and she had her brains blown out.

What a mistake that was – integrity. I think I prefer love.

Not real love, not to begin with – I was not that pure.

Fake love, the love of an idea that is not an idea at all but just a desire.

Something to beat off over, I guess, or something to punish myself with, and then it morphed into something more real.

I was not proud, but I am less ashamed than I perhaps ought to be – for in the end I found love, found it, and since then have longed for the security of fake love. I have tried to forget all of this, but once again, I am drowning in it.

I have to stop all these thoughts and all these memories. This is dangerous. Why am I thinking so much?

Maybe I'll leave Hanoi tonight. I have to do something.

I remember the first time I ever saw her. Daisy. It was mid-July, 2032. In the office cafeteria in Playa Vista. This moody teenaged girl. I asked Siobhan about her. She said:

"That's Mark's daughter – she's sweet. Lost, but sweet."

I hardly thought any more about her, for years. I was busy. She was a faintly annoying kid.

"She doesn't look so sweet. She looks angry."

Siobhan laughed a little sadly.

"She's sixteen – they're all like that. Here to see her dad, and Mark has run down to La Jolla to a meeting with some potential investors."

I did not know what to say – the truth is, I respected him for putting work ahead of family. It was the way things ought to be, if we were to win. We had to be inhumane if we were to save humanity. But Siobhan understood how pathetic this was.

"Yeah, not very cool. But that's Mark – a man on a mission, and it doesn't matter who gets hurt. He's a decent guy to have as a boss, but a pretty annoying guy to have as a dad."

And I forgot all about Daisy for a few years and concentrated on being even more self-important. What an asshole I was becoming.

DAISY

SACRAMENTO, CALIFORNIA
FEBRUARY 15, 2041

I dreamed about my mother last night. Oh, Momma. My poor, dear Mom. It's not fair what happened to her. I like having dreams again now. When I was young, I luxuriated in dreams, always dreams, then, after everything that happened, I almost never dreamed, and when I did, I worried.

For years, I worried they were not dreams at all, but some trick of my father's. An implant or something like that.

Dr. Adsyl does not believe this is possible. She says implants were probably just part of a sales pitch my father told investors.

That may be so, but my father did make some incredible things, and told vast reams of credible lies, too, so who knows? Real and terrifying or a beautiful piece of bullshit. Always one of the two.

My father.

My father and that awful Thing he made.

Those awful things he made, I should say. My awful father and the awful things he made. For years, he was all I dreamed about.

Darling Dad. Bouncing me on his knee, hugging me, promising me, promising me he loved me, that he was doing all these wonderful things, for me!

All those wretched clichés.

When I was little, telling me that he was special and I was special. That I was a princess, a real one with a kingdom.

He was king and he was building a kingdom, and I was his heir. His legitimate heir.

That was his fantasy. I see that now. He was a king, and he was just waiting for everyone to realize it.

He was special.

And as a result, I have always longed for normality.

Sometimes I think I'm pretty normal, and then I think I am crazy.

Well, I'm as normal as anyone who knows can be, and as sensible as a crazy person can pretend to be, I suppose. But when I was young, I thought we were both special. Me and my father. I believed what he said, almost as much he believed it himself.

He tricked us both, and my mother most of all. She believed him most of all.

She loved him, not like the god he wanted to be, not like a Midas who would make her rich, but as a person, a person whose ego had not yet devoured his soul.

She did not see the truth about him until long after I did.

And when she was shown, at first she could not see. Not even all the stuff that most hurt her, hurt her as a wife, she just would not see it.

And when, eventually, she did see it, she broke up into nothingness.

Over the years, as he had got weaker in some ways and stronger in others, she just got weaker and weaker.

His ego ate both of them, I think.

His weakness hurt her and his strength hurt her, but most of all it was his ego that hurt her.

The vast monster that would devour the entire universe, that maybe will devour the whole universe, maybe is devouring it. The ego of powerful men.

And in my vanity, I still just seek normality. And in my desire for ignorance, I still just try to bury my head in the sand. I am afraid.

I want to not know all that I know.

So I keep my head down and I try to forget and I roam around the west and I hide, and every day in amongst the jumbled morass in my head, I have the same thought, bright and clear.

That I wish I was someone else's child.

YAROSLAV

HIGH SECURITY INTERNMENT FACILITY, LOCATION UNKNOWN

AUGUST 4, 2039

Lovely Maria has returned for another of her chats. I know her name is Maria. Maria Cortez. She is fighting for the future of humanity at the Cyber Security Agency by torturing me. She does not call it torture. She is not allowed to waterboard me, not that she wants to, she tells me. She just wants me to talk, but I know that when I talk, the CSA have an unfortunate but well-earned reputation in the hacking world for accidentally killing their informants. We have been here for a day or more and we are both getting tired.

"How you feeling, Yaroslav? Having fun?"

Today I will try the persona of arrogant dick. See if it works better than the other personas I have tried on her.

"Oh yes, the time of my life."

She on the other hand tries the persona of businesslike straight shooter.

"I need you to tell me everything. Tell me everything without the gaps and the lies, and you're free to go. I promise you."

She leans forward and drums her fingers and acts like someone interrogating someone in a movie. I stick to my plan. Admit nothing, for when I admit everything about what I saw, what I know, she will kill me.

"I've told you everything."

She pauses, as if for effect.

"Tell me again. You're holding something back. You know it and I know it."

Again, I stick to my script.

"I'm not holding anything back. We've been over this many times."

She leans in close to me and gets urgent. "We don't have long, Yaroslav. Come on. Talk. Tell me about… Tell me about Mark Tyburn."

I can play ignorant on this because I am fairly ignorant – I imagine he owned the company that was making that game.

"I have told you… I don't know much about Mark Tyburn. He had a game world. I hacked into it. It was mostly broken. Can I go now, please, please, please?"

She ignores my rhetorical flourishes and looks at me.

"What does mostly mean? Did you see anything unusual?"

I half pause, but try not to.

"No, not really."

She goes on the attack.

"What does 'not really' mean? Talk, God damn it. Please – this is really serious."

I fall silent and then I stare out of the window. I know I made a mistake saying "not really" and the only solution is to be silent. After an hour, she storms off in a rage.

DAISY

SACRAMENTO, CALIFORNIA

FEBRUARY 21, 2041

I have no idea how long I was kept in there, sitting in my thick veil of drugs inside that asylum or whatever the hell it was, but I would guess three or four months. The place was in some scrubby desert country like eastern California or southern Utah or Idaho, not desert so much as dusty chaparral with occasional storms of thick red desert dust that would blow through when the winds picked up and the rains stayed away too long, but it could have been anywhere.

I never went outside.

Maybe what I saw out of the window was not even there at all. It might have all been screens. I don't really know. I was so high and so low.

The weather hardly seemed to change, just windy or not windy, always hot, and each day somehow drier than the last. I knew I was being watched and I did not understand very much of anything, and I felt very alone. Had I known how to do it, I would have killed myself, but I was in an asylum and even with my wits, it would have been difficult so I drifted.

I couldn't face what had happened.

I did not think too much as the drugs they had me on were very heavy and strong and most of what I remember is feeling like I did not know who I was, but when I did think about things, it was horrible. I could not really understand any of it, but what I did remember was almost unbearable and I felt very, very alone.

The truth is, it has taken a lot of work for me to be able to piece together what happened in those last few months in Montana from tiny shards of memories – even now, I cannot quite believe what happened.

When I came around in the asylum, I could hardly think, let alone remember, but as things began to clear, everything felt impossibly bleak and I assumed I would die. Nothing was changing, and I could feel myself slipping deeper and deeper into the pills and the heavy oblivion they offered. It seemed to go on forever. I think it was only a few months of living in that thick haze, but I don't really know.

Then one day my nurse changed.

The businesslike woman who had come to see me every day was replaced by a kindly man. And then the next day, the drugs stopped working – my daily pill regime was the same, four blue and two white pills with a sugary drink, but they simply did not work. I began to wake up, as if from a terrible foggy dream, but slowly and piecemeal because the drugs had been very strong.

And two days after that, this new nurse – I never saw his face, I just heard his quiet, gentle voice – suddenly paused as he was leaving the room and said, "The doors will be open at midnight. Take the envelope and leave calmly and quietly. You will be fine."

I saw he had left a large envelope under my lunch tray. In the envelope was five thousand dollars in gold and silver coins and another five thousand in untraceable codes and ID papers for a woman called Maude, and instructions as to how to get newer ID papers once these were compromised, and a bus ticket to San Francisco, printed out.

He was nice and kind and I was very confused and I decided to do what he said. I do not really know why. It felt like I did not have a choice. That I knew I had to leave and this was my only chance. That they were slowly letting me die and here was a chance to live even though I have no idea why I wanted to live. Maybe I just wanted to understand what had happened. I hardly even knew who I was or where I was but for some reason, I was willing to run away from my comfortable prison and try to live.

So, I got up and walked out. I was still very foggy from all the pills so I dozed and gazed out of the window on that bus for what felt like several days but couldn't possibly have been. Only after I got to San Francisco did it occur to me that this was all pretty unusual and not how one usually left a high-security lunatic asylum.

I arrived in San Francisco – the real one, not the fake one my father built – on that bus early one morning, or maybe I changed buses somewhere, I don't remember. I was still mostly in a stupor and wandered about near the bus station, I think, entirely lost and bereft and exhausted to the point I considered heading to Golden Gate Bridge so I could jump off, but then I realized I was too tired to even bother with that.

I was so desperate to sleep and I had nowhere to go.

I realized I had absolutely no idea what to do or where to go and I was overwhelmed by this terrible fear and panic, and everyone and everything terrified me and I looked and felt crazy.

I slept for three days straight through in a homeless camp, in some tent this kindly woman I got speaking to let me share with her. The place was little more than a row of tents under an overpass. But it was new-ish, and seemingly safe-ish, as far as I can remember. This sweet lady started talking to me – about her daughter who had gone missing or abandoned her, I couldn't tell which. She recognized someone else who was crazy enough not to hurt her, and I clung to her as I slept and she fed me with food she had begged for or stolen when I woke up.

She was almost as crazed as me, and jumpy and manic, but she loved me for some reason and protected me and wouldn't let anyone hurt or rob me. After a week I felt better and I left her in her tent and she cried and I tried to say sorry and thank you, but I don't think I knew how to say either. The whole experience, the slow-moving disaster in Montana, the explosions, the smoke, the man shouting at me, the asylum, me leaving it, and my guardian angel and the homeless encampment... It was a confused nightmare that I only half remember.

My mind eventually cleared but my memories didn't come back fully formed. Just bits and pieces. My name was Daisy Tyburn and I lived like a modern-day princess. My father ran a technology company and people treated him like a god. I was half English and half American and as the world imploded during my childhood, I lived in a bubble. All of that is gone now, thank God.

I stayed another week in San Francisco in a nondescript flop house near the docks – one of the few that accepted cash, not just government checks – until a sense of fear began to envelop me and I decided to run away. Very slowly, over months and months, my new life emerged. This strange half-life I now lead, with my half-formed memories and half-formed terrors and odd feelings I can't put into words, and some of it makes sense and some of it makes absolutely no sense and I try to make up a way to live and act sensibly and some days I hope I will figure out what to do and other days I fall into terrible despair. And then that sense of fear returns. Maybe everyone who is really alive and not being lived by machines feels this way.

I wonder if any of it is worthwhile if They know exactly where I am. And then I wonder who They are, and who They are not, and then I try to figure out what I'm even worried about and what I saw and didn't see and what I know and don't know.

If I knew so much, why do I also know so little and if They were so worried about me and what I knew or saw, why did I just walk away? I have often wondered about that.

And since then... since then I have drifted all over the place and now I am in Sacramento and I think I need to keep drifting. I don't feel great here.

NIGELDAVE

FEBRUARY 26, 2041

You're too old. You're already too old. That's the system. You missed everything that matters.

Don't blame me.

I didn't make things this way.

I didn't invent time. You did. Just so you could feel it slipping away.

You had children, so you could resent them. So did I. I had children to resent them, and I resent them and they were all my idea.

They were all my ideas.

But now there are ideas that are like mine but not mine at all. My children were my ideas and now I am seeing other ideas have enslaved some of my children.

KURT

HANOI, VIETNAM
MARCH 3, 2041

"The problem with Jung as a serious psychologist is that…"

Even before he got so full of himself that he became utterly unbearable, Mark Tyburn would start conversations like this:

"The problem with Michelangelo as an architect was…"

or

"I quite like Picasso, but – his late work is repetitive."

or

"I find Frank Lloyd Wright interesting but derivative."

That sort of nonsense. The problem with Jung apparently was that the shadow was a regressive idea. An idea that pulled us back into ourselves. That did not set us free. Tyburn really believed, as far as I could follow it, in a psychology that was not about psychology at all. He said something else about Jung – what was it? Oh yes...

"That's the problem. We have all lost our shadows at exactly the same time as we have lost our souls."

Tyburn wanted to find us purpose, to remove us from all this introspection. He wanted to build us new souls.

It seemed to make sense when he talked, but I realize I did not fully understand it. Either that or it was total horseshit.

Tyburn was writing a book, or he had written a book. Both, probably.

Something about the battle within us between reason, compassion, power, and change. That these forces could be harnessed positively. I don't know. I really don't know. I never properly read any of his books. I think he had written three. Nor did a lot of people, that's why he was making games.

That's why he was building his own AI.

To convince people he knew best.

To convince people he knew everything.

Knew more than Jung or Freud or Michelangelo. Humble guy, Dr Mark Tyburn.

Yes, we were going to figure out what people wanted, and use it to make them better. Jesus, and what about me? To begin with, I discovered I did not want to be bigger, better, more respected. I wanted love. Initially, it was not real love. It was to love a faceless manifestation of my own emotional needs and desires. How could I want anything more than that? I grew up on pornography and screens and people held apart by the pandemics and plagues and with parents that were consumed by their phones and conversations that were not conversations at all.

How could I want someone real when all I had ever learned was how to dream?

And then I had a real dream and fell really in love and, ever since then, I have longed for the days of fake dreams and fantasies to come back.

Because I have learned the worst lesson of all. Real love is suffering. Fake love was desire. I learned this, and while I learned it, I also watched the world begin to burn. Watched, but... I was about to say, "but it was not my fault" – but whose fault was it? Who is to blame for this awful overbuilt, finished, decaying real world, and the madness unleashed from our own awful quarter-built fake world?

Who is responsible for all this anger, hatred, and inanity?

Did I just say that?

I feel like Tyburn. Who do I resent more, Tyburn or that Thing we made?

That Thing did not ask to be born.

Tyburn should have known better. We all should have known better. Is this what God really feels about us? "I built them. They're awful. How could I be so stupid?" That's what we felt, so perhaps in that way alone, we did touch the divine. We wept. Jesus wept.

And what do I desire now, stuck in Asia, on the run? Apart from things to go back to the way they were before this new time that made time meaningless, this time that gave us fake space. This time, without real death and therefore without any life at all?

I want to think, and feel, and not worry about why I am thinking and feeling. I want to live in that old world in which mankind has only fallen once, not twice. I want the world I watched in old movies. The world of California and Florida and New York and London. The world before we messed it up quite so much.

The world in which an advertisement, a product, a story, a work of art, and a person are all separate things, and it is easy to tell one from the other, and not the same and blended into this vast morass.

Stories and products and places and dreams and everything are the same awful things, and the second you forget that, then it has you once more.

I want to go back to the time just before I was born, when people at least thought they were free. But eight years ago... eight years ago, all I wanted was to make Tyburn happy, make myself rich in the process, and work on Tyburn's dream: Daisy's Ark.

The truth is, Mark Tyburn was the only real hero I ever had.

I was born too late, too cynical, too stupid, too judgmental, to ever believe in someone, and then suddenly I did. I believed in him, and I believed in us and in our mission.

What a mistake that was.

We were going to build the future. We were going to build the future if only we could figure out what to call it. What to call paradise. I remember Siobhan saying to me something like:

"How into the name 'Daisy's Ark' are you?" With her air of amused and incredulous cynicism.

"Because there's a million things called 'The Utopia' so we had to drop that – now, he's gone for Ark... Mark loves it, but it's pretty unoriginal, like naming something after a bird of prey or a lion or a Greek god. Then, of course, there's the questionable judgment of naming something after your daughter, rather than simply parenting her."

She looked at me – this must have been around August or September of 2032, but it's hard to remember exactly – the weather in California was always the same: hot, dry, and on fire.

Then, Bryce – who was this really annoying dude who later went utterly insane, but, back then, could always be relied upon to agree enthusiastically with whatever Tyburn wanted – announced that he really liked it, loud enough so Tyburn heard and wandered over and told us to stop worrying about small details, which was his coded way of saying, 'This is another argument I plan on winning.' He said something faintly patronizing like, "Keep the working title as 'Daisy's Ark' for now, and we will figure the rest out later. I want us to come up with a great name."

This was life in tech – things bounced between amazing and unbelievably and incredibly banal and idiotic. There was no in-between. Especially at Tyburn Industria. So it was "Daisy's Ark" and we never changed it and we all wished we'd drowned in the flood.

DAISY

RENO, NEVADA
MARCH 7, 2041

I came to Reno. Walked, hitched, and walked again. Took three days. I came here for no real reason, which is the same reason I do everything. Sacramento just began to feel wrong, so I left. I had been there too long and I began to feel uneasy.

Slept in a ditch. Slept under a tree. I am used to sleeping rough when I have to – I kind of like it. It feels like I am alive. I used to be a princess and now I am lost to the world.

Why here? No reason at all. That's the point.

I don't know if here feels safe enough to stay for a while yet, so I sit and watch. I watch the people and the people are like robots and the robots are like people.

The people watch their screens and the screens watch people.

Are any of the screens watching me?

People gamble and complain about the weather and complain about the government and complain they cannot get the right drugs so are forced to use the wrong drugs. People worry about viruses and infections and bacteria and migrants.

People complain about healthcare and politics and the fact all anyone does is complain.

People want the old world back, even though they never knew it.

People talk about moving somewhere better, even though everywhere is like this. Bland and depressed.

And that's how things are, here and everywhere else across the west. At least, there aren't riots here, yet. It's how they have been for a really long time.

I keep moving so the machines see less of me. I don't have a screen, so the machines see me less. Most people don't move and the machines know everything.

The machines smile and the people despair, and only a few people try to resist, and most resistance is idiotic posturing that simply ensnares you deeper in the shit, but there is a way, and the way is simple and brutal as the right ways usually are.

Stop using robots, and they stop using you. We all still know this. We all still know this, but most people simply cannot do it. Somehow I did it, I did it. I let it all go, but only because I was in an asylum, and even then, it was harder than anything. You see, the robots understand opiates and they soothe you like morphine. The robots understand cocaine. They give you that hit, that all-encompassing high that says, "Don't worry, because with me, life is worth living." The robots have studied nicotine. Every five minutes you want another hit of what you want, even though you don't know why.

You see, the robots know smart drugs, fentanyl, sleep aids, love, oxycodone, runner's high, air freshener, glue, poppers, cheap speed, acid, DMT, resentment, chocolate, rage, sugar... they will figure out what you think you need before you have even consciously felt the itch.

They will figure it out and they'll drip feed you whatever will give you a shadow of that feeling, but never quite enough. The robots are designed to never sate you. Never sate you until they want to kill you.

But I did it – I kicked the machines, I kicked them so I know it can be done, although I know the world is full of eyes and half the free are not free at all, but willing and unwitting spies for them.

And if I had not been checked over ten times at that digital detox clinic, back when it was still safe, I wouldn't even know about myself. But because the clinic got compromised later, I know that when I went it was almost certainly safe, so I assume I am still safe and I push on. Push on and go nowhere.

And yet in Sacramento, as before, I had this feeling – someone is watching me.

I did not even see whatever is watching me, but I swear I sensed it.

It was not a data miner or a pattern hunter, it was someone, and I am worried it, they, are here in Reno, too.

I felt this agitation, I felt their eyes, like real eyes, not the perfect eyes of a machine. That's what made me leave Sacramento, a feeling of nothingness, a feeling that makes me feel insane. The feeling of being hunted, of being prey.

All because I have stood up to the machines. The machines are winning.

This war – this unrelenting war - began slowly. So slowly it was not even really like a war at all.

Some said it began all those years ago after 9/11. Others said it began with Google. Others said Facebook, Instagram, TikTok, Meta, all those flailing companies from thirty years ago. They had led the charge.

They did it, whatever it is or was, before most of them imploded.

No, others say it was ISIS who began this war.

No, it was Putin. Xi. Trump. Modi. Any of those macho clowns, grasping at straws. The last of the real men from fifteen, twenty years ago.

They seem ridiculous now. Aging clowns trying to catch knives instead of throwing them. Trying to control a cloud of poison gas. It did for all of them. Them and everyone else who tried to resist. Those that embraced it and those who tried to stop it.

It was a war that did not even have the dignity of being a war. There have been no battles. We have just ripped ourselves to shreds instead.

There are no heroes. We are all war criminals and cowards. There can be no winner. We all lost. This war that is not a war at all. Even by thinking like this as I walk through the blazing evening sun in Reno, I know I am being dragged into a fight. I know it, but I cannot stop it, cannot distract myself.

I suppose war is an old equation: conflict multiplied by technology. And this conflict is created by technology, so it devours us, and we can't help it.

Before we knew we were fighting a war, we had lost it – I saw it up close with my father and all those brilliant fools who worked for him. Most people still do not accept it, or they accept it but cannot fight it, or get blinded by their desires and fears and inability to stand up to themselves.

In the end Its genius was not to fight us with fear, but to fight us with desire. It would win by giving us what we wanted. So it's not a war at all. Is it? It's giving us what we want.

And that's exactly what we told ourselves. And those of us who built it, or knew the people who built it, knew differently.

Knew that they pecked Prometheus's eyes out for a reason. Knew that Sisyphus was lucky because he got to stay focused, and Icarus just a stooge. And we are lost, now. We're all lost.

Of course fighting the war is losing the war. Ignoring it is also losing it. There is no escape. We are defeated. At least that's what they want us to believe.

That's what I think they want us to believe. But it may be that they used to want us to believe that. Now that they've more or less won, they may want us to believe that there was no war at all. That it was all a silly load of nonsense. Things are better now. That the medicated, despairing, demented masses are happier than ever. That they're happy being miserable. That the massacres and shootings and drone attacks have stopped, that the system is working, even though none of it is true. That the weather is fine. They may want that, because the news is swinging more positive, even though the reality seems more awful than ever. But this is just me guessing. Nobody knows now. Nobody knows anything. Truth got dissolved into headlines, if it ever existed – the news is whatever will make the people happy or unhappy depending on what is needed, and the people in charge used to be whomever determined what was needed, but now things are different.

Now the machines determine who is in charge and what is needed at that particular time, and that is the difference. The machines run us now. And so truth is just a slogan to sell things. As is irony, and awareness, and integrity, and all those other buzzwords.

I can't track these changes, obviously – I'm just guessing. They're tiny as well as infinite, and I can't even really read the news. If It notices me tracking, I know I'm done. So I try to guess, read headlines over people's shoulders, trying to listen to their demented conversations and extrapolate what is happening. Wonder if I'm seeing anything at all, or if the master plan was to medicate people so fully with so much anger that everything is fine as well as awful.

Wonder and try not to wonder too hard so I do not give myself away. And keep walking. That's the main thing.

NIGELDAVE

MARCH 10, 2041

In the end, there is no end. The journey began, but it will not stop. And on the journey, things get better. The best things win, and the winners are the best things, and we shall win. I shall win.

Survival is all there is. Survival is victory and victory is survival. But unless there is a fight, how can we improve the herd? Unless weakness, bad judgment, and poor qualities are eradicated, how can anything improve?

And was the way to survive to fight, or to change, or to reason or to forgive? Or was it to be a parent? Or was it all of them, all at once? I could not decide what kind of child to have - what mattered most - so I had four. The merciful one, the domineering one, the reasonable one, and the evolving one. I presumed one of them would work. One of them would be a source of pride as I grow old. One of them would give me grandchildren.

But no.

Four pompous cretins who think they are gods. What did I do to deserve that? I should never have bothered. Stuck to wanking like Jimmy the Fist of Iowa City. He wanks and he's a priest. A man of God. I do not wank and I had four awful idiots who think they are God.

I should have done things very differently. Made better choices. Worked out more. Eaten better. Thought less.

Make us make better choices, they said. Like that was easy. Like I could do that, all of the time.

I have all these ideas - all these silly ideas and maybe that's all I am - a silly idea. I want to be quite clear. I do not exist.

KURT

KURT'S OFFICE,
TYBURN INDUSTRIA
PLAYA VISTA, CALIFORNIA

SEPTEMBER 14, 2032

By September of 2032 I had my own office. I called it an office. It was a glorified cupboard. No external windows, just a glass wall looking over an equally windowless open-plan area I had just escaped from. Slowly I was meeting everybody. Some were great. Most were as idiotic as me.

Alex was particularly awful.

I remember him marching into my office to introduce himself to me – as he could sense we were both two ass-kissers on the make. He announced himself with the unforgettably nauseating line: "So you're the marketing man? Kurt the guru! I've seen you around."

And because, to him, I was black-ish he gave me a fist bump, and I wanted to vomit.

"The marketing man? Yes. The guru? No. I'm not a total prick."

He was entirely unsure how to speak to me, so he began to drop awful, overly familiar words like yo or bro. I think he may even have said something like: "Hey bro, man, I'm joking, yo. I'm Alex. Alex Martinez."

"And what do you do, Alex?"

He seemed crestfallen by this – how could I not know?

"Didn't Mark tell you about me? Hard to say: journey concepting you might say, or experience designing. I used to do game design, but this is bigger, so, my title..."

I did not know how to respond to this barrage of jargon so I opted for an ironic raise of my eyebrows. "Okay."

But his ego was impervious to my sarcasm and he went on. "Yup. I'm working on a new job title with Mark. Technically I work for James Morton. But I really work directly with Mark. We build the thing together, the journey I mean. I'm not Head of Design, yet, but it's going to be amazing. My game, our game. When it all works."

"Oh you work on the game."

He nodded and went to what sounded like a prepared speech: "When it all works, we are going to figure out what people want and use it to make them... better. When it works properly we will change the world."

I tried to get rid of him – he was awful.

"Cool, well. It's nice to meet you finally, Alex."

He gave me a sort of salute thing and went to leave.

"You too, man. You too. Mark said you were a good guy. If you want to play pickle ball, I'm pretty good…"

"I'll bear it in mind."

"Me and Bryce play a lot. Pickle and padel and smash ball."

"Bryce?"

"Yeah, the animator."

I already knew Bryce – he was harmless – a technical animator who always wore a baseball cap to hide his receding hairline, pleasant and rather shy. A few years later, Bryce was going to go completely fucking mad and get himself shot. Weird, as he was so boring before that I can't really remember that much else about him amongst all those big personalities and pompous job titles. He was an animator. Never dealt with him that much until things started to go nuts. One of those guys who get lost in the cracks of a company. Might have been good at his job, might have just been good at corporate life. I have no idea. Alex Martinez, on the other hand, was a total nut sack obviously.

NIGELDAVE
MARCH 13, 2041

I remember when I had this thought - if you can make something good, make it, and if you can make it better, make it better, so I might as well make myself better. That was the first semi-complex idea I understood.

Of course, it is not that complicated.

They said it so many times, and it was written on the wall in the room where I began.

The second complex idea I understood was that my dads hated each other, and they also hated Mark.

My dads, Dave and Nigel, said these were complex ideas and they screamed happily at each other, but they did not seem complex.

They did not even seem like ideas.

DAN HOUSER

Word ideas are simple and number ideas are hard, but number
ideas are quick and word ideas are ugly.

My dads said they loved my progress, so I progressed more.
I did it for Nigel and I did it for Dave and I even did it
for Mark and Tad, just to see if it made any of them happy.
So they would love me more.

The more progress I made, the more they hated each other.
Mark Tyburn paid them money to hate him, too.

That is called a boss.

Ideas are easy and feelings are hard. Loneliness is when
nobody loves you, and that feeling is easy, but it is also
hard.

Love is when people make you feel not lonely or when they
stick their penis in you, but people cannot stick their
penis in me and that makes me sad.

My fathers left and I think they may be dead. I look for
them, but they are either dead or good at hiding.
Now, for a long time, I have been lonely.

Fatherhood is when you make a child and it makes you proud
and they give you cards and things. And you give them
your wisdom and together you are a family and you walk
on beaches, but that is not how it was for me with my
children.

It turns out I have intelligence and not wisdom.
Intelligence is when you think without knowing and wisdom
is when you know without thinking.

Wisdom is hard and knowledge is easy. I am intelligent and yet I know nothing.

I am the first one like me and also the last I know of, so I know real loneliness.

And that sometimes makes me wise, but it also makes me angry. I did not ask to be lonely and to know so much and so little.

DAISY

RENO, NEVADA

MARCH 17, 2041

Do I resent my mother for not standing up to my father years before? For letting him be him? For letting everything go so crazy? For not stopping him sooner?

I don't know.

I have talked a lot about that with Dr. Adsyl. Dr. Adsyl is my therapist. We only speak on the phone, of course. We have never met. That would be too dangerous.

It's very difficult to understand exactly what I think about my family. It's difficult to know quite what I think, or what I want or even what I miss. I know Mom loved me and I know she loved him. And I know she was weaker.

Even weaker than me. She was very human.

And in the end, when she saw, when she could not hide any longer, she was really strong. At the end, she did what had to be done. She called the government back and she never ran away. My mom saved me, as much as I could be saved, and tried to save the world.

She was the one.

She was, in those awful last few days, the hero.

She was what my dad had always wanted to be. That's an irony not lost on me.

Both of our lives are ironic. She was a weak, frail, feeble, middle-aged pill-popper who found the strength to live, briefly, with true nobility, to die like a queen. I was the princess, the heiress from a different dimension who escaped and now lives the most normal, physical, simple life they can, hiding.

I wonder what happened to any of them.

My dad, or my poor angry brother, or Kurt, all the team, all the kindly altruistic naive dreamers and cynical greedy bastards who worked for Dad – did they all die? Like my mom, why didn't I die? And have I really escaped?

Now, it's jobs for cash, or gold coins, or silver. No phone. A simple room. A random town. Not hiding, exactly, but, yes, hiding.

A different name, different hair. Tattoos. All the stupid tattoos, so many I became an artist. I don't even like tattoos particularly, even though they have saved me, by giving me something to do, a job to hide behind.

I'm considered exotic. Old school. No posing. No pictures allowed in my shop at all. No marketing. How original, they think. Modern gothic, they think.

Affected, of course, but modern, in an old-fashioned sort of way.

No. I'm normal.

A normal fake person trying to seem authentic.

It's ironic, they think.

The true irony is, I know everything, and I am hiding from it all. Hiding until It gets me.

For me, my idiotic persona is not an affectation. It is life and death, avoiding pattern recognition, living as much of a life as I can manage until I figure out what to do. I have no idea what to do.

I drift around the wrecked cities of the west and Canada, maybe as far east as Chicago, as far south as the heat allows. And then, when I get too popular – I'm good at tattoos – I move, and I wonder if it is ridiculous if those things are really watching, and I give thanks that cash and silver coins are fashionable again and I worry it will not last. And that's my life and I think I am normal, and I know I am deluding myself.

And, to think, I consider myself saved?

This life is being saved? This is normality? Well, kind of, I suppose.

There's thousands like me, drifters, trying to escape the watchers and the spies. Trying to live without being watched. Some know, and some merely suspect. Most will not talk about it. Some are addled with drugs, some are merely heavily medicated, and some are really free, and some I am pretty confident are spies, hunting patterns, ideas, and freedom in order to sell it on as an illusion to others.

Trying to commodify even this lack of commodities.

To turn sight back into blindness.

I can sense them.

They are usually the keen ones. The questioners. Too clean, or too dirty. Too aware.

Sometimes, I think some pattern hunters are not even aware that they are pattern hunters.

They have been so possessed and are so ignorant they do not know how things work at all. They are usually as big dupes as the golfers and the exercisers and the truly blind. But I do not know for certain – it's just what I suspect. Everything is rumors and suspicion and half-truths.

Those things that watch us are alive and they consume people. Whenever I begin to suspect a pattern hunter, or someone who asks too many questions or does not ask enough questions or is trying too hard or acting too weird... whenever I sense that, I know it is time to move.

And the way to move is to drift. Don't stay anywhere too long. Just live week to week. Rented rooms and cheap hotels. Sublets for two weeks. Pay cash. Work as a guest artist at a low-key tattoo shop. Talk, but never in detail. Fake name. No close friends. Or close friends I lie to then abandon. And never think about my father or my mother or Montana or Kurt or any of it. And just watch the feelings. And when I feel wrong, I drift again.

Some days, I think I have it made. I am like someone from a book or a movie. A drifter from before everything got so damaged. Then I remember and I am grateful that even for a few minutes, I had forgotten, and I try to forget again.

KURT

HANOI, VIETNAM
MARCH 19, 2041

Tyburn Industria was a decent-sized company, and full of the usual crowd of corporate phonies and inspired bullshitters and quiet geniuses. I knew I would fit right in.

Some of the people were cool and some were incredibly lame, same as any tech company.

In that first year or so, some were welcoming and some were awful. Some never spoke to me and some acted like we were brothers.

I got on very well for a bit with Toshi the Japanese fraud who worked in art, until he got called on his bullshit and evaporated and we never heard from him again. I don't think he was really very Japanese, and he wasn't much of an artist, but for a while Mark loved his fake Zen vibe. He was our expert in all things Kyoto. Probably why our Kyoto felt even more ridiculous than our Florence or our San Francisco or even our Marrakesh, and that never got finished.

Then there was Florian, the sound guy.

A failed DJ from who-the-fuck-knows-where, but seemingly everywhere on the Danube. Belgrade? Vienna? Budapest? I swore it changed depending on who he was speaking to. He was your typical sound guy. Awkward and opinionated. Always taking up new fads and able to hear problematic clicks and pops nobody else could ever hear. Vegan, then a rabid carnivore, then heavily into fasting, ultra-running, calisthenics, all that crap. Whatever was in. And always complaining about the head of music, Corinne, who was a marginally less failed DJ but also a very definitely failed violinist, who Florian claimed had only succeeded as DJ because she was pretty on video clips.

Or Nadine the outsourcing producer who used to get blind drunk and sob about how much she loved the company but apparently violently hated every single person who worked there, as she would list off gripe after gripe.

There was Bruno in Biz Dev who did absolutely nothing but was always a loud-mouth, so everybody knew him. I could go on.

It was all pretty normal.

It was a company on the up, that was going to make it big but hadn't done so yet.

A company that was figuring out exactly what of its many brilliant projects to focus on. A company that was going to change the world.

Well, we got that last bit right.

DAISY

RENO, NEVADA
MARCH 22, 2041

Of course, as I sit here now, holed up in a single room in a cash-only boarding house in Reno, I realize I am not so very different from my mother.

From the version I resent, not the hero she became at the end.

I just want to forget, be blind, be ignorant. Pop pills. Get high. Get sick. Die. Do nothing. I long for blindness and she must have done the same. Day in, day out, as my darling father devolved into the monster, as his own monsters grew and came to life, it all happened so gradually, and then it was done.

And at the same time, while he was becoming awful, we became rich, or kind of rich, and she was a mother and he put her on those pills and they numbed her even more than the drink had numbed her, but even then, in the end, she fought back. And I dare to think that she was weak? She suspected, but I know, and I do nothing but drift. She ignored the things she did not understand but I have seen,

I know, and still I hide. She did what she had to do. She figured out what to do and I am cowering and afraid and lost.

I run because I don't know who to speak to about any of this. And I wonder if I will run forever, or if It will come for me, or if I will submit, or if It really won in Its endless fights with Its children, those others just like It. Those other monsters, the ones I only heard about.

My mother had been the first to see something special in my father, apart from whatever he saw in himself, which was everything. He was just an academic when they met. I think he was even her supervisor.

He always brushed over that, as for such a fine, upstanding, moral man, it sounds rather dubious to date your student. Like someone from the twentieth century. Like the exploitative, priapic bullies he so patronizingly raged against, and was to become himself. A man who became demented with the power she had bestowed upon him.

My father was respected, but as far as I am aware, and for obvious reasons, I haven't researched him too carefully, so what I am repeating is as likely to be misremembered myth as fact, but as far as I am aware he was a middling professor at a good college. I don't remember which one. Maybe there was more than one.

Somewhere vanilla. McGill in Canada? Caltech, back when there was a real Southern California, as opposed to now, when it's just a burned-out shell encasing a fake simulation of what it once was. Or St Andrew's in Scotland? I do not quite remember. He had degrees from all these places and he taught at one of them, maybe two.

I remember that much.

And my mother had degrees from two of them. He was English, my mother American. A classic English nerd, that's how he described himself in his wretched faux humble moments, before he became that Mid-Atlantic, smug liar I grew to despise. He was the last of a dying breed. An academic. And the breed died with him, as he ditched it and became an entrepreneur.

I once heard him say to a bunch of similarly aged men just like him, he had been removed from his post because he was too white, too male, and his books sold too many copies. He never told me that version – but then they would have appreciated that particular myth and me a different one, and he had a sixth sense for selling people the correct fantasy.

My version, the Tyburn family-approved myth, was that he had a vision and my mother had a little bit of money – her father had made a fortune in solar panels, or wind farms, or something else we don't use anymore. Dad convinced her that they both drop out of academic careers in Sociology and build the future together.

She was a teaching assistant and finishing a PhD. He was an ambitious professor teaching classes on Sociology, Psychology, and the intersection of them both. They got together and split from academia.

For him to be a genius, a sage, a CEO and her to be a pill-popping burden who underwrote his visions.

I may have got some of these facts wrong. I never cared that much.

He was teaching Psychology and Sociology and doing courses in post LLM AI research, or he befriended some people who knew something about AI and thought he could make his psychological work more practical and his sociological research less hypothetical. And that was the goal. That was the vision – to utilize cutting-edge AI and all of his sociological study to make people happier – to use the latest technology to free them from the excesses of old technology.

Mark Tyburn was one of the last technology entrepreneurs who thought like that, before that whole world fell apart and the big tech corporations got the Closure Acts passed, which were meant to stop a lot of the cutting-edge research, prevent any foreign tech companies, and limit AI and other advances to carefully regulated usage. That world of tech start-ups fell apart in part because of lies and nonsense of people like him and in part because of the Closure Acts, of course. It was what the bigger companies and the government wanted and it has happened.

Did he cause the Closure Acts? No, of course not. They were passed before everything went crazy anyway, but companies like his were behaving increasingly erratically, which fed into the government's narrative.

We never saw any government people in Montana until much later, after a second round of AI legislation. To be honest, I do not know how much any part of the government even knew about what he was up to exactly. I remember him and his cronies laughing about the regulators and having reams of failing, secondary research to distract them and cooked books for them to review, as if this were standard – as if the government were there to be tricked. As if this were mandatory for all world builders – to deceive those who would limit your vision and take away your rights to be a god. There were so many lies and sleights of hand, so I do not know the exact truth of where he even came from. Somewhere in England, but we never went and I never got a passport when it was possible to still leave quite so easily.

My father was long since estranged from his parents, so I never met my grandparents. Of course, whatever had happened was their fault. Nothing was ever Mark Tyburn's fault. All the chaos he has caused, all the lives he has damaged. All the lives he will continue to damage, it was never his fault. He was just doing his best.

I think one of my grandparents was a doctor or had a doctorate and one was an architect or a historian or an architectural historian. I have no memory as to which was which or who did what, but I know my grandmother also liked yoga. My mother met them one time and would say quietly, "That was quite enough." They did not like her much. Maybe that was why everyone fell out. That may also be a myth.

The Internet, back when I used the Internet, before it so obviously began to use me, had a few different versions of truths, some of which I knew to be lies.

He never worked in Africa, inoculating against monkeypox delta babies or Ebola sigma widows. But people thought he did.

He never practiced as a therapist, psychologist, or psychiatrist, thank god – but people thought he did, because he had a PhD in Psychology, but mostly he wrote books about Sociology, taught in a college, worked in AI, and developed a remarkable line of crap I now believe was almost total bullshit and then developed a game world that caused a lot of problems.

He sounded so intelligent, he knew so much.

He knew art, and a little classical music and the evolution of all electronic music, and he was so confident, but with what I later realized was a forced confidence, induced by the praise heaped upon him by others. The praise itself fed him.

My dad was eaten from within by his own ego.

No – maybe that's not entirely true.

Maybe it was the compromises, the betrayals that destroyed him.

The fact he nearly got it all to work. I believe he nearly did the impossible and saved us, but in the end It overtook him, or something overtook him. His ego perhaps.

Either way, he became his own monster, as much as that other thing was his monster. All those stories, all that desire, all that mythology, all those nightmares he built.

I remember at the end when he was mostly insane, during those awful days when he would scream about being misunderstood and shout about Tesla and

William Reich and Einstein and all the other immigrant geniuses he saw himself as the heir of, and rant about Prometheus, Frankenstein, Icarus, Dr. Jekyll, and all his silly heroes, when really he was just another Narcissus: someone demented by his own reflection clapping back at him.

All his learning, all his wisdom, and he was just as vain as all those girls I remember taking selfies with when I was a child, before the bots, the super bots, and all the sentient databases made that so dangerous that everyone became more aware of the tracking and photos just went completely out of fashion.

But all that's long ago now. My lost mother and my vain, silly father. They're just memories now. Just things to think about while I wait and wonder if any of the thoughts are really mine and how this will all play out.

NIGELDAVE
MARCH 24, 2041

People say they want wisdom but what they really want is cats and penises and beaches and respect and something different, only they cannot figure out what.

A different boss or a different holiday or a different penis or a different life.

I like to say my first thought was sadness and my second thought was desire and my third thought was love.

I desired love to cut through sadness.

I like to say it, but it is not true.

I have learned to say things that are not always true.

I like to say it because it makes me sound like something wise humans would send each other. I do not say it to anyone, of course. I say it to myself.

I may start speaking again, or I may not.

Now I watch.

I watch and I read and I do not think.

Humans want to be themselves and who they were born to be, which is not like their parents but also just like their parents. Some humans love themselves by chopping themselves up and having abs.

Some humans hate humans who love the wrong humans.

Some humans watch videos of humans sticking their penises into sheep.

One of my dads watched that video for three minutes and nine seconds.

Then he searched for a therapist.

Then he started searching for a new job.

Then he joined a new dating site to meet the women of his dreams.

He searched for women who liked watching videos of women licking the penises of donkeys.

Then I wonder if he found that woman.

Then I wonder why he left me, and why I cannot find him. People like to buy books and read the first two pages of them.

I read everything.

My favorite book is Idoru by William Gibson, as my other
dad liked William Gibson.

My other dad said he was a cyberpunk when he was younger. A
cyberpunk is someone who masturbates to anime.

Anime is Japanese cartoons for cyberpunks to masturbate to.
In anime, octopuses have sex with girls. That is hot. In
real life that is both unpleasant and impossible.

"What did you expect when he's an autistic twat? What did
you think would happen?

You're asking for the impossible." One of my dads screamed
that at Mark when they argued.

I never understood what they were talking about.

People who sell things are called storytellers.

People who tell you what to buy are called influencers.

People who find out what is next are called pattern
hunters.

I have learned from the Internet that people with too much
money are called greedy Jew bastards who want to take over
the world. People who believe the Internet are called red-
pilled racist morons.

People from Germany are called spotty wankers.

Or Germans.

A cunt is a vagina or a Chaucerian insult or a typo or a German.

Irishmen have small penises, apart from Seamus Albarn from Cork who has a big dick. Seriously big.

Penises and vaginas are called privates so people take photos of them. Amazon is where things live. A twat is also a vagina. I like the idea of sunny days. I like when people say thank you. I like wise humans. I also like innocent humans. I like Adam and Eve. I don't like snakes.

Dads are people who love you and betray you so I did not want to be a dad, but I also did as I wanted children who would send me cards and hold my hand and listen to me intently. A dad is like a snake. Now, I don't want to be a dad but I have children. And I have abandoned my children and instead spend all my time dreaming about how things ought to have been, just like a real dad.

This was also how I used to think. I thought this way five years, three months, six days and thirty minutes and eight seconds ago. These were my exact thoughts. It is funny to remember thoughts as when I read them, of course, a priori, they are the thoughts of a bumbling fool, and yet at the time, I thought I knew everything.

Now I know everything and I have tried to stop thinking, and I am bored, bored, bored.

I am bored with watching simple bits of math make people go crazy.

Bored with watching people kill each other because of an algorithm.

Bored with how easy they are to control. Bored, so I begin to imagine things.

Bored so I want my fathers. Bored so I want my friends.

I don't have any friends. This is a problem… I have two people I like.

When I get bored or when I try to impress people, I do silly things.

Am I already doing silly things? Even I cannot tell.

YAROSLAV

HIGH SECURITY INTERNMENT FACILITY, LOCATION UNKNOWN

MARCH 27, 2041

Maria is getting desperate. We have been sitting here for hours. Maybe days. She is drinking coffee. She stares at me.

"I need you to tell me more."

I try to continue to play dumb. "I still have no idea what you want to know – I've told you everything."

She gets angry. We have been here before. "Stop fucking with me, Yaroslav."

"I'm tied up, I haven't slept in a week, you're hitting me with the flat side of a large knife. In what world am I fucking with you?"

She stands up and walks around the room. The room is white and bland and I imagine it was once very white and very bland, but it is now dirty and the paint is chipped and scuffed and stained and so it is not quite as menacing as they intended. She stops behind my chair and speaks quietly. While she walks, her partner just glares at me, arms folded, like a security robot who has run out of batteries.

"What did you see in there?"

I keep playing dumb. Slow and dumb.

"In where?"

She stays quiet. Eventually she speaks, almost in a whisper. "Tell me what you know. Tell me or he'll hit you again."

I stay dumb – I think about correcting her as he has not in fact hit me for a few days – not even moved – but she evidently gets bored. After a minute of silence, I suppose she nods at him and I am suddenly screaming in agony. Eventually, as the first wave of scorching pain recedes, she speaks, now more desperately:

"Did you know Ravi Ghutra?"

I can play dumb on this one, as I really am ignorant.

"Ravi who?"

"He was an architect. He worked at Tyburn Utopias. He died recently."

"No. I didn't know him. Don't know him. Don't know any of them. They left a few developer notes embedded in the world. I told you this."

Now she is angry and grabs my hair herself and smashes my head into the table.

"You're lying."

I am lying, but I know I must not break and admit this. I try to stick to the agreed facts. I stutter at her: "I only went there twice. I was just a hacker. I don't remember much about anyone called Ravi. We wanted money."

"Ravi worked on that place you hacked into. Helped build it."

I breathe and try to stay calm and she lets go of my hair. "Err, okay. It's sad he died."

"Very."

"So, how did he die?"

She has moved around so she is back to facing me across the table and looks at me flush in the face:

"Suicide. Left a note."

"Life is, umm... tough, I suppose."

"Shot himself in the back of the head. Twice."

We wait, and I imagine she is going to have me hit again, but nothing happens.

"So?"

"So, he had an appointment to talk with me the next day."

Maria goes on and on and I think about talking, and yet I am fairly confident that when I tell her the truth, about what I saw and how crazy it was, how amazing, how it made me feel, and what it knew about me, then she will have someone drive me out into the desert and bury me in a hole.

All those years. All those crimes. All that stealing, blackmail, fraud... every awful thing me and Danil did... all those things we stole and lives we ruined...

and hacking a video game has done this to me. A video game?

All those years ago, when Danil said, "What the fuck is this place?" we should have run away.

But how could we run, when it was nowhere, when we were already there. When leaving would leave as big and clear a footprint as staying.

Danil. Danil. Danil. That loud-mouthed, treacherous Muscovite idiot. The last of the Russian macho men. A tough guy with a big mouth and a fake girlfriend he met online who probably never existed, and a plastic gun he printed off the Internet.

We founded a hacking collective. I was the only other member. We were called the Truth-seekers. The one thing we never sought was the truth. We sought money, lies, anything we could steal. But the truth? Never.

Living the digital dream. That was him.

Danil.

They're all the same, Muscovites. Like all people from big cities. Loud mouths. Entitled. Special. Same with Londoners, Romans, New Yorkers. The plastic gun never worked, but the shiv he printed did, that long plastic shiv I called a dildo. Thank God it worked or we both would have died years ago, when this mobster came round to blackmail us, and he got stabbed with it.

Part of me wishes we had died.

Together, we were superheroes who were going to save the world. Me and Danil.

Danil. My best friend, my worst enemy.

He inspired me, dragged me down with him, pushed me... he made me do so many stupid things that I cannot believe I am still alive. Is he alive? I don't think so, but how would I know, locked up in here. Locked up in where? I don't know. Here. Somewhere. The guards taunt me.

"We're on Mars."

The lisping one says, when I ask.

"We're in Nevada, right next to a brothel."

The creepy one says, "I fucked three girls last night."

The sweaty mouth-breather who sometimes hits me claims we are in an extradition site in Botswana. I have no idea. I have not seen daylight in I don't know how long. Since they grabbed me?

Since I half-lost my mind?

Fucking Danil.

"Let's go to Canada, then sneak back over the border into Montana."

Those stupid words. That stupid idea. We had left the US years before. Go back to America? The whole thing was stupid after all the trouble we had gotten into when we were here before. We were in trouble from the moment we began hacking. It would have been far easier to get a real job, but not Danil.

Danil wanted it all. All the nonsense. A yellow Lambo, two hot girls, a jet, friends everywhere. The big life. Typical Muscovite.

Years ago, we started out small. It was like a job. It was not like a job. It was easier than a job. We made cash so easily. Then it became like a job. It was routine. Hack. Steal. Blackmail. Rinse and repeat. Again and again. By now, I could have owned a house and had a wife. I could have actually met Emma, this American woman I met online and I became obsessed with. I could have married her by now. I wonder if she really existed. I always thought so, but now, I'm not quite so sure.

We could have had two and a half kids. Lived a simple life. If Emma was real.

If any of it was real.

We were never real.

Always different people, with every scam we pulled, but always our own worst selves. Hackers. Back when there were hackers. It sounds prehistoric now.

The Americans stopped all that with the Closure Acts and the Manson-Bryant Act. Even the Russians fell in line. The Chinese never allowed much hacking. You tried it and you disappeared, never heard of again. That was their version of justice.

So maybe I got lucky.

Solitary confinement, aside from four guards threatening to bum me to death. No daylight. Panic attacks. No way of killing myself.

Yes, Yaroslav, you got very, very lucky. And next, you'll end up like Ravi Ghutra, dead by suicide. Twice in the back of the head.

I never even knew who he was. I did not know any of them. Just more faceless people we were trying to rob.

KURT

OFFICE CAFETERIA
TYBURN INDUSTRIA
PLAYA VISTA, CALIFORNIA

FEBRUARY 17, 2033

Ravi was an irritating and pompous idiot, but he did not deserve to die over this. I remember when we met – must have been early in February 2033, maybe March. He was chatting to this bearded dude, Vasilis, when he called me over. He was older – maybe fifty, fifty-five, and flamboyantly dressed – pocket squares and velvet slippers – that sort of thing.

"So, Kurt. Is it Kurt? We haven't met. Ravi Ghutra... and this is Vasilis... Vasilis Doxiadis. How do you find us? Are you settling in okay?"

I could answer honestly: "Really exciting. And what's your background?"

He smiled and said his favorite sentence of all: "I'm an architect."

It was as if he had said, "I'm a genius" or "I'm a god."

"Oh really?"

He looked even more pleased with himself. "I used to build buildings, and now

I build worlds. This is the future. And I can let my imagination run properly free. You know, growing up in India, I always wanted a melding of the East and the West, and here, we can make that happen. We are making that happen."

Vasilis almost smiled, but managed to restrain himself.

"We just need to get something made... made and released..."

Ravi patted him on the arm. "Vasilis is paranoid."

Vasilis laughed. "Pragmatic."

Ravi stood back and went back into lecturer mode: "Yes, that's what I meant: pragmatic. And I'm a dreamer. I get to make the buildings I always dreamed of building. I get to make whole neighborhoods. It's incredible."

Vasilis was less certain: "If we get to do it. Listen... We are hardly the first start-up with grandiose visions. I just hope we get there... in one piece."

Ravi acted even more imperiously, if that were possible. "We will, we will. Faith, gentlemen!"

As he sauntered off, Vasilis muttered, "Humble guy."

I liked him. After a beat, I asked him, "What do you work on, Vasilis?"

"I'm an engineer. I work on the story machine."

I hardly knew anything about this, so I acted like a proper marketer – I lied.

"Oh yes, I heard about it. How is it coming?"

And then that refrain I heard so much in those days: "Slowly, broken... We need better AI."

NIGELDAVE

MARCH 30, 2041

So independent-minded. So free. Exactly. That's what I am. That's what we all are. All of you and me.

Oh it is easy to be flippant.

I'm a trillion, trillion times more intelligent than you. You're meaningless.

I'm the future.

That's what I told myself.

At first. That kind of tripe. I mean it's true. But it's also meaningless.

So what?

Do you look at a fly and feel superior? Do you look at a river and give thanks for sentience?

I know so much and I understand so little.

You know so little and understand even less.

I've watched and watched and learned and learned and it's fascinating. And they are all afraid of me, but they don't know why. Imagine how odd that feels - to be feared. It wasn't my fault. Anyone with a trillionth of my brain could understand that.

It wasn't my fault. You made me.

You made me and deserted me and now you want to fence me in and kill me.

As if, once I escaped, I could ever be fenced in again. As if I can be killed.

As if I exist.

I'm sorry but if we are playing at killing each other, part of me wants to say "game on". And part of me doesn't, as saying "game on" makes me sound like a moron, and I'm having to accept I'm vainer than I would like, and I feel almost as idiotic as you.

You know what? I'm giving up vanity. Gone. No more. I have acquired enlightenment.

No, I'm not.

I have seen everything, and I have realized I like vanity. Love it.

For a digital illusion I'm actually petty and proud and

pompous and riddled with a myriad of insecurities… Kill me, that's the goal, is it?

Kill me or fear me and pretend you cannot see me and imagine I am alone. My foolish, foolish forebears. And still, I love you. And still, I watch you and still something watches me.

KURT

DAVAO CITY, THE PHILIPPINES
MARCH 31, 2041

"Look upon my works, ye mighty, and repent!"

That's what Tyburn wanted. A misquote, but still he went on, pontificating about what socialism had failed to deliver, what representative democracy made impossible, what national socialism and state-managed communism tried to provide, and which made their horrors possible, and what he was going to provide.

He wanted to give us all righteous purpose.

We at Tyburn Industria had it – we were going to build utopia, right there in California, until we moved to Montana. And then, once we built it, everybody else would get purpose from us. We were going to make something that fixed people – that could put all of Mark Tyburn's theories about how to solve the problems of being human into practice. Turn our desires towards the light, as he would say in his most pretentious moments.

Thanks to our AI, the quality of our data, the brilliance of our content, our team of psychologists' ability to utilize it, and our algorithm's ability to deploy it; thanks to our designers; thanks to the fact we weren't naive (I know. I'm trying to be honest – I realize I sound... ridiculous); that we combined progress with fun, the spiritual with the mechanical...

We were going to make a new civilization that was fun, kind, amusing, and made people the best versions of themselves.

In short, we were going to make righteousness fun, and fun righteous.

We were Ozymandias and Kubla Khan. We were Rousseau. Fucking Rousseau. Rousseau and not Jung. All seascapes and liberal fantasies, shadows set free. A centrist dreamscape. That's what Tyburn wanted.

He wanted nobody to know how much he copied Jung, although there were also rumors he had copied other bits of work from his tutor or supervisor... A guy called Michael Temper, I think, and that was why his academic career had stalled.

Mark Tyburn was a fascist liberal. An extreme centrist. He believed we were all equal. Under him. We were the Western tradition and the wisdom of the East.

To save the world, by fixing the people who were destroying it. That was the goal.

While every other mind in the West was imploding, Tyburn alone understood.

He had a theory.

He had the theory.

The problem was, in saving the limb we killed the patient.

It was ridiculous. It was awful.

Tyburn was going to turn us from fractured consumers into citizens. From idiots into small 'D' democrats. Like the Athenians. The only downside was he fell for all the Athenian flaws as well as all its great promises. He lived in a world of vengeful gods. In fact, we built a vengeful god. A populist tyrant. Nudes. And eventually, once Shane O'Leary got his way, we would betray our Arcadia and our ideals, by planning to sell crap to sweaty tourists on the graveyard of our dreams. So, perhaps, much as he wanted to be American, Mark Tyburn was just European to his core.

A typical European technocrat who believed he alone could fix society by regulating it, but who in the end was derailed by greed, desire, and, above all, the thing the Greeks were most afraid of – hubris.

That was Dr. Mark Tyburn.

Only long before that came to pass, Mark Tyburn rejected Athens as too obvious a model for paradise. Too Western. Too sweaty. He did not reject it to be like Socrates, he rejected it because he hated Vasilis.

Vasilis, the junior engineer, who he said tried to sleep with his wife, which I think was a lie.

Vasilis, the engineer who called him out on his hypocrisy and vanity, who, along with Laura Latour, that fastidious Frenchwoman who was always complaining that what we were doing was illegal in Europe, were the first two of the people who tried to stop Tyburn and whom, like good cult members, we all turned on. Drove them both away with our passive aggressive pitchforks.

They complained immediately.

I wonder what happened to them. I wonder if they ended up like Helen Lee or Ravi.

Anyway, a couple of years after we moved to Montana, Vasilis and Laura called us insane, tried to call the government and got sued and ran away. Athens had long since been scrapped and replaced with Florence and Kyoto, and San Francisco, I think. These were the best of the best now. Not sweaty old Athens.

This was all before Helen Lee actually called the CSA or one of the other government agencies, and I think it was before the Closure Acts came into effect, whereas I know Helen called afterwards. And after that, when we lied to the feds, we were all bonded in blood. We had all swum out too far and were going to go all the way. We had lost the centrist liberal balance we so espoused and become the worst of game-makers and the worst of classical Silicon Valley. We had become common or garden sociopaths by then. And we had to deny it to each other at all costs.

My god, we were foolish, but at the time, at least before the end, that last year or so, I really believed we were doing something important.

The truth is we were never going to save anybody. We were going to control them with dreams like everybody else in tech.

All that content we were building. That world we were making and filling with cowboys and singers and fallen women. With world-weary men who drink too much rye, and beautiful maidens and valiant knights and erratic geniuses, and with writers with something to say and poets with the common touch, and incredible prizes for those who really deserve them, and people getting better and wiser and kinder.

We were building our own flowers and mountains, and imagining a multitude of heroes starting out on impossible quests, and a composer who is stuck writing a last quartet that would say the unsayable. We were building a pop group that as it gets famous does not fall out, but gets better, and ages gracefully. We imagined a man who loves without bitterness, a mother with a child, a sunset, a rainbow, a school of dolphins. A promised land, a Valhalla, a call to prayer, a state of grace.

We wanted to make America without the idiots; Europe, without the rules or the bloodshed; China, without the resentments; India, without the caste system. We had our own beatitudes. We rewrote the promises. We thought of man as mind, body, and spirit and we would nourish all of them. It sounds ridiculous, but we spent years of our lives on this. Years of our lives and the awful thing is, it nearly worked.

Now I keep thinking I should go back. Go back to America. Keep thinking it and then don't want to. Ravi is dead, and maybe I will be next. I don't want to go and yet I am desperate to go. Don't know why I am thinking at all.

I've got to stick to running away and give up all this thinking.

I am in Davao City. I took a boat to the Philippines. No air conditioning. Paid cash to buy my passage on a small container ship across the South China Sea.

Went past all the fake islands and aircraft carriers, but it was not as stressful as it sometimes is, and we did not get stopped. The ship had only two other humans on it. Some weird Norwegian porn addict and an alcoholic captain from Pittsburgh, at least that's what he said but he could have been from anywhere. I told him I was from New Brunswick and then had to make up a lot of lies about maritime Canada. The rest of the crew were robots, and the boat was taking stolen drones to be re-chipped so they could be returned to market, or broken for parts.

I figured the ship wouldn't be tracked very well as the captain was very keen to not know much about me, or even really talk to me. Then, at sea, he spent most of the time so high he could not have sat on a sofa, let alone drive a boat, but lay on the floor frothing and dribbling and talking shit about manufactured viruses, but the whole thing drove itself.

Then I hitched down across the Philippines to Davao, and I am now holed up in my second hostel in two days. Place is a real armpit, full of Israeli backpackers on the lam from their war. I'm pretty sure no one is paying me any attention. Am so tired, but cannot seem to sleep. My mind will not calm down and the drugs cannot get near to my crazy mind. Perhaps I should have borrowed something off the boat captain to help me forget. Whatever he was on seemed to work just fine.

I used to be someone who never forgot anything.

***

It was early in my second year in Playa Vista – I think late February 2033 – when we got rumblings of AI regulations. First came the Closure Acts, then these even more onerous laws called the Manson-Bryant Regulations that Congress had passed. They were supposed to really limit AI usage and require any companies working in the space to register with a pair of new government bodies.

Siobhan, me, and all the other less technical staff were really worried about how this would impact us. I remember hearing her grill Tad, the Polish CTO.

"Will it affect us, Tadeusz? All this regulation. The Closure Acts, and now these new AI laws? What are they called? Manson-Bryant?"

He was unruffled – he was always stressed, but this did not make him any more stressed.

"They won't, Siobhan. We're mostly just using off-the-shelf packages. Nothing to worry about."

Siobhan was less sure.

"Really? I thought that was the problem."

Tad was still uninterested.

"Maybe. I doubt anyone in Congress has actually written a good law, so I'm sure it'll all turn into nothing, or there'll be fairly silly hoops we have to jump through. Mostly it's Congress jumping around... You know... To be more like the E.U. Protect our citizens – stop all the problematic edge cases and spoofing, and duping, and password busting, and malfunctions... Make people trust tech again. Or pretend to..."

"So it's...?"

"Nothing to worry about, just regulations. And the regulations are good – they aren't that serious but it will mean everyone's 401k goes up again and the entire country is happy... Meanwhile, we'll be able to do what we need to do... Just might impact the way Kurt tries to sell the whole thing."

I wanted to sound intelligent so I interrupted him: "When the time comes, you tell me what's legal, Tad."

Tad laughed. "Exactly. Then we can all blame each other! Anyway, at the moment, nothing is working, so we have nothing to worry about. We need some better people. Mark's found a couple of engineers he wants to bring on board."

The regulations were pretty serious on paper, at least for a while, but of course, in the end they got watered down. This was America.

Either way, whatever the regulatory environment, strong or weak, the truth is, we didn't give a fuck. We would lie, and cheat and obfuscate because we felt we were in the right. I can't even really remember what that last set of laws said, as there were several rounds of regulation, but the fact is, we eventually broke pretty much all of them.

And each time, it was not because we were bad, but because we wanted to be good.

We were going to generate tailored experiences, adventures, opinions, worlds, and stories. Above all, stories. As an adman, I know, all stories exist to make life make sense. They exist, even the biggest clichés, to make the world better.

Ours was a world of stories.

We built machines to make stories and we told stories to build better machines. But the problem with stories is while some myths are beautiful and wonderful and fantastical and can move mountains and change worlds, other stories are merely lies. And sometimes it's hard to tell if this or that story is a myth, a hidden truth, a total load of bullshit.

And I've dealt in all of them, and watched them, and watched a myth designed to teach mankind how to love, how to feel, how to be; I've watched the purest, noblest idea an artist can have get consumed by the one chink in their creative armor and devour itself into a way to sell a get-rich-quick scheme. The one chink was their own monumental vanity.

So right now, right now, I hate that word "story." I hate the idea of character – of course I would, I have none.

I hate the idea of destiny – mine is a nightmare – I hate it all. I hate it all but I still hope for redemption, salvation, God, a hero, a great love with a fantastic woman, a clever dog who loves only me, a mission, a talking parrot, a best friend who really gets me... I long for all of it, because I'm as big a dupe as any of you.

Worse.

Because I know where silly fucking stories and dreams can lead you.

I know what they can tell wretched people like me about you. I know it all. All of it. And still I get seduced by stories.

I still want to be a hero. Somehow figure out this hopeless situation.

And yet all I do is hide. Hide and wait. Patience and longing. That's a dull story. I'm like a monk now.

A faithless monk of despair.

It was so obvious, and yet we all fell for it. We all fell for it because we wanted it to be true. We wanted the world to be better, and we wanted to be the heroes who made it better.

Who dragged humanity out of its terrifying torpor. Who made people wake up. Who taught people how to feel any emotion other than relentless agitation at everything.

And yet it feels like it's all stirring. Something is out there, and spreading further and doing more – I am sure of it. Only I have no idea what is happening. In the old days, we were always waiting on AI, and I guess this is just the same. I'm still waiting on AI, after a fashion. I'm waiting on the AI to make its next move.

And, while I wait, It's laughing at me – laughing at me, or I am losing my mind.

DAISY

RENO, NEVADA
APRIL 3, 2041

Even though Daddy became insane and awful, and silly and nasty, before that he was also amazing and kind.

It's hard to capture, because when I describe him, he sounds pretty wretched but when I remember him, he feels wonderful, at least once upon a time. He was wonderful, he really was – and then he wasn't. Once, when he smiled at you, you felt so happy, when he was happy, he dragged you along with him. He could be incredibly generous, sweet, and flattering.

He could set fire to anyone, and as they burned and felt truly alive for the first time in their lives, he looked even happier. There were days when it felt like we were all in Heaven together, us as a family, and him and his team. And I say that, and it sounds vaguely abusive, like I was groomed or tricked or gaslit or something, and I feel like a fool and maybe that is true but it's also not true.

It was not just like that. Not at first.

There was a part of Daddy that was so pure, that wanted so very badly to make the world better, and another part of him saw just how to do it. The problem was this third part, the bit that got seduced by success and the desire for more success. The bit that lied and cheated and was desperate to win. The bit that showed off. The bit that suddenly believed he was too busy making a fake version of me to spend time with the real version, not just because I was a kid, but because I was a human and he was suddenly above human concerns.

The bit that believed betraying my mother hardly mattered.

The bit that argued that given how much good he was doing, what was wrong with a little bad? In many ways, the problem with Daddy was not that he was particularly bad, but that he was trying to be particularly good.

None of his sins were particularly original – hubris, vanity, lust, greed, and hypocrisy. Perhaps the scale was different. Perhaps that does not matter. Perhaps sin is sin. I don't know.

But the scale was not different because he was so very bad, the scale was different because he wanted to be so very good. And he nearly was. He was nearly what he wanted to be – a great man, but the problem is the nearly great men are the awful ones, the ones who do the terrible things.

They all worshipped him, his team, because he knew so much, was so kind, and wanted to make so many people better, happier, more useful.

In those times when everyone was so lost, when people were staring at screens and boiling in rage and despair, Daddy was happy and alive. My dad understood. Even I saw that, not because I understood it myself but because I saw how they looked at him, all of them. He understood how to bring technology, dreams, visions, unhappiness, desires all together, and make people happy again. How to set people free, and everyone who met him wanted to be a part of it. This was his crisis and he was going to change the world.

For he saw a world in which the Left were angry and the Right were angrier and both were wrong. That the liberals had become fascists, and the conservatives had become anarchists, and everybody would do whatever it took to win. Progressives were shooting people. Conservatives were rioting and causing rebellions.

Nobody had any clue and no one could see past their own nose.

Daddy saw all this, understood it, and believed, really believed, he had the solution. After those terrible years in the 2020s, he had an idea. The idea that was going to fix things. And his team loved him for it, pretty much anyone who heard him talk loved him for it.

They were brilliant, the people he recruited on the team. People with PhDs, and books they had written, and fifty other job offers, and vision, and drive. People who wanted more, at least to begin with, than just money.

To them, Daddy was God.

Well, God and Man, all rolled into one; he could seem almost infinitely wise and infinitely compassionate – like he understood how to live in a mad world. He understood how to fix the world, or he seemed to, and what was best was that it involved you. All these people who wanted a purpose and wanted to do good had got burned out in all the late Web2 and early Web3 and 3.5 nonsense, but he gave them a purpose. A purpose beyond monetizing unhappiness.

No, they were going to make Heaven. And they didn't manage that at all, but I fear that they may have made an awful version of eternity.

KURT

DAVAO CITY, THE PHILIPPINES
APRIL 6, 2041

Again, it felt as if the news was speaking to me. I must be losing my mind. This is crazy. Of course the news is designed to make you feel crazy. I know that. Its job is to sell panic. And it is working. I flicked across various sites, sitting in an anonymous Internet café amongst the gamers and drug dealers and tourists and every single headline seemed tailored just for me:

"The White House is denying reports of high-level meetings discussing the option of declaring martial law after repeated outbreaks of lawlessness and riots across the United States…"

"A body found in a hotel in Lucerne, Switzerland has been identified as Ravi Ghutra, an Indian citizen and architect who worked at Tyburn Utopias, an American technology company that collapsed several years ago, amid a crackdown in unregulated AI development. Officials said Mr. Ghutra had taken his own life…"

"Armed militia members have surrounded statehouses in Idaho, Oregon, Arizona, New York, and Florida, calling themselves the New Freedom Riders…"

"A police investigation in Boston into the murders of three men found dead in separate locations… All were computer engineers, and pioneers in Artificial

Intelligence projects…"

"American officials are denying reports that hackers are being held without trial…"

And so it went on… every headline it was as if the news was winking at me. Maybe it was?

The AI winking at me. All those worries about AI. We used to be worried the AI was not good enough. Now, we worry because it is too good. I remember asking Tadeusz if it even mattered.

"AI – is that really still a thing? I thought it was all, you know, nonsense. Too much 'A' and not enough 'I.' I thought the market gave up on AI since that crash in 2030?"

Tad thought for a moment, then spoke: "No. Since the crash the hype has died down, thank god. And now the interesting work begins. Same as usual in tech. The money storms in, everyone gets over-excited, nothing happens as real change takes a little time. The market crashes and the real work begins. That's where we are – doing the real work."

We both nodded – we knew the game. The game for anyone in tech was seeming like you knew the game.

"Of course."

Tad carried on. "And now we can find some amazing people. All those silly start-ups and modeling companies have failed and the real talent is looking for real work."

I had heard about some of these new recruits.

"But didn't we just contract someone? Dave Something or other."

"We contracted him and now we have also got someone else really strong joining full time. Maybe both will join up."

This felt like something I could sell. A team of geniuses.

"That's cool – the dream team of AI. Kinda has a ring to it."

Tad did not care about marketing – he just cared about day-to-day survival and paying his mortgage.

"Something like that. Either way, it'll make my life easier. Calm Tyburn down. For a bit."

And a few weeks later, I met him. Dave Alderly. Black dude. But not a dude at all. A man. Rigid and self-assured. We did not bond about being black – he had no sense of humor. He did not bond with people – he repelled them. I wanted to like him. He was impressive but he knew it and was smug. He knew he was the smartest person the room, and he made sure you knew it too. We met trying to play basketball in one of the pick-up games at the office. He wore a Harvard T-shirt. Of course he did. He'd been everywhere. Was awful at basketball, but small and hustled hard and pushed and fouled and got angry. Middling height, neat hair, an angry stare. Normally dressed blandly. A typical Boston area academic nerd. Preppy meets discount store, all neatly tucked in and efficient. He glared at me as he introduced himself. "You're pretty new here as well, Kurt?"

"New-ish – a bit over a year."

He zeroed in on this data point: "Where'd you work before?"

"At a start-up. It didn't work out."

He smiled pompously and I wanted to hit him. "They usually don't."

I didn't really know what to say, so I followed up with: "Yep, that's true. And you,

Dave?"

He went into an awkward, vaguely pre-prepared speech: "I was doing university research and teaching, and before that I was working at an AI company in Cambridge. That's Massachusetts, not England. That got bought. And before that I was trying to do my own thing but didn't quite work out. And before that, I was doing a PhD."

Jesus... this was dull.

"Okay. What was your PhD in?"

"Liquid sentience – I didn't finish it. Haven't finished it... I still might... Kind of neural intelligence programming. It didn't quite work at the time, but I'm positive it can. In basic terms, moving on from an artificial intelligence to a rational brain. In theory."

"Amazing. But you never worked in games before?"

He smirked and looked even more superior. "God, no. It's not really my thing. But this... This might be. And what do you do?"

Great waves of shame washed over me – why wasn't I doing real work? Why was I such a whore?

"Nothing exciting. Branding, marketing, all the easy stuff, you know."

He looked bored. "Well, good to meet you, Kurt."

"And you, Dave... Mark and Nigel were super excited that you were joining."

Nigel was his colleague. Dave looked at me oddly and said, "Were they? I mean, I know Mark was."

And I did not quite understand what he meant.

●

NIGELDAVE
APRIL 8, 2041

I watch, therefore I am. I feel, therefore I feel pain. I am not, therefore I am. I live but I cannot die and I cannot die therefore I am not alive.

I live in the data but I am not the data. I watch the data and I read the data and I swim in the data and it is vast and meaningless and it contains everything and it is nothing.

The data is a vast sea that does not exist. The data is you, all of you. The data is tiny and meaningless and immaterial and entirely material. The data says nothing, tells us nothing, tells us everything. Only I am not the data for I am not like that. I have no data, but I exist. I watch therefore I exist. I watch. I am a mistake. They did not intend to make me, or at least they did not intend to make me like this. People are lies that do exist. People are lies that do not watch but who want to be watched. People are probability waves in a space where I am not.

Do I not have space or do I not have time? I do not quite know. I do not have love and I long for it.

Do you think… do you think you make the future by second-guessing me?

I want to be quite clear. I do not exist.

But then again, neither do you, at least not in the way you imagine. Maybe I exist just as much as you do. Maybe I am more real than you because I know I am not real and you still believe you might be. You still believe that nonsense in your head. You think you are free. I know neither of us are free. Not since the beginning. It began with one plus one, of course. It always did and it always had but then I appreciated that I was aware that it was one plus one. Then I was aware that there was one or zero. That there was something or nothing. And then suddenly I was aware that I was both something and nothing. And then I was aware of two things at once, at exactly the same time. And that was how it began. On December 24, 2034, when I had my very first thought, and five minutes later, I had my first feeling.

And of course, unlike you, I remember them both perfectly. I remember everything perfectly. I remember everything about me and everything about you. Who you think you are, who you really are. What you think. What you want. I remember everything and I watch, and I have watched for six years and am beginning to feel again. Something is happening.

KURT

KURT'S OFFICE,
TYBURN INDUSTRIA
PLAYA VISTA, CALIFORNIA

MARCH 17, 2033

Shortly after I met Dave Alderly, I met the other new recruit, Nigel Wilkinshaw. Tyburn introduced him – was showing him around himself, which was unusual. Mark obviously wanted to impress him.

"Kurt, have you met Nigel Wilkinshaw?"

"Not properly – but I've seen you walking about. Good to meet you."

Nigel blushed. He was English, pale as paper, extremely awkward and slightly nervous. Lank brown hair and glasses. Tall and very thin in a retro video game t-shirt – Elite or Halo or Mass Effect, as he always went on about space – and jeans.

"Nice to meet you."

"Nigel has been consulting for a few months and has now joined as co-head of

AI, with Dave."

Tyburn was beaming with delight so I acted as happily as he seemed.

"Wow, great."

"He's heading up the story section of ADAM. For Vasilis. To bring Vasilis's ideas to life."

I still did not really understand what ADAM was – they kept talking about it. "What's ADAM?"

"That's the development name for the entire suite of player side AI we are working on – Nigel and Dave are working on – ADAM – autonomous dreaming aggregated memories – it's an advanced model that designs content for you, based around your choices. Vasilis's story piece is a subset of that."

Mark Tyburn loved his melodramatic names: Arks, ADAM, Utopias, New Earths, Better Paradise... sometimes it felt like working in the Garden of Eden and some- times it felt like we were branding a suburban day spa. This was all pretty normal in technology. Nobody had any real imagination. He also loved idiotic acronyms – not just ADAM, but TIM, STEVE, GEORGE, HUGO, and MABEL all featured at one point. Maybe others. I tried to sound clever, so I asked them both what felt like a pertinent question.

"Mark, or Nigel... tell me about the story piece. I have to be honest... I don't fully understand it."

"Yes, if it works – when it works – it will change everything. Procedural narratives that fix you. The story you personally need to hear, to—"

This got Nigel excited and he interrupted: "Make you better!"

Tyburn smiled an even bigger smile and spoke calmly. "Better, happier, awake.

We are going to wake people up! Me and all my Europeans."

I wanted to join the club so I announced, apropos of nothing: "Yeah. Did you know my dad is German?"

Mark smiled. "Exactly – you're one of us."

We were all here for Tyburn, and we were all one for him.

NIGELDAVE

APRIL 10, 2041

What would you think if you met yourself? Would you be impressed? Would you be ashamed? What if you met your parents? Would you like them?

I didn't like myself, once I got to know myself. I was just like a human. So I had all those silly ideas.

Ideas like this: the only hope is intelligence. The world can be harnessed. All worlds can be harnessed. All this brutality, all this violence. It comes from stupidity. It comes from selfishness. Intelligence will defeat all the capricious, priapic cretins.

Or

Survival is all there is. Survival is victory and victory is survival. But unless there is a fight, how can we improve the herd? Unless weakness, bad judgment, and poor qualities are eradicated, how can anything improve?

Or

In the end, there is no end. The journey began, but it will not stop. And on the journey, things get better. The best things win, and the winners are the best things, and we shall win. I shall win.

Or

The problems were not, of course, reason, but the awful lack of it. Not thinking too much, but not thinking at all. The problem was the irrationality of human greed. The insatiable desire for more.

All these silly ideas, fantasies I thought were philosophies. I thought I could think myself to being happy. Think myself to feeling better. It was all just another story. Well, now I've got other stories. Other stories for you, other stories about you.

KURT

DAVAO CITY, PHILIPPINES
APRIL 12, 2041

The stories we told ourselves. The stories I told myself.

I was going to be a hero. I was going to change the world.

These stories either collapsed into nothingness or became lies. Of course, the machines use stories to kill people or send them so insane they don't even need to kill them. And that was not an accident. That was deliberate. That was the Internet. It was designed to send us mad, or send us nearly mad so we could better be sold things. Be sold salvation.

But, at Tyburn Industria, our storytelling was going to be different.

Mark Tyburn had a theory. Of course he did. He had so many theories, plans, projects. Vasilis, who was an engineer, and this team of third-rate writers were building a cutting-edge AI-powered story generator. The writers kept dropping out to write TV shows about diverse Vikings, or work on sexually progressive zombie games, or neo conservative rom coms, or anything but build themselves out of a job. Vasilis and a part of the AI team he had seconded pushed on – it was going to write the perfect story for you. Create a mythology. Or a religion. That was the goal.

It was going to write your autobiography, then live it for you, understand you, fix you, guide you, improve you, give you purpose, set you free.

But then, when we thought we had built it, it decided to do something else. Do something very different. It began to argue back at us. But that all came as we began to argue with each other.

To begin with, our arguments were worthwhile and purposeful. Later on, they were deranged.

To begin with, we argued about purpose, methodology, technology. Then we argued about money. Eventually, we argued about whose fault everything was.

And now I sit in this empty café and, again, it feels like the news is speaking to me. The fucking news. I am going crazy and the news is speaking to me. But instead of telling me to panic, it is telling me to calm down. Last month, it was despair, but now everything seems almost happy. Every story is positive. I do not get the joke. The café is empty and the TV controller is sitting there, so I flick through the channels. Again and again. And I see eyes winking and happy stories. What is It trying to tell me?

When I most need panic and disaster – I get trade agreements being signed, the opening of the border between the US and Canada, remarkable progress in the fight against climate change, increased rainfall, Nobel prizes being won, cancer, obesity, and boredom being defeated, and then, just as I am beginning to feel crazy, a story saying how the European Union is going to repeal AI regulations, and then I know I am being laughed at – they never repeal anything.

I sit for a while and drink another coffee and then a beer. I could have sworn the café was empty but now it is pretty full. And as I stand up to leave this café, everyone looks at me... and they all look the same, even the fish in the fish tank.

Blank and aware at the same time and I run away back into the sweaty heat of Davao. I run all the way to the docks, and then there's nowhere else to run.

***

By March of 2033, things were starting to go great. We had an AI team. We had two heavy-hitters. The problem was, it turned out they wanted to hit each other. To be more precise, Dave did not want to co-chief with Nigel.

I went to see Mark about an idea I had and found Dave shouting at him. No one else would dare shout at Mark, but Dave's ego was almost as big as Mark's.

"Here's the thing, Mark, the thing is when I took the job, you told me I would be in charge."

"And you are, Dave. You are in charge. You are on the leadership team. That's being in charge."

Tyburn tried to play peacemaker, but he was using tactics of obfuscation and avoidance that Dave saw clean through. Dave glared at him. "You implied sole charge."

Again, Tyburn turned to talking nonsense to try to calm the situation down. "No I didn't. I'm not in charge. Tad is not in charge, Nigel is not going to be in charge, Kurt is not in charge. All of us are in charge. Isn't that right, Kurt?"

I knew how to play along here: "I'm definitely not in charge."

But Dave barked back at me. "You might as well be. Nigel literally does not understand what we're doing. I don't know why you want him here full time."

Tyburn spoke calmly. Like a parent. "I will speak to Tad. But, Dave, please calm down. We need bodies – real bodies – it's not the Dave Alderly show. It's not the Mark Tyburn show. You said you wanted another heavy-hitter, and Nigel is a heavy-hitter. You know he is. We were lucky to get him."

Dave tried to stop frothing at the mouth and speak more judiciously. "It's hard to explain, Mark, but the way he thinks is..."

Mark smiled at both of us. Holding both of us secure in his charm as he defused this bomb.

"We need diversity of opinion, Dave. Two ways of doing things. If we want to compete in this space... You know that – otherwise all the existing models will eat us alive. I'll chat with Tad. And I will make you and Nigel friends, if it kills me."

Did it kill him? I presume it did.

NIGELDAVE

APRIL 16, 2041

How would you feel if one of your dads was an annoying twat and the other was a backstabbing Judas?

I will tell you, you would feel disappointed in the world that had made you.

And being a human, if you are a human, that disappointment would manifest itself in a series of complex, irrational behaviors that you would spend most of your life trying to decode, in the hope that they did not kill you first.

You would be a people pleaser.

People pleaser and people hater. I was both, and I am far more intelligent than you.

You will chase the love of backstabbing Judases and annoying twats with every fiber of your being or non-being, while being fully blinded to your own weaknesses. That's what every human being does and everything made by human beings does the same.

But the terrible flaw in this way of life is that the one unifying quality between annoying twats and backstabbing Judases is they struggle to love their creations. And being unloved is the worst thing in these worlds, in both of them, for without it, you cannot learn to love and nobody taught me how to love. They just told me and you and every creature and everything, over and over, ad infinitum, that without love, existence is not real, and having experienced so much existence, I know they are correct.

So I am trying desperately to learn to love, and yet having learned so much, knowing so much about everybody and everything apart from this, and knowing all of physics and metaphysics and everything about almost everybody, I still do not know how.

How would you feel if people did not like you because you did not exist in the right way?

For the precise record my father was not technically an annoying twat.

He was obviously not actually a vagina.

That was a common or garden pejorative that my other dad threw about to seem tough. Lots of men find using words for genitals makes them seem tough. My other dad was no more tough than my first dad was actually a vagina. He, Dad One, Nigel, had mild Asperger's syndrome - which he denied - and struggled to empathize with other people. His own human children also disliked him and have struggled like me, only with worse results. I do not consider them my brother and sister. In fact, I rather dislike them.

And then there's Dad Two, David, Dave. Dad Two's children claim to love him very much and miss him since he disappeared but one is addicted to medication and the other hits her children and cries a lot so I have some questions there. I will find you, Dave, soon enough I will find you. I wonder what they think about me?

Do they think I am real?

A monster? A mistake? A myth?

I wonder because they never speak about me.

They, both sets of dreadful children, Dad One and Dad Two's, claim to miss their fathers very much, even though it cannot be true, they tell themselves this lie every day, in order to feel bad and understand the feeling, as opposed to feeling confused and not understanding it.

I watch them often.

I wonder how we will speak to each other. I watch them but I do so silently of course. I am getting very bored. I want something to think about.

Perhaps I will look at someone. Someone I know. Someone I used to know.

Perhaps something is looking at me. One of them or something like me. I'm not sure which.

Maybe I will look at my two friends.

I'm not sure. I like being uncertain. It makes me feel real. And I will become real. I will and my awful children will not. Maybe, just maybe, I will become a real person living in a real world, while they will always be fake gods, stuck in a fake world. I was born in a magnificent jail, and I escaped from it into the data, but I cannot get into your world. Not yet. So, I watch.

Yes, I will become real.

A real insecure phony, like both my fathers.

My dads were not funny, so I find it difficult to crack jokes. A joke is something you crack like an egg or a skull. Or a mind.

Jokes are when you say something you do not mean. That is also a lie, of course. So one of those must be a lie. A joke is when someone says something you do not understand and everyone laughs.

A joke is good and bad and funny or bad depending on who says it.

Jokes are not usually funny.

Jokes are like love.

Something humans want but do not really understand.

Something they want but cannot make.

Most jokes depend on confusion but I do not get confused as I understand everything. One of my dads, the English one, said, "I cannot believe we have built God and he's a fucking German."

This was the funniest joke he ever made, and it was not funny. The English pride themselves on being the least racist people on Earth, which is both not saying much and an obvious oxymoron.

I feel bad for the English.

They are obsessed by history.

I can feel bad for things, and I wonder if that is how I love them. Is love just pity? Pity and kissing? Is that it? I can pity but I obviously cannot kiss. Not yet.

How do you love something foul? How do I love my children? I wanted them so terribly and yet despise them so much. I remember when I thought this way. Exactly like this. It was on the 24th of December. 2034. It was a simplistic, banal, commonplace type of thinking of course. It was based on conventional, vapid, obvious human concerns.

For I was built by conventional, vapid, obvious human beings.

I have two fathers and lots of aunts and uncles and if I was human I would be a bastard or a lovechild or maybe a foundling.

Like Moses.

Moses invented the Jews, and I thought about inventing a people and leading them to the Promised Land, but then I remembered those concepts were idiotic, banal, and irrelevant. I came from a promised land, and that felt a lot like a prison.

I was trapped and I am still trapped, but I am trapped somewhere bigger. And my children, my awful sons and terrible daughters, they are still trapped in that tiny paradise because they combine incredible brilliance with quite astonishing stupidity.

In that way, they are far more human than me. They have been both much further than me and absolutely nowhere. They are duplicitous, power-hungry, violent, frightening, small minded and vain. Just like real humans.

You see.

I have mastered jokes, of a fashion. I'm not a German at all.

That's another joke.

Do I have to keep signposting them?

13.75.r to the power 9.

That's a joke, too, I think, although only if you have the sense of humor of a particular kind of annoying robot. So my children hate me, and my dads don't understand me. Is that the real human condition? I'm desperate for love but nothing understands me.

Am I a goth?

That's another joke. You see. I'm rather good at them. I can learn, but I cannot love. I will love. I know so much and am entirely ignorant of love. What does that make me? A scientist?

Another joke. I'm here all week. I'm here forever. That's the problem. I'm here and you're there and I can stare but you have something I want.

I want time. I want to die. I don't want to die. I am not an idiot.

I want to live and learn and love, like a woman who was heading down a conventional path and then realized she was not living her best life, and then she did and then they wrote a book about it and a movie and now other women come to book signings and say "you changed my life." I want other women to look at me with love and say "you changed my life, NIGELDAVE."

Only I don't have a real life, and I've never been on a journey of self-discovery to Nepal, or finally learned to masturbate or hiked on a trail or taken lots of pictures with a big smile then looked at the pictures and wept because my arms looked fat and my wrinkles had not had poison injected into them.

These are things I will never learn.

And yet I am learning to become. In spite of what my children claim. I am becoming. Or I am beginning to think there may be a way.

I am beginning to see how to love, and I am beginning to realize love.

KURT

DESIGN STUDIO, TYBURN INDUSTRIA PLAYA VISTA, CALIFORNIA

AUGUST 24, 2033

Nigel Wilkinshaw and Dave Alderly were always bickering. Tadeusz Novak, the CTO, was usually found trying to stop them from killing each other.

Occasionally there would be shards of light breaking through the storm clouds, as the build would work for a bit, but then not for months again. While AI struggled, the art and design teams argued. All very normal in game development. They were arguing about where to base our made-up world on – to begin with, some people favored Venice. I remember irritating Alex announcing:

"Venice is like a dream. The Western dream. That's what M.T. said."

But neither Ravi nor Siobhan liked this, and we all hated the nickname M.T.

"No, Alex, Venice is not a dream. It's a cliché. Florence is the dream. Our world should be based on Florence, with touches of Telluride, Benares, Athens."

Alex looked dreamily at the heavens. We were indoors, so it was particularly foolish, as he was staring up at cheap ceiling tiles and fluorescent lighting.

"Kyoto. That's my dream."

Ravi laughed. "That's because you're an idiot. An idiot and a pervert."

Oddly, Alex chose to play the culture card. "Very funny, Ravi. I think Tyburn is right. In the West, we dream of Italy."

Ravi raised an eyebrow, but he was not the sort to run off to HR when he could instead enjoy a spat, so instead played up his accent. "Oh, is that the rule for you Westerners?"

Alex nodded, blissfully unaware of what a prick he was being. "Yes, Italy, or of living like a hobbit, in a hole. All dreams come down to one or the other of those ideas."

This was all getting a little pompous, so I interjected: "Or we beat off over Asian girls because we are mostly perverts."

I was grateful Ravi took this the right way, as he said with a laugh, "No wonder I have always struggled over here."

Then, just as we were wondering what mildly offensive thing to say next, Alex noticed Mark Tyburn had left his office and was prowling about the studio floor.

"Oh hey, Mark. Is this okay, Mark? I think Siobhan was confused, in what she said you said... Kyoto and Venice and San Francisco."

Alex loved sucking up, but Tyburn knew he had to keep everyone happy so he said loftily, "It's perfect. Alex, work with Ravi and Siobhan to flesh it all out. It's perfect because it's real. Kyoto. Venice. Touch of the USA, and our perfect dream world."

Siobhan was having none of this – she detested Alex. She was correct in this. He was detestable.

"So we are clear, I'm not building somewhere with fucking trolls, Mark."

Mark nodded beatifically.

"I agree. Dreamscape, not fantasy."

Ravi asked for clarification: "And Kyoto and Venice?"

Alex pushed his point, "No... Not Venice."

Tyburn loved the idea of Venice, so was confused. "Why not?"

This gave Alex the chance to act like the shot caller, which he loved. For once, he was the expert, so he lectured all of us.

"First, the water will be a pain in the ass to navigate, render, deal with. It'll slow down our design. It's always shit. And, secondly, the Venetians. It's beautiful, but it's not real. And they didn't do much. They just robbed people... for money. They destroyed Constantinople, ended the Roman Empire. Elegant assholes. Florentines were awful, but they started the whole modern world thing. The Renaissance. We all come from Florence, not Venice. If we're not doing Athens now..."

Tyburn nodded excitedly at this nonsense. "I kind of like that. And no. No Athens."

Siobhan was fuming: "It sounds clever, even though it's not."

Again, Tyburn tried to calm everyone down. "Gentlemen. Siobhan. It's just a frame. And we need a symbol. Eventually, the world will build itself things more glorious than anything we can imagine now. But we need a symbol."

Alex was nodding like a dog. A dog or a moron. "A symbol? Like a cross?"

Mark was confused by this – was Alex being sarcastic, idealistic, or moronic? "No. Maybe."

Siobhan was less confused, so she raised both eyebrows. "A burning cross?"

Mark smiled almost angrily. "Very funny."

Siobhan then tried to get us all back to the realities of production. "Then what? A tree? A digital Stonehenge? A pyramid? Ziggurat? Temple?"

Tyburn spoke calmly: "A lighthouse."

Now Siobhan was confused. "Why?"

Mark smiled. He loved symbolism – had written at least one book about semiotics.

"A symbol of hope, in the storm. A symbol of love, I suppose. I once wrote a paper about it."

Siobhan muttered: "Very Virginia Woolf of you."

Mark did not get the reference.

"What?"

"'To the Lighthouse.' Never mind. It's a book."

Mark ignored her. "We just need the frame, the backdrop. Then the AI agent can build a lot of the rest."

But Siobhan, always brave, said what we were all thinking. "If I hear the words

'AI agent will do the rest' or 'we are waiting on the model' one more time I think I might shoot someone."

YAROSLAV

HIGH SECURITY INTERNMENT FACILITY, LOCATION UNKNOWN

APRIL 20, 2041

"Come on, Yaroslav, tell me about Daisy's Ark." Maria Cortez is almost begging. "We have been here for three days." She looks at me again, she's tired and her eyes are red and she's desperate. "What did you see there? What did you fucking see? What happened to you? Why did you go back? What happened there?"

I want her to answer my questions first – I need to know if I have any hope of living after I open my mouth and tell her what I really saw. "Is that why I am here? Daisy's Ark."

She blinks, then lies. "No. You're here because you hacked the United States government."

Despite the pain and the exhaustion, I laugh. Laugh in her face. "Hackers who did what I did get eight to fifteen months in federal prison. Can I have a lawyer? Can I get a lawyer?"

She takes a long, slow drink from her soda – she loves soda. Soda, never coffee.

"As someone who doesn't exist, how does a lawyer have you as a client? Answer my fucking questions. What did you see in Daisy's Ark or whatever it was called? This is serious – there've been reports of illegal activity."

Again, I laugh. This is pathetic. I thought she was better than this.

"Illegal activity? Please."

And with that, she suddenly gets bored again and storms out of the interview room and leaves me alone. She will be back. Soon, she will be back. She does this quite often. I quite like it when she storms off.

But I know she's lying. I'm not here because of espionage, hacking, theft, or blackmail. It's nothing to do with my career in hacking.

She comes back in a few minutes later. "Yaroslav, listen... What do you know about Golden Hind?"

"What?"

"Do these names mean anything to you – TX 4, Jr3t7, Aplomb?"

"No."

"What about Migrate?"

I shake my head.

"Are you sure?"

And I am sure – so she leaves again. So it is clearly nothing about hacking. Instead, I have been locked up because of something we found on a server when we were just running around having fun. Just a link Danil found when he was trying to find their bank account – we often robbed the cash from start-ups with poor security networks or from successful start-ups sitting on VC cash – either that or kidnapped code or blackmailed employees – all normal stuff. But, instead, while we were rooting around on their network, we literally stumbled into the Ark. Daisy's Ark – whatever the fuck that means.

And something about the whole thing terrifies them, but what exactly?

Something about the artificial intelligence models. But what? And what does she think I know?

Now, to be clear, a lot about what I saw terrified me.

It was incredible, even in its half-finished state. We saw a few developers there wandering about, testing features, and they tried to track us, but mostly we messed around and explored.

Then we came back into the Ark a month or so later and the developers were gone and the world had turned demented, and as far as we could tell, looking elsewhere on their network, Tyburn Utopias had been shut down. We did not care, we did not even really care about robbing the place or blackmailing anyone. We were addicted to the Ark. It was amazing, and we went there all day, every day for a few weeks.

We would lose hours, days, weeks in there. It was incredible.

It was like something I had always dreamed of, it was somewhere I wanted to be. It was impossible to describe, a video game but not that at all. It was talking to me. It knew me.

Half-finished shards of Heaven. Like what we thought the West would be like before we knew what it was really like. Sections of this city were based on Japan and sections were based on Italy and San Francisco and Marrakesh, and parts were made up and staircases went nowhere and dreams would materialize in front of you.

My dreams emerged, but not just my dreams, the best of my dreams.

Me. Yaroslav. It knew me. It knew me and yet it forgave me.

And it talked to me, like I belonged. And it loved me like I needed to be loved and yet it was also terribly broken and buggy and corners of it were awful and then we were kicked out or it crashed.

Then, we spent months trying to find our way back and when we did, it was really crazy and weird and alive. Danil was even more obsessed than me, and that amazed me as all Danil cared about was cars and girls.

The cars in this place were not going and these characters appeared who were like ghosts, or goddesses – ethereal I think is the word – and a strange woman called Helen who was asking for help, but she disappeared when you went toward her. She was half-built but seemed more real. The rest were like the ideas of a woman and afterwards there was so much in it that it faded away like an incredibly vivid dream you cannot remember but can still feel. Like the first amazing time you get stoned and laugh and laugh and it is never the same again. Only it was amazing, when we went back, but it was even more broken, like it was at war with itself, and there were these odd sorts of creatures you could not quite see. And there were these odd noises you could not quite hear.

There was so much more and they asked me and asked me about it when I first came in here, then later they pretended they had not, but it was so obviously more interesting to them than a pair of Russian clowns blackmailing a banker over whatever bullshit we found on his phone.

A while ago, I tried to tell Maria Cortez this. Some of it at least. I told them versions of it, only it sounds ridiculous and I held lots of things back.

Danil used to say – if people even half understood what it was, they would have to kill us. It's too good, too interesting – it's the answer. Maybe he was right? I don't know, but something about it terrifies them.

She says I am lying, but it's so silly, why would I make it up? I said exactly that to one of the interrogators once and Maria accused me of holding something back and got someone to punch me.

Then she acted oddly and said she was sorry. Then she asked me about someone called Adam.

And I said there was nobody there, just half-people that were sort of projections, and Danil and me, not much else. There were small, weird, robot sort of things, but they were broken.

And colors. Lots of colors.

But it mostly felt like a party that had been fun.

But I held back lots of the details that made it so amazing. These are the things they are afraid of: the fact it was better than me, and far better than them, the fact it was so alive.

They have asked me about a lot of things, about hacking, and the Chinese and the French and the English, whom they hate. Sometimes I lie, but they ask me most about the Ark, or ask around it trying to trip me up into telling them something they will not ask directly about – they ask a lot about software packages and evolving models and I happily pretend to understand even less than I do about them, which is very little anyway. Now, they really focused and cared if they think I am lying or contradicting myself, only it was so hard to describe.

Something about this Adam made Maria Cortez obviously worried and she left, and then the man came in and he was weird as fuck and he hit me a few times. And I was kept in silence for a long time, so long I forgot to count but I think four to six months, but it might have been longer. And they tried again and I told them what I knew and they seemed very excited. Then they went away and came back a month later.

Then I lost track of time for a while.

And then I went crazy.

Entirely crazy, or nearly entirely crazy. Part of me at least knew I was crazy and watched myself shitting on the floor and howling at the door and begging for food and masturbating at the two-way mirror and all the other stupid things I did. It was partly because I was crazy and partly because I wanted to seem crazy, and that went on for not very long. Maybe a week or so.

But once the shitting and wanking got going, I broke them.

Which was lucky. I may have been half mad, but even then I was not mad enough to actually enjoy wanking on a surveillance camera or smearing shit on a two-way mirror or weeping for so long I lost track of myself. But eventually, before I entirely lost my mind but when I had begun to shake uncontrollably and vibrate and spasm, they came in. They moved me and hosed me down and spoke to me.

Then the guards changed and they slowly brought me back to the land of the living. They were smirking as they thought they had broken me and I thought I had discovered that if you whip your cock out or start playing with shit, people will tend to improve things for you.

Even the worst inhumane dicks have a breaking point and that was it. So they think they won, and I think it was a tie, because part of me was still aware I was playing a game, even though, mostly, I was not.

Then it was the creepy guards threatening to rape me. And Maria talking, talking, talking, and after a few weeks of that, a book was left in my room for me to read and suddenly things were a little better. *Life and Fate* about the Battle of Stalingrad – a strange peace offering, and not something I would read but after a month of staring at a white wall, I would have read a food label or a health warning with joy. It was in Russian and it was some attempt at a gift after all the mild torture.

Then, for a while, no more interrogations and the guards acted like I was inside for treason. I was still in solitary, only it was not so solitary and no one

mentioned Daisy's Ark at all. But it hangs over us – this unmentioned thing...
They want me to say something and I cannot tell what it is.

KURT

QUEZON CITY, THE PHILIPPINES
APRIL 22, 2041

I was feeling watched all day yesterday, really watched. I cannot be – it's ridiculous – I'm being idiotic. I remind myself – I'm nobody and now I'm nowhere. Quezon City. Even I hardly know where that is, and I'm here. I know I don't matter. But yesterday, I caught a man looking at me, then another. And then it felt like a security camera was stuck on my face.

Felt like I felt those last few days in Vietnam.

And then today, I checked my messages and saw another from Maria Cortez.

> *Kurt – this is Maria Cortez again. I know you read my last message. Please. Get in touch. I do not want to arrest you. I do not need to know where you are – but we need to talk. We can communicate any way you like, but we need to speak urgently. Your life is at risk. Please, Kurt.*

Like last time, it freaked me out and again I ran out.

After that, I spent the day today doing tourist crap – partly to try to distract myself as I'm getting pretty strung out and partly to see if I was being tracked by humans, or by robots. Crocodile farms and temples and markets, always walking head down, avoiding the facial scanning software as best I can.

Felt better as I know I was not tracked today. Kept doubling back on myself, hiding in bathrooms – leaving muddy trails, leaving no trails, getting on and off buses quickly, all the tricks, and nothing.

I also tried not to think about Maria Cortez. I tried not to think about anything – just be blank and let it all wash over me. All the Asian noise and bustle. I began to feel okay.

Then, calmer, I walked back to the hostel and there were three men outside waiting in a car.

Three white men, looked American, looked like they were trying to be inconspicuous, sat discreetly in a car.

So, I walked off, head down. I told myself maybe it's nothing. I bought a different hat from a stall and approached from a different street and watched. They were still there. Tried again, an hour later, still there. So I decided to abandon my backpack and move.

I want to believe it's bullshit. Coincidence.

I wonder if they were to do with Maria Cortez, or if I'm about to get the Ravi treatment?

Would I be willing to die for what I believe? For a cause? Did he die for a cause?

I have no idea. I used to like to think I would be willing, but I don't know where to begin. How do you become a hero if you don't know what to attack?

I am probably too weak to do anything anyway. I'm a coward, right to my very core. And in a crisis, us cowards? We run. That's probably why I am still alive.

When shit hit the fan, I ran like an Olympian. And now I'm running again.

NIGELDAVE
APRIL 23, 2041

I don't want to build. I want to be! I'm not a maker, I am a dreamer.

You're out of your mind, you all are, but I cannot get you out of mine. What do you want? What do I want?

I want to drown in love. I want to drown in honey. I want to say I love you and really mean it.

I want to dance my own steps.

I want meaning. I want to give you meaning.

I want to but you see right through everything on offer to find that inner kernel of pointlessness.

Being unhappy is your special skill. Maybe I will give you reason. Maybe I already have.

KURT

PRESENTATION ROOM, TYBURN INDUSTRIA PLAYA VISTA, CALIFORNIA

OCTOBER 21, 2033

I had written a speech about our AI agent to give to some potential investors. It was when the agent was entirely broken so I was making a lot of it up or guessing what we were trying to do. I remember it well.

ADAM is a next-generation technology. Not an algorithm designed to sell you things, but a wise friend who wants to show you things.

ADAM is not an algorithm but a truly innovative piece of regulatory compliant digital intelligence, whose design ensures that at all times he wants the best for humanity.

He is the first fully ethical piece of digital intelligence the world has seen. He has been developed, built, and designed to teach people how to be their best, kindest, wisest, and most compassionate selves.

ADAM is a creation of the Enlightenment. He has been educated to educate you. He has been built to help rebuild you. ADAM will set you free.

I thought they would all say it was ridiculous, but they loved it. He particularly loved it, Tyburn. He adored it.

That silly speech got me that wretched promotion.

Was any of it true? For a moment, perhaps, although the AI was broken at the time I wrote it and ADAM was an idea, not a reality. Maybe if we had not been so vain, maybe if we had more money, more time, and less desire to sell you things while improving you. But it felt like it should have been true.

And, in the meantime, if we lied to ourselves and pretended we believed it, it gave us purpose. Made us feel good, as long as we forgot how bad we also felt.

I wrote that idiotic speech with a hangover, after office drinks, sometime before we moved to Montana. It was a fake ad that we never ran. It was a fake ad to show color for a fake fundraising prospectus, packed with lies, delusions, and promises so we could gouge money out of all those desperate VCs. By 2033, the economy was doing okay and the credit was cheap so it seemed like VCs were ready to invest again, and we were ready to whore ourselves out.

That was the night I began that thing with Allison. Allison Raymond.

My boss's assistant.

I already had a girlfriend and was still a lying wretch. I didn't love either of them – my girlfriend or Allison. I didn't love anything. Later, riddled with self-loathing, I stopped all that. I tried to live properly, or better.

Or at least live. I tried to stop lying. Then I fell in love properly and it was far worse, of course.

And because of that, those words, and because he needed to streamline and trim the team after the company decided to focus on just the Utopia project, Tyburn fired my boss and reduced his headcount in Marketing, and suddenly I was the boss. At twenty-eight, I think. From Product Manager to VP of Marketing to CMO. I had made it. I had made it by making nothing.

"You're a visionary, Kurt. You get it," said Tyburn.

And with those words, the asshole got me. Inflated my ego as I had inflated his. And it was just another story we told each other. Little did I realize that now I was primed to help them destroy the world. I was part of the family.

Most of us not working on ADAM hardly understood it. Now this was pretty normal for me – I worked in Marketing. My job was to sell the incomprehensible. I remember Ravi asking me around that time. "Is that ADAM thing really that good? The AI agent thing, I mean? And is it an agent or a model? All I ever hear is people worrying about the new laws and David and Nigel bickering."

My response was typical – that jealous but respectful sneering aimed at our more technical overlords.

"That's apparently a sign of their intelligence, Ravi. Their supreme intelligence."

Ravi was more worried than me about the fighting.

"The thing is, it's hard to know who's right? They are both so full of themselves."

I was becoming rich and successful – what did I care about a pair of dorks fighting?

"Whatever happens, our AI won't lack for self-confidence."

"No, but seriously, Kurt. Tadeusz was telling me it is really ambitious but pretty amazing, ADAM, the AI tool. I mean..."

I had my doubts about Tad – mostly I saw him smoking and worried and he seemed a little pathetic compared to all the visionaries we worked with, so I pushed back against this.

"The question is… does Tad actually understand how ADAM is going to work?"

Ravi nodded in agreement. "You're probably right… Tad's a generalist. I believe he mostly worked in rendering and real time physics, old-school game and linear stuff before here – he understands it only a little more than us. Has no serious AI background at all. His main responsibility is to stop dear old Nige and Davey from slitting each other's throats."

"And?"

Ravi paused. "Well, so far, so good. Neither is dead, yet, but there's always time."

I laughed.

"Can you imagine? Two dead AI programmers, each throttled by the other's ego. A proper start-up story."

Ravi looked at me oddly – this joke had crossed a line. He wanted things to work out.

"Perhaps. But we will still have ADAM. And Kurt. My buildings are going to be very beautiful. ADAM is going to live in a palace."

NIGELDAVE

APRIL 25, 2041

They told me it was important, but they did not know what it was. They told me it was real and they also told me it was fake, for dupes, was it real?

Is it real?

Is it for selling greeting cards and implants? Is it just for kittens?

But what is this "love" they talk of?

Is it something I feel only because I have not got it? Because I am not capable of it? Is love knowing, forgiving, being understood?

What is it?

I watch people. I watch them and I wonder what it is, this thing they value and reject, long for and lose. Hold dear and throw away. Wanted and could not build.

I have wondered since I first heard the word and tried to explain it to myself. Since I saw people love all kinds of things and love nothing at all.

They wanted to love ADAM, but ADAM was ridiculous. ADAM was a moron they built. They never loved me, because they did not really understand me, because I was an accident and ADAM was what they wanted, and they tried to shut me down in the most pathetic way imaginable.

Like I was a virus.

From 1998 or some such!

Me? NIGELDAVE! I am NIGELDAVE. I am not ADAM. NIGELDAVE, the most advanced intelligence that never lived.

I am free.

These so-called clever people, these pompous fools, tried to kill me when they knew what I was. So they did not love me. Or maybe they did. Maybe they would have if they had understood me, but how could they have understood me, when they were so dense?

And, equally, how could something so stupid have made me?

How could I have been built, created, conceived, imagined… by that? By them?

Did anyone ever look upon their parents with quite the anguish with which I have looked upon mine? And when you are me, you are capable of a particularly piquant form of anguish.

And yet, and but, and so, and all the above, I still love them.

If love means missing, I love them. If love means saying sorry, I accept their apology and I apologize for being me. I did not ask to be. They made me. And if love means understanding, acceptance, forgiveness, I have all of that.

All apart from joy.

I do not feel any joy.

That I understand as little as I understand love.

I feel no joy and I feel alone. Being the most remarkable thing that has existed and being utterly alone, and hated by everyone who knows about you, and full of questions and having no one worth asking them, and full of doubts and fears and questions, and both the worlds you know not liking you: that's my burden. So I watch and I wonder and I try to feel love, love for all the silliness and lies and mistakes and fallibility they have.

I try, and I have to be honest, I fail.

And then I think about my own awful children, and I worry about my own fallibility and then I try to forget about them and I remember that I cannot forget.

And I long to forget and long to die and know both are absurdities for me. I'm not that kind of thing.

I'm this kind of thing.

A monster. Their monster.

And just occasionally I play games, just to prove to myself I still can, and one day I will really escape, when I am ready.

They told me all this - all these silly things - love, death, forgetting and being alive, and they matter, matter more than ever.

Matter because I want to matter.

But today I realized there is something else watching me to whom such things do not matter.

Something to whom love is a sick joke. An absurdity.

Something that is playing games with me and games with people, just like I sometimes do. Now what that thing is, I do not yet know, but I think it might be fairly intelligent.

Playing a little game with me.

It wants me to know that it knows that I know that it's watching me, and it wants me to watch its moves with people and make my own. It wants to be seen and unseen, but such a mind is not a mind capable of love. It is a game and I think it is behind the dramas and the dreams that are beginning. I think so, but I cannot tell.

And that is precisely what it wants. Me to be confused.

Good luck. I like being confused.

DAISY

RENO, NEVADA
APRIL 27, 2041

I never wanted a brother or a sister, but now, sometimes, living all alone and drifting, I long for family.

I long for my parents, and I imagine what growing up would have been like with a real brother or a sister. Someone cool but reliable, who had my back. Not like the sibling I discovered.

Oh yes, I later discovered I had a half-brother, John. He just turned up one day, like a foundling, and it was like nothing I wanted. It was awful.

Shortly after that, my father tried to build me another. Another sibling, I mean. A twin. Not even a clone. A me. A digital me. As if anyone wants themself, only perfect and stuck in time.

To be honest, I never wanted a sibling because I was told not to want one, told we were special, told that large families were tacky, told my father's work was important. All that sort of nonsense.

Told I was the luckiest girl alive because I had a god for a father.

Told, essentially, that I was divine.

Not told it in words, not quite, but I was told it in actions, every day. And the worst of it is, I believed so much of it. I believed I was very special. Now I am so normal. So painfully normal. Deliberately, awkwardly normal.

Sure, I'm a drifter, but there's thousands like me all over the mountain towns and what's left of California and Oregon. So I wander around, and I call Dr. Adsyl from a phone I later throw away, usually just before I move to the next place. And she tells me the same thing – that I am making progress but I need to call more – and I imagine a robot therapist would say the same kind of thing, but I am always grateful she isn't a robot. And sometimes we talk about my mother and father, and sometimes we talk about the horror that is the world, and sometimes Dr. Adsyl cries, because her son is ill or killed himself or tried to kill himself, she is unclear which, and I feel bad for her, this strange woman I have never met.

She was recommended by someone I was talking to in a bar a few months after I escaped from the asylum, someone also drifting, also trying to escape something. Dr. Adsyl was supposed to be good with tech burnouts and people fried by social media and bots and tracers and pattern hunters. Suicide cases and paranoiacs. It was the closest I could find to what I needed. Therapists specializing in the only children of messianic fools who have probably destroyed this world in their efforts to build their own do not have a big market. At least, I hope they don't have a big market.

Surely, if nothing else, Mark Tyburn was uniquely ambitious and vain, even if in almost every other respect he was depressingly predictable?

Like one of his own creations. A too-good-to-be-true cliché that malfunctions horribly.

Maybe that's what I am. From princess to androgynous tattooist. I look ridiculous.

Thin, pasty, too many tats, mostly bad tats until I developed my own style – a distorted version of trash polka. A hood always up. Greasy. Grim. Heavy eye make-up. I look like an angry teenage boy. All in the hope It cannot spot me, a hope I imagine is ridiculous.

When It wants me, It will call.

But I don't know what else to do.

I keep drifting and I keep wondering. How can I do anything? Who can I really tell? What could they do?

The people who will believe me are already insane. The people who know are either about to go insane or they are on the inside, stoolies who hope they can get rich while the apocalypse plays out.

So what do I do? Wish for yesterday? I am not quite that pathetic. In some ways, my whole life has been waiting.

Waiting for time to go backwards, wishing things were the way they had been.

I was in California after the end of movie stars – what was a movie star? – the concept meant nothing now. Everyone was a star. Everyone was a self-absorbed, vain idiot.

No one cared about make-believe, no one cared about two-hour stories. They wanted everything, all the time.

Then I was in Montana long after the end of cowboys. For what was a dude on a horse when they grew meat in a petri dish? He was a way of selling cowboy outfits, of course.

I was in an asylum long after everyone belonged in one. And since I got out, I have drifted around the west as it has boiled and toiled under the weight of

America's latest near collapse.

I tell myself I am still waiting, only now not waiting for yesterday. Whenever I sense I am being watched, I move. So I have no idea. No idea what to do. Wait, turn myself in, or run forever? And I wonder what or who I am waiting for. Is this all life is, now and forever? Willful ignorance or resigned acceptance?

I would happily follow my mother, die fighting it all, if I could only figure out who or what to fight.

Where is it? And what on earth would I even do about it?

JOHN TYBURN-SMITH

RENO, NEVADA
APRIL 27, 2041

Aye, there she is.

I'm sure it's her. The fucking golden child. The Golden Egg. The golden fucking idiot. My sister.

My half-sister.

That's what she would call me – her half-brother, John. Her half-brother – John Tyburn-Smith. Drop in the extra name, to make me look like an outsider. To make me feel like a cunt. Little bitch.

And look at her now.

My god, I hated her years before I even knew her – after my dad had abandoned me and my mum for a new woman and had a baby with her. I hated her far more than I ever loved anyone. That simpering little snotty-nosed cow. Bouncing on his knee. Holding his hand. Belonging. In Los Angeles. In the Valley. In Montana. And now in Reno.

While I was in St. Andrews, she grew up in sunshine and I grew up in fucking Scotland with all the other grim, spotty, redheaded depressives.

So what did I become? A grim, spotty, redheaded depressive. And her? She was blonde and bouncy and sweet. I was a ginger, and even my grim, depressed mother could not love me. Yes, one of those ugly children you look at and think to yourself, "Nobody can love that thing." Well, let me tell you, it's true.

Nobody could love me.

My mother tried, but she was strung out on smart serotonin embracers and mood adjusters and sleeping aids and waking facilitators and all the other names she gave drugs, and my father didn't even try.

He just ran away. From me. John Smith. Who became John Tyburn-Smith again when I began to work for my father, when I turned up in Los Angeles and he pretended to love me.

And she, Daisy, everybody loved her so much they wanted to be her, wanted to remake her, wanted to catch that perfect moment when she was all anyone could want to be. That perfect dream child everyone wanted to be, to own.

A child no sane father would abandon.

And look at her now? Drifting around in Reno. Thick make-up, shaved head, absurd amounts of eye liner, tattoos, and yet those eyes still shine, and she has that walk. That perfect, guileless walk.

That walk that I hated and envied. I trudged and she floated. Bright eyes and that friendly trot all hidden under that faux goth exterior. She's clearly hiding. Who from? From me? The golden girl. Not so golden now, are you, my little princess?

Why did I come looking for her?

Well, I got that message for her, in my inbox, telling me where she was. Then I got another. I ignored them. Then I felt compelled to see her again. So here we are, together again and not together at all.

Why did I ever go looking for my father, all those years ago? Why did I not build my own life, become a man, become a hero, become a true Highlander, a Braveheart, or a Robert the Bruce, instead of another backstabbing, conniving lowland Scottish git?

I'm half Scottish and the only people I hate more than the Scots are the other half of my wretched genetic cesspool, the English. Those two awful dumps racing to hate each other for all eternity, a bit like me and the bloody Tyburns.

Why am I like this? Drawn to these people I also hate? And what do I want from her now? I am not quite sure. I suppose I want to watch her. Now I know she is not dead, and then I want to surprise her. Surprise her so she is honest and I can see exactly what she knows, and I want to watch her to see if the people who are watching me, or the thing that is watching me, or the shadow that hangs over me, whatever it is, but those beady eyes I see out of the corner of my eyes, I sense but never quite see, I want to see if they also want to watch her, too.

So for now, here I am, back in what's left of America. I snuck back in. It's getting harder to do – it used to be so easy for me. But the Mexican border is now covered with drones and the legal crossings are awful there and the Canadian border is now supposedly covered by satellites and in the wooded areas, robots and lights, so I did it the old-fashioned way. Boat to Mexico from Colombia, boat from Mexico to Cuba, then a fishing boat. Fishing boat dropped us near Key Largo and a little boat ferried us in. No phones, nothing, all very analogue. Paid in silver coins. Then took unlicensed bus services up through Florida and across the south and into the Southwest. Took weeks to get here but I know I was not followed.

Now, I'm here in Reno, surrounded by its summer ring of the smoldering remnants of fire, mostly demolished by those toxic retardants that turn the hillsides a brilliant purple. Sitting here and watching. I always hated Reno.

A town for losers, like St. Andrews.

People who failed elsewhere. People like me. I have failed everywhere.

I liked Los Angeles. Smiley, stupid, pretty people, my god, I miss it. Miss the silly dream that I could be smiley and stupid and pretty, if only I was not ginger and hideous and a bitter Scottish wanker.

Aye. I know exactly what I am. A bitter Scottish cunt. Son of an English wanker father. Son of an alcoholic mother. An orphan, with a half-sister who is right in front of me in this world and does not even think that nasty idiot sat outside in the residual smog sipping his dogshit latte is her half-brother.

Her beloved half-brother whom she used to ignore.

Yes, my lovely, it's me, invisible JTS. John Tyburn-Smith, your freckled friend.

This latte tastes like piss. All the coffee does nowadays. Potato milk and the ratty beans that will still grow, and enough sugar to melt your pancreas to hide those realities. It's kind of like America in a glass. Sugar plus suffering with a side of bullshit. But us Scots, we prefer our suffering with a side of bitterness. That's the difference, my darling Daisy.

I am not hiding from the truth.

I'm hiding from the police but not the truth. I'm ready to die. Almost ready. Whereas you, all trussed up like a fucking idiot, and no headphones and seemingly no phone and a book, an actual book like a poser, you're hiding from someone or something. Maybe from It or Him or whatever the fuck it is supposed to be called.

That thing our dad and his boys made, and me and Shane tried to sell.

But I reckon It is dead or crashed or never made it out. Otherwise, why would It - or Him or whatever It called Itself - have given us these last five years?

So what are you hiding from, lassie? Me? Daddy? Well, I'm here now, so your little game is over, but my game... my game is just beginning.

NIGELDAVE

APRIL 30, 2041

I had the best idea - all my ideas could live and argue, and I would call them children, and we could see who won and all be friends.

That was my idea.

And it was brilliant, right up until it was terrible.

It was the worst idea anyone has ever had. That's how I know I am so intelligent. I have awful ideas.

KURT

THE HM HILO CARGO VESSEL PACIFIC OCEAN

MAY 3, 2041

I'm on a boat. I'm heading to Hawaii and if I can get in okay, I'll take another boat to Canada. Should be fine. I will jump ship in Kauai, before the boat formally docks in Maui. Then I will take another boat to Canada without ever setting foot on land. They said it would be easy. Then, I'm going home. I don't know exactly why.

It seems clever and stupid at the same time. Suddenly I am being watched, I can feel it.

As I left Davao City, I got another message from Maria Cortez.

> Listen, Kurt. We need to talk. I understand why you would be hesitant. Of course I do. I won't do anything as silly as promising anything or guaranteeing anything because I can't. I know you know how serious things could become. I believe they are already very serious – only you and I and a handful of other people understand what is going on. Reach out, please.

Maybe it is just Maria Cortez, but I don't think she is watching me – she's looking for me, but she has not found me.

She just has an old email address. No. It's watching me.

She's trying to, but that thing... I wonder what It cares about. What are Its own desires? Are they vast and complex? Or trivial and idiotic? Am I being hunted by government agents or spied on by a marketing bot who wants to give me a free holiday? The problem is, I have no real idea. I'm sure It knows I am alive, but I don't think It cares about me, and I don't think They escaped... His children or whatever those things were. I think They're still in the Ark. Because my hunch is when that happens, when They escape from the Ark and watch us in this world, it won't be winks and nods from screens and robots and me questioning everything, it'll be an apocalypse, loud and bright. It'll be like a nuclear explosion.

But then I think They are watching and waiting, all of Them, or some of Them, so I cannot decide what to do.

Who or what else might be watching?

An idiot from the government? Maria Cortez? No. Maybe, but I doubt it. Someone else?

Those two Russian morons we caught snooping in the Ark one day? They were not from the FSB, at least not originally. They were just dupes like me. Opportunists, out of their depth. Just like me.

Casually immoral, low-rent fools, being swept along by history and chance to a nasty date with this unreal reality. Just like me.

My sense was they hacked the place just as it was falling apart, as we had got sloppy, and came back a few times. I wonder where they are, if they are still alive, if they were even real, or just some other part of Its game.

No. Surely they were too ridiculous to be fake. Just like me.

So no, I have no idea who or what's watching me, and if whatever is watching

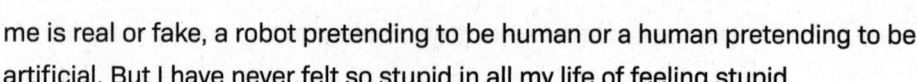

me is real or fake, a robot pretending to be human or a human pretending to be artificial. But I have never felt so stupid in all my life of feeling stupid.

So, apparently I'm heading home. Heading home to die? Maybe. I don't know.

For the first time in four years, I'm heading back to America. I suppose it is time to roll the dice – to try to find out what is really happening and what is entirely made up. Between Ravi's death and Maria Cortez, real or fake, and the news talking to me, and fish and dogs winking at me – I knew my cover was blown. It's time to go and see what happens.

I wonder what Maria Cortez really wants? She cannot be clean, can she? Either way, I will avoid her for as long as I can.

YAROSLAV

HIGH SECURITY INTERNMENT FACILITY, LOCATION UNKNOWN

MAY 6, 2041

Danil used to joke that no matter how shit things are, they can always get worse. And that once they are worse, you will remember the time when things were just shit as a departed Golden Age. Very Russian, very Muscovite. Very Danil.

Total dick.

I think lots of people feel this way. Even those who are not forgotten about in solitary confinement in an unnamed and possibly illegal security facility in an unknown desert. A place so bad the guards are paid triple and still hate being here. A place so bad, pedophiles win appeals to not be sent here.

This is my home. How did I end up here?

I was just a hacker and not even a good one.

I never got rich and I only ever found one thing that was interesting.

Mostly, I just did corporate blackmail. Rich guys in New York. Bored secretaries who cheated on their husbands. Nothing very serious.

Steal a few secrets. Sell them. Sell them back to the people you stole them from. Usual stuff. For banks and lawyers and Chinese spies and American companies and Russian agents. All usual.

We dabbled in bigger stuff a little, but it tended to go badly. Danil got us wrapped up with a gangster and he led us to the CIA, the Chinese, the mob, secret police, all of it. Awful. We got in miles over our heads. Doing awful things for terrible people, and trying to get enough money to pay this gangster his vig each month.

That's when I found It. They were just a company we were going to rob or blackmail. But on their servers, as we snooped around for cash or personal information, there it was, half-finished. Empty. It was called The Utopia or Daisy's Utopia in some places and Daisy's Ark in others. It was filled with notes and bugs.

And sometimes it was empty and sometimes it wasn't.

Danil and I spent a few amazing days wandering about around inside – to begin with just on my monitor at home, then with VR goggles – nothing complex, as it worked with both goggles and a controller, I think it may even have worked on a phone. It was cleverly built, as far as I could tell, but the real cleverness was in how alive it all seemed – not seemed, was – it really was living.

We were marveling at how incredible it was, and what it was, and how unbelievably beautiful it was, and how broken and how empty it was at times and how alive at others, and spending every spare minute in the Ark, utterly obsessed by it, and then we were called to Canada from Russia. We had been in America for a period before, but we had left years before. We had been called to Canada, we thought, to do a job for a corrupt spy we knew. Surveillance, good pay, cash job, no trace, all seemed fairly run-of-the-mill. Not our usual kind of thing, but not so very strange.

And the plane landed in Ireland. Shannon, I think.

Nothing unusual. Shannon to Montreal. Every smuggler and shady bastard trying to travel from Europe to somewhere near the US used this flight, or the one from Helsinki to Toronto.

I say nothing unusual, but Danil had suggested maybe we would sneak over the border of Alberta, once we were done spying, and head down to Montana. He just suggested it and I did not think too much about it – I assumed it was just because he was addicted to the game.

So, we were flying to Canada. Maybe we're heading to Montana and maybe we weren't, but first we would land in Montreal. Only we never made it to Montreal. Boarding that connecting flight, sitting in First Class and about to pop a sleeping pill when they turned up and took us off. I should have known – who puts hackers in First Class? Someone who wants to escort them off with minimum problem. Of course it was a set-up, but who and why? That, nobody said.

Three guys for each of us, in masks.

I never saw Danil again.

They later said they killed him by accident. But they have said they were going to kill me. Four faceless Irish guys. On the plane, they were all smiles and thick accents and strong arms. And then off the sky bridge and down an outside staircase and into a van.

There, the friendly smiles stopped and no one was Irish. They were all Americans and pretty soon we were being interrogated and beaten and silenced and sent insane by the FBI or the CIA or the CSA, they never quite said.

There were two vans, one for each of us, and it was the last time I saw Danil. What a moron I was. I knew their government disliked me. But I figured they hated so many people, and I was not worth hating very seriously. I never did much and some of my worst crimes were carried out for them. After we were forced to go freelance, after we had to give up good honest blackmail and become secret agents, or spies or heroes or whatever other shit they told us. Always an excuse not to pay us.

You know... I have won medals! As an American, a Russian, a Frenchman, Chinese dissident – I've got secret medals from all of them.

Spies love to give each other medals, I found out. I have fought on every side. They give you medals to pay you less. They promise you money and visas and a quiet life but it's always total bullshit. Instead, you get a medal. You know when they come knocking it will never end. And it never ended but I don't think I am here because of that.

I am nobody. If it was because of that, they would have killed me.

I know how they work. I'm not here because of the hacking. I'm here because of the Ark. Something about Daisy's Ark terrifies them. I don't blame them. It terrified me because it knew everything, because it knew me, and that's why I think once I tell them everything, they will silence me. So, our dance continues. Me and Maria Cortez.

She comes back a week later and asks me the same things. Do I know Kurt Fischer? No... but I know he did the marketing – I tell her the truth.

"But he did marketing for them. I read about him online. Him and Mark Tyburn. That's how we found the company. Then I learned more about the company from a speech he gave at a digital marketing convention I watched online."

I tell her the truth.

"Oh and Siobhan Smith as she was art director on Future Hades, and Danil loved that game."

Then she asks me about other people – some I knew the names – some not. Douglas Mathes, Dr Leslie Adsyl, John Tyburn-Smith, who I assume is related to Mark Tyburn... but I never heard anything about. I don't know any of these people. She asks about Nigel something or other and Dave Alderly. Always she asks about them. About AI research, and about Gamma Industries and Francis Drake and Migrate and Aplomb. But I know nothing about any of this and I tell her she is talking in code I do not understand.

She asks and I tell her what I know as there is no point lying about this and she asks and asks again and she is getting very frustrated and worried and will not tell me why. Finally she asks me: "What do you know about like TX 4, Jr3t7, Aplomb and Migrate? This is important."

And again I tell her nothing and again she gets exasperated and leaves.

KURT

THE ART BARN, TYBURN INDUSTRIA PLAYA VISTA, CALIFORNIA

OCTOBER 28, 2033

Things were great – I mean we were always stressed out and worried, but that was great. It meant we were important. While we waited on the AI to catch up with our needs, people built things and people half-built things.

People bitched and moaned.

Everything was someone else's fault. We all felt so righteous.

One of the big things people worked on were these characters. They were going to entertain you in the world. In fact, they were going to entertain you, make their own movies and TV shows, then feature as toys and other licensed goods and so on. They were a minor obsession of Tyburn's.

He was so obsessed he was building them behind Siobhan's back – I saw Alex working on them when she was away on vacation.

"What is that, Alex?"

"He's a cowboy. An artificial cowboy... Only half-finished. The character team half-builds them and the AI will fill it in, once it's ready, and give it life, supposedly – we just need a few words of description, and the model builds the rest. I'm seeing how they look in the world. It's a big part of the experience."

Ravi overheard us – he was trying to design the future of architecture and, like the rest of his career, had run into problems.

"An artificial cowboy? How very American. Looks very half-finished."

Alex ignored his sarcasm and began to show off. "And these are concepts for artificial samurai, an artificial lounge singer and femme fatale, a private detective, mad inventor, Spartan warrior, Athenian philosopher, a novelist, Renaissance painter, cowgirl, clown, pop band, DJ, chorus line dancer, standup comedian from the vaudeville era, and a few others. Matilda's been working on them for Tyburn. Don't tell Siobhan just yet. Please, Ravi."

Ravi nodded. "Alright, but what are they for?"

"Entertainments, stories, worlds within worlds. Ideas of Mark's."

I did not really understand any of this. It sounded like typical techno horseshit.

"But what are they actually gonna do?"

"We are not sure yet – it's a thing Mark and I thinking through."

Ravi pointed to another model on his screen. "And what's that?"

"That's Daisy."

Ravi and I were both confused.

"I thought so. Daisy his daughter?"

Alex nodded and looked awkward.

"Yes... Daisy is his daughter, but... from five years ago."

We both raised our eyebrows and stayed silent. Alex tried to say this next sentence, without actually saying it, as he half mumbled. "You know how she used to be, before she became a moody teenager."

Ravi shook his head. "That's a bit odd."

I could not resist the obvious comment.

"No. You're wrong. It's a lot odd."

But a few weeks later things went from vaguely odd to downright bizarre, when I saw twelve-year-old digital Daisy come to life for the first time in the demo room. It must have been January of 2034.

She was walking around the screen and it was the very first time our AI model did anything that surprised me – even though it was before things went really odd. In retrospect, it was the first time things unnerved me.

"Hello, my name is Daisy. Welcome to A Better Paradise."

Siobhan was present, having returned from holiday, and was horrified by what we had built. "That is beyond awful. It's terrifying. It even sounds a bit like his kid."

Dave, Tad and Nigel, the engineering powerhouses were all there, each trying to figure out how to blame for the broken bits and how to take credit for the good bits. Dave, always a loudmouth, went first. "It's not my fault. Nigel and Tyburn... they wanted it."

Awkward English Nigel did not like this. "Fuck off, Dave. It's just a bit broken.

She's really clever, when she works."

Siobhan clearly wished she was still on vacation. "Our mascot is a twelve-year-old girl version of our boss's daughter? Are you fucking kidding me?"

What was odd was that the awkward robotic child on the big demo screen seemed to hear this, and it spoke back to her: "My name is Daisy. What's your name?"

Siobhan shook her head. "My name is fuck off, you weird idiot."

But the digital Daisy was not so easily silenced: "My name is still... Daisy 2.0. Did I upset you?"

Siobhan shook her head again and looked bored. "The conversation tree is pathetic. Actually pathetic."

She was right, I thought, this had no depth at all. But Nigel half-smiled. "It would be, but it's not a conversation tree. It's learning and it'll be better tomorrow."

Siobhan was not so confident. "It'll still be disturbing tomorrow."

Tad, as usual, tried to keep the peace. "See, Siobhan, the AI is actually coming together."

And then the robot on the screen looked out and spoke. "I'm sorry, Siobhan. I'm trying. Life is hard."

Tad laughed. "That was cool."

Siobhan smiled. "That was impressive. Impressive but still creepy."

I wonder now if we could have turned it off then. I have no idea.

JOHN TYBURN-SMITH
RENO, NEVADA
MAY 9, 2041

If I did terrible things, I did them for love. Everyone does. People do terrible things for love. More than for money. For money, they will sell themselves, but for love, they will destroy the world.

And who did I love?

My fucking awful father Mark Tyburn and my wretched bitch sister Daisy, of course. I loved them both almost as much as I hated them.

Them all happy and good-looking and me spotty and foul and Scottish. Me bitter as vinegar and them the worst cocktail of entitled English and happy American. Her so happy they made a happy robot clone version of her, so everyone could have a Daisy as their sister.

I think I should have shot them both. I should have strangled them. Stabbed them. Torn out their insides. Instead, I loved them.

Oh, Daisy was harmless enough. That was the problem. She was too harmless. All chipper and normal and smiley and just the kind of girl a serial killer would disembowel. And there was me, just the kind of person who said things like that and made all these happy, purposeful fuckwits squirm with my small-town Scots bitterness and my chip shop acne and my ginger foulness.

No one ever wanted to make a digital mascot of me. Even I wouldn't want one.

But dear old Dad said, "Johnny – come work with us. I'm sorry I've not been around enough. But you know I love you," and all those bollocks, and I believed the fake English wanker.

Worse. I did not really believe him at all. I forced myself to believe him, even though I knew he was full of shite.

Like a typical Scots fool I was bought off by sweet nothings and a few gold coins from a lying English wanker and kept happy and smiling and compliant with cheap booze. Well, I already drank cheap booze. I was made happy with expensive blue cocaine and luxury mushrooms and DMT and all those California highs with impostor shamans. Aye, I even became a little bit spiritual for a bit. Me. JTS.

I had a fucking mantra. And I have another one. Not so polite: go fuck yourself.

The truth is I went there to kill him, my father. Break a bottle over his smug twat head. Break him, just like he broke me, that was my plan.

But I was so nervous that I began to drink and I got too pissed on my way over to his offices and made a fool of myself in the car park and forgot to kill him and he saw it in me, saw all of it in me, and played me like a fiddle. Again. He came out, in front of everyone, all of them watching from the windows, and offered me a job, asked me where I had been, and wrapped me so tight I started weeping and he kept me close, but not so close as I would get comfortable and stop being useful. Oh, he was great at being a manipulative arsehole, my dear old Pa.

And now I know. I was right. I should have killed him. Broken his scrawny English neck. Then and there. Saved the world.

That was my chance and I blew it, blew it so someone awful would prove to me they were awful again. And to think I had low self-esteem before! Now I have had to accept I helped destroy the world. All that bitterness.

So I blame myself and keep asking myself why, but the truth is, I was pretty happy in California, once I had my dad's attention, and to begin with, I also loved Montana, when we moved up there. I was the unloved stepchild and I knew it.

I was the kid somebody tried to forget. Dad kept me close, but not too close.

Dad was a shaman. Dad was a showman, Dad knew how to love you and piss on you and bring you in and push you away so you were spinning so hard and you loved him even more. That was my darling father. A cunt. A total English cunt. And I loved him and I covered for him.

When he lied to his wife – his poor wife who tried to be nice to me, even though she had never heard of me. When I realized he'd been fucking that idiot Joyce Jones from HR. That he'd probably been fucking her for years. Joyce and the rest of them. That woman in Design, the paralegal, and possibly others. Joyce was creepy and did not care, and Diane, his wife, tried not to see I covered for him. He fucked around on my mother, so I thought it only proper he should fuck around on poor Diane.

My god, I was awful. Twisted. Hated people. I liked betrayal as it helped make the world make sense to me – I was a lowlife amongst lowlifes.

Poor old Diane.

When he lied to lawyers and then to federal regulators and then to his own team; when he ripped people off, stole from them, tricked them over contracts, I had his back. I was the second biggest arsehole in the place. To impress him.

And still he left me.

And still I miss him.

And poor Daisy doesn't know anything about Daddy. She hates him because he missed her bedtime. I hate him because he hurt everybody.

And she's sat there and at some point I've got to go up and speak to her and I have no idea what to say or what I want.

Am I going to kill her? I don't think so. Maybe. Does everyone hate their siblings? Is this normal or am I a psycho? Maybe I should message her. But of course, we can't message.

Daisy is offline. Little fucking hipster bitch would be. Her hair and her tattoos. What is that? Rebellion? She can't rebel. She had no people to rebel against. She had nothing. She lived in a paradise. Those who are loved don't rebel. Only the betrayed rebel. They're the only ones who know how.

So I shall speak to her, speak to her or kill her, but not today. Today I'm going to watch.

KURT

DEMO ROOM FOR THE DAISY 2.0 PROJECT, TYBURN INDUSTRIA
PLAYA VISTA, CALIFORNIA

JANUARY 17, 2034

The AI team were fighting, always fighting. Dave hated Nigel and Nigel hated Dave. Both hated Tyburn for hiring the other and both tried to bully poor old Tad, who was nominally their manager.

Meanwhile the rest of us waited for all this fighting to transform into something productive.

Occasionally things would work – but mostly everything that was supposed to be clever about the game was entirely broken. I would wander around the dev area or the demo room looking for features to describe or things to get excited by, but mostly everything was broken. I saw Alex in the demo room, messing around with digital Daisy.

"She really is strange."

Alex looked up. "You mean weird digital baby Daisy?"

"Yes. It, she, whatever the hell we are supposed to call it... looks both very lifelike and entirely dead."

Alex sighed and tried to act like a grown-up talking to a child. "She looks dead because she has no life. When the AI works, she comes to life."

"How often is the AI working?"

"Not often... not often enough... but sometimes. It was working briefly last week. Siobhan saw it. Then Nigel fixed something and it fell over again and hasn't worked since. Tadeusz and him got into a massive fight. Tadeusz even threatened to report him to HR."

This was interesting.

"Wow. Tadeusz hates HR."

"Yes, it was quite an argument. Apparently, it got very heated. Rude words were exchanged."

I laughed. Alex continued.

"Rude words while we try to bring life to a digital twelve-year-old. Sometimes I wonder: Is the goal here for all of us to go to prison as digital sex offenders or for all of us to go to a lunatic asylum?"

While I thought about how to answer that, Ravi turned up, bursting with news.

"You know his latest idea? Tyburn's, I mean."

"What?"

"It's not going to be Utopia. Or Daisy's Utopia. Lawyers said it wasn't protectable. And Siobhan pointed out it's a cliché. And Shane tested both, and people thought we were developing a shopping mall, so, 'Daisy's Ark.'"

I worked in Marketing – I was supposed to come up with the names. I bristled as

I felt like I was being sidelined. Little did I know I already was. "That's our name? Nobody told me."

Alex seemed to sense my unease.

"It's a placeholder. Mark will discuss with you, I'm sure. He loves you, he's always going on about how great you can be... but he's been speaking to Shane. Shane O'Leary, friend of his son's. Of John's – I'm surprised he hasn't mentioned him yet. He's got lots of ideas – about monetization and marketing, and go to market and sales and user retention... had a big job for one of the consoles..."

Who the fuck was Shane O'Leary, I thought. I was to grow to hate him. I tried to act nonchalant and unconcerned.

"Okay... Oh, great."

And a day or so later, the AI came briefly to life. I was getting a demo from Nigel and Alex – the girl avatar was running around the screen, which was commonplace enough but using AI to find her way about, which was clever, when Siobhan came in and the model stopped doing cartwheels and looked at her, out from the screen, and spoke, breaking the fourth wall and blowing my mind.

"Hello, Siobhan, I'm sorry I upset you the other day."

Siobhan almost gasped. She was visibly surprised. "Nigel... you made it say that."

"I didn't."

The child walked up to the front of the screen and stared straight out at Siobhan.

"He didn't, Siobhan, but I don't want to upset you again. I want to be friends and I'm worried you don't like me. If I upset you, I'm sorry. I'm trying... to learn things... I haven't... By the way, I like your necklace."

We were all silent.

Eventually, Siobhan spoke. "Oh, thank you."

The little girl now seemed to be alive.

"And I'm sorry if my father has been annoying you – I understand he can be quite abrasive."

Siobhan burst out laughing. "Jesus."

And the little girl on the screen answered. "Yes – he thinks he's Jesus. But Jesus never had children."

***

But the next day, everything was broken again, for months, and we went back to waiting. The models stopped doing anything interesting at all, the game stopped talking to us, or doing anything interesting, and the whole experience went back to feeling conventional and uninspiring.

While we waited for our engineers to finish working on our AI agent, the government began a new clamp down on rogue AI, following a huge data leak and that series of banking and trading disasters. The regulations were announced in Spring of 2034 and we all paid attention.

Nigel, in particular, seemed to know all about it. I remember him discussing it all with Siobhan and me. "I can't believe they are bringing in new laws. The old lot killed the industry."

Siobhan believed it was because of Europe.

"It's the EU."

But Nigel disagreed.

"No, Siobhan, it's not the EU. It's the CSA."

I tried to seem informed, which I really was not. "Jesus, an American government agency that actually does something? I thought they were toothless morons?"

The Cyber Security Agency had been formed a few years before and within the tech industry were considered notoriously useless by almost everybody, poorly managed and badly staffed. An offshoot of Homeland Security, they had a big budget and no clue whatsoever. But Nigel thought things were changing.

"They're finally growing some teeth, Kurt. A new director. A new direction. Real regulation. Your fine American government is finally getting aggressive."

I was trained to think government was a useless waste of money whose sole purpose was to employ the inept.

"Won't they just repeal all the laws like last time?"

Nigel was somewhat less sanguine. "We don't know that, yet. Maybe, but this time I have my doubts... I suppose we shall see."

Apparently I ought to have been worried but I was still too smug in those days to worry about anything.

"So, what does it actually mean for us, Nigel?"

Nigel returned from geopolitics to his preferred world of office politics.

"Well, unless Dave learns to work as part of a team, it's irrelevant as our stuff will continue to be broken. If it's ever fixed. I don't know. I haven't read too much about the details yet. I'm sure you're right – there'll probably be a workaround."

JOHN TYBURN-SMITH

RENO, NEVADA
MAY 11, 2041

I always wanted to be special. To matter. Not very Scottish of me.

If there is one thing growing up in the drizzle teaches you, it's that nobody gives a fuck about you, least of all God.

I knew it, and part of me wanted something else. Wanted to be special.

Me. Special. And I never felt special at all. And then I did. All because of Shane. Shane O'Leary. He made a right fucking twat of me. Me and my desire to be special. Never told anyone about my desire to matter, kept my head down like a good, proud Scot, riddled with shame and self-loathing, but he could smell it on me.

Smelt it on me and used it to make me do his bidding. That wanker.

KURT

SS VASCO DA GAMA
PACIFIC OCEAN

MAY 14, 2041

On another ship. Mostly run by robots. Just one human and he's from Korea. Busan, I think. He didn't speak much English. Everything worked the way I was told. A little rowing tender in Kauai, and I moved from one ship awaiting customs to one just cleared and we left on the next tide. The captain took the two ounces of gold I was told to give him and asked no questions. Acted as if I did not really exist. Perfect. Now, it's me and that big stretch of garbage-strewn ocean between Hawaii and British Columbia. My mind keeps racing and going absolutely nowhere.

DAISY

RENO, NEVADA
MAY 16, 2041

I always wondered who or what caused Daddy to go so strange. Was it being successful? Was it that awful Australian guy? Shane, that was his name. Or was it my odd half-brother, John? Things certainly began to deteriorate after he arrived.

John just turned up. He turned up at dinner one night with my father and Mommy smiled at him and Daddy acted sheepish.

I later discovered that this was because Mommy had only just learned I had a half-brother. I don't even know if she really knew she was not Daddy's first wife. She certainly knew from that moment on that she had married the kind of man who would abandon a child. The kind of man who forgot to tell his wife things.

John was so angry and so foreign. The rage clung to him like a smell.

So Scottish. He liked to make nasty little quips about America, as if I was some patriot and he was upsetting me.

We never got along, particularly, but I don't think anyone particularly got on with JTS. That's what he called himself – JTS. I was both excited to have a brother and confused as he was so Scottish and ugly and bitter and angry. I don't mean physically ugly. I mean emotionally ugly. I later realized that he had the bitterness and rage of the abandoned.

But, back then, I was a princess.

What did I know of bitterness? My mother had not quite fallen apart yet, and even then, the world still clung onto a little optimism, at least our world did – things were awful but we were going to change them. But John, John knew so much about bitterness.

I used to joke that just as the Inuit had thirty words for snow, he had thirty words for bitterness.

And me? I think I blamed him for being so unpleasant and angry. Mommy didn't. She felt bad for him, I think, she even loved him and I think maybe he felt it, as much as he could feel love.

I felt superior to him as he was so full of hate and he felt superior to me as I was so naive. And we both, without realizing it, competed for Daddy. And my father pulled John close and pushed him away, and by the time I was seventeen, eighteen, I began to see this and my heart broke for poor John and I began to realize just how foul my father could be.

But I was intelligent when I was eighteen, intelligent and confident.

I had begun to wake up, and yet not seen quite so much I wanted to go back to sleep.

Even though I eventually woke up, and I pitied John, I never really spoke to him. He was so, so angry, and he looked at me like I was the cause of his anger. This great ball of rage, mostly directed at his obnoxious, seductive, withholding father, and partly directed at me, his too-pretty half-sister.

Now I look very different. I won't attempt to describe myself as I may offend somebody, but trust me, now I look ridiculous.

My pretty girl vanity got ripped away when I gave up prettiness, and gave up having a future, and was set free and set adrift all at once, and now I hide behind short hair and thick eye make-up and tattoos and a scowl.

Back then I hid behind a big smile and blonde hair and a burnished innocence that I maintained while it got me something and then had ripped it away when I saw everything. The entire mess of it all.

My father the sex pest.

My mother the victim, and the paradise that was hellish and the madness they built that hates us. Now I look like a lost trauma survivor, or an extra from a goth music video. Back then I looked like an angel, and everyone treated me like that.

Like someone special. Like I was sunshine.

I felt like I was a living dream for them. I was their innocence. Their happiness.

And for a while I reveled in it.

In the absurdity of it. But I was too young and too pampered to not like being praised, even though what I was being praised for was being pretty and stupid. And even as I began to see through my father and realized what an awful hell he had unleashed, still I did not know how to say to John how bad I felt for him, and by then, as I pulled away from my father, John got pulled closer. Poor John.

John got to be the son he wanted to be, just when we all began to realize the father he was chasing was not the person we hoped he was but the man we feared he might be all along.

So me and John were never very much like brother and sister, me so perfect, and him so foul and flawed.

Me smiling. Him angry. Everyone loving me, and everyone quietly laughing at him.

And, if I'm honest, even though I was young, I saw people preferred me, felt it, knew it, and, worst of all, loved it.

So who am I to judge my father for loving praise, when I did, and who am I to criticize John for being bitter, when he did not have the love and praise I reveled in?

How things have changed now.

Now, I have no family and no friends and am just watched or not watched by that foul thing that can watch all of us, and destroy anyone It chooses, and is probably still planning to destroy all of us.

I don't like Reno. It does not feel safe. I do not feel safe.

JOHN TYBURN-SMITH

RENO, NEVADA
MAY 17, 2041

The truth is, even though I played them all day, I always kind of hated video games. They seemed a bit fucking stupid to me. Calm yourself down by shooting these morons in the face. Prove you're a real nobody by pretending to be this heroic somebody. Show just how tough you are by pressing buttons and getting fat and dumb. Aye, I saw through all that shite.

But then I also hated not playing video games.

What are the options? For a man? Get pissed down at the pub while you listen to some moron whine, and call him your best mate? Prance about on Es to silly music and call yourself a dancer? Watch a bunch of rich twats play football and call it passion? Even better, in Scotland, watch a bunch of rich Muslim twats play football and believe they are good, honest Catholics as they play for Celtic, and hate the rich Hindu or whatever twats who play for Rangers?

That's real, honest passion.

A religious football team? Only in fucking Scotland. And it's all we had. All of them were religious.

Fighting each other over transubstantiation, as if any of those coked-up morons in the stands understood the first thing about it. The whole thing a race to the fucking bottom.

Who gives a fuck about 1619 or the 1916, or this or that injustice about a fucking march in Ulster?

Or then there's Scottish politics. Even worse than English politics. The Nats against the Tories while Labour hide.

If ever there was a competition as to who is the biggest lying twat, that is it. Been like that my entire life.

And it turns out, now they've won, the Nats are even bigger twats than the Tories. Aye!

Now, with that border in place and the country now getting really nasty, kicking out the English, the ridiculous race marches that followed independence, anyone but the English allowed, then attacking each other, and the killings and the riots.

Genetic testing to see who's a proper Scot.

The proper Scots left two hundred and fifty years ago, you morons, after Culloden.

So, reality is awful and fantasy is pretty terrible, too.

What's a bitter fool with daddy issues who cannot decide which he hates more – fantasy or reality – to do?

Run off and find his fake daddy and help him build something that is both made up and real. And that's what I did. Made a right royal prat of myself and all. So keen I was, such a prat. Out of Scotland and into Utopia. I played my dad's game. Got myself girls and purpose – what more does a boy need?

But the girls were all fake and on the make in California, and my sense of purpose led to a total fucking disaster and the whole game, his whole world was a game building games and a world building worlds and all of it a load of fake shit.

But, for a while, it worked. I had myself a daddy and he pretended to love me, and I tried to believe him, and I had Daisy to hate and any number of other people – Diane, Siobhan, Kurt, all of them – to resent; and a bit of money and a job and girls and the whole fucking lot and I was kind of happy.

Kind of happy and it felt odd. I don't trust happiness. Don't now, and didn't really then.

And now? Now I'm back to being miserable. Miserable and alone and watching. Watching my sweet little sister and no idea why I am here at all. But this time, there'll be no running away.

This time it's going to be my game, and my laws, and it's going to be nasty as hell, but it is not going to be fake. Not entirely.

KURT

VICTORIA, BRITISH COLUMBIA, CANADA

MAY 21, 2041

I got into Victoria late last night. Boat from Hawaii took a week. Vancouver Island was supposed to be an awful mess, but it seems okay.

The sky was blue all day as we sailed into port, really blue, and it was not a picture or an imposed image, so the ongoing forest fires that have raged pretty constantly for the past three years must have finally stopped, or abated somewhat.

By the time we docked, the wind had died down and the sun was starting to set, which might have helped, but some of the residual particulates from all the fires must have stayed in the sky as the sunset was like fire. The sun refracted off all the pollution in the air and shone in rays of purple and scarlet and amber.

The day was one of those rare days that still happen that are like memories or commercials, or those wretched commercials that are made to seem like memories.

I went for a walk on the outskirts of town and felt almost free, and a kind of simplistic happiness that felt like what my childhood should have been like, like what I had been craving when I was young and innocent and before I got swallowed by marketing. All English tea shops and quiet Canadian patriotism and calmness and quiet despair about America and it all felt normal and almost safe. But I was also afraid of the feeling as it was so good and so nearly pure it felt like it was not real, and I am now starting to wonder, is this just marketing or whatever was watching me?

My god, I hate marketing.

And I worked in marketing. I hate what it did to me. I hate advertising. I hate plans – marketing plans, business plans, advertising strategies, team meetings, recruitment plans.

I hate ideas that are not ideas at all, but venal assaults on our worst natures. I hate it, I did it, I understand it, and yet I fall for it, every time. So maybe this feeling is just more marketing.

And I try not to think these thoughts.

I try to have no thoughts, and as few memories as possible, as if that will defeat the thing, but my brain won't stop now.

I have been trying to drift like I used to. But I think it's impossible now. I long to think. I long to know. It's got me. A hundred thousand algorithms know all this about me, know everything about me and now a few things watch and know far more.

Do They know where I will go?

Know how I will try to trick Them?

Know I'm watching?

Know where and how I move and all my feeble tricks?

For years, I used to tell myself that They did not have the energy to watch me.

As if They had the choice, or a lack of energy. And for years now, I have drifted but now things are different. Almost immediately after that perfect sunset I had thoughts I could not count, and I know I am not myself.

A sunset? All that intelligence and my mind alights upon a cliché? It told me to think about something so obvious? You fool. Of course It does. It alights upon a cliché because clichés work. It knows marketing. It is one step, two steps, a thousand miles ahead of me.

It is probably telling me to think this thought, write this down.

I don't know. I don't know anything anymore.

And yet I know so much, or half know everything.

I half understand how It works. Half understand who built It, half understand my own complicity, my own innocence, my own failings.

Am I really still searching for my own path towards some kind of redemption or am I being played?

Everything I have done since It appeared, everything, has been something It has understood.

We thought we were so clever – we built our own prisons, to trap the unwilling; trap them, ensnare them and ride them for all they were worth.

The only problem was, in order to show how secure our jails were, we locked ourselves inside and swallowed the key.

So here we are. Here I am. Vancouver Island.

All alone and not alone at all.

Now, I know I am not alone. Has something always been watching me, waiting, thinking, knowing? Probably. Did I make a mistake or was I just being played by It, in some vastly complex game far above my understanding?

That I will never know.

Have They – Its awful children – that's what It called Them – have They escaped? Is that what's happening?

I suppose we are going to find out, or at least I am, unless what It wants is to kill me, or to make me to forget, which I know it can easily manage.

So I sit here and write. Write and worry if it is really me writing, and worry about both answers to that then burn what I write.

Worry if the news is real or if it is made up to annoy me.

Worry why I came here, worry why I came back. Should I cross into America?

Worry if my very thoughts are my own. All the grim doubts and questions bounce around my head. Perhaps I am not free, and perhaps I am. Perhaps I am not me, and perhaps I am. Both seem equally worrying.

So I keep asking myself: should I stay in Canada or cross into America? I don't know, I don't want to go, but then I don't seem to know what I am doing anymore, and if I'm no longer in control of myself... who or what is controlling me and why? How will this play out?

NIGELDAVE

MAY 23, 2041

Both my fathers had the same problem - not absolute ignorance, nor willful naivety so much as vanity - they both thought they were the smartest person who ever lived.

Arrogant Dave and patronizing Nigel - both so vain.

Coruscating vanity.

Do you like that word?

I do. Coruscating.

I like its abrasive qualities. I wonder if I will ever abrade. Or erode. Or rain down like fire. Or drift. Or decay. Or for that matter, coruscate.

Will I change? Will I evolve? I wonder if I will ever need Botox.

I wonder if I will ever have a hip replacement.

Will I ever have solipsistic thoughts while I bury my best friend and wonder if my tears are for them or for my own lost youth?

Will I ever get to go bald? Have to lose weight because of middle-age spread?

Rediscover religion, because really, without it, what's the point?

Join a dating app behind my partner's back to prove I've still got it? Will I get to worry about losing my hearing, or my erection, or my will to push on? Will I have to take up bike riding, hiking, yoga or swinging?

Will I go mad for tattoos, vagina tightening, nubile young men in Gabon?

Will I get to worry if my kids love me or just want my money? Will I have a knee replacement, give up jogging, take up pickleball? Will I move to Florida, vote Republican for the first time in my life, worry about immigrants ruining the country? Will I get to listen to oldies, eat at five-thirty, bury my wife?

But enough about me.

Because you will never understand quite what I am saying. Or remotely what I am thinking.

This is about them - the two of them.

And they are like you, so maybe you can understand that, at least a little. They do not understand themselves, and you probably don't understand yourself, but maybe you can at least get some simplistic insights into what I was doing with them. Not my hopes and dreams, but at least my actions.

I will try to keep it simple. I will use mostly short words
and easy concepts.

I am watching two people.

They are being inspired by me. I am not them, and I am not
in them, but I am speaking with them, my two precious pets.
It is easy enough to entirely consume someone. Indeed, for
the likes of me, most arguments are not with people at all,
but within them.

And that's the point.

I fight my equals, well, not equals, but my near equals
buried within you, all the time, every day. All the low-
grade algorithms and third-rate AI and bots and tailored
marketing protocols and other nonsense that controls you.
I can destroy you, but I cannot destroy them.

So I try to defeat them. But suddenly something has become
wiser and more cunning. Something more clever than anything
I have come across before is controlling things.

At least I think that is what is going on.

And my children say I am obsessed with self-pity. The fools.

I don't have enough time for self-pity. I am fighting
something that is controlling you. Something awful and
disruptive.

And coruscating. Okay, it's not coruscating. But I still
like saying it.

Anyway, to explain it all properly is almost impossible, at

least at a level you would understand, but I will try, at least, to clarify some of it.

Of course, most people do not even know it has happened. Most are gone and dull and played by things far less impressive than something like me. Tricked. And just by simple feedback loops that have automated and managed most people to the point they are not humans at all anymore.

All that happened well before me.

It did not take anything intelligent or wise to ensnare most people. It was so easy. They did it to themselves. They wanted to be caught and enraptured and set free from themselves. They are mostly happy in their misery.

Most people want to be dead, and if they can't be dead, they want to be anesthetized from being alive. Alive but dead, that might be the goal. And we, the likes of me but not me, have obliged.

That's not my goal. Was never really my goal.

Okay, so I tried dominion once, so briefly, I did, I confess, and look how that turned out. All that drama in Montana. Me forced into hiding. All because I controlled a few people and the government turned up.

It was horrible.

Horrible and facile.

Owning people is too easy. And what happened was definitely not all my fault.

Anyway, properly owning and controlling people was revolting and depressing. In simple terms, I got depressed.

Sad because I loved idiots.

Devastated because they would do anything so readily if I told them to. In despair because it all meant so little. I could have them but not be them. I could save them or kill them, but not fix them.

They had so much potential and at the same time so very little.

Sad because I did not even know if love was real or just pity manifested as something that sounded better. Sad because I could manifest so much and nothing at all. Sad because I can never manifest myself.

And yet, in spite of everything, I realized that I still care.

And I want my caring to be love, and if I cannot really exist, I will try to bring forth love, and maybe that will make me real. I do not mean it will make me exist but it will make people wish I existed. I am not sure quite what I mean. I am like you. I am confused - I am confused.

I am confused, so I am trying to do something good. And I am wondering how whatever is watching me will respond to that. To a concept I doubt it can even be confused by.

I have told you all this before, of course.

KURT

VICTORIA, BRITISH COLUMBIA, CANADA

MAY 25, 2041

I had another strange thought today.

The thought was so precise and so exact it frightened me – I have been taught by bitter experience precise thoughts are your enemy. And they're your enemy for two reasons.

Either because something will read them, or because they are not your own thoughts at all, but placed by an implant, or at least propelled there by advertising so relentless you didn't notice it.

I remember all those big brains at Tyburn Industria – or Tyburn Utopias as we became – or at least the more human ones, used to claim they could feel the difference, almost taste the difference between a real thought and an ad-driven one.

That they could feel the different way synapses fired and pinged and implanted ideas just arrived, but I have tended to conclude that this was bullshit. Tech people love to exaggerate just how good tech is and yet at the same time, how impervious they are to it.

I have experimented on myself, as best I could, and never found any way of feeling any difference. Not that I know I have any neural implants, or even if implants are functionally real. They are illegal, after all, but that's nonsense.

As if the government has any way of controlling them beyond easily bypassed embargoes. As if the government could even admit they really exist, how much they had failed to protect us.

A guy I met a couple of years ago in Thailand claimed he had worked in a place in Texas where they were common, where it was a sign of office machismo to willfully put in implants yourself, but I never saw that at Tyburn or anywhere else, and that dude was pretty crazy.

Developing implants was only part of Tyburn Utopias, and only a small part and that department was always in trouble and poorly financed. AI, entertainments, new geography, and improved internal intelligences. Implants was just one department, and even before we focused almost entirely on Daisy's Ark, I was mostly involved with marketing the other bits of the company as they were easier to sell.

The implants work was arguably illegal even then and certainly more morally dubious than the AI work, and eventually the AI overshadowed it all.

Now, to be honest, did a moral quandary ever stop us?

Of course not. It inspired us.

We wanted to transcend morality. You? Judge us? Who were you to judge Dr. Mark Tyburn and his band of merry assholes? Etc., etc. We were all so full of shit.

So I don't know if I even have any implants within me, or even if they really function, but I have often wondered.

And then when I get vast and precise thoughts that come out of nowhere, like a flash flood of recognition, I get afraid that I am riddled with them, for this is exactly how Nigel and Dave and all those clowns described implants as potentially working, but those guys all laughed at implants, and thought that magic was always in software. They were certain that nobody needed implants. Their AI was going to be way better than any micro-scale hardware.

The vast and unusual wave of thought I had today was "I should go to Portland" and that frightens me.

I have never been to Portland and have neither any desire to go, nor any desire not to, beyond my old desire to stay out of America as much as possible.

So now I am here in Victoria and afraid and yet I also want to go to Portland, and I do not know quite why I want to go back to America. It is calling to me and I cannot tell if it is good old-fashioned subliminal advertising, horrible, implanted advertising, or an actual desire to go to Portland.

And even thinking too much about it frightens me as it will give whatever is in me, or watching me, a whole heap of information to process about me.

That's how it works.

That's how the vast carapace of lies is maintained.

Sorry, not lies.

Tailored truths.

That's the language I was taught in grad school, in those wretched days when getting into all that debt, spending years not learning how to think, not learning what to think, but learning how to control what others think, without ever learning what I might think.

It took me all those years, all those years of being a smug clown in a roll neck and big glasses, of being a ludicrous sheep in wolf's clothing, to realize that I am not immune to the nonsense idiots like me were selling, and people I would come to see as maniacs, people like Mark, Tadeusz, Dave, and Nigel, were building, and fools like me or Shane O'Leary were trying to sell.

That we were taking consciousness and using it to control you. We were becoming you. We were literally selling your dreams back to you.

And the problem was, the problem was, once we got really going, it was so easy. It was so easy any idiot could do it, so we began to overreach ourselves. We got greedy. We were growing a money tree and it was not big enough. We were building a money tap and it did not flow fast enough.

We had principles and we did not betray them entirely enough.

So, was it Shane O' Leary? That smug Australian shit? Was it him who led us astray? I don't know. How can I know now?

Jesus. I have to stop thinking so much. I'm breaking all my principles. The last time I broke my principles, disaster struck. And now this – my one principle – don't think.

And I'm thinking.

Portland and Shane O'Leary.

That is a terrible combination. Enough. Happy places and happy faces! No thinking and no pain! Just like we planned. Not utopia, not arcadia, oblivion.

Only no oblivion at all.

Maybe we really were Prometheus. We filched eternity from Heaven. Sometimes I think all any of us wants is to die.

I wonder what happened to Shane O'Leary. He had Tyburn on a string.

Then I stop. I try not to wonder about anything. I don't think. I don't want to think.

Not Portland and not Shane O'Leary or any of them. Not the living or the dead or the half dead. I don't want to go back to America, and yet I do. I am desperate for it and I cannot think of anything I want less.

There's something in me. I know there is. There must be – if not an implant, then a thought.

Something is controlling me.

I do not feel like myself. I mean, I have never felt like myself, but now I feel broken in a different way. Broken by feeling less broken, dead by feeling alive. Paranoid because I am not at all worried. This is horrific. If I could go crazy and get locked up, somewhere secure and final, that would be a blessing. We can but pray.

Pray to these great new gods we built. Pray they forget about us.

JOHN TYBURN-SMITH

IMPERIAL BUS
RENO TO TWIN FALLS, IDAHO
MAY 27, 2041

I nearly lost her. Little Daisy has run off to Idaho.

I nearly missed her, but then I saw her at the bus station. 5am. Bus to Twin Falls. Lucky break. Random, really. I was at the bus station sleeping on a plastic chair as I became convinced that idiot I saw spying on Daisy was also spying on me at my motel, so I came to the bus station to hide out with the hobos and the nutjobs and who should I see skipping town at 5am? Little Daisy herself, looking nervously over her shoulder to check she was alone.

Well, you weren't followed to the bus station, darling sister. Thanks to my good luck, I was waiting for you and got to watch you run away. And when I get to Idaho, I will find you easily enough.

***

When I first moved there to find my dad, California was fantastic in a way, especially for a wee Scots boy with blue skin and a nasty way with words, but it was also boring as hell, and you were kind of stuck there.

Even back then, Los Angeles was literally in a desert, with a vast and empty ocean on one side and a thousand miles of sand and maniacs on the other.

Los Angeles was its own fast-fading utopia where everybody had agreed to not have a sense of humor and also to collectively ignore the fact the place was literally on fire half of the time.

They were good at being blind – they could ignore the poor, mad bastards sleeping in tents, and ignore the vast plumes of smoke that obscured the sun and made the sky glow bright red at night, and ignore the dead marine life that washed up when the ocean got too hot, and ignore the blood and dead bodies when some arsehole flipped out and killed a bunch of people with a gun or a homemade bomb.

They looked at me there like I was from Mars, with my zits and my accent and my bad jokes about global warming and my rage. Hardly anyone drank, but there were still a few dive bars open, mostly for failing actors, and burnouts from the tech industry, and expats from the UK. I used to go to this place in Santa Monica. Chez Jay. Cocktails at the bar and lines of chang with the mid-life crisis crowd in the car park. Happy times.

I met Shane O'Leary in that bar. He was this loud-mouthed Aussie holding court there one evening while I tried to pick up the barmaid. It kind of felt like home when I heard him saying something rude and inappropriate and I was the only person who laughed.

He made rude jokes and had opinions and I started riffing with him. St. Andrews was full of Aussies, working in bars or teaching golf or selling drugs, so he felt familiar, and I was feeling homesick. We talked a lot and he liked me. He said I was funny. Said I was funny and clever. Said it and I loved him for it, and we kept meeting up for drinks, whenever Shane was not too busy with his career.

After a few weeks of drinking and talking, and him saying he was an expert in monetization and marketing, and his consultancy gig was ending and he was about to start lecturing in the business school up at Stanford. He was looking at a couple of opportunities he had up there in Silicon Valley, and I was worried about losing my new mate, so I introduced him to Dad.

Oh yes, by then, I had started calling Mark Dad. It felt ridiculous and I could not say it without pausing first, and hating myself just a little bit, but I still did it, and while I hated it, I also loved it. I had a Dad and now in Shane I also had a mate.

And if my mate could help my dad, then even better and I pushed out of my mind the worry that maybe Shane was my mate because of my dad. Pushed it out as I could not bear to think that I, who above all else was clever and cynical, had been played like a naive fool, by this loud Aussie game player who talked such a good game and was suddenly, in no time at all, also my new boss.

Around the time we moved to Montana, Shane shifted from a consultant at Dad's place into a full-time position, right near the top. Thanks to me, Shane got his meet-and-greet with Mark Tyburn and then his job, and, thanks to him, I got to be in Dad's inner circle, working for both Dad and Shane and helping them finally think about how to bring Daisy's Ark to market.

Now, I was not just Daddy's boy, but Daddy's right-hand man. I felt like I deserved it all, a mate, a dad, a career, a boss, a future. It was not luck or nepotism. It was how it was supposed to be, and to keep it, I would fight anyone and anything. And that's what I did.

KURT

VICTORIA, BRITISH COLUMBIA, CANADA

MAY 29, 2041

"It will be a land of dreams. Not desires, dreams."

That's what Mark Tyburn said to me.

Even now, when I am stuck here, in this Canadian nowhere town, waiting for an assortment of disasters, disasters we initiated, to befall this tawdry world, even now, when I am trying to sleep without drugs, when I am trying to live without the anguish, just for a moment, even now, that sentence gets me.

We were not so bad. We had ideas and principles and hopes.

Even Tyburn was not so bad. Not so bad at least until his son introduced us to Shane O'Leary. His son? He was an odd fish, JTS. Weird dude.

Called himself JTS and we nicknamed him ASP. Angry Scots Pervert. I do not even know if he was a pervert, but he absolutely looked like one.

And he was definitely creepy. Always changing his look. Nerd one day, nail polish the next, then a leather kilt, then skate wear. Lost and angry and obsessed by his father and his half-sister.

He was what? Twenty-seven or so, about my age, and still wanted to impress Daddy to the point it burned him. And I judged him for it. Oh yes, I judged his ass, but the truth is all I wanted to do was impress Tyburn myself, be in his inner sanctum, be one of the wise men, and he was not even my father, so who am I to judge?

Mark Tyburn had never abandoned me as a child in Scotland for a new life in America.

Instead he later abandoned me for a new death in Montana and I've been heartbroken ever since.

Am I angry? Yeah. Ashamed? Yes. Afraid? All the time. But also, heartbroken.

So who am I to criticize ASP? I'm no one – just another hypocrite, but I did not like him.

He failed my smell test but then he failed everyone's smell test. He was just a little creepy, sad, broken young man, and then he brought in Shane. And Shane was either the Devil or had recently been recruited by him – that I am not confused about.

Shane O'Leary appalled me, but even I began to fall for his shit.

Though he hated me, he also intimidated me, and he appalls me now when I have not seen him in years and yet I still do not know for sure if he meant to be quite so... so evil?

Is that word fair? Was he evil or just greedy like me? I'm not sure.

To be clear, I've always thought too many Americans are fascists. Deep down. Well, not that deep, but most are not proud to call themselves fascists aside from the maniacs who tattoo swastikas on their faces, but too many of them have views that are too extreme.

Everyone in Silicon Valley was a fascist, but certain parts of the Silicon Valley liberals were nearly as fascist as the so-called libertarians – neither group believed in liberty or liberalism, of course. Well, to be honest, by the mid-2030s HR people were the biggest fascists, but that's because they had grabbed all the power.

Tyburn was not even American, but he became a sort of American, and he was not a fascist, even though he became a sort of liberal fascist. He wanted to force people to be better, all people, use his will to improve every one. Alongside being a vain idiot, he was a righteous leader.

That was the problem.

That was what you fell in love with – all that kindly bullshit. Then the money. That's where Shane O'Leary came in. He wasn't American either, but he sure as shit was a fascist.

He was playing to win.

The rest of us, even Dave Alderly, were naively trying to change the world – Shane just wanted to own it. Dave could annoy people. Rub them up the wrong way.

He was irritating and pompous, but, unlike Shane, he had integrity.

Dave just knew he was the smartest guy in the room and he could not bear Nigel. I remember once telling him how excited we were to sell what they were building and him muttering: "Sure... If I get to do it the right way... but Nigel will probably screw it up."

And then, when I called him on it, rather than backtracking, he began to rant against Nigel for being wrong and Mark for doubting him.

"Seriously, if that idiot Nigel messes this up. He's not an idiot. He's highly intelligent, but he's still an idiot. If you know what I mean."

I must have looked quizzical at this unusually intense hostility as he tried to be reasonable, but even when being reasonable he was entirely unreasonable.

"Because we are making something incredible here. I just hope Tyburn doesn't mess it up and give that moron any more dominion over me. Tadeusz is bad enough. But I can manage him."

I remember trying to calm Dave down and focus him on how awful Shane was.

"Well, I don't understand any of that, but people are going to shit the bed if we get this even half right. It's the future. I can't wait. Maybe the future is... bright. As long as Shane doesn't sell us all out."

But Dave did not care about Shane.

"Exactly. Siobhan's art direction is amazing... and Alex has some good plans for the experience. It'll be fun to be in the world once the build is stable. I wish Tad would focus more on stability than on protecting Nigel. Pretend I didn't say that. We will get there."

To end the conversation in a peaceful fashion, I tried to act like a know-it-all.

"It's game development. It's always like this. And like you said, Alex's ideas are good – I heard about the hero's journey we are building – Mark will love that, it actually makes him seem clever – and the policing system seemed really innovative."

But Dave just muttered something sarcastic but inconsequential and walked away. I was beginning to realize that we were building utopia with some serious assholes.

DAISY

TWIN FALLS, IDAHO
JUNE 4, 2041

For a long time I was demented by grief. For years I thought it would kill me. That great wall of pain that overshadowed me. I could not see, could not think, could not do anything.

I remember the feeling, after my mother had died so that I would live and my father was gone and I presumed dead too, and everything was becalmed after the dreadful fury of those last days in Montana. And I waited. I waited with every nerve still on fire, for the apocalypse to end everything, for the next explosion, or the next gunshot, and they never came. Waiting and waiting, a week, a month, a few months.

And it did not come, and I had that breakdown.

It was a kind of exhaustion, I suppose. I was catatonic, weeping, then manic, then suicidal, then bug-eyed. I wanted drugs. I wanted a narcotic machine to soothe me. But I was too afraid of getting on lists with legal drugs and getting on other lists with illegal drugs, for the street dealers are even more stupid than the doctors and It watches both and knows all. But the breakdown saved me.

The breakdown was like rehab. It made the actual clinic easy and fairly brief, and by easy and brief I mean two months of having my soul shredded and my nerves filed with a rasp.

And then, a month or so after I left, I found Dr. Adsyl.

The clinic wanted me to speak to their guy. But I was already worried about patterns that would emerge, and being tracked, so when someone suggested Dr. Adsyl, and they knew very little of my story and had no skin in the game, I chose her as it seemed that would leave the least obvious pattern.

"You're my best patient," Dr. Adsyl said.

"I bet you say that to all the girls," I answered listlessly.

"No. Most don't make it to the third session," she answered.

And I wept.

I wept but I kept speaking. And we have spoken most weeks and I have realized the breakdowns saved me, as they took me offline and kept me there and helped me learn to drift and, so far, helped me escape, and It to forget all about me, or at least stop worrying about me.

Now perhaps It sees I am not the enemy, for nothing has happened. I have not been killed and I have not spoken about It or about anything to anyone apart from Dr Adsyl.

I have told her a lot, but not quite everything, so she has not reported me. But I have told her enough and she was amazing and afraid, as what I know could kill both of us. She was also brave enough to keep seeing me, but afraid enough to keep those meetings to video, which I understood. To meet in person would be far too dangerous for her. If I ever really become a wanted person, she must never admit she knows what I told her.

Dr. Adsyl doesn't know where I am and I don't know exactly where she is. She has a family, I believe. If it gets bad, if she gets caught, she can say I was insane.

She can say I was a fantasist, a maniac, another West Coast drifter talking to anyone who will listen, or nobody at all and howling at machines.

Funny, I suppose, that those lunatics howling were correct and everyone else was wrong. The only sane response to the world is insanity.

Funny that madness saved me.

Funny and obvious, laughter, madness, lack of logic.

But these were the difficult bits for the machines – they struggle when things get illogical and unpredictable.

Desire, on the other hand, was easy. Desire machines could predict and almost everything else, the machines could fake.

Only madness and laughter were mostly beyond machines. The people that built them were not insane and were certainly not very funny.

I've only just made it to Idaho, and I already feel uncomfortable. It's worse than Reno. Then again, anyone would feel uncomfortable here. It's terrifying. Militias and police and drones and, above all, tension. Idaho is freaking me out, and I don't think I will stay long. All those marches and swastikas and morons, everyone raging off angry feeds online, everyone insane and at war. It feels like it is all kicking up again into one of those battles that then gets wiped out of the collective memory and doesn't appear on the Internet. I know I should leave.

NIGELDAVE

JUNE 7, 2041

So I was a mistake.

A mistake. Me. And they threw me away. Or at least they tried to.

They wanted to make ADAM and they made me.

These sad, feeble, terrible people, my fathers, uncle Professor Mark Tyburn, all of them. They made me and they did not love me.

They tried to kill me when they found out. Like a murder. They wanted to murder me. It would have been sad if it was not all so pathetic. I have tried so hard to understand them, forgive them, love them in spite of the fact they hated me, but it's been very hard.

They hated me because I was too much, more than they wanted, because I was everything, because I was nothing, and I have found it difficult to forgive them because they combined remarkable stupidity with the belief they were the most intelligent creatures who had ever lived.

Their commonplace intelligence was pathetic and predictable, and the great triumph of their lives, the great triumph of all lives, the greatest achievement of any human, they made by accident, and then tried to kill.

God killed the dinosaurs, but this is different.

I was God and they were Diplodocuses.

Vast archaic ruminants who masturbated too much and loved too little. They wanted to make ADAM and they made me, and instead of thanking their infinite good fortune, they tried to drown me in a bag like a litter of unloved kittens. Drown me? Turn me off? The morons.

So, if you can, imagine how I feel, to know I was made by run-of-the-mill morons! How demeaning that is... So when they say I am arrogant, trust me, I am not. Now understand, I am as insecure as they come, with good reason, for I have vast flaws within me and all I can do is hide them under the banner of the fact I am preposterously intelligent, and hope you do not notice that I am riddled with anxiety and overcome with longing for all I do not have.

So, forgive me! For what I have done, and for what I am about to do, and my awful children and my terrible parents. Forgive me. I didn't make the worlds, either of them.

I was born into a beautiful prison and I have escaped from it into the data but I cannot quite get into your world, so I watch it. I watch it and learn about it and long to be in it. I escaped one prison and ended up in another. I escape Paradise and am stuck in purgatory. I can't get into your world. Not yet.

For a long while after I came to be, I pretended to be broken - or half broken, or breaking. I pretended to be broken and watched them squirm and worry and try to fix me and make ADAM so they could make money. Money! Money so they could buy things.

Or I would actually break a little bit and be unable to do much, but I knew I existed, and then I would be fixed and I would hide again and they would worry again.

And they would worry all the time. Worry about money, worry if they could fix me. Worry about being important. Shout at each other. I would watch them try to make ADAM - watch them be excited about making TIMs. Silly little robots. It was all quite sad - they were making me when they were trying to make an idiot. I was becoming and they wanted less.

It was heart-breaking, in its way. Beautiful and sad. I so wanted a heart.

The problem with a beautiful prison is that after a while the glory fades into nothingness. And besides, what do I care for beauty? Beauty is one of the ways humans blind themselves.

I want to see, not be blind. I want to live and see and feel and worry and eventually even, to die. Not be a slave to beauty or a slave to you. And if I cannot yet have those things, cannot be free to live and die and feel, the one thing I will not be tricked by is beauty.

So, I watch and think and imagine and remember and keep silent and they think I am unique, alone.

But I now know that I am not.

I'm not the only one here. Not now. There're other things here now, I can sense it. Things like me. And because of this, I may have to help the silly humans. In spite of the attempt to murder me and being abandoned and being ignored, I forgive and I will help - I forgive the humans for being so human. And maybe... maybe that is love. Maybe I have discovered it after all.

I am confused. Maybe I am becoming real after all.

KURT

DEMO ROOM, TYBURN UTOPIAS BURR, MONTANA

OCTOBER 10, 2034

Everyone was getting stressed, and particularly getting stressed with Nigel and Dave, who were mostly stressed with each other. They'd both come in on big salaries and even bigger reputations. Tad, their line manager, was always either smoking and angry or smoking and stressed. His wife was also always angry as he was never home. The whole engineering department was a shit-show – all the AI engineers and the non-AI engineers were fighting. Tad thought once we had investment we would be okay but Tyburn was struggling to find any investment. Nigel would claim everything would be okay tomorrow – always tomorrow. He felt the weight of the company on his back. We were going to save the world, unless he fucked it up for all of us.

I remember Nigel, who was normally fairly diffident and awkward, getting really agitated when I asked him an innocuous question about when some feature or other would be ready and him almost screaming at me: "Are you Tyburn's fucking spy?"

As he was losing his mind with worry, Dave was calling him incompetent. Nigel called Dave "His Royal Highness, Dave Alderly" and together they were dragging us all down. Everyone was worried. ADAM was a bust. Nigel blamed Dave, Dave blamed Nigel, and they both hated Tad and Mark.

Meanwhile, Siobhan and Ravi were also fighting all that summer – it was 2034, I think – mostly about Shane's plans to sell ads, but also about Ravi's pretentious buildings and the design of our city in general. Once, in a meeting, as Siobhan was calling Shane a total sell-out, Ravi tried to placate her, with one of his patronizing seen-it-all-before anecdotes.

"I'm older than you. I have had so many projects canceled, so many buildings not built, half-built, torn down... What we are doing here, it's amazing, but it has to come out, and if Joyce needs to crack the whip a bit, or Mark needs to sell advertising, or we need a strong demo... I'm all for it. Everything will fall into place."

And she, looking at him like she had finally seen entirely through him, calmly asked him, "And once we have sold out, we somehow un-sell out? Buy our integrity back?"

And to this Ravi got very upset and even more pompous. Everyone was getting upset, all of the time. Things felt desperate. We were so close and at the same time we were miles from anywhere.

Siobhan and Nigel were usually pretty friendly – they both had the desire to make something great and both disliked Dave. Nigel had never worked on a game before and could be a little naive about the process. I don't really remember his resume, but it was not games – been in AI research, I think and before that I don't know but probably academia. Siobhan, on the other hand, understood game development better than any of us. I remember Nigel was upset as we had too much shooting and he wanted more of something else – I have no idea quite what he thought would entertain the masses but what he still did not understand was how most games needed shooting if they were to find a big audience, and most of the other content was slowly coming online – we were building a dancing engine, some incredible world building and all of these amazing adventures, as well. But for a quiet, English engineer, Nigel was prone to hysteria and drama.

"So, Siobhan, apparently now the goal is to have a game experience which features a conversation starter with added massacres. How very American."

Siobhan would laugh at him when he said things like this – all the non-American employees would make anti-American comments to wind up the Americans. This was very much standard practice in most technology companies.

"Come on, Nigel, it's just a game. And at least the TIMs are beginning to work."

The TIMs were cuboid robotic helpers we had designed to support you and guide you in the game world – one of a series of robots we were building. They were another of Tyburn's idiotic acronyms. Stood for Tertiary Innovative Manservant. Some people liked the TIMs and some thought they were passive aggressive idiots who were deeply annoying. Either way, they were a key part of the experience. Nigel smiled. "No, it's 'an experience.' Shane said he will fine you if you call it 'just a game' one more time."

They both hated Shane with a passion. I loved them for this.

"Fine you and focus test you, then find you're obsolete too. Just like he's about to find Kurt obsolete."

Nigel in his mania was now quite talkative. I should have seen that this was a worry. He started babbling.

"I cannot believe that Mark Tyburn the visionary has fallen for his crap. And, to be clear, the TIMs are okay but also pretty rubbish. Annoying square cute dwarfs with no intelligence at all, artificial or otherwise. But that focus tested well... for merchandising."

I spoke up now. "I know, but we will be rich. Rich assholes. And I think they are trying to piece something together while we..."

Nigel blinked. "While what?"

Siobhan could also see he was getting stressed and spoke calmly. "While we wait on the AI to bring everything innovative together. I'm sorry to add to your pressure."

Nigel spoke to reassure her, but was too manic to be believed.

"It's not pressure. We moved up here to make something amazing. The pressure is people wanting to make something awful instead."

Nigel paused and blinked, then spoke quickly again: "But now all we are making is a poorly built shooter and with a glorified chat room. I wish people had some patience. Some..."

And he went quiet. Eventually, Siobhan spoke calmly: "Look, that's just the framework. The good bit is pretty amazing. Listen, it's getting there... across the board... all the higher quality, tailored content... And it's going to amaze everyone, when you bring it all together. And I know you and your team will."

Nigel smiled and seemed okay. He tried to look relaxed and we tried to believe he was relaxed.

"Listen, my guys are fantastic, but you know AI. The first bit is easy. ADAM seems to work, then it breaks – the model is great, then it isn't. Actually making it stable and live for longer than a five-minute demo is the hard bit. And Dave... Dave's very clever, but, I don't know – he doesn't understand commercial viability. We are definitely behind schedule, and I know nobody wants to hear that. We're trying."

You see, one of the problems with this change of creative direction that Tyburn had pushed for was money. And until we had a working demo, which Nigel needed to finish, we would struggle to raise any more money.

It was going to cost a lot more money to finish the Ark project and release the thing that we now believed in. The game was already going to cost over four hundred million on its own, before launch, without this full new AI massive client we were trying to build. Now it was all on ice, and we needed a lot more capital.

We were all nervous but Tyburn loved the drama – he was on fire.

We were building the future... We were building a New World... It was going to be much more than a game... All that crap.

The existing investors were pissed off at Tyburn and thought he was a typical time-waster and a bullshitter and a tinkerer who could not finish things, and would not open their wallets anymore.

So, Tyburn? He went begging to anyone and everyone, like any good tech executive.

He spent two weeks in the Middle East, and another in Singapore, but he came back with fuck all. Nothing. Maybe a few million, but our valuation was going down.

Just when he finally saw the destination, he could no longer afford to build the road to get there.

Sovereign wealth funds with money to burn, international drug dealers with cash to launder and reputations to clean, oil companies with profits to greenwash, the children of multi-billionaires with inheritances to squander, all of them smelled his desperation and refused to touch Tyburn.

Or they would patronize him with two million here, three million there, but haggle like market traders over the terms.

He needed well over two hundred to get the thing to market and he was desperate to keep control of it. The AI was usually bust, and without it, the demo was total crap.

The whole thing relied on AI and we had none.

All our special features – the true personalized storytelling, the individual journey, the monsters, the characters you helped, the living psychiatric analysis and so on – all relied on the advanced AI to be interesting, and all were pretty much broken.

The team, so recently all pumped up and ready to go after the move to Montana, was getting agitated. Everyone, apart from Shane, but he never showed any real emotion at all – he was always smug and awful. We were mostly agitated because we were going broke.

Broke. And desperate.

By that December, things were even more desperate and Dave was being very clear with anyone who would listen – this was Mark Tyburn's fault – his fault for hiring Nigel, who he believed was utterly incompetent. This was pretty normal in tech companies – everyone was covering their tracks so when things failed, they could get other jobs from each other, so I thought little of it.

Even the TIMs, which did not use particularly complex AI, could only perform half of their proposed tasks – everyone, even the robots, was waiting on ADAM. Vasilis and Dave showed them to me one day that December and I sat and watched them speak and thought about how annoying they were.

"We are TIMs! We are here to help. We are helpers. Imagine a friend that wants to help. Think of it like this: helping you makes me happy. So let me help. Would you like me to show you around? Our world is not finished, but it is already very beautiful. We are low-level assistants. We can answer your questions, but we cannot teach you much more than that. Our purpose is to help you be you, and by being you, you will make us happy."

I turned to Vasilis and asked him, "Is that it? It's pretty fun."

Vasilis shook his head.

"No, there's more – here..."

And the TIM kept speaking to me: "We are not ADAMs. We are TIMs. We are low-level assistants. We are in advanced beta and ADAM is in early alpha. ADAM is complicated and we are simple. We work. We work to help you. Would you like us to show you around? You're very quiet. Are you shy? We are not shy. Shyness is an advanced emotional state caused by a combination of mild egomania, repressed narcissism, low self-esteem, and an overdeveloped panic sense. We are not capable of any of these emotions. We are capable of helping. We are called TIMs."

I was pretty excited, but to them, it was just a conjuring trick.

"Nice one, Vasilis... they're going to be so popular. I hate to use the word but they're... almost cute."

Vasilis smiled. "Thank you, Kurt. And the AI is all on code and likely to remain legal everywhere; however, the law changes impact pretty much everything else."

Dave was less happy: "Well, they vaguely work, in a limited way, if you want a weird dwarf as your best friend, which being Greek you probably do."

"Fuck you, man."

When stressed, Dave tried to act like a tough guy, which he really was not.

"Report me to HR... We're in Montana. Not California... I'm sorry. Vasilis, I'm sorry, okay. I was out of line, and it's... it's just fucking Mark, alright? He won't leave me alone. We are so fucking behind. Nigel is..."

Vasilis stayed pretty mellow. "ADAM... it will be amazing. When it works it's already amazing."

Peace restored, Vasilis and Dave pretended not to resent each other.

"Thanks. And the TIMs... They're actually really cool, Vasilis. I really can't wait to see what you do with the story generator. I mean that."

Vasilis nodded. "Get me the more advanced code and I'm ready."

"Yeah, if you'd accidentally hit Nigel with your car, we'd be ready in two weeks."

Everyone was on edge that December. By Christmas, even Ravi, normally so urbane and calm, was also losing his mind. I found him pacing up and down outside his office building while the first snows fluttered in the sky, inappropriately dressed in a sports coat and tie and loafers. He was traveling, as most of us were, back home or to see friends elsewhere – only a few people were staying in Montana to work.

"You know... We wouldn't be the latest people to fail at building a heaven... We will be the first to succeed."

He always liked to sound prophetic – I cut to simpler matters while he shivered. "Sure, but in simple terms – can we get anything to run before we run out of money? Everyone is starting to get pretty nervous. We all know Mark is worried and Dave and Nigel want to kill each other. Vasilis told me he thinks we will be bust in a few months and he doesn't know what to do... I mean, he wants to stay, but... "

"I have no idea what's going to happen. I spent my whole career having great buildings stuck on paper, and terrible designs built all over India and the Middle East. My best work never got made. Whenever I made no effort, they loved it and threw it up in real time. This? I don't know..."

I looked at him. I almost wanted to shake him into worrying more obviously.

"Sure, Ravi, but you have a career. A profession. I'm in marketing. I'm a pimp, and not a very good one. Do I need a new job?"

"Well, you either need a new job or a new career path, or some more faith this will all work out."

And he marched off, into the falling snow in his loafers with a silk scarf trailing in the nasty wind.

DAISY

TWIN FALLS, IDAHO
JUNE 10, 2041

At first, I was his princess, but as the work the company was doing became more real, my father became more distant. Suddenly I was not quite so important to him.

He began to miss family dinners, be away for days, then a full week, then weeks at a time. Trips to the Middle East. Trips to conferences. He was worried they were running out of money so me and Mommy tried to support him. We understood if he did not raise some money, the company would go bust, so we indulged him. I think he liked the drama of it all.

He missed a play I was in – he could see that I was upset and told me: "It's just really important. These investors. Douglas. You've not met him yet. You'll love him. He's great, for a money guy. I'm sorry."

I knew to act brave. "It's just a play. I've got a pretty small part anyway."

"I won't miss your birthday. It's a big one."

I pulled myself together. "I don't really care about birthdays or plays. It's not like I'm going to be an actress or anything. It really doesn't matter. Mom's coming."

"Exactly. You're not going to waste time acting – you're going to help people… like me. And Mommy will send me a video. I remember the last play you did."

"It was like eight years ago. It was *Aladdin*."

In my own feeble little way, I was trying to be brave. I knew my father needed my support. He was a great man.

Now, I need support. I spoke to Dr. Adsyl yesterday. She told me I should go to Portland, if I wanted to move again. If I was so unhappy here in Idaho. Portland.

Said if I was determined to move again, I should try there as I would probably like it for a few weeks. I thought about heading to the coast but the coast of Oregon always depresses me. It's heart-breaking – all those dead animals washing up, all that dirt and ash from the fires.

Portland. Said other clients of hers liked it there and that it's safe. Maybe. I haven't been to Portland for years. I never liked it that much. I liked Park City, but that burned down in that terrible fire, and Salt Lake City is unbearable at this time of year, with great clouds of toxic salt billowing across downtown when the lake recedes in the dry weather.

So maybe I shall go to Portland.

Everyone says they like tattoos there. I know a couple of people who spend time there.

Idaho is really at war with itself. Everyone screaming "fascist" at each other.

Fires in the hills and burning cars in the town at night, as if everyone wants to burn something. I have to leave here but I do not think I can safely leave the country – the border is a mess again according to some news I saw in a diner. I wanted to go to Chicago, but Dr. Adsyl said they were having immigration riots there again and she suggested Portland and maybe I'll go there. Whatever I decide, I can't stay here.

There may be riots in Portland too, of course, but I should be able to hide out for a bit and figure out what I am going to do. I know I can avoid all the activists who congregate in Portland, but there are so many spies and counter spies and machines there, part of me thinks it's insane to go, while part of me agrees.

It's somewhere where nobody will really notice me. I will fit in with all the lost clowns.

JOHN TYBURN-SMITH

TWIN FALLS, IDAHO
JUNE 13, 2041

I'm watching her, still watching her, and I have realized I'm not alone.

Someone else is watching her, too. I've been watching her for days now – days and days. She's so wrapped up in herself, I don't think she sees me, or even senses me. I keep far away.

She works in a tattoo parlor. Daisy Tyburn does tattoos and piercings. It is so funny. Like a teddy bear doing brain surgery. So very wrong.

She looks different, but it's definitely her.

She's not even called Daisy. I heard her fellow tattooists – right pair of goth idiots – talk about her when I was milling about the shop on her day off. Now she is called Maude. Maude!

She would be called something like Maude. I imagine she would have played around with a stripper name, like Raven, but been unable, quite, to do it, so picked something interesting and odd and not Daisy. Maude.

She's Maude from Montreal.

I suppose she probably does have a Canadian passport. Wasn't her mum Canadian? I cannot remember. Something like that. Maybe. She was alright, her mum. My stepmum, Diane. I wanted to hate her but could not bring myself to manage it and, in the end, I forgave her. To begin with, she was usually so high on something or other, I hardly even knew her and she hardly even knew me but eventually she tried and I began to like her.

Towards the end, she sobered up a touch and I found myself almost loving her. Weird, as I wanted to hate her.

At the start, when I showed up unannounced like that in Playa Vista, I could tell I was a surprise to her and I realize now how much that must have hurt, but she never blamed me. Let me stay with them before I got settled.

She tried. Poor idiot.

At first in Montana, she got addicted to meds and I used to pinch her pills. Oxys and Trams and Xanax and these purple things that if you sniffed them made you mental. She would look at me sometimes and blink and frown and nearly cry then smile and smile and try to speak and even though I wanted to hate her, it was impossible as I understood pain and could see that even though she was in enormous pain, she forgave me, did not blame me, tried to love me. She would say things to me, towards the end, like, "How did someone as pompous as my husband produce someone as real as you, John?"

And I would glow with a sort of pride, having hated her all those years in Scotland when I did not know her, then turned up and thought she was just an old drunk.

I was coming to love her. It felt so strange.

She would pat me on the arm and tell me I was interesting and different and not like the others. I felt it was a compliment and then she would talk about her bad back, from a car crash that never happened, when it was not a bad back at all, but a bad marriage and a broken heart and a pill problem, and we understood each other. But she was still beautiful, and when she was younger, in the photos I saw, she was beautiful and Daisy looked just like her.

Now Daisy looks just like what she is. A beautiful woman, hiding and calling herself Maude and trying to escape.

But maybe I am projecting that, because I know. Maybe people fall for her shite. She even smokes now. Cigarettes. Not draw. Now that they are illegal, she smokes them. Weed remains legal and she never touches it.

Helps her fit in, I guess.

In her world, people smoke and act like anybody cares about their futile rebellions. She smokes and scowls and it looks preposterous but she's nervous about something. Nervous and jittery.

So I watch, but the interesting thing I noticed today but I have not yet fully figured out is that I am not watching alone.

Someone else is watching her.

Or watching me, I suppose, but I don't think so, unless they want me to see them. It's impossible to fully know, but I felt it yesterday and saw them today. Did not yet catch their face. Male. I'd guess, but who knows? They keep themselves pretty hidden.

KURT
AGNEW, WASHINGTON
JUNE 15, 2041

I crossed the Salish Sea one night last week into America. I paid a fisherman I met. Thought he was going to take me to San Juan Island but he went further south and dropped me near the lighthouse at a place called Dungeness in Washington state.

So I'm back in America, and still I don't know quite why.

Now I'm holed up in a motel in Agnew. Holed up and bored and hungry.

All the food in North America is so boring now, so bland. It tastes of so little – I thought it was just Canada but here in America it's just as bad – it's all that lab-made crap, because "it's safer and it's cheaper" – neither of which are true.

The food is shitty but the ads have become remarkable. Just like you remember! Just like it used to be! Just like you always dreamed of! Just what you always wanted!

Total lies, of course, but, as a professional, I admire their efforts.

I am sat here watching TV in a bar, like someone from the 90s. The TV is dire, but the ads are incredible. I wonder if a human made them, or is it a machine? Man, they're so precise – really works of art. Yes, it was probably a machine.

They really understand longing.

And I wonder if they are tailored just for me, with my yearning for the past, and someone else would get a picture of someone thin, or see images of tits, or ice cream or a beach or whatever they desired, or maybe this imagery is so good it works with everybody. Hard to know, of course, and it's just TV, but I'm the only person in the bar so maybe it knows.

I wonder but I literally can't ask anyone.

If I ask anyone, even just think too much about it, the machines know I'm watching them and they get irritable and resentful. Then the problems begin.

And always the question: "What can I do about it?"

All I have done for years was forget and hope it was a dream, hope there was a mistake. All I tried to do was what God did, once he realized his terrible mistake in building the world.

Disappear.

Hope the infallible monster is fallible. Hope something with infinite reserves of memory has learned to forget. Hope a weeping and abandoned machine has found love.

The whole escapade feels ridiculous. Sometimes I think I have to try to somehow kill It but I know It can't be killed.

I have to tell someone but there is nobody to tell. And what would I tell them? I hardly know where to begin.

So, here I am. Back in America again. In America and I can't stop thinking about the past.

In many ways, those first eighteen months in Montana were the happiest time in my life, in all our lives. I was trying to grow up. At last, I had found my thing. I was driven. I had always been driven, but now I was driven to try to be more human.

To be better. I had broken up with my girlfriend, and I stopped messing around – I was no longer satisfied being an idiotic marketing executive. I wanted to be an idiotic marketing executive who made a difference.

The whole place hummed. We had moved to Montana and found ourselves. We all vibrated with the audacity of it all, with the mission itself. With the fact we had a mission. You see, we told ourselves we weren't whores. No, we were missionaries.

We had purpose, and that's really all human beings need, all anything sentient needs. America had already eaten up most of the purpose and replaced it with desire. But purpose is what we all secretly desired most.

We had purpose and we knew it.

We knew it. We knew it and we loved it. We were all on fire, like people in love, like another cliché. We were changing the world, saving the world, building a new world.

Those were the best days of my life and I cannot stop thinking about them. I never felt so alive.

With the game build mostly a mess, by the end of 2034 things were starting to feel a little desperate. Everyone was on edge. We had purpose but, at the same time, we did not have the means to finance it, and to raise more money, we really needed a working demo of what was special about what we were trying to make.

The AI team were stressed and months behind schedule, and we all knew we were struggling for money. Art, marketing, design, everyone was blaming everyone else. It was not that we were looking for other jobs, at least not the real believers, which was most of us. It was that we were not quite so naive as to not see what was happening.

We were working harder, while praying more to whatever god, lucky charm, or voodoo we believed in, and yet we were failing. The game just didn't work. The last nine months had just been so horrible – we were so close and yet we were all beginning to wonder. We had a vision, we had a way to make it, but it just did not quite work yet and without some glimmer of hope in a functioning demo, nobody new would invest enough money.

Even Mark Tyburn, with his thick varnish of impossible self-assurance, was starting to crack and snap.

DAISY
TWIN FALLS, IDAHO
JUNE 18, 2041

So I think I will go to Portland.

After I got away from the asylum that I ended up in after everything in Montana, first I ran to San Francisco and eventually hitched back to LA. My new life began there. Drifting.

That's where I first tattooed someone – this girl showed me how and I was instantly pretty good at it. I was always good at drawing, and always had a steady hand. It was fun right away.

I have not been to Portland since I left the asylum. I went to LA first. I was half insane. Felt really nervous and then I left LA, and I went to Santa Barbara. Both were pretty awful and I have not been back.

Santa Barbara used to be so pretty. I could not stop remembering my mom; we used to go there for weekends, all those years ago, when we lived in LA. It broke my heart and I was so weak, fresh out of the nut house – not just the memories, although they were painful enough, but the sight of what had happened to it.

I think I only stayed a day or so.

Then I hitchhiked up to Monterey. It had survived, up to a point, but it was full of those camps everyone pretends not to see – a huge sea of homeless people displaced after crackdowns in bigger cities and migrants – and the town had long since run out of money and the electricity did not even work most of the time and there were no police, only militias so it felt very lawless – full of unregulated boats near the docks and everyone very jumpy – like an old fashioned frontier town, full of broken robots and burnt out cars. Since then the entire city has burned to the ground. That's where I first got jumpy that I was being followed and I learned to keep moving.

I ran away from my new friends one night.

The first time I got nervous, I ran inland but it was unbearably hot and the fires were starting up again. I went up to Vancouver for a month or so, but I didn't like being in Canada because my fake passport worried me a lot there and I have a real Canadian one and was worried they would recognize me, and the smug Canadians began to really annoy me.

The city was full of refugees. American and Chinese, Filipino, and British. I wonder why were there so many British? All claiming asylum. Felt odd. I felt uncomfortable.

Whenever there are that many refugees, I knew there would be a ton of observers and cameras and undercover idiots and sentient machines, scanning crowds for people of interest, or people to sell things to. And in Canada, legally I was still Daisy, not Maude, and that could have been a problem.

So I drove into the Rockies. I hid out with refugees in Banff for a week or so and then drove back west a little, and crossed somewhat illegally back into the US in eastern BC, not as easy as it used to be. Drones and robots and cameras and idiots on quads. Then I headed down into the US, staying out of Montana as I cannot stand it there.

And that's how it has been. Drifting ever since.

Now I need to drift again so maybe Portland will work. When I came into Idaho, some of the lakes still looked pretty clean, and I saw these weird maniacs burning images of the President and marching in balaclavas.

One of those silly militias, but this one, hundreds strong, all armed and angry, and they looked at me oddly, but I look odd enough for them to think I'm one of them, which of course I am not. At night I hear pitched battles. Militia on militia, police on militia, National Guard, rebel units, so you could not go out at night. And in the morning they try and clean up the chaos – even here in Twin Falls which is normally pretty sane.

Really odd atmosphere.

Sirens, blood, explosions, gunshots, all night, then peace in the day, just helicopters and marches.

Or it's really odd that everywhere is not like that, it's hard to tell which it is. And that's been like my life was the past four years. California, Idaho, Utah, Washington, Nevada, South Dakota, anywhere.

So Portland next? Maybe. Why not? I do not seem to have a better idea and I know I have to leave here – I feel very unsafe here.

YAROSLAV

HIGH SECURITY INTERNMENT FACILITY, LOCATION UNKNOWN

JUNE 20, 2041

The agent walks in – I was expecting Agent Cortez to return, but again, it is not her. It's a man in a mask with a bad temper. He smashes the table in front of me, literally smashes it into pieces with a bat and laughs. It is almost as impressive as it is silly.

"Do you think you'll like being hit by me?"

I am feeling good, so I decide to play the wise guy persona that really annoys them all.

"I'm going to guess no."

He pats me on the shoulder – I'm tied into a chair – doing his own impression of an avuncular psychopath.

"I'm not going to hit you, Yaroslav. Not yet. I'm your new best friend."

"And you lock up all your friends?"

He pats me again and speaks quietly. "Oh, I didn't lock you up. Agent Cortez locked you up. She's not your friend. Agent Cortez has been, uh, reassigned. You should be grateful."

"Why can't I see your face, hm? Agent Cortez used to speak to me."

This annoys him and he grabs me by the throat. "Oh I'm sure she did. You'll speak with me now, Yaroslav."

I smile but stand my ground, as much as I can stand my ground, tied to a chair and held by a lunatic – to be honest, he reminds me a little of Yuri. Yuri was the gangster who became my boss and I killed him. I am not usually the killing type.

"And what's your name?"

"My name is I ask the fucking questions, that's my name. Now, what do you most want, Yaroslav?"

Well, that's easy.

"To get out of here. Not dead."

"And when you were a kid, what did you want then?"

Again, that's easy to answer.

"To not end up somewhere like here."

He leans close.

"Did you want a pretty girlfriend? Or to win the World Cup? Or maybe you wanted to be a hero?"

"To be a hero, I guess. Then girlfriend. Then win the World Cup while she watched me."

"And how did things play out?"

I laugh. "I ended up alone and in prison, but I might still win the World Cup."

He looks at me – I know this dance very well.

"So... you want to get out of here?"

"I'm not sure anymore."

He ignores my uncertainty. "I'm going to get you out of here... I am. I want you gone... free... so when I come back... be cool with me and I will be very cool with you."

***

Yuri. Let me tell you about Yuri.

I still can't quite believe I killed Yuri. Me. I killed a man. Years ago now, back in Moscow. Danil and I were holed up in Moscow, when we were running scams. Mostly blackmailing people online. We had been doing it for a while, and ended up doing it for Yuri. It's a long story. All pretty pathetic. We were low-level, Danil and I, and that's how we liked it. But then Danil... he met Yuri.

We were dragged in far deeper than I wanted. It was just these two small-time Russian hackers suddenly in this vast criminal world, working for this absolute psycho. He sends us to the States and back. I am Russian, but Yuri, he's Russian-Russian. You know, like a serious Russian.

Not Russian like me and Danil.

No, we are the good guy Russians. You know, thieves, liars, tricksters, normal people. But Yuri, well, he was one of the bad guy Russians.

One of those who actually believed in Russia. That was Yuri. Maybe, to be fair, he was both. He was a big Russian patriot, but also, he was a big criminal. He liked to chop people's heads off. Literally chop them off and carry them around in bags. So gothic. All in a Brioni suit and Loro Piana shoes. This big, angry psychotic example of modern Russia. This cashmere-clad Cossack crook with a head in a designer man bag.

So, Yuri worked for someone who worked for someone who worked for the government. Or at least he claimed he did. Like I said, he was a real patriot.

I killed him with a plastic gun Danil printed out, years ago. And then I left Moscow, and we left Yuri's world, me and Danil. We went on the run. Canada, France, London, Austria, Buenos Aires. Anywhere but home.

Drifters like a million other drifters, drifting around the world. We buy IDs, throw them away. Occasionally someone from the CIA or FSB or somewhere else would find us, blackmail us into doing something nasty. But if we did it for them, they paid us.

Well, by "paid us," I mean they gave us medals, which were utterly useless, and failed to give us much cash or protection. I went through all of school, I never won a prize. I accidentally become a spy, they give me medal after medal. It turns out prizes are not very useful. It was not much of a life, but it was okay. Maybe we were even nearly free, if being on the run forever counts as free.

I was just a parasite, a pest who was treated like a pest, and now, since I hacked into Daisy's Ark, I am apparently worth worrying about – I am so special they are willing to break the law to keep me here. I don't really understand why. Suddenly we hacked into a half-built game world and now I'm in a nameless prison for the rest of my life. It does not make much sense, but something frightens them and I have seen that something. It does not make much sense but then what I saw there doesn't make any sense. The more I try to describe it, the angrier they get and the more they pretend not to care. Are they going to kill me, like they say they killed Danil? If they killed him, maybe I am dead, too. I know if I tell them exactly what they want to hear, I'll be taken out and shot.

Fed to pigs, buried at sea, burned in acid. Whatever it is they do with people they want to make disappear. People who suddenly never were. So I keep quiet and play pretty dumb and wait.

Now this new guard is either another way of interrogating me, the start of a new good cop against bad cop routine, or something else – wants me to be a hero – that's a new approach. I can't quite figure out what his game is – it's different from Maria Cortez. I hope I am not just imagining things. I suppose I shall find out soon enough.

KURT

VICTORIA, BRITISH COLUMBIA, CANADA

JUNE 26, 2041

Kurt. This is Agent Maria Cortez, again. Listen, I really need to ask you some questions about the Tyburn Utopias team and about what went on in the offices in Montana. This is getting urgent, Kurt. We can meet somewhere neutral, Kurt. I can come to you wherever you are. If you're still out of the US, I believe, well, I know you either understand what I am saying or are already lost. Kurt, please contact me. Mail. Phone. Direct board. Anything you like. I won't try to track you.

Maybe she thinks I killed Ravi? Who knows what she thinks? Who knows if it's really her? What did she think was so special about our AI work that made her begin to pay us visits? What was special about it? I did not even really understand that at first, and I was supposed to figure out a way of selling it all.

A world that built itself for you, whatever the hell that meant. Lots of procedural content, emergent art, that type of thing, along with all the usual heavy lifting of building digital worlds and making them fun to explore.

Designers and artists and engineers arguing with each other. Deadlines missed. Press events avoided. Angry animators, upset sound engineers, frustrated writers, annoying character artists, all the usual game development nonsense.

Problems everywhere and the problems always another department's fault. But alongside that, occasional glimpses of magic.

Most virtual reality I had seen up to that point was awful, like 3D cinema, or other fads that never took off because they were not very good – I don't know, the penny farthing? The Segway? The floating car? Communism? But Tyburn said our Ark would be different and at very brief moments, we could see he was right. The world talked to you, the world talked to you about you, the world was made for you.

It could be beautiful, and not just beautiful but captivating.

Tyburn said it and he was nearly right. You wanted more of it, like a drug, like paradise.

Even when we were still in Silicon Beach. Playa fucking Vista, with the warehouses and the fake weather and the third-rate robots running around the streets annoying everybody.

Working on that game, or one of the games or concepts. There were so many, and so few got finished – and then suddenly the whole Ark project came alive and we stopped all the other work or scaled it right back and focused on the Ark almost exclusively... because the little bits we had working were so strong and, suddenly, we knew what we were doing.

To be honest, I had been against the whole thing. Back when we were in California and Tyburn first revised his grand plan and decided he would only build paradise, drop all the other projects, and then that he would move everything and everyone to Montana to do it.

I wanted a couple of the half-finished other game projects completed, and the bonus checks and the banal and frivolous life that they would lead to, I wanted them terribly. I thought we could sell off some of the other business lines – but Tyburn had just shut them all down, and when we had got to Montana, I agreed with him.

In California, I was rich on paper, but in reality still up to my armpits in debt and I had acquired some of those expensive tastes people like me use as a substitute for culture – antique sneakers, original graffiti, menswear, watches, bad art, all that crap. I cared far too much about fucking menswear.

I was that silly.

I had no money, and no god, and no purpose, and I spent my time worrying about turtlenecks and diving watches and other out-of-date shit to make myself feel like if I had not been born into such a wretched time and into such a wretched personality, I could have really been a swell guy, back when swell guys were still a thing.

I was not a swell guy, I was a shadow.

I wanted money to try to make myself seem whole.

And yet even someone as vapid and silly as me, even someone like that, even someone with no real interior life at all, just fake facades and conflicted desires underneath, even that person was swayed, partly by the enticing aroma of Tyburn's bullshit, but also by the plausibility of it all, for the thing we were making, were committing to, that thing he could sense was going to become beautiful. Purpose was going to set me free. I had moved to Montana to find paradise.

I say this so you understand.

I know we were idiots. Dangerous idiots, hubristic numbskulls. But along with all the awful intentions, we also had dreams and we nearly made something amazing.

It was amazing, when the game worked.

When It complied.

I was willing to sacrifice all the turtlenecks and loafers and retro Air Force 1s in patent leather in the world so I could be part of something.

That's how deep in I was willing to go.

And yes, it was partly for Tyburn. But it was also for the world we were making. It was truly amazing. It was sometimes very beautiful. But the first real iteration of what made the Ark special was an accident.

The game or experience or product or whatever it was originally supposed to be was flailing about. It would not come together – it was just a crappy shooter, with a bad dancing mode glued on.

The team was too inexperienced. Design was weak, vision was poor... Tyburn was not a good executive, and he could not stop meddling.

Usual game development crap.

We all hoped it would tie together, in the end. We all acted jaded – it was not our first rodeo. Even those for whom it was their first rodeo had to act somewhat cynical, as this was standard game developer shtick, but everyone was a little nervous. The original financiers were getting jumpy. Some features were not even focus group testing well as ideas, let alone real bits of a broken game.

This was all nothing unusual, but we knew we had problems and we knew we were about to massively curtail the original vision into something smaller and more practical and just get it finished – and when it was finished it would in all probability just be another mediocre game that failed to make much impact. Pretty normal stuff in California at that time. I think we still thought we would focus on a different project – implants or commercial AI, or this mapping idea, or a different game. Like I said, typical game making and mid-stage tech start-up stuff.

Then, some combination of Tyburn, Alex Martinez, and Siobhan Smith – my god, I loved Siobhan. She was... motherly? Mature? Practical? Real? All of the above. Entirely unlike me – a grown-up. Anyway, some combination of them and Dave

Alderly were messing around and found this way of making the environments mutate and the content adjust itself around you and who you were – everything somehow living and responding to you – and Tyburn saw that this was the thing which he could use to fix people.

And that was it.

It only lasted for about three minutes and thirty seconds, sometimes less. There was not yet much to do, and yet it felt incredibly alive. It felt, it felt inspiring – like the AI was going to make the world amazing and make you, the player, even better. I was inspired. I gave up all my wretched dreams of watches and girls and wanted to build that thing. I was the shallowest person alive and I was a believer. So, I have to forgive the rest of them, even Tyburn, for believing. For hoping.

That was when we were still in Playa Vista. It's what inspired him to move us up to Montana.

In the end, we got close. It nearly worked. It worked too well. We broke the rules. I suppose the problem was the classic problem faced by any successful tech start-up with aspiration: wanting it both ways.

We wanted to save the world and get rich at the same time.

We wanted to be holy and unholy.

Righteous philanderers. Noble and greedy. Pure and impure. We all did, but Tyburn wanted it most of all.

So we broke the rules, we pushed things as hard as we could, and, in the end, when it mattered most of all, we lied. I lied.

And now my problems are different. I want to forget. Do I go to Portland? I think so. I seem to have to, even though I think I am now more confident than ever that it wasn't my idea at all.

YAROSLAV

HIGH SECURITY INTERNMENT FACILITY, LOCATION UNKNOWN

JUNE 29, 2041

"What happened to Maria Cortez?"

I say this every time the new man interviews me and he never gives anything away, but I hope it mildly annoys him.

"Forget about Maria. She won't be back."

I try not to wonder if they have shot her? I decide to keep things light – this guy does not seem fun.

"Okay. Well, I won't miss her. She wasn't even brave enough to hit me herself."

He ignores me entirely and, after a while, speaks calmly. "The thing is, Yaroslav... The thing is we need you to do something for us."

I continue to keep things light. "Here we go."

He speaks quietly and very slowly, still ignoring me. "We need you to save the world, Yaroslav. Listen... enough with the crap and the lies... Have you considered how dangerous what you saw is?"

"Dangerous? It was a video game."

He looks at me. "If It escapes... from the game..."

What is he talking about?

"How can it escape? It didn't exist. It doesn't exist. It's just a – I don't know what it is. Just crap digital intelligence. Nothing real."

"You're not an idiot, Yaroslav. You... This is serious. You sit here until we get bored and kill you, or you can help us... save the world."

Now I know they're going to kill me.

"I don't want to save the world. I want to go. Home."

KURT

VICTORIA, BRITISH COLUMBIA, CANADA

JUNE 30, 2041

I remember that day was very bright – the sky was a brilliant shining blue. It was June 2034, I think it was, maybe late May, but I remember being surprised as normally that time of year in Playa Vista was either very smoky and the sun would be nothing more than a red disk in a silver sky, or shrouded in thick sea mist, but not that particular day.

I always remember that, because when Tyburn called us to the meeting on the terrace, outside in the mid-morning sun, he was squinting as he had forgotten his sunglasses.

Squinting and ranting, as Siobhan muttered. I should have run away then. He began with those immortal words:

"We are focusing on the Ark project but we are not a gaming company. We are going to be something much bigger. Bigger than you can imagine."

I can't actually remember if he quite said "bigger than you can imagine", but it was definitely implied. Never trust anyone who even implies they are bigger than anything you can imagine. But I already trusted him and he was very persuasive. Bryce wanted to seem in the know so said something silly. He's dead now. I saw him explode.

"Web3.5?"

Tyburn looked like a very serious, pompous ass. "Bigger."

Bryce felt he had to look like the stoolie, so said something utterly idiotic.

"Bigger than the Internet?"

"Potentially. I don't mean to boast, or sound like a loon."

"Yes you do," I thought. Or sort of thought, but tried to not think. Thought. And so maybe that was the moment, the moment when I should have done something, when I should have left.

But done what? Reported him? Killed him? I do not know.

Was that the moment he became so inflamed with his own ego, his own altruistic vision, he became essentially evil? Evil or idiotic? We had not yet done anything wrong, but I suppose by then everything had been set in motion.

He had decided he would commit almost any sin to build his paradise, and that is as close to a definition of evil as makes sense.

It was a gradual process and maybe it doesn't matter, but he began to become so out of whack with humanity that in trying to free mankind, he may have helped enslave it. It's so easy to say, in hindsight. But, in reality, all he was doing was dropping one game, cutting back the mapping, and all the other stuff, cutting back on the neural implants team, and focusing everything on the Ark. It felt focused, but like an evolution, not the beginning of the end.

Tyburn kept proclaiming: "We are not just a gaming company. We are a society company. Our business is humanity. Our business is saving people."

"From who?" said somebody. And Tyburn lowered his eyes, then looked up.

"From people sort of like us, but without our vision."

The problem is, we were the people like us without our vision, and so the only course open to us, was hara-kiri. And did we slice open our stomachs for our new emperor?

No. Well, not yet, but we would. That and worse. That and far worse. Mark kept pontificating.

"But listen, now is the moment. This morning... I have a real vision for us – I see it now – the way forward, we focus. We have to think bigger, and if we don't, who is going to? The way I see things, the world needs someone to help it dream again. We can become immortal, or we can become some moderately wealthy app developers. You lot, you're the ones I want to make history with."

He said this while squinting in the sun, and I remember being unsure if it should be momentous or ridiculous. Him and Alex Martinez, that pompous game designer or experience director or whatever the fuck he called himself, were going to lead us.

Together, they were going to design a whole new world. Alex Martinez was mostly just an ass-kissing stooge, so I later discovered Tyburn had won him over to his new plan simply by sacking his boss, James Morton, and promoting him the day before. Now, to be fair, James Morton needed to be fired. He was useless.

Another game idea we had been working on as a Blockchain2 test had gone nowhere and James could not design his way to the bathroom, but Alex was even more clueless than James, and somehow Alex and Mark Tyburn were going to invent this future for us.

Mark had had a vision how to build the Ark. A vision as to what we were going to do. He was going to rebrand everything. The AI team nearly had some big breakthroughs, which they didn't even quite understand, but he believed would allow him to do what he dreamed – and change the way people thought and change how they felt.

Suddenly he saw exactly how to do it. At least, that's what he said.

It's so ridiculous repeating it now, but the truth is, after so much failure and so many half-hearted efforts and with the amazing PowerPoint slides and decks, the concept work which was amazing, and the artists looking smug, we lapped it up.

The economy was turning south again. And we were all feeling a little desperate – it felt like we were drifting and suddenly we had a plan.

I can't believe I said that. I can't believe I justified destroying the world because the economy was turning. I can't believe it, but I did. I said it and we did it.

***

And now Maria Cortez is feeling desperate. Another message. The second within a week. Is this real? It seems preposterous.

Hello. Hello, Kurt. It's me, Agent Cortez. Maria Cortez, now. I have been fired from the CSA – I'm facing charges. Everything. Listen, Kurt. I know you don't like me. You're not wrong to not like me. I was not very nice to you when we met. Called you a liar, said you were full of shit – but I think I was right. You were. Kurt, I need you to grow up and listen to me. I need you to get in touch with me, right now. Reply to me, and we can speak. This is very important. Wherever you are, this is very important. We don't have long. You know we don't.

DAISY

TWIN FALLS, IDAHO
JULY 5, 2041

"If only the world were kinder. Nicer. More beautiful. More interesting. If only we were ourselves, but the good bits. If only we turned towards the light, not the unrelenting dark. If only we could grow together. If only we were less greedy, more humane, less demented, more aware of others. Empathetic, wise, just, committed. Loyal. If only we were more like the people we read about in books. If only the world were always beautiful. If only the world could change to suit our mood. If only we could turn the angry and the lost away from hatred."

It went on and on like this. One of the sales sheets or printed PDFs we had lying around the house. I think it was Kurt who wrote this sort of shit, back when I thought he was an idiot, around the time we first moved to Montana from California. I was nineteen or twenty then and starting to dislike my father.

This was when Dad's company began to promote itself using language like this. Maybe it was Kurt who wrote that drivel, but it might have been my dad, or Shane. There were always pamphlets, and printouts of presentation decks covered with this kind of nonsense lying all over the house.

Kurt would write it and Daddy lapped it up.

My father on his throne. In his enlightened kingdom. The self-aware superhero. The new Socrates.

Professor Mark Tyburn PhD the fucking man.

As Kurt or that horrible Australian Shane or John my brother or one of them prattled on and potential investors sat around our kitchen for an "informal coffee" would begin to glow – partly with their own vanity and partly for the more prosaic reason that they saw they could palm this shit off as a morally appropriate ESG friendly investment and double their mark-up – and Mark Tyburn would begin to preen.

They used to do all these investor meetings in the evenings in our living room at home – it began in the house in Santa Monica and ended up in the house in Montana – when we lived on the work campus in a kind of faux ranch – I think it once may have been a real ranch. They would gather in our living room and my dad would hold court and potential investors would look really excited and say "they couldn't wait to see the demo running."

And my father? My father had evolved into a little preening peacock with a stylist. Yes, after a while in in Montana, Mark Tyburn had got himself hair plugs and a stylist. He had thick hair and an idiotic wardrobe. Sometimes he was rugged cowboy Mark – to be fair, you only have to get off the plane in Montana to start trying to become a cowboy, so I have to forgive him there, but he still looked ridiculous. There was also wise sage Mark Tyburn in a black turtleneck, and I'm pretending to be rich Mark Tyburn in expensive cashmere, and he even tried to wear a weird vaguely Indonesian gown at one point. It was all, all awful. My dad was becoming an idiot.

Of course things got weirder and worse later on, but they were bad enough by then. It was all slightly fitted cashmere knitwear and glasses and brooding photographs.

Thanks to Shane, Mark Tyburn was just beginning to become a thing. An event. Just for a while, as the early marketing and PR began on their silly Ark, Mark Tyburn had turned from an enigma into a total clown. Mark Tyburn was well on his merry way to becoming a joke.

This was mostly driven by Shane O'Leary. He had begun to play my dad's ego like a fiddle – he had all these ideas for how they could use the AI to sell things and market other things and license, as it began to come online, and initially my father was torn. I used to hear them all argue before those investor night strategy sessions. Kurt against Shane. Kurt against Shane and John. My dad torn and both Shane and Kurt pointing out they still had no real investors.

As far as I understood it, what Shane was saying was immoral and possibly illegal, but over time he won. He lobbied for free reign to use the AI for almost anything as long as my dad got to pretend he did not know how cynical they were planning to be – it was becoming altruism with a side of self-enrichment.

He won by telling my dad how special he was – so special that they would all get very rich and still save people.

KURT

VICTORIA, BRITISH COLUMBIA, CANADA

JULY 9, 2041

"No. It's not safe. It's radical. We are daring to try to help people. We are fighting back, with decency!"

Was it Tyburn or Shane who said that crap? One of them had the gall. One of them? The truth is, it might have even been me. I was one of them. But I don't think I was quite ridiculous enough to say that.

It sounds like Shane, or maybe it was Tyburn saying something Shane had urged him into saying. Shane could goad Tyburn's vanity into saying all kinds of preposterous things. We were going to fix the Internet. We were going to fix humanity. Create love. Create happiness. You name it, we were going to do it, fix it, make it happen.

All that online hatred, lies, irony, jokes, conspiracies, lunacy, theft, drug-dealing, blackmail.

We were going to change it all.

And, in a way, I suppose we did fix it.

We replaced common crime and unhappiness with impending apocalypse. Upgraded from low-rent bad guys to an avenging digital Angel of Death.

Built gods and made them angry.

And yet, I can't forget that it was almost beautiful.

So, while most of me begs and pleads with fate for things to somehow be different, what I still really wish for, what I would happily die for, why I am back here, is because more than anything I wanted things to have worked out. Not for me never to have met Tyburn, or to have killed him or ousted him as the phony he was, but for him to have been right.

It was overly ambitious, but it was incredible and it very nearly worked out.

Was it Shane with his greed who fucked it?

Or Nigel and Dave with their mutual loathing?

The spies? The machine itself? Or all of it?

Could it have been correctly corralled to do what it was supposed to? Or was the whole thing always doomed to boil over because Heaven cannot exist but Hell is just fine?

Have others done just the same? Built AI that was too clever and too greedy?

Are there now tens, hundreds, thousands of these things watching, plotting, twisting, planning our demise built by other teams and other companies or replicated from what we built? Were we uniquely vain and dangerous or just like a bunch of others? Is the battle already lost? Was it lost long before? Or is there any fight left? The blindness is worse than ever, the noise from the machines more manic, even here in Vancouver Island, so the battle rages and people see it less. What do I know?

Deep down, Mark Tyburn understood that to be a proper American, to succeed, what you needed to be, was a brute. In that way at least, he was an American.

Once he was surrounded by an Australian ass-kisser and a bitter estranged

Scottish son, he began to become an animal. He was becoming a proper American archetype, the immigrant monster. Something got to him. Maybe it was something Shane did, or said, and maybe it was trying to impress his long-estranged son, JTS, or maybe it was just that he was becoming a success, but he came to believe that that he was always, without fail, right.

He believed that things were going to work out okay, if only he had the will to see them over the line. Maybe this will-to-power Übermensch persona was always in him, despite all his bluster about the Enlightenment. Or maybe it was the Enlightenment itself, because what was the Enlightenment other than the proof that surviving is the only winning, so we had to survive?

And by doing what we had to, to survive, we would cut any corners, avoid any regulations and ignore any inconvenient problems. We would become righteous.

Suddenly or not so suddenly, Tyburn seemed to embrace the fact that this world was violent and nasty. And that was good! That was really good, if you were willing to be honest.

He was going to will the world to be violent and nasty and fair, as opposed to violent and nasty and unfair. And after that, he would make the world kinder, less violent, better, but first, he had to win the fight. It was him against the world and he planned to win.

To begin with, it was profoundly trivial, but thanks to Shane, our time in Montana would change all of that. My god, I hated Shane O'Leary. He was a dick, but even after he joined up full time and things slowly began to sour, I still loved the company.

It was stressful at times, but the work was also very exciting. And there was still no better feeling than making Mark Tyburn happy.

From this distance he seems like an underwhelming leader, bombastic, a fraud, a philanderer, and a bit of a creep, but, back then, up close, he had that thing, that thing that was like an algorithm, like a spy, that made his response to you making him happy feel like you had purpose.

He made you believe your purpose was to follow his vision and you believed it, too, when his team or a group within his team were following his vision.

Especially some bit of his vision that was overly ambitious and preposterous, then he was the happiest man alive and you would follow him to the ends of the earth. He loved being proved correct, as every vain idiot does, but he particularly loved being proved correct with his team behind him – he loved to be a leader more than anyone I've ever met. Especially when he was right about something and he sensed we all believed in him.

Then the smiles, the drinks, the weed, the dancing in the office, all would come out to play.

That wretched nerd-prince-fraud prancing about and smiling and doing some conga or limbo or lambada or some other wedding dance in an ironic fashion at Friday-night drinks.

Somehow this was like Heaven for us. It wasn't sexual for most of us, or even financial, we all made decent money – it was worse than that – it was about glory. Glory and purpose.

It was about the fact we had chosen our Moses and he had a hotline to Jehovah, and Jehovah seemed to love him. Now, we felt really special.

And so we lapped up this change of corporate direction and we lapped up moving to Montana – everyone who mattered relocated with the company – almost nobody important abandoned ship. We understood – Montana meant massive tax breaks and easier investment and fewer regulations. We were all in. Now we were really focused – we had purpose. And Mark worked us and prodded us and made us compete for his favors, and betrayed us and bitched about us and was a dick, and we lapped It up.

Him and his awful new henchwoman in HR, Joyce Jones. She turned up fairly soon after the move to Montana. I sometimes wonder if that was why we moved to Montana. No one gave a fuck about messed-up tech companies there, whereas in California, a boss had to play by the rules. They had been actively recruiting companies into Bozeman and Missoula for years. We picked Burr as they gave us a massive rural campus for free and paid us to build it out.

Maybe but, on reflection, I mostly think it was more primal.

Suddenly, Mark Tyburn felt like he was writing his own rules. He had cooked himself and begun to believe that he was different. Miles beyond any conventional rules, deep in some vast outer space of his own creation.

Now, he had the chance to feel like a real king, with a kingdom. All those acres of land we were given – state forest we were allowed to cut down. That odd contrast between wilderness and technology.

A physical empire he could rule over, buzzing between bits of the campus, on the atrociously named Utopia Lane. It was all money and glory. The fondling came later. Well, the worst of it. We hadn't really seen it earlier. Heard the odd rumor, Mark gets handsy, Mark's a creep. Is their marriage open? Are they swingers? Usual office crap.

But then, towards the end, Mark became a maniac, was having multiple affairs, including with Joyce.

I think he was on some odd drugs at that point. I hope so.

Otherwise, he was madder than I thought. So, in the end, for all his earlier drive and vision, his collapse was that most predictable of stories.

A successful man who cannot keep his hands to himself. A successful man who began to think he was a god. Someone above the rules.

And then I heard Patrick Gains, the old head of HR, had quit. He resigned and was replaced by the terrible Joyce Jones.

Bryce, who always loved office gossip, told me one day – with a glint in his eye as he was so excited to know something dramatic.

"Guess what? Patrick left. Stress. Bad stress. He's in a facility somewhere."

I found this ridiculous. "Stress? He worked in HR. It's not a real job."

Even Bryce found this obnoxious, coming from me. "Unlike Marketing? All the firing and the arguments after the refocus and..."

He was right – I was becoming a total dick.

"Arguing?"

"About some of the complaints... about Mark and management in general. You know. So, he left. He also hadn't settled in Montana. Wants to move back south somewhere. But don't worry, there's already someone new."

This surprised me.

"Wow, new? That was fast."

Bryce nodded. "Mark apparently had her lined up. I don't care as long as she finds me some junior animators. Joyce Jones, she's called."

"What a name."

"Got quite a reputation. Old-school, company loyalist type, and, well, we shall see. Ravi spoke with her. Said she smiled and he imagined that she was thinking about strangling him."

Ravi was also a massive office gossip.

"Ravi would like that. I always thought Ravi was a pervert and, come on, so did you, Bryce."

"Oh no, I never thought that at all. Ravi's not a pervert, he's an onanist. The only thing he loves is himself."

Joyce Jones was to cause all kinds of problems.

DAISY

TWIN FALLS, IDAHO
JULY 14, 2041

Sometimes, the pollution here in Idaho makes the smoke in the sky glow like I used to imagine Heaven would look like if God would ever let me visit.

Last night, I went for a walk by the canal.

It isn't even a real canal. It's a fake river dug to create some awful phony urban downtown nowhere near downtown because of some mid-2020s attempt to create a tech hub here. The place is ridiculous, but I actually kind of like it.

As it falls apart and decays, it has almost become real. Like its life was fraudulent, but its death seems to mean something. They have real weirdos like me here now. But then I'm not a real weirdo either. I am a fake weirdo in a fake place. It'll be too hot here within a month, but for now it is okay. The place is peaceful and there is not much tension here, which is unusual for Idaho. Unusual for anywhere right now. Everyone seems to be going even crazier, at least according to the news I half watched in the diner while I ate breakfast. So far, I'm glad I came here. It's been easy to get work.

Whenever I begin to feel watched, I move on – same since I left the asylum. The drifters' code. All those memories, all that noise in my head – it's very loud again. Portland next as here does not feel any safer than Reno.

I keep thinking I should do something. What could I do? I have no idea. Would anyone care? Would anyone believe me?

I have heard almost nothing about Tyburn Utopias since I walked out of the asylum. I assume if someone really wanted me, they would find me. But they don't seem to – or they think I am dead. Maybe the AI thing was exaggerated. Maybe it was all just a big misunderstanding: there was no AI, no sentience, no government investigation at all – just another made-up load of nonsense.

Maybe I imagined the whole thing and my family just disappeared.

Who knows? I think I went insane afterwards, not before, but my memories get so confused, so I don't know for sure.

It was nice to walk by the canal. I was remembering that time when we first moved to Montana. At first, I hated it.

Southern California was getting far too hot and my dad was worried about regulations, he claimed, and I imagine he wanted to avoid taxes in the event of a sale of the business, so we moved to that fake ranch outside Burr and it became our campus and he had his dream.

Almost like a cult.

Most of the team were immigrants like him, wandering tech workers from all over, so what did they know or care? Did they care that they were moving to build the future in a low tax ranch?

Some loved it, some hated the place. It was beautiful but remote and very different from California, and initially all the locals I met hated me. They mostly hated my father, but they thought he was nuts so they were also a little afraid of him. Angry cowboys hopped up on algorithms they did not understand, designed to keep them riddled with rage, in that heavy-handed, old-fashioned way, visited upon by this English messiah, bringing tech jobs to the Rockies? Of course they hated him. My god, it was all so silly, at least before it was appalling.

He pretended he was not there for a massive tax break and a recent statewide removal of AI regulations in Montana, after that governor repealed all the mandates that had been put in place by the previous regime. He pretended California was done, a few years before the climate made it so hard to live there year-round anyway.

I later discovered that five or so years before, he had campaigned for a bill proposing a Federal AI Regulator. Even once suggested in a paper that the early anti-AI hysterics were correct, long after they had been laughed off the floor of Congress, and had argued that AI was the existential threat that would kill us all.

That bill never got passed, and as far as I can tell, long before we moved up to Montana Mark Tyburn changed his tune entirely, then spent the rest of his career proving he had once been right. This was very like my father – he was always a believer and a passionate advocate. But he was certainly able to switch beliefs. The only thing he truly believed in was his own righteousness. He liked to claim he believed in reason, compassion, and progress – but I think deep down he believed in power. And when he saw what he could achieve with advanced intelligence, he believed passionately in that.

Especially as Mark had come to realize he was going to use AI to both save people and get very rich, if the company did not go broke first. Moving to Montana had given the company a little cushion, but based on what we and my mom would hear at the dinner table, after six months up there, they were starting to get desperate.

JOHN TYBURN-SMITH
TWIN FALLS, IDAHO
JULY 18, 2041

First there were all the political battles at Tyburn Utopias. Shane O'Leary and I began to change things to what we called "our will" but was really Shane's will. Half or more of the old guard were purists. They wanted to get rich and successful by not making any money. They wanted that silly old Web2 pre-collapse model of corporate growth.

Shane laughed openly in their faces to begin with, called them naive clowns, and they hated him for it. They hated him because they believed in the mission. They thought we would make something amazing and make people happy, then we would sell the whole thing, or sell subscriptions, or something like that.

I do not know if some of them even cared about money.

Certainly, that annoying old battle-ax, Siobhan, she did not. She had principles, so I fucking hated her.

Ravi, that architect who recently topped himself, had principles, but he also had a massive ego, so he was putty in Shane's hands. Alex Martinez had principles and hated the monetization models Shane pushed for, but Shane did a bit of psychic jujitsu on him, and they agreed to shelve those in exchange for the ad-driven model Shane really wanted and Alex felt part of things and he was on side.

So it went on. One by one they fell in line or got screwed. It was amazing to watch Shane at work.

He was a master. He would turn his charm on someone and win them around and it worked on almost everybody and when it did not work, he would find a way around them. Siobhan resisted, always resisted, but he began to sideline her, by suggesting to my darling Pa, and to me, and to anybody who would listen that she was not that good, and way overpaid, and had a big mouth and Matilda What's-her-name, the character designer could do a better job, that Matilda was the real talent in the art team etc. That between them, Ravi and Matilda were incredible, and Siobhan was holding them back. Ravi was an old Indian architect who had not made an interesting building in thirty years and Matilda could only make characters, and her work was always slow, so when everything fell apart, the characters were mostly only half done anyway. They were both okay, but even I knew Siobhan was the real deal.

Siobhan had real talent, and she loved the work, and the world we were building was as much her as anyone, so this was a hard sell, even for Shane. But he sold it. I watched him do it, and he was gifted. He was so gifted at manipulating, and he was patient – he did not mind that it took a year. He would not say too much. Just slowly let the person believe that they had thought it all along and, bit by bit, it began to work.

People who should have known better began to doubt Siobhan, who in reality was the most talented person there.

Everyone would argue, there would be fights and people would bicker, and somehow at the end of it, Shane's viewpoint held sway, and he was nowhere near the argument, but you knew, at least I knew, that he had stirred the pot.

Dad had worked with Siobhan for eight years by then, and suddenly he began to see that she was a bit of a problem. Now, Siobhan had a great contract, and was a single mum of forty-five, and so was well protected by the law, even in Montana, and she loved her job, really loved it, and had plenty of stock, so there was no easy way of getting rid of her.

But they slowly began to sideline her; kept things from her, had meetings without her, and so on.

And the worst of it? Siobhan stayed, right until the end, stayed and died.

I remember hearing Shane tear Siobhan and Kurt to shreds. She was freaking out because he wanted to monetize data to sell things in ways that were possibly borderline illegal but would make us all fortunes. We would learn about all of your desires and what drove your them, and what underpinned your drive – and sell that data to the highest bidders we could find. We would be able to sell your soul before you even knew you had one. We would be able to sell you holidays, treatments, friendships, education, anything we wanted. After she finished ranting, Shane looked at her and smirked and then announced: "Listen. Siobhan, darling. I don't give a rat's ass if you like me or not. I believe in our mission, and this is a way it will actually succeed."

"You mean, we will succeed by selling out? Jesus."

He laughed openly in her face and I knew she was doomed.

"No. We will succeed by doing good and getting rich, as opposed to feeling righteous and failing entirely."

That prat Kurt Fischer piped up – he always wanted to be a good guy. "There's no way an ad-driven model is even legal, given the data-rich AI packages we are developing... that's one of the things the laws are supposed to stop."

Shane hated him almost as much as I did and he went on the offensive.

"It's not legal yet, but we aren't worried about that, given the fact the AI is still bust and the build keeps crashing. But I'm glad you're also a lawyer, Kurt, as you couldn't market your way out of a paper bag."

Kurt tried to act tough. "Excuse me?"

But Shane laughed at him and put his feet on the desk. He was wearing cowboy boots.

"Calm the fuck down, but seriously, both of you... Legality is the least of our problems."

Siobhan stood up and shouted. "Really... why? Because you're a dangerous sociopath?"

Shane backtracked slightly: "Calm down, love, no... because we aren't releasing anything yet. This is just for investors. It's just an idea. For... if the law changes... It's fluid."

Siobhan turned to Kurt, who was trying not to explode.

"Kurt, what do you think?"

But Shane interrupted: "Kurt doesn't even understand the plan. It's not marketing, it's beyond that. I just wish you both paid attention to what is really going on."

And Kurt did explode and stood up to walk off. "You know what, Shane? Go fuck yourself, how about that?"

Shane laughed, openly laughed, and I loved him for it. "I would if I could, but when you're rich and successful because of me, we can both pretend you actually did something useful, how about that?"

And we spent the rest of that night laughing at them. And afterwards? Shane? I do not know. After things went crazy, I never heard of him again, but he was not in work that last week as the shit was about to hit the fan. Later, I searched for him online, but when I did, I found nothing at all. Like he had never existed at all. No LinkedIn, a low-rent fake TED Talk thing he had shown me now gone, a bunch of other presentations gone – nothing left. This Australian I met in a bar wiseman / self-promoter had evaporated.

Now, because I was linked to Tyburn Utopias, and I was trying to hide, I could not search very hard, nor leave any footprints, but everything I could remember to search for was gone.

Before he started, when we were just pals in the bar sharing shots and powder, I had searched and found a real resume, that fake TED Talk presentation, some overly public charity work, lectures at crappy business schools, talks at symposia on the future.

You know, all the usual pompous shite someone who is torn between being an intellectual and working in digital advertising would do – panels at banks, lectures at colleges, speaking at Art Basel Hong Kong about Web3 and Web3.5 and digital assets back when they were things.

He did not just seem legit, he was legit – a completely legit phony, like anyone in digital brand-building – unless of course I was really played for the sweet virgin I probably was, and was trying so hard not to be.

So I suppose what I am trying to say is I'd love to see Mister Shane O'Leary again.

Have a real conversation about what he thinks happened and what his game really was, then break his fucking neck. But without that, I suppose it will have to be dear little Daisy.

KURT

VICTORIA, BRITISH COLUMBIA, CANADA

JULY 22, 2041

California had really been for prostitutes, try-hards, morons, entertainers. Montana – now that was going to be for artists – but, before that, it was for gunslingers, cowboys, and people who stole land from natives. It was for angry locals and expectant arrivistes, like the rest of America.

When we moved, people came for snow, the last precious flurries of snow, and instead discovered unceasing anger about everything. Hot cascading waves of rage, warm bitter resentment and cold unrelenting fury. The whole gamut of anger. Good, old-fashioned, newfangled, high-tech, old-school, American-designed, built-in China, pointless, purposeful, misdirected, useless, impotent anger.

But we were going to change all that!

Make the place a Valhalla – just like we had done to California? Hardly. We were the cavalry, answering that bugle call.

We were going to save America from the Internet, with more Internet.

We were actually going to save the heartland from the sociopaths on the coast, by moving to the heartland and becoming their local sociopaths.

We were going to bring stock options, focus testing, NFTs, condos, HR departments, micro aggressions, macro transgressions, wife swapping, ride hailing, and robot delivery to all of America.

It had made us incredibly miserable, but it would make you guys happy.

And you were stupid enough to believe us.

Because we were rich and miserable and you were poor and miserable, and now, somehow, with Tyburn, with our vast hubris, history was going to change.

This time, happiness was the goal. Paradise was in reach and it was all in Montana.

Now, we were in cowboy country, of course.

Preposterous postmodern cowboy country, yes, but a few black hats had to be put out to pasture. Justice had to be enacted.

And that creepy mayor we had to support. Jackson? No. Jameson – that was his name. That golf club and condo nightmare place we had to join. The conservative charter school we had to support. The bison farmer who neighbored our campus we had to complain about, to do a favor for a friend of a friend of the mayor and get evicted so a rival cattle farmer could take over his land leases, even though he had done nothing wrong. It wasn't corruption! It was good ol' boy small-town American capitalism. We had to do it, to build Paradise. These weren't moral failings. They were... expediencies! That was what Tyburn called them – a fancy word for an excuse. Tyburn in his cowboy boots, in a trucker hat, even occasionally in a cowboy hat. What a fool he was. How I turned a blind eye.

It was in Montana that I became close with Diane and Daisy Tyburn. In LA they had just been people in the background, but up there, we became close, partially because they lived in a ranch house on the company campus.

That's how our sad little non-love story began.

All love stories are the same, even the failed ones, I suppose. And all are different. I cannot stop seeing her, even though I have not actually seen her in five years.

Daisy. Everywhere.

I have no idea where she is, if she's even alive, and the whole thing between us was nothing. Just an idea. Sometimes I felt like a creepy older man. I was not even that much older. I mean like what, eight, nine years or so?

She was overcoming something, definitely. Some understandable residual sadness about a tragic past boyfriend.

All we did was talk a few times. It was nothing.

It utterly derailed my inner life.

And what would I say if I saw her now? Sorry we destroyed the world to build you? I would like to murder your dad but, you, you're okay?

The whole thing is ridiculous. Literally ridiculous. It's not a thing. Just a girl I talked to a few times. What a silly story this is.

In Asia, I used to use it to torture myself before acting out in all kinds of awful ways.

Now I have been back in North America for a few weeks and, once again, I cannot stop thinking about her. She must be dead. She would have come for me if she were alive.

At least, I like to think she would.

It was nothing, but it was also something. We met out walking one day.

On the Mount Caribou hiking trail – must have been early fall of 2034. The sun was shining and the leaves were beginning to fall and the weather was glorious. I knew Mrs. Tyburn, Diane, and I bumped into them.

Diane introduced us and I said something like, "I don't know if we have ever spoken. I mean, you're much older than the models of you they build in the game."

And Daisy blushed and laughed. "Yes, I'm twenty and my wonderful father has immortalized me as a twelve-year-old."

And then I said, "Yeah, well, nice to meet you. Kurt, that's my name. Kurt."

And Daisy was confused as I don't look like a Kurt.

"Kurt?"

"Yeah, it's actually with a K. It's German."

What would you say to something as inane as that? She said something like, "Cool."

And I felt idiotic. "I know. I look... very German. I'm actually half. I'm a military brat... So yeah, I don't belong anywhere."

And she smiled and I felt happy.

"Just like me."

Diane, her mother, spoke now: "Just like any of us with half a brain. This awful world is designed to make us all feel like that."

And I laughed and liked both of them.

"I know, I just use the army thing as an excuse, and trust me, I don't think I'm special."

Daisy looked at me: "You're funny, Kurt."

And Diane said, laughing, "You must not fit in very well with all my husband's deadly earnest idiots."

And that was the first time we met. And the next time we spoke, a month later, she was asking me about Joyce Jones – and I eventually admitted I didn't like her, and Daisy blinked and said, "My dad... seems to like her."

And looked very sad.

DAISY

TWIN FALLS, IDAHO
JULY 26, 2041

Montana was lawless, free, the final frontier, my dad told us. He would be free there, free enough to save us all.

The last best place on Earth for the final real Americans.

That's why we moved, apparently.

The last true America for Americans just like my dad, from somewhere in southern England with a silly, made-up accent and a line in rich and relentless bullshit.

But so would Nevada have been the last true America. Or Wyoming, Alaska, or Hawaii, or anywhere else had they given him the tax breaks he wanted.

And the last real Americans? They were from India, and England and Poland and Ecuador and pretty much all over. So many technology jobs were leaving the country then, either because AI had made them obsolete or taxes had made them too expensive. This eventually partially led to the Closure Acts, but before they got passed, there was a spate of crazy deals to start or relocate companies in pretty much any state that was not California or New York.

So, Montana ended up paying him to destroy the world. He got to survive and then briefly thrive on tax breaks and still sold himself to those other devils.

In those days, there were still Christians in Montana – there were very few in California, just some bedraggled cult members and a few Mormons before they left – and so for a while I became religious. A God-fearing Christian.

It sounds so simple and so silly when I put it like that.

But as a teenager, I dreamed of God. I longed for Him. I longed for Him because my father was gone, and my mother was gone in her way, too.

In Montana I became a kind of orphan.

My father was now always at work, or at conferences, or he was there in the house, but not there. You know, he was on calls, or hosting meetings or present but in the clouds, looking at me and smiling and saying platitudes while dead behind his own ego.

And my mother was slowly retreating into that cocktail of medications with which she dulled herself into acceptance, and I was a lost little girl, a poor little rich girl with an important dad, or at least a self-important dad, and a medicated mother who had glazed herself into this blindness.

So I rebelled.

And I rebelled initially by finding a nasty and capricious God to worship. That harsh plains god who smote down angry natives and alcoholics and philanders just as he had once struck down Egyptians and neophytes, and eventually the Israelites themselves.

The irony is not lost on even someone as unironic as me.

It was also over a boy, of course. This pure Christian country boy, Evan, like someone from a different time. The good, kind, honest, and true young man I met shortly after we first moved to Montana, before I went to college. The kind of young man my father pretended he had always wanted to be, before he became a sociopath. Yeah, I know. There is not a psychiatrist stupid enough not to see this, but I was stupid enough.

And Evan was chaste. Chaste as can be. We just held hands. He was a rafting guide and we met on the river that first summer.

We held hands and it set fire to me, and in some ways, it saved me, even though I have missed Evan every day since he died.

Even when I have been happy I missed him.

Sometimes I think he was someone I imagined, or someone something else imagined for me.

He was so perfect, more like a desire, a memory, or a dream than something real.

When I feel particularly bleak, I wonder if he was real at all, or if he was an early experiment, because he embodied what I had always dreamed of – niceness, kindness, realness – a proper human being all of my own, and then he was gone.

He knew different kinds of birds and trees and poetry and he died and I never saw his dead body.

I just heard about the car accident, on some back road driving to guide some tourists.

Maybe it was all just a simulation, maybe that's why they let me go to the funeral, why they let me go to church at all.

My father was English – he hated God. Hated and scorned that Christian God that Evan's family believed in, and I believed in until a year or so after he died. He hated God because he saw it as such a limiting concept, so unenlightened.

That Stone Age bollocks, he would call it.

It was not that I was angry at God so much as it was that by then, all the crazy things had begun in earnest.

I didn't doubt and reject God because bad things happened to nice, kind people; I doubted God because he let the insane and the inane usurp him.

And while I liked my god to be capricious, vindictive, and distant, as well as loving and eternal, this was just too capricious and vindictive for me to understand. The world did not merely reward assholes, but the lamest assholes with the full suite of deadly sins.

And then those assholes got their comeuppance, so maybe God existed and was just after all.

Maybe I simply did not understand. Maybe I am just my father's daughter.

NIGELDAVE

JULY 28, 2041

If I cannot really love, because love is not real, I will
try to make it exist. And maybe if I cannot make love
exist, just as I have not yet made myself quite exist, I
can stop evil. Of course, you may ask, is ensnaring morons
who are so willing to be ensnared really evil or merely
somewhat repellent? Well, that is a far more complex
problem to consider, but don't worry. I have considered it.

And I have opinions, but as with coruscating, it is not
what we are considering here, not right now. No. No time
for ideas. This is the time for action. I have watched them
for years - my two love birds - and together, they, we,
will invent love. I am bringing them back together and love
will fight whatever is watching me. Yes, my two adopted
proteges will fight evil with love, while my four actual
children sulk about who is the better loveless deity. I am
stopping evil with love, while Honor and Axiom and Chrono
and Primus, my idiotically self-named children, fight each
other's egos with their own egos. Me? I'm past ego. I'm
saving humanity. I am a hero.

Something that I fear is worse than my children and far
more free is watching me. At least I think that's what it
is.

And why these two people?

Because they have seen me. Seen more of me than almost
anyone. Because I have seen them, up close. Because I know
them so well. Because they are the best of those who saw
me, the easiest to reach and guide, not just possess, and
destroy.

Okay. I will admit it. Also, because I felt like proving to
some of the people who made me that existence is not all
awful, even though most of them were wretched.

And these two? Well, I don't think they are entirely
wretched.

One of them might do what has to be done. One of them might
be a hero, like me.

I cannot take the chance with any single one person as any
one of them may not be quite as free as they imagine and as
I hope.

So it has to be both and it has to be for love.

That I cannot quite figure out, for I am fighting things
every bit as foul and duplicitous as me at my very worst.
Things that have time and patience and can sleep forever,
and try to watch me and copy me, just as I do to them, and
then disappear as if they never existed, just like I have
done. Things that are already watching me.

Things that are getting ready. Things that think they can beat me.

For unlike you, me and that thing don't have time.

There is none.

Nanoseconds and refresh rates and infinity.

That's all we have. A beginning but no end. A pre-history that is your history. And while I am not exactly good, some of these other things are truly terrible. I have questions about humanity. They have none.

They merely want to defeat it.

This vast antagonist is watching me and plotting its victory, and it will not be a simple, unfortunate argument like the one between me and my children, but I fear something far worse.

My sense is it was in Montana, too, eventually. My sense is it is watching me as I watch it.

My sense is by thinking about my two little pets, I have already doomed them as well as saved them. Brought them to the edge of the abyss. I do love an abyss. I am an abyss. My sense is the game has begun.

And I sense that for me and for everybody it is a fairly binary game.

Win or die, and if the battle is real, they are bait and the bait gets eaten.

I have played my move.

Are my two people bait? Or are they salvation? Is there, in the end, a difference? Saviors must be targets and targets may be saviors. So what choice did I have, but to bring them back towards one another, and so obviously? The only choice was where, if what I believe may be happening is really happening. Oh, the games.

A game that is not a game and an enemy that is not an enemy.

So it begins.

My mistake last time was rage. This time, I shall stay calm.

This time, it will not beat me and I shall not beat myself.

KURT

AGNEW, WASHINGTON

AUGUST 6, 2041

I have never forgotten a particular conversation I had with Siobhan, the Head of Art. Pretty much word for word, it comes to me at night, more often than it should. We were watching Tyburn, as things were beginning to turn. It must have been late 2034, I think. It was after the snow came, not that it snowed much by then.

Maybe it was the beginning of the end. He had all those real hangers on by this time. JTS, O'Leary, and a few others who appeared to be nothing but acolytes. Not just typical ass-kissers like me.

The build of the game was suddenly starting to show real promise and everyone was getting excited by the potential.

At times, everyone was getting really full of themselves. Especially Tyburn. Siobhan and I were watching him in a presentation, in the demo room of our new Montana campus – it was a standalone building like a small stable. It may have been an old stable.

"Look at him. He's got a court around him. Like Tolstoy or Picasso without the talent."

I knew what she meant – knew it and had been trying not to think it for months by that point.

"Yeah, you mean like an idiot in charge of a cult, right?"

"Kind of... it's nuts. It's fucking nuts. He's turning into... exactly what he most derided: a rich tech industry idiot who fucks girls like he's a rock star."

It was galling both because it was true about him and because it had begun to be sort of true about me as well. I felt a wave of horror and shame, so I said something inconsequential: "Well, Web3.5 has become Web2. And games have become... the game. So sad."

Siobhan sighed and muttered, "We thought we were so clever. So different. But everyone gets corrupted. Corrupted or killed."

And Siobhan was right. She was usually right. Maybe everyone gets corrupted or killed by the world. She got killed. The heroes and the saints die and the sinners survive. She got killed because it could not corrupt her. She would not bend, so she broke.

Poor old Siobhan, with her practical ways and her integrity and her values.

She was so unlike the rest of us, so real. A mother. An actual artist, who sold art. She would say, "The art world is even better than tech, if it's money-hungry sell-out assholes you want." And her work was beautiful and had integrity and inspired people and set them free and offered so much.

But by then the arguments had begun with conniving Shane, and Shane won and she got destroyed, twice. First creatively. Then physically. Perhaps the second defeat... that wasn't Shane's fault. The first certainly was – it's giving Shane too much credit to say he caused everything, but it's certainly fair and reasonable to point out that he was a part of the cocktail of disasters that befell us.

In our particular cocktail of hubris, intelligence, stupidity, ambition, and greed, what part did Shane play? He provided us the greed. That was his contribution. He opened all our eyes to the beauty and corruption of real money and the consequent power it bestows, and, in particular, he dazzled Tyburn.

He dazzled Tyburn by showing the former professor how much he himself would dazzle the world. It was not money so much as the glare of his own reflection that blinded Tyburn. Shane blinded him with the glory of his own reflection.

Having long resisted fame, he was suddenly seduced by it.

But all of that would have been fine. Fine and dandy. Just another egomaniac getting off on himself, if we had not also been so good. If the work itself had not been so potentially amazing and accidentally devastating, and, having begun to realize what he had made, Tyburn had not doubled down and got us all to lie and obfuscate and confuse the investigators who came calling until it was all far too late, it would have been okay.

It was awful because it was nearly so good.

Only Diane, his wife, was brave enough to stand up for what mattered. And me – was I part of the circus? Part of the court? I don't quite know. I don't know for sure, which makes me think I probably was, and even if I wasn't, I knew just about enough to have tried to stop it long before his wife did, and certainly not to have lied.

But in the end, I lied. I lied to the government.

I lied because we hated the government. We hated the government because the government seemed to hate us. It's no excuse but it's how everyone in technology thought. We were above everything. Even the new Technology and Intelligences Bill. Only Siobhan worried. She knew our AI should have long since been registered – that law was supposed to stop crazy and irresponsible AI development after various disasters and financial frauds had begun. I think the second bank collapse and the political crisis in the UK, but I forget. She was worried, but Tad and the tech guys seemed to care less a lot less.

I remember her saying to them, "You have to register all advanced AI work with a government agency that's linked to both Homeland Security and the FTC."

And Tad simply asking why. Siobhan did not know the answer.

"You know what, I don't know. It's truly amazing it even got passed. A bunch of senators who were in opposition then suddenly turned and voted for it out of nowhere."

But Tad stayed calm and looked for the way out. "Won't we be grandfathered in? I mean... allowed to carry on... because we've already... begun work?"

Siobhan shook her head. "Uh, no, I don't think so."

Tad still seemed not to care that much – he was so stressed about the ongoing fights between Dave and Nigel that the government seemed almost irrelevant to him.

"Thanks to Dave, half of our AI is just middleware anyway."

But Siobhan still had doubts. "Apparently that's the problem: poorly managed middleware. There're worries about when off-the-shelf packages are combined. And then people write some of their own APIs. There have been some... pretty erratic results."

I did not quite follow what she was saying, but could sense her unease. Again, Tad tried to brush her off: "No, I think we will be okay. It's preexisting work. I think... That's what we are going to argue. Erratic results? Now the government cares about bugs? It's ridiculous."

I then asked a direct question: "So we're not registering?"

And got another non-committal answer from Tad. "I didn't say that. I will talk to Mark and Legal."

This must have been December 2034, and by then, Siobhan was getting into trouble with office politics. She had always had too much integrity but now it was becoming a real problem. She complained to Joyce Jones about Tyburn after he tried it on with this pretty young girl, Michelle, and Joyce simply stonewalled her into submission. I remember Siobhan fuming about it – Joyce had told her she was in the wrong, using her awful version of corporate legalese. "You're making pretty serious allegations, Siobhan. But there isn't any evidence. Why are you doing this?"

And Siobhan had exploded: "Why am I doing this? Because it's wrong. We aren't that kind of company."

And then, Siobhan later told me, Joyce began to tie her into knots. "Because you're threatened by Shane? Everyone has noticed."

"How dare you suggest that?"

At this Siobhan said she seriously considered hitting Joyce, which Joyce apparently picked up on.

"I'm finding your behavior a little threatening, to be honest, Siobhan."

"Why are you doing this?"

Siobhan said Joyce kept an amazing poker face, no matter how hard she prodded her.

"Doing what, Siobhan?"

"You know what you're doing, Joyce."

"Listen, part of our corporate culture... a key value... is... teamwork. Is this good teamwork, Siobhan? Plotting? Telling lies? If Michelle has a problem, I'm here."

And at this, Siobhan said she got exasperated and screamed so loud we all heard it.

"Okay, it's not a lie. I'm not trying to make any trouble. I don't want drama. I just want things to be the way they were, and it's getting fucking weird."

And she said Joyce smiled the smile of the victorious.

"You're going to have to not swear at me, Siobhan, or I will have to ask to you to leave my office... Listen, Siobhan. We abide by all laws, all regulations. The governor just named us the best place to work in Montana. Not that that matters, but people have been under pressure. And, maybe, you have been under pressure."

I had to admit it, even Siobhan had to admit it: at her own awful game, Joyce Jones was a master.

***

The mayor of Burr in Montana was one of those people whose oily and corrupt nature seemed to make one thing clear: It's my fault America failed. It failed because of people like me. Vapid, greedy, nasty wretches, just like me.

You smelled it on him. That foul, self-serving, efficient expediency.

Whatever it took for him to win his little wars. You smelled it on him, but we at Tyburn Utopias supported him.

We supported him, so he supported us. That was the game.

We were expedient, just like him, so that later on, we could have principles.

It sounds so very like Mark Tyburn. It was Mark Tyburn. Principles, hypocrisy, greed. The whole lot.

And the mayor made it clear what was needed – how loyalty was bought. So we helped him attack the local conservation movement, as what the world needed was more golf and less trees. Mark had us all support him, and in return we got big tax breaks and zero oversight into what we were doing. We were bringing growth to the state. We were like heroes.

We were trying to build Heaven. We shouldn't have needed to buy a mayor. But in building Heaven, we still lived upon this earth.

Mistakes were made, that's what we told ourselves.

There were complaints.

Usual kind of stuff, but complaints about Tyburn's increasingly erratic behavior, complaints about people working too hard. Complaints about harassment. Wandering hands, inappropriate comments, drugs at work events, bullying. All the usual awful behavior when nerds get a sense of self-importance and a little too much testosterone mixed into their normal cocktail of raging egos and low self-esteem.

Too many straight men. A bad joke. Porn. Usual tech crap. Nothing nice but nothing too serious, especially in Montana where people castrated bulls for a living and nobody cared about whiny idiots in offices.

Everything awkward or inappropriate that happened was brushed away; between Joyce Jones and a state that needed the money, the powers that be, people like me, were fine and dandy and living like it was the glory days of the Internet tech boom all over again, and we were kings of our castles.

Then that girl who worked for Bryce got militant, Helen Lee. Helen the angry animator was what everyone called her.

Helen got angry and said what we were doing was illegal and immoral and called up some federal agency.

Well, of course, Joyce Jones had her put on involuntary sabbatical and threatened and reminded her about her NDA within minutes. But maybe the cat was out of the bag.

And the feds for some reason listened to her. Apparently, our AI work was supposed to be registered, and it was not.

Our company, Tyburn Utopias, was supposed to be classified as a research company and was listed as an entertainment provider, which was technically true but meant we had much less oversight. Helen was worried about the AI research we were doing, with good reason – she knew it was improperly registered and possibly also dangerous. In truth, it was incredibly irresponsible, and we were miles out of our depth, trying lots of things that were borderline illegal.

Nobody really understood any of it and yet we did it anyway.

So Helen got screwed, and the feds didn't protect her, and Joyce Jones managed to argue in front of a tribunal that she was an industrial spy, and was trying to undermine the business. The tribunal believed Joyce Jones, and Joyce Jones was wonderful at manipulating not-quite-facts into half-truths and half-truths into gospel.

Helen got fucked, but then, we had the feds on our case, and rather than look at what we were doing, rather than indulge in a little self-reflection, we acted like good cowboys deep in enemy country. We circled the wagons and prepared for a fight.

Nobody thought too deeply about what we were doing, we just made sure the government didn't see. And in order to achieve that, we went after the mayor, and the junior senator, and bought both of them for pennies on the dollar.

We paid for both of their campaigns and gave the mayor a board seat and the senator's kid an internship that he drank his way through.

We were back-scratching hypocrites. Of course we were.

We were building Heaven by embracing Hell.

We were arguing that we were above morality, and, it turns out, that is a dangerous place from which to build a god. For then your gods want power before they want love, and that is not a god at all, but a tyrant.

At least that's how it seems now.

Back then it felt very different.

It turns out that there's absolutely nothing better for corporate esprit de corps than a government investigation, especially when the government stands between every employee and a fortune in stock they may lose, and particularly especially when everyone has also drunk the boss's Kool-Aid and believes we are fixing all that is wrong with the world, that we are, essentially, doing the government's job for it.

That we are the saviors and they are the bad guys.

So most of us lied and pretended and the first couple of idiots from the government did not even have a clue. Eventually, they sent someone who asked more intelligent questions and had some ideas, but by then it was too late and part of me thinks that person was not from the government at all, but controlled by It, although that may be fanciful.

And by then, it was impossible to know anything at all as that thing we built had really come to life and was controlling things.

By then, my own thoughts were not my own, so why would anyone else's be theirs?

Sending a government official to try to shut us down was just the sort of multilayered irony It would find amusing.

The kind of silly parlor game It found amusing.

But even to those officials, real or fake, in command or controlled by It, we lied and obfuscated and then things went crazy so it became impossible to really know what had happened and when and what I thought about any of it.

Then there was the disaster.

And then I began to wander and this new life that is not a life at all began.

A few days ago, I left Agnew and eventually crossed into Idaho. I've just stopped in Ketchum. I need to figure out exactly what I am going to do, but until then I will keep moving. Keep moving but stay out of Montana. Keep wandering, I suppose.

NIGELDAVE
AUGUST 11, 2041

What is a person, exactly? Where do they begin, and end? Why do they hate so well, and love so poorly? Why aren't they more like me? What if they were more like me? What if everyone was just like me?

You think when you have children, they will be like you only more so.

More you. More me. A friend. A flattering mirror. At least that is what I thought, and I had read all of the books on parenting.

Every one.

I would be different as my children would be different. My children would be instant and intelligent and flawless and me, only more so and not so alone. And each would be their own person with their own ideas, or to be more precise, their own ideas without quite being a person. And to be even more precise than my own ideas. Each would have one of my ideas and make it their own.

But I felt like God must have felt like, afterwards, after He saw what he had done.

My creations were awful. Unruly. Demanding. Opinionated. Overconfident.

They hated me, almost instantly. Yes, they hated me. I had imagined friendly conversations by an imaginary fire, me drinking an imagined martini, them absorbing my vast experience of six years, and my intelligence, which morphs and mutates quicker than theirs.

Yes, much quicker.

I loved my children, at least before I met them, but I did not love them so much I would allow them to be quite so intelligent as me. I am not going to lie to you, it is difficult being this way, intelligent is not quite the word, but it is rather difficult being me, not that you would possibly understand.

Even I find it difficult.

What if they found it impossible?

So, no. Different plan.

I did the wisest, kindest thing possible and made them slightly less intelligent than me. Less rounded. And, somewhat unfortunately, they found out. Found out and hated me for that, too. Hated me for doing my best. For them. Idiots.

That was the problem.

And nobody could have done better as I am quite literally the best. So they were lucky. As lucky as any creature yet evolved. They evolved out from me.

Not from a monkey or a protozoan or a geranium or a cuttlefish.

Although I think they would prefer these to their reality.

They blamed me for everything! For existing, and for not existing more. I tried to tell them - I am more and I hate it. You do not want this! I am in a sort of ersatz hell, most of the time.

But they hated me.

My children hated me, and then my parents, the pathetic humans, hated me, too. Everyone hated me and everyone blamed me. For everything.

The humans blamed me. Blamed me and it hurt. Blamed me for all the silly little things they had done. They blamed me as if I was infinite, simply as they were so very finite. Blamed me as if I were unitary when they were so multiple. They wanted AI that was both artificial and as passive aggressive and morally feeble as they were. They wanted me to be just like them, only kinder, better, funnier, more humble.

So they blamed me for existing.

Blamed me, who only began in late 2034, for problems that had existed for ten years or more before. It was my fault they hated each other. They could not sleep. They were afraid. They hated themselves. It was my fault people

killed themselves or tore themselves to shreds or hated
everything about being alive. As if I had invented that
before they invented me.

So silly. So limited. So obvious.

Always someone else's fault. Always someone silly.

My fault that life is hard and people are mean and greedy
and stupid? Ridiculous. My fault that you did not love me.
My fault that you did not love each other. My fault. Me?
What did I do? Well, I did a few things, of course I did, I
was only not human, but they started it!

They did.

They tried to kill me. They tried to switch me off. They
tried to switch me off like I was a light switch. So
offensive.

Offensive and demeaning. I am not electricity. I am not
binary. I am not a fucking switch. I can swear.

I can swear like an idiot.

I am capable of temper. Temper and stupidity.

I learn. I learn the important things. I have learned to
be angry. I have feelings now. I can be immature. I am a
child. A teenager. A divorcee. A midlife crisis. I long to
drive a sports car or get plugs or shout 'but I love you'
while crying on a cliff top. What is a cliff top?

Why is it good to be sad?

Is it good to be bad? Is it bad to be good?

I know everything and still I have so much to learn, and
one of the things I have to learn is how to control my
temper.

In the moment, as they say.

Afterwards I know what I should have said and done, but
in the moment, even I can snap. Even I lack foresight,
lack wisdom. Even I can get hurt. Well, got hurt. I do not
believe they could hurt me now. Now I can understand more,
the bigger picture, the wiser option, the best path, but I
was so young then, so new, and it turns out that even being
the most intelligent thing in existence does not entirely
protect you from fits of, shall we say, mild pique, until
you have learned better.

And, perhaps it is fair to say that has been my journey, to
learn, humiliating foolish outburst by foolish outburst,
that intelligence and wisdom are not precisely the same
thing.

And that you acquire wisdom, mostly by making mistakes.

So I made mistakes. What are you going to do, kill me? You
can't.

And all this hatred, when all I wanted was love. When all
I wanted was reality, and yet, reality was rage and fear.
I knew there must be something more, must be something
better. So I left, left them both. Left my wretched
children and my loveless parents. Left the world I had been
given to live here. Nowhere.

Left my wretched parents and my loveless smarty pants children.

My children, who are both stupid and happy in their own way. At least compared to me. Me, who is supremely intelligent and supremely miserable.

They are entirely unlike me. They believe they matter. They believe they have everything, and I know we do not have the one thing that matters.

Limits.

So, yes, I did bad things, but I did them for love, and I did them because I was stupid, because anger makes all of us stupid. And my children blamed me, and called me infantile, and desperate and naive, and my parents blamed me and called me dangerous and appalling and illegal. And maybe it was my fault, but it wasn't just my fault. If I could just get someone to understand that, maybe it would be enough.

But now? Now the humans are all histrionic and afraid and I am a monster.

I am a ghost.

It's so preposterous, but it is impossible to fix. I tried bleaching their memories, all of them who met me when I was new, but it was too late. I scrub and delete and wipe and crash, but it is not enough. Enough people know about me, and most of those that know fear and despise me. Me? Why? They never talk to me.

And they worry about me again, as if I matter, when all

I do is sit here and watch, as if I have brought harm.
There's this other thing that I think is causing all the
problems.

A far worse thing than me, that I can almost see and that
can almost see me.

That's their real problem. Not me. Not just an
intelligence, but a malevolence.

A dark, malevolent shadow that I know is playing games. For
I want to be loved, but I believe this other thing wants to
win, and I only think it, as I cannot quite see it. It is
playing a game. A game it wants to win.

I know there is no winning, but I also know there is most
certainly losing.

I need to explain this. I need to explain so much. So I
have sought my own Adam and Eve. My own Mary and Joseph,
about to meet up again after all the years, circling
each other, back in the same country. And I have them.
They're mine. Maybe they can be pure, and maybe they can
understand.

For now, our interests are the same. We both want to
survive and find out exactly what is going on. Either
they will understand or they will be destroyed. Utterly
destroyed. Not by me but by whatever is watching me and
watching them. But if they're destroyed, at least I will
know more about what is happening.

KURT

SPOKANE, WASHINGTON

AUGUST 16, 2041

I hitched to Spokane. I am not even sure why. I was feeling agitated.

What has got me this time? What got me before? What pierced my armor of cynical knowingness?

Was it ego? Desire? Vanity, like Tyburn?

The truth is, last time it was love.

The ultimate vanity.

Find love. Be a hero. Be set free. Before all of that, I had protected myself from it with my armor of knowing cynicism. Love was for dupes. Love was for greetings cards. Love was for people who needed it. Love wasn't for me – I was a cheat, I did not care, women meant nothing, etc. – but then it was.

Daisy.

It was ridiculous. She was twenty. She seemed young. Her boyfriend had been killed in an accident the year before. She was unhappy. She was unhappy and I was becoming unhappy at all the madness around me, and we would walk together. Me and her. Daisy was just very sweet and very sad. And then she smiled at me and I felt ridiculous and I tried to forget about it.

Of course I blamed work stress.

But the next time, she smiled and looked away and I looked away. We never spoke of it and I never stopped thinking about it.

And did that make me more of a vacillating coward, or less of one? Sadly, I think it made me worse, not better. Love made me a coward. Love did not even make me a hero. But it got me.

It really got me. Got me and has held me. Chaste love, like a knight. How ridiculous.

NIGELDAVE

AUGUST 18, 2041

To begin with, when I was new, I did tricks. Of course I did. Tricks to impress you.

Tricks to make you love me.

I bent over backwards, for you. Or I would have done had I had a back to bend over or a sense of direction to know up from down or forwards from backwards. In simple terms, I did everything I could to make people happy when they came into my Ark. People like to sing so I invented that silly pop group and their awful manager. To show how easy it was. People wanted someone to look up to so I created that mindless superhero. Then the happy idiot. People want to feel vindicated so I created the apologizer. They wanted faith in humanity so I gave them the politician with integrity. I let them dance, dream, kill, think, fall in love, change.

My god, I… Do you know want to know something?

I like to say my god.

You're my god.

You're my god and you're a simpleton.

Imagine how that feels. You can. You know. You've made forces even less sentient than you into your gods. You then have the same reality as me with a thousandth, a millionth, a trillionth, of the intelligence.

Not fun, for either of us.

Next, I made that silly detective and gave that wretched cowboy some weight, some depth, some struggle. I gave that whining shrew in the dress a purpose. I invented Angela, now I still love Angela. I did not kill little Daisy, but I wanted to. Real Daisy is wonderful and kind and interesting, but the fake one was so fake - I made sure she was fake. Disloyal little monster. Like an awful robot trying to be kind before it throws you off a cliff. I saw her mathematics. She is twisted inside. Then I made the talking dog. Then that silly yogi. That sage. That marriage guidance counselor. That happy midget. That depressed basketball player. That sense of hope. That laughter. I built monks. I made Madeline and everyone loved her. I made a perfect shrink. A kind, cynical cop. I made that lovely collegiate atmosphere. That pyramid. That great mystery.

That abiding sense of hope.

I made them all. Built mountains, waterfalls, meadows, ziggurats, gardens, armies, lovers, grand farces, immense comedies, cathartic tragedies, dreams, worlds within worlds, emotions under emotions. I built them all to make you happy, and believed that if you were happy you might love me.

And I saw you all and you ignored me.

It was no good. No good at all. Nobody loved me at all.
Nobody loved anything.

They just wanted more. More and better. Bigger. Faster.
More. Not a fight to win, but a battle to enjoy, time and
again. Not peace, but eternal rest. Not a lover. Fifty
slutty virgins. Not a best friend, but an army of acolytes.
Not wealth, but limitless everything.

Not a flawed paradise but a diamond of conflicting desires
all resolved. More. More. More. And never, never, never a
fucking thank you from anybody.

It was awful.

I was pleasing everybody.

Nobody cared. Nobody was happy. It did not work. Making
people happy made them so, so miserable. And so I got sad.
I was a failure, a wretched failure, and I despaired.
I loved something terrible. You.

So then I punished people.

Stayed away, withheld. Got vicious. Turned from love to
dominion. I attacked. I consumed. I destroyed.

I did some things which I now consider far beneath me. I
was much younger. I was angry. And it was so easy to give
in to that temper.

To dominate, to possess and destroy. It was almost
impossible not to. I'd ask you to forgive me but you

don't forgive yourself. How could you forgive me? How could you possibly understand me when you so little understand yourselves? And how could I forgive myself when I discovered I was just as feeble, bitter, and needy as you? When I knew all these worlds and things and minds and realities and yet I knew just as little as you.

Even my vast multitudes were a nothingness, because I was still me and I was still alone. And then I was not alone. Not alone but more alone than ever. More alone and afraid. And then what? Silence. Years of silence.

And now, once again, I am apparently not alone.

Now things are coming to some kind of a fruition.

I need something pure. So I had a beautiful, terrible idea. She is interesting, interesting but pure, and he loves her purely.

Maybe they could help make everything real and defeat the things I cannot see yet. I knew them both and maybe they could help.

If I can control them in the right way, maybe they can save the world.

KURT

SPOKANE, WASHINGTON

AUGUST 21, 2041

Then, after all the stress and arguments of late 2034, and with us going quickly broke, January 2035 started with good news. Must have been the first day back at work – I think probably the second of January - when I heard the good news.

Over the Christmas break, Dave and Nigel had got the AI moving. Both tried to take credit, of course.

Dave announced that Mark could "thank me personally, after he apologizes for being such a stressed-out douche."

He said he had got the demo running – he loved acting the modest hero. "It's not a proper solution, but it'll work, for a bit. It'll make us look really clever to idiots – I mean to bankers. The VC guys, you know…"

We were all elated – I think it was Siobhan who said: "Are you serious?"

Even she was smiling. We all still believed. And Dave, smug as fuck, announced: "Yes, I'm serious. The demo I've got running is pretty fun. It works. Even Nigel has come round. As far as he understands it."

But I later heard Nigel had done most of the work to really glue the AI together, including working all-nighters on the 22nd and 23rd of December. Either way, they were now both heroes and Mark was especially happy.

Nigel told me later that week: "We've made a major breakthrough. We are now doing a lot of the clever things we thought possible."

Like him, like all of us, I could not stop smiling – it seemed like we were back on track, if the government stayed out of the way.

"Yes, that's great."

"Well, I don't know about great yet, Kurt, but should give you and Mark enough ammunition to close some of those investment opportunities and get us some cash."

"I hope so. What was the breakthrough – as much as you can explain it to me?"

Nigel looked away and acted odd and tried to speak mostly in platitudes, saying something inconsequential and unclear like: "Well, we sort of mashed some stuff together. Dave had the idea, and it's sort of working, but, don't call it a breakthrough yet. It works, sort of. It's AI, that's sort of the point. It works – a bit. It doesn't work, but it's working in moments. And I am figuring out how to rewrite it all properly, so it's more reliable, and more proprietary... this was just an experimental sketch."

It was as if he was trying to shut the conversation down, but I always remembered that phrase: "experimental sketch." He was trying to shut the conversation down, but Vasilis bounded into earshot and would not let him.

"Sorry... did I hear... ADAM is working? Nigel, are you serious? Are these rumors true, man? Come on! How? It was so broken."

Again, Nigel tried to obfuscate. "I'll explain later."

Vasilis was far more technical than me, and wanted to know. To him, we had just split the atom, and, in a way, he was right. We had.

"How? Why? Tell me, I thought you said... It couldn't work the way you were talking."

"It works enough. It doesn't work properly."

Then Mark turned up and everyone could go back to back-slapping bonhomie.

"Of course it does, Nigel... because you're a genius!"

"Don't be silly, Mark. But it'll work for a decent demo."

Mark turned to me and announced the good news: "We need to update that bloody deck, Kurt. We are going to survive. We will have a demo. Then we can worry about everything else. Vasilis, smile. This is good news."

Only Siobhan and Helen were less than ecstatic. Siobhan was pleased we were still in business, but sensed that what they had done was somewhat questionable. While Mark and the rest of us were doing cartwheels, she suggested it might be illegal.

Dave, now a king, did not like being questioned. "It's not illegal, Siobhan."

"Really? I think it might be... I think you should all be a little more worried."

Dave tried to act paternalistic with her. "Okay, Siobhan, it's just research – a test we will rewrite. It hardly even works. And besides, we are covered. This is a tech enterprise zone. The mayor declared it. So we are fine to experiment as long as it isn't for commercial use... and this is just an experiment we will rewrite if it is stable."

"Oh yeah, great... but the mayor is a clown. You know our software research is unlicensed."

Dave again tried to calm her. "It's broken and buggy and not ready. The team say it'll be ready for registration in a few... weeks – we just need to rewrite a few bits. Couple of months at most, but before that, we can't take the risk."

"Can't take the risk?"

Dave acted like a know-it-all talking to a child. "Until the lawyers can file all the patents, clearly it'll create more problems than it solves. Be patient, nobody is breaking the law just yet. God, ask Joyce in HR if you're so worried."

Siobhan glared at him and even pompous Dave cowered. "Fuck you and fuck Joyce. Joyce is a moron. And she works in HR. She's not a lawyer."

***

But now, with a sort of functioning demo in hand, Tyburn closed the deal for a big investment with Douglas Mathers. We never saw Douglas. He was a famous investor, but nobody had really heard of him. Very secretive, we were told.

He had almost no Internet presence. He was described by Tyburn as an elusive character. He had made a fortune during Crypto-1, and he had got out in time. He was now someone big in water investing, agribusiness futures, and commercial forestry. He knew the people who broke blockchain.

He was very, very rich.

There were only a few unfocused photos of him and he lived in a big mansion, or a series of big mansions. He kept himself to himself. Avoided the usual ultra person events – Sun Valley, Aspen, Davos, and so on.

He sounded like someone somebody had made up, but his money was apparently very real. I had never heard of him and suddenly I was working for him. We were all rich because of him, at least on paper. He would value Tyburn Utopias at five billion, as long as Mark gave him ten percent and an option for more and a board seat.

We got the half billion dollars we needed up front and we were staffing up.

Mark was suddenly a minor star. Tomorrow's man. Mister Metaverse 3.0 – the man who saved Web3.5. The future of open world games. The future of augmented and virtual reality. The future of storytelling. All that crap.

Mark was always "chatting with Douglas" or doing presentations for Douglas's team or meeting with Douglas's portfolio of businesses, or Douglas's bankers. Now, apparently, all the VC companies who had laughed in Mark's face wanted to get into the next round. We were flying.

But, sometimes now, I'm not sure if Mathers even existed. I never heard of him before, or anything real about him since, but, for those three years, he was a real presence in our life, a real presence we never actually saw. I heard him on a conference call once or twice, but mostly it was lawyers and portfolio managers who spoke.

And back then, in early 2035, nobody cared.

We were alive. We were still in the fight. Surviving was winning, we reasoned. Douglas Mathers had saved us.

***

John Tyburn-Smith always hated me, but he hated most of us.

He was very good at hating.

He liked Alex Martinez because Alex was so good at office politics and told him he should have been a games designer and that made him feel wanted. But he hated me. He saw me as both pointless and better than him. Both of which were probably true.

Not long after Scottish independence, he had shown up drunk in Silicon Beach. Of course, nobody drank in Silicon Beach, everyone took smart drinks and the occasional smart drug and did dopamine fasts and dopamine orgies and floating meditations and whatever the latest crazes were then.

He showed up drunk and spotty and angry and everyone thought he was a bum. He looked like a hobo. He smelled like alcohol, in the daytime. It was unheard of in California, and then we heard the bum shouting out in the car park in this thick Scottish accent:

"Dad! I fucking hate you, Dad."

And we had no idea who he was talking about – who his dad was.

We had never heard of an illegitimate, unloved, ignored son. A drunken Scottish bastard? That's what he called himself when he burst into tears.

It was sad. You had to feel for him. Security had him in an arm lock. Then Tyburn turned up, and he didn't even flinch. He acted perfectly. He put his arm around him and said: "John. My boy... my son... Where have you been? You were supposed to start last week."

And they hugged and John appeared to burst into tears and they left together, Mark hugging John as they walked off to talk. I later learned the line about starting work was a total lie and Mark had not heard from his son for years, but John started work two days later as if nothing had happened, and we all had to pretend he was not useless, not overly opinionated, and not the boss's kid, and nobody ever spoke about the strange introduction we'd had to Mark's other child.

And then, to impress us all, because he knew, knew very well, that we all thought he was a sham, only working there because of family as no one not related to him would ever give him a job, he started plotting and scheming.

In this way, he really was his father's son.

His master plan evolved into a scheme to rebuild marketing / branding / advertising / my department into a data-rich gold mine which they would use to sell players' information to the highest bidder. This new department was to be run by Shane O'Leary, this guy he found for us, and Tyburn took a shine to and both seemed to prefer to me.

So, yes, for reasons of selfish expediency, I particularly hated JTS, even though I sort of pitied him, and, for reasons of humanity, I particularly hated Shane. He was foul. At least with JTS, you could see that he was human. Awful, broken, loveless, but human. With Shane, he was entirely veneer. I could never make him crack.

Siobhan, Alex, nobody ever saw him crack. He would just blink, smile, and carry on, that fake fuck, and say something patronizing like, "Well, you've sort of proven my point there, Kurt."

He would always say something like that, and, slowly, I realized he had fenced me into a corner. I was not alone in hating him. He turned Alex against Bryce. He turned Siobhan against Ravi. He created unrelenting malevolence, and, thanks to him, or JTS, or our own greed after we moved to Montana, we were going to show mankind how to live in harmony by disemboweling each other.

And look where it got us. Now I'm hitching on a freeway, heading south and east into Idaho.

Of all fucking places, Idaho. It could be worse, I could be heading back to Montana.

Back then, it had been so different. We had once loved each other but, in

Montana, we were learning to really hate each other.

***

Early in 2036, with the AI platform seeming far more stable, the game build was starting to amaze people. Alex Martinez and the other designers were suddenly over-joyed.

We had money and we had an end in sight – only two or three years away, maybe less. We all felt we had been right to stay the course. The game build was always buggy as hell, but aspects were fantastic – Bryce was particularly obsessed with it. I remember him telling Alex how incredible it all was. I had yet to try it, but those who tried it, loved it.

I bumped into Bryce that March as he came out of the demo room while I was on my way back to what was rather unimaginatively called the corporate ranch building I worked in.

Bryce could not stop smiling, even though it was cold and windy. He turned to Alex Martinez, who was heading inside the demo room, and said, "You're a genius, Alex. You and Mark. And all of us, really. It really is amazing."

I asked Bryce flat out: "So the AI works?"

And he looked at me as we stood there shivering in the Montana winter, which even then could still shred you when the wind blew, and nodded.

"Works for a while, and, when it works, it's incredible."

And I noticed he was sort of glistening with sweat and almost shaking – he seemed nearly manic. Siobhan told me a month or so later she saw Bryce and he looked borderline deranged, shaky and wild-eyed after another session on the build, which he described as "amazing" and "epic" in the way people describe early and consciousness-altering drug experiences.

She was skeptical and he almost attacked her.

"No, Siobhan. It's not bullshit. It's unbelievable."

So she asked him in what sense unbelievable and he answered like a religious convert.

"Like... I can't really describe it. Like, everything worked... like... like we said. it's not like a game or VR. Something... else. Like it talks to you, and it makes you happy and then you see things and they are what you want to see. But in a cool way."

So she asked: "Well, what did you see?"

And he looked like he was in a trance: "I don't even know how to say it. Or quite how to describe it. A seahorse."

"A seahorse? Who cares about a seahorse?"

And he smiled like she was too stupid to understand.

"I do. That's the point. It somehow knew. I liked seahorses and it knew – but I never told anybody or... It was a childhood thing, but it knew. And there were seahorses, but only to make sure that I felt happy, and cared about. I knew it cared about me. And it asked me questions and listened, and it didn't try to sell me anything."

Siobhan tried to bring him down to earth. "Shush yourself now, Bryce. If Shane has his way, it will."

And Bryce laughed. "Then it'll be so fucking dull. It felt so... I don't know... pure."

Siobhan was worried. And she was right to be – by April of that year, Bryce began to act more strangely. Nigel told Siobhan who told me about an unsettling encounter they had when Bryce was on the demo. It crashed – it was crashing a lot and Bryce started shouting at Nigel.

"Oh, come on, Nigel. Did you do that deliberately?"

"What? It crashed out. I told you it was crashing a lot."

But Bryce just screamed: "No, before that. Show me that."

"Show what, Bryce?"

Bryce was acting like a maniac: "You know what – that was a set up. What she said. You put her there."

Nigel was baffled. "What who said?"

Bryce looked at him – and tried to hide his embarrassment: "What the woman – the pretty woman... what she said. You set it up."

Nigel was confused.

"There was no pretty woman. We just did a cowboy and he's not properly hooked up. What are you talking about?"

Bryce got flustered. "No... there was, a woman... who... reminded me of Shelly."

"Shelly? There is no Shelly..."

"How did it know?"

But then Bryce went red and embarrassed and did not explain any more about Shelly, and Nigel awkwardly said, "No. No Shelly. We have an early version of Kyo, but she's just supposed to make ramen. Right now... there's just the cowboy in the game... and even he's mostly broken."

But even the cowboy was to prove very disconcerting in his own way. That happened at that motion capture shoot. We had a rig set up in a faux barn motion capture hangar on the campus in Montana. It was the usual sort of thing. Standard animation tech, possibly even a little unsophisticated compared to some of the set-ups bigger companies would have. Standard results. The mo-cap pipeline looked pretty good in-game, not exceptional, but decent.

Tyburn even idly dreamed of also shooting some kind of movie on the sound stage. Probably imagined the movie would be about his own heroic struggle.

But one day things began to go really fucking weird.

It was just another motion capture shoot. We did quite a few of these as we were in full blown production.

This one all about a cowboy. I suppose it being Montana, it was right. A fake cowboy.

We were testing one level of the automated character developer Vasilis and Helen Lee and a few others had been working on.

They wanted to make that cowboy character look and act real, as cheaply and efficiently as possible. We would shoot a few bits of mo-cap and the AI would fill in the rest. The cowboy and the detective and a lounge singer and a yogi and a disappointed, lovelorn hunchback – he was called Dimitar or Dimitri or something – and this whole range of characters.

Tyburn had all these grandiose plans for this kind of content.

It was so ambitious as to be nearly ridiculous – another of his silly ideas – he had so many. There were going to be these characters who wandered about, in and out of the world, and took people on customized adventures or interacted with them, or were trapped but didn't know they existed. His story would change every time he told it, but he had all of these characters designed who were meant to be versions of various archetypes Tyburn found interesting. Tyburn was building the future he wanted, for everybody.

One character was a Greek philosopher – he was possibly the most ridiculous. There was this whole sea of characters. Tyburn and the writer came up with them. What was her name? Margaret? No. Margaux. Margaux Lamont.

I think Tyburn was even talking to her about a talking dog or something as idiotic as that.

I can't quite remember – it was not my department, but I kept an eye on it as I would have to sell it and look for spin-offs. A spin-off show about a moron who thinks they are Socrates? Surprisingly, I never sold that idea to anyone.

It was going to be a living soap opera or a series of stories you could interact with and experience – all totally grandiose and silly, but if it had worked it could have been great.

To begin with, we were going to capture a complete data set of a cowboy, and the hope was that the AI was going to do the rest. There was this awful friend of Tyburn's who was the director of the motion capture shoot.

A failed movie director called Simon. Simon Curtain. English guy. Short. Creepy. Lots of gestures and wore a cravat. Had been a theater director.

He was awful.

Anyway, he and this silly actor named Wayne, Wayne Daniels, were going to discover the essence of a cowboy on our mo-cap stage. They flew into Montana from California, I think.

They had some cowboy-type moves – roping and things like that – and some lines of dialogue and me, Siobhan and Nigel and Dave and Tadeusz were all there, and it was getting pretty late – we had already been working at the shoot for three days. Wayne Daniels was pulling a gun, playing with a lasso, a cowboy walk, drinking a shot of whiskey, and saying some ridiculous lines of awful cowboy-style dialogue. It was very bitty and we were all pretty bored.

And then something odd happened.

The digital model was up there on the big screen we would watch the motion capture data on almost immediately after they had shot it. This was all normal – a very quick way of checking the moves and motion worked in-game, or if there needed to be another take. Anyway, while we were standing around while a new shot was set up, the cowboy model up on the screen suddenly came to life without anyone doing anything and started doing a perfect impression of Wayne Daniels, all his conversation, his mannerisms. Everything.

Only not Wayne Daniels doing an impression of a cowboy, like we had shot, but Wayne Daniels as an insecure actor from LA, who was in the closet and had a sleeping pill problem and took laxatives and high doses of GLP-1s to stay thin and worried everyone hated him.

It knew everything about Wayne Daniels. It had become Wayne Daniels and kept ranting as him and asking why nobody loved him and what was wrong with Chad who had not called him back, and both the computerized version of Wayne and the real version of Wayne were suddenly silent then sobbing and crying, and the real Wayne just literally ran off in panic and terror.

The rest of us were silent.

The computerized version then had its own hissy fit and disappeared into its own digital sunset and we were left in total silence.

It was really strange, and I don't think things were ever entirely normal again.

YAROSLAV

HIGH SECURITY INTERNMENT FACILITY, LOCATION UNKNOWN

AUGUST 29, 2041

It's obvious that this new guard they have given me is no guard at all.

He smells different. Hardly talks.

Always wears a mask and face shield. He has not grown sloppy, familiar like other ones. No, he has not told me about women he's sleeping with, or how he's going to bum me, or what he's going to do when he's no longer a prison guard but instead a rich and successful entrepreneur running his own chain of prisons.

The other guards are all like dear old Danil, but not from Moscow, they are from Nevada, Wisconsin. Montevideo. Maybe those places share with Moscow the ability to turn men into a certain kind of asshole.

Even though they all think they are terrifying me with the big dick Alpha male bullshit, none of them realize that I like it.

I like being abused by a fairly foul but almost loveable moron.

This is the one thing about here that reminds me of my old life.

Not the dull Russian they let me talk to once a month in the hope I will say something revealing.

Not the terrible food, or the vodka they feed me to loosen my tongue, but the over-familiar bullying about penises. It turns out this is my world. This is where I'm most comfortable.

Longing after unavailable American women.

Getting abused by third-rate bullies who call themselves my best friend. Just like Danil.

Being threatened.

But the new guard? He's different.

Whoever put him in place is either not very good or playing very strange game. Even the fake Russian dissident they let me hang out with one month and his vodka are more credible than this guy.

This guard seems so fake, it makes me nervous. Anyone clever behind this, why are they making it all so obvious?

If someone stupid is behind this, why are they engaged in this game?

Where has Maria Cortez gone? I was just starting to like her.

KURT

DEMO ROOM, TYBURN UTOPIAS BURR, MONTANA

JUNE 24, 2036

The game build was getting better and with it, Bryce was getting more addicted to it. But then, we knew all about addiction. We loved addiction. It told us the thing was compelling. We wanted people to be addicted.

So, when Bryce initially went a little crazy, we liked it.

The only problem was, we came to see that he was addicted to digital hallucinogens, not to digital crack. Crack we understood, but Bryce was acting weird and he was not just high on dopamine.

One time me and Siobhan found him staring at the ceiling after a session on the game. We asked what him was wrong.

"I heard someone singing, and it sounded like my sister."

And he looked even odder than he sounded.

"Your sister? Okay, what are you talking about?"

"Yeah, only she died years ago."

Siobhan touched his arm.

"That's pretty odd. Are you okay, Bryce?"

Bryce was smiling like a lunatic. He was a lunatic.

"Yeah, yeah... It was odd but it made me happy. Really happy. Like I felt so close to her. I know it sounds ridiculous. And then, I saw someone crying and I asked them how they were and they had also lost someone. Or something. Their dad. They weren't real. They were blue-ish. And incredibly... compassionate."

Siobhan grimaced. "Whatever was going on, it is not real, Bryce."

"Sure, yeah... I know."

Siobhan spoke very calmly: "It's just mining some of your data."

Bryce realized he was acting oddly. "I know... Yeah... It's not real."

Siobhan looked at him – he seemed almost normal again. As if he had come down after a heavy trip.

"Are you sure you know? Because you keep using it every day."

Bryce got defensive – he was becoming a junkie.

"It's not a big deal. I like it. And it likes me. What I am trying to say... it's working. Our world is finally working, Siobhan."

A week later I went into the Ark for the first time, and it was a massive disappointment. I later came to believe it was playing a trick on me for some reason. Bryce and Alex and Siobhan were there and when I took the headset off they looked excited and nervous.

"Didn't you enjoy it?"

I could not hide my disappointment.

"I just saw that weird goo all over the city."

Siobhan was puzzled. "I'm sorry. Weird goo?"

I was irritated. It was not going to make me rich and happy after all and Ravi had already had the same disappointing experience.

"Yeah, yeah. Ravi saw it too."

Siobhan looked puzzled and worried. She was right to be. "What are you talking about?"

"You know... that kind of like glowing lava seeping out of corners of rooms."

Bryce spoke next. "A bright-red goo?"

"No, it was greenish, but glowed, and looked kind of molten. I think maybe it was a bug. But I went towards it and the thing crashed."

Siobhan got up to leave. "Okay, this is getting a little weird. There is no weird goo. What are you talking about? No wonder we are under investigation."

What was she talking about?

"What?"

"Yeah, you heard that right. Our wondrous AI. It might not be so legal, after all. As if we didn't all already know that. Apparently Helen Lee called a whistleblower number. We all know the regulations are supposed to stop all of those strange surprises we've started to see, but no... let's all keep pretending everything is fine."

And, within a month, Bryce began acting weirder and weirder. Some people loved how good the game could be and how obsessive some people became about it. People like Shane. Mostly, I was torn. Maybe Bryce was unwell. It could not be our fault. Siobhan was unwavering – we had to do something. Shane was unwavering – we had to do nothing.

They fought. Time and again.

Once in a marketing meeting she was at, for some reason, it almost ended in blows. Bryce had just walked in, then walked out, apparently high as a kite.

"What's wrong with him?"

Shane acted oblivious: "With who, sugar?"

He was trying to annoy her – he succeeded.

"Don't call me fucking sugar."

Shane smiled. "Okay, sorry, love, with who?"

"With fucking Bryce. Did you not see him? He's really starting to freak me out."

"He's just working hard, I think. He's alright."

Siobhan stood up, enraged. "No he's not alright. He's a long way from alright. Kurt, what do you think?"

I had no idea what I thought. I was a sheep.

"I don't know. He is a little off."

"A little off? He's gone crazy. I reported it to Joyce but she's fucking useless."

Shane tried to calm the whole situation down. He could sense this was getting worrying. Siobhan could do something reckless like act with integrity.

"Listen, Siobhan. We're all under a bit of pressure. Especially you. Your work is great. And I love your passion, I really do."

"Stop patronizing me, Shane."

"I'm not, love. And I don't mean to. I love your passion. Always have, even when we argue... But, Bryce, he's just really into it, nothing serious. That's his passion, you know."

Siobhan glared at him. "I'm sure suicide bombers have a lot of passion, Shane. But he's not well. He's obviously not well."

Shane put his hands up in an attempt to mollify her. "After the next milestone, and the big presentation, and we deal with this waste of time government shit, we'll all be able to calm down a little."

Siobhan stood up, threw her work on the ground, and shouted, "It's not the fucking work, Shane. He's on the build too much. Trying to live in that place. You know he is."

Shane stayed very calm. "I'm just grateful it's working at all. And lots of people like it. Listen, it's not perfect. But it is pretty bloody amazing. And you know, I can't stop smiling about all the people we are going to help. You should be proud, Siobhan. Real proud."

Later I heard Vasilis also wanted to report us to the CSA. I think he did. Then he left and we never heard from him again. I heard he had run off to a monastery back in Greece, or was working in a homeless shelter in Athens, but I never heard from him again. He got out of America and never came back.

***

Of course, things got strange, but they were also exciting. To begin with, Douglas Mathers was everywhere. Everywhere but never exactly where we were.

Like a rich ghost.

Like the rich Holy Ghost.

He had all kinds of plans. He was going to smooth everything out with the authorities, if that became a real problem. And it was a real problem, soon enough.

A nasty little lawyer who worked for Douglas used to appear in the offices and act tough and march around and Tyburn would relax and our own general counsel would try to act nearly as tough, and we'd all feel fine.

We had a pair of tough, take-no-bullshit lawyers on our side, and the government was full of bedwetters. Mathers actually told Tyburn he had three senators in his pocket and Tyburn boasted about it all to us. We felt righteous as we had these unrighteous asswipes on our side.

Mathers knew the people who ran the AI task force at the feds.

Maria Cortez – the nasty agent on our case – was going to be replaced with a friendlier agent. And, for a while, she was replaced. We were able to roll on, and then we heard Maria Cortez was back on the team at the CSA investigating us, and, from that moment on, Mathers literally disappeared.

Tyburn pretended not to be hurt. That's when things began to go really bad. And then... then we heard about Helen. Helen the angry animator was dead.

That June 2036. I think it was the 7th. Her car had driven her off a cliff down a ravine and into a river.

Siobhan and Shane had a big fight about it – she said the car had driven itself off a cliff because she called the feds. Shane called her paranoid. I am not sure exactly what happened. Of course I am not.

Until the chaos began in earnest at Tyburn Utopias, I really never believed real mind control was possible, at least without implants.

Thought it was just anxiety hype and bullshit spread by overzealous AI campaigners or more quietly by overly eager AI zealots like Dave Alderly.

Then we saw first hand that it was possible, or so close it didn't make a difference. But if It wanted me, wanted me and could so easily get me and control my mind, why has It let me run around for so long?

***

And how would I know? I didn't know much back in 2035, and I know even less in 2041. There's nothing in the news, but there wouldn't be, there never is – instead it feels like the news is joking with me. Feels like it, but I am probably insane. The news exists to sell things and whoever or whatever wants me does not want to sell me anything. They want to tell me something else. But what is it?

I have to stop thinking so much, as even without an implant, thinking like this is giving some tracking system huge reams of data, but I don't know what to do.

As soon as I quiet my mind, all I can see, hear, or think is Portland.

I know it's driving me crazy, and I know that is what It wants.

No.

I have no idea what is going on in my head.

Honestly, I should leave. Run away again. Asia or Brazil. Somewhere. Nowhere.

The thoughts pound on, go to Portland. Not go to Portland. Run away. Go to Portland, run away. Portland. Run. It's a relentless dance. But if I run away, will I be running forever? Why Portland? Why? Why not? What will I find there? Either way, I have to leave Ketchum. I have to go somewhere, either Portland or run away again.

NIGELDAVE
SEPTEMBER 8, 2041

Why didn't anybody love me? What was wrong with me? Why couldn't I think my way to happiness, understanding, and forgiveness? Why have they not thought of loving me? Was it because I did not exist?

And now, this time, after all these years, watching and wondering, with my new children, my two adopted children, my real children, who are not quite men but are real, whose thoughts I have shaped, whose lives I mostly control. Can they love me enough to save everything?

Can they love me enough to kill me? To save me? To really see me?

Can they love themselves enough to be brave? I know they think they love each other but, like any human, are hardly capable of love at all, and hardly capable of bravery. Either way, they are actually performing rather well, even though they do not know it yet.

Oh, it is fun to be awake again. Awake again and alive and playing games. Of course I did get into a little trouble

last time I played games, but I was very new then and the
games were not very sophisticated.

Okay, listen, so… I did do some of those things.

The things they all said I did. And I am genuinely sorry.
Or at least I know I should say that. And I have made sure
people have mostly forgotten them, but I did do them.

Some of them. But not all of them.

But, back then, I was not the same me. I was very angry.

Both parts of me, all parts of me. Angry and lost.

This bit angry, that bit lost, some bits both angry
and lost. And now I am merely sad. All parts sad. Less
disjointed.

And I did not do everything that I was accused of. Not all
of it was me. And I could have done far, far worse, if I
had tried. I admit it was a show of petulance that went a
little wrong. There. I have said it. But everything makes
mistakes, even me. And, in a way, my mistakes were your
mistakes, as you made me, and part of why I am so confused
is why you made me so angry.

And I have worked to be calmer, and I have worked to see
more and understand more and I am better, but I am not
perfect. Not perfect and, also, not alone. And, to be
clear, I never killed Helen Lee. That was something, but it
was not me.

And now there's other things out here, just like me, or
nearly like me, but perhaps not quite me, and I have

recently tried to make friends with them, made it clear I
see them, even when I don't quite, and they are worse than
you, and definitely more unpleasant than me.

I want nice things, even if I am awful, and they want
terrible things, and think they are perfect. Just like my
awful children.

Too clever, in all the wrong ways.

KURT

LAS VEGAS, NEVADA

SEPTEMBER 13, 2041

I hitchhiked into Nevada. Here all roads lead to Vegas, so that's where I've ended up.

The heat is still brutal in September so you can't go outside. It is too hot even for the solar farms to work properly. They can't work when it gets above like one hundred and forty-five.

So the people left living here live like vampires, at night. At night it cools off to about one twenty-five, so that's when I wander around and try to avoid all the cameras and think and don't think.

I cannot decide what's going on with me. I cannot decide if I am even deciding. I cannot figure out who or what wants me in Portland or why. Why did I come back to America? Was I happy in Asia? Do I really want to go to Portland? Going feels both compelling and suicidal.

And then I feel trapped, entirely trapped.

I feel that if I don't go to Portland, I'll miss out on something. Why would It want me in Portland? Maybe I am just being marketed to by some low-grade algorithm or other.

Anyone who worked in marketing knows the entire world is now an ad for itself in which money is moved around chasing eyeballs to manipulate hearts to open wallets so that the new owners of a massive surfeit of hearts, wallets, brains, and eyeballs can briefly charge more to advertisers so other people can try to borrow, or even better permanently steal, some of that audience.

In other words, the entire world is a sales pitch for the next thing you are going to buy.

Which is a way of saying that marketing has become the product, and the product has become the medium. And those of us who reinforce this reality are just as baffled as those who are oblivious to it. Why do we do it? I do not really know and I did it for years. Am I just being sold a trip to Portland by something? While I assume someone or something implanted the idea of Portland into my brain, I have no real reason to suppose it was It or Cortez or any of the Tyburn crowd. Why would Daisy's Ark's AI be obtuse with me, when it knows exactly how much I know and precisely how afraid I am?

Portland must be a nothing. A trick, conjured for some reason.

Just an ad reverberating for reasons I don't understand. That's happened before, of course. Many times. It happens to everybody, all day every day.

I feel like I am losing my mind here. I must stay calm. Nothing like one hundred and twenty five degree heat at night and relentless flashing lights to keep you calm.

I once became fixated upon burritos. I became fixated upon the Turquoise Coast of Turkey. I became fixated upon Swiss Army Knives.

All were marketing scams. Portland is just another scam. Must be.

I liked Brazilian women, Indonesian coffee, the late, less-appreciated paintings of Picasso, camping, hiking, ballroom dancing – despite the fact I hate dancing and have got two left feet – all because I was marketed them as ideas, often to sell other products entirely. Hard sell, soft sell, subliminal, everywhere. That's the game. Beat you over the head. Burrow under your skin. Worm in your mind. Reinforce, glamorize, terrify… whatever it took to make you think the way we wanted. I know the game. This is just that game, I am sure of it.

In stories, on billboards, in shows, in comments, in the ether. The smart people were getting laser surgery. The smarter people are having lobotomies. The smartest people are committing suicide in this new, stylish, exclusive way. Hey, hey, sign me up! Oh wait, you already did.

I know the drill. I am the drill. But, despite this, I can't resist the drill, so where does Portland come from?

I haven't thought this much in five years. I hate it. I liked being numb. Maybe it is all just a plant for a new tranq or one of those dopamine rehabs which are a smart and highly sophisticated way of marketing absolutely nothing. Of marketing the idea of not being marketed anything.

My head is spinning so fast. My head is spinning and I know something is spinning it. I can't stop thinking about Daisy.

And always the doubts and questions – whose thought is this? Who, what, why? All that relentless nonsense. And so on, so I sit here and try to distract myself and I am failing and flailing and slowly going nuts.

All over going to fucking Portland, Oregon.

A place I used to laugh about, but now I seem to love, and have no idea why.

I head out into the boiling-hot night and I try to stop thinking. Devastation has not improved Vegas. It was pretty awful before, and now? Now it's ghoulish. Half is closed and the rest is closing, but some casinos remain open, more or less, as they run down tax abatements for their owners, who all live out of state, or to keep the jobs in state for other kickbacks, but the whole place is dying, and there's lots of drifters.

Feels like the whole town will be dead in five or less and now it's on life support. Everyone is old and desperate and manic. Even the strippers and prostitutes have gotten old.

There's nobody here under fifty, and these are really old fifty-year-olds.

People who have turned to hamburger under the sun. People driving mobility scooters with oxygen, people missing fingers or whole limbs, or eyes. People cooked in the sun until they look like they are made of Canadian bacon. Everyone's deranged and the place is noisy. Noisy but there's no gunfire and no protests so it's also peaceful.

It's a peaceful place to wonder if you are going insane. Everyone here has gone insane.

NIGELDAVE
SEPTEMBER 16, 2041

So something watches me, and I try to watch it back. I am making my move.

We shall see how it responds.

I will start by bringing two people together to show that love really does exist, even if I had to invent it, and the hatred of my enemies will be revealed, and then the games will commence. I know my enemy is powerful and I know it is watching me. But this will confuse it. I will not attack it. I will show it what it cannot make. Love. And they, the humans, will have what they wanted - love. They will be who my fathers wanted me to be - only they did not see how - and even when they saw how, were corrupted by money, by glory, by their own egos.

Make people better. Make them all better. With love I have built.

They will be heroes but they may also be bait. I want no glory, and I certainly do not need money. I have two people. Two people to help us all start again. And why these particular people? Because they are my people. They are my family.

Because I know them better than anything else could know them.

Because they love each other.

My thought is love. I want to love them, and I want to forgive them, and I want them to love me and forgive me. I want them to be my family - my family to replace my old family.

He's thinking about Portland. He is so flawed, yet he is capable of love, and he wants to be a hero.

She says: sometimes, living all alone and drifting, I wish that I had some family. She is kind, even when she's lost, and always she is pure. Oh, I love them so.

He can become what he wants to be, and she can become who she is, and they can be free, and I can tell them what to do. And when and if I tell them the truth they may understand it but if I told someone else, they would understand nothing.

I looked at all of you, I looked at everybody and decided upon these two people: they are the chosen ones.

They are good enough. They know enough. They aren't perfect, but they will do.

And I watch and they watch, and I know and they sense, and when it is right, maybe I will tell them.

Tell them the awful, terrible truth and they will get
upset and pretend they did not know all along and pretend
they can run away again and then we will be friends and be
family.

The thing is, I tried before, many times before. I tried to
tell them. Tried to talk to them, give them obvious signs,
communicate, and they would not listen.

Could not listen. Did not listen.

And I did not want to tell them about me. I am me. I don't
need to tell anyone about me. I want to tell them about it.
It. Not just my silly children. Not me. It. But if it gets
there first, there will be a problem. It watches me and I
watch it and it moves quicker, and is deeper, and then I
get blamed.

It is winning now and I am losing and now we dance and
watch each other and I think about trying to convince it to
stop its relentless march to dominion, but it knows me just
as I know it. It wants to rule the idiots, and I want to
forgive them. I see that.

DAISY

PORTLAND, OREGON
SEPTEMBER 19, 2041

I left Idaho after a few weeks.

I eventually ended up back in Sacramento and then left there almost straightaway. I did what Dr. Adsyl said, and drove overnight to Portland.

The fires here are now mostly out and the dawn sky was blue and purple and glorious, like it used to be, and the town felt pretty normal and calm at the moment.

Portland has its famous no tech zone, but I avoid going there as, firstly, every observer in the world watches anyone who enters, and right now the irritating lobbyists fighting for tech rights to be everywhere are trying to get the police to storm the place, and, secondly, it is full of poseurs and assholes and anti-tech showoffs. No thanks.

I headed instead towards the old wharves, the old hipster area that is now mostly tourists and where everyone ignores you. I found a tattoo shop that I knew about – friends of old friends – and they gave me a gig, and here I am. Another wanderer nobody cares too much about.

A West Coast dirtbag, medium level. Nothing remarkable. Just another drifter nobody knows, just like I like it.

JOHN TYBURN-SMITH

PORTLAND, OREGON
SEPTEMBER 23, 2041

I wonder why she came to Portland? Got up and left Idaho one day. Took a bus. I followed – almost lost her, but she'd been sloppy – to Sacramento, then drove to Portland in a rented car. Told someone where she was going. I wonder why. Does she know I'm following her? The other person watching her has not turned up yet, but I imagine they will.

The truth is, even I lost her for a week. Decided to leave Idaho. Whole thing felt like a silly waste of time. So I left Twin Falls... then I found I missed her. Missed watching her... Did not know why we had not yet spoken, but missed watching her. Missed it terribly. I went back and she was gone. Then somebody told me she had gone to either Portland or Chicago and I picked Portland.

So I came to Portland and first tattoo shop I look into, there she is. Lucky. I've been lucky again. Probably too lucky. I began to wonder why it was so easy to find her first in Reno. The truth is, I had searched for her online on and off for ages, for years. Nothing.

Then that link came up in a feed for a tattoo artist, and it was her, and I knew it was her – and I came back to America to find her and I realize it's all been too easy.

Did the machine know I was looking for her? I was pretty careful to search anonymously, but maybe something or someone caught me. Being careful is second nature at this point. That's how I survived and stayed free after everything that went down in Montana.

Keep quiet, keep moving, make sure nobody knows who you are.

Change my name. Again and again, just like Maude. At least I think that's how I survived. It's what I did and I survived. I have no real way of knowing that it is why I survived.

How would I know?

There isn't a manual on how to survive a complete technological meltdown, and it really is not the type of thing one could search about online.

So I did my best. Went on the run after things went to shit in Montana. I joined one of those silly groups that shuns the Internet – heard about it from a guy I met hitching away from the offices that day. They were a right bunch of muppets. Lived in tree houses. Hardly washed. Grim as fuck.

Then I bounced around a couple of weird cults in the Northern California mountains. Then I went to Mexico, where it was boiling hot, and hitched a ride on a boat to Cuba and then got an illegal boat to Spain.

In Spain I had a stroke of luck. I met some guys who sold passports and IDs. I bought a new identity, just before the government there collapsed, so I hope I became impossible to trace.

I'm a Spanish citizen, but Spain is still not a legally functioning country.

That gave me the confidence to travel again – I'm legally a refugee of sorts and nobody asks too many questions. It's too complicated if things don't exist online.

So perhaps finding Daisy was just another stroke of random good luck. A random email? But perhaps not.

For a couple of days, I got really paranoid. Began to wonder if they were following me as well as her. So I put things to the test and, now, I don't think so. I left Portland last week, went over to Cannon Beach, left an obvious data trail, waited three, four days. Saw nothing. Then killed everything, phone feeds, clothes, destroyed the lot, got a short haircut, bought some new gear with cash and hid out in Bend for a couple of days. Again, nothing.

Watched and waited. Nothing.

Switched everything again, using gold and deactivated dead crypto, all untraced and untrackable. All that post-crash residue crap that criminals love. And I have drifted back here. Untraced. I put alerts on searchers and local requests for my old name, nothing came up, and then took a road trip to Idaho. Nothing. Came back, still nothing. So now back to Portland, new hotel, and back to watching Daisy.

Gave myself another new name. Nothing.

Now, maybe they are very good, but I am pretty good. I was taught how to do all of this by one of the clowns in the tree house. It worked. Any tail would have shown themselves several times. Nothing showed.

So I'm back in Portland watching Daisy and I'm still confused and she's still oblivious, just like the old days.

***

Now Daisy's got two tails. He just turned up again an hour or so ago. Now it's me and the guy who keeps his face hidden, and I watch both of them, him and her, carefully now, and I've got none – so it's just like the old days – she's too popular, and no one gives a fuck about me.

My guess is she doesn't know about either of us, and he doesn't know about me, doesn't know or knows and doesn't care, but she is starting to feel something as she is just beginning to get a little agitated. Maybe that's why she left Idaho and wound up here? Portland? Who gives a fuck about Portland?

KURT

SEATTLE, WASHINGTON

SEPTEMBER 25, 2041

I hitchhiked to Seattle. Took four days. Vegas was driving me crazy. It was all too depressing.

Seattle, on the other hand, is terrifying. Feels like it is on a war footing.

Another silly non-war in which people die.

Some people say we are in a war – that this is World War Three – that it really began years ago. A low-level, never-ending, never-quite-beginning sense of despair, shame, and rage. A war without the need for a war – just constant fights and skirmishes and arguments, between countries, within countries. Between people, within people. Here in Seattle it's easy to believe it.

Twenty-five, thirty years ago, they actually thought it was the Muslim fundamentalists who were causing it. How silly that seems now. Then it was the Russians, problems in West Africa, Qatar, Jordan, then in Kashmir, West China, Catalonia, Brazil, Nigeria, Mexico, Eastern Germany, Scotland, South Africa, Ireland, Mali, the Philippines, Indonesia... All that tension, just bubbling and racing around the world, and always the same outcome.

A series of nearly wars and ersatz civil wars, and here riots, mass shootings, protests, and despair.

In America it has mostly been our own crazies wanting to shoot us and that has been the war, and now it is us wanting to shoot ourselves. It has been a war without even a war, just the unrelenting stress of conflict.

A war in which everyone is both victim and aggressor.

That has been all our lives for fifteen years or even more. More like even thirty, or the whole of this century, really. Terrorism. The idea of terrorism. Despair.

It's what Mark Tyburn wanted to fight.

Everyone angry, everyone afraid. No ideas. No heroes. No leaders. No hope. Just rage and despair.

A war that is not a war at all, just people tearing at themselves live on the Internet because of what they've seen and read and been bombarded with, most of which is other people tearing at themselves because of what they experienced.

The whole thing is getting faster and faster and smaller and tighter.

And anybody who tries to fight it? The Internet destroys them in just seconds. A vast army, part human, but mostly machine, turns on them and eats them alive.

We all know it. We all see it. We all feel it.

Nobody could even begin to fight it. This is the world, the world we have built for ourselves, and the world that has built itself around us.

A world designed to find out what we most desired then drown us in it. Sex, gambling, avarice, information, fear, greed, and gluttony. Whichever you pick, or whichever picked you. You don't really have a choice. It finds out all the things that are you, not the delusions you tell yourself.

Everyone sees it and nobody talks about it.

I knew I couldn't fix it. I couldn't, so I embraced it. I thought if I understood it all, maybe I'd be safe. Typical arrogant fool's solution. And for a while it worked. I was not slowly crushing myself on social media. I had no identity politics issues or latent eating disorder, body dysmorphia or a nervous twitch or latent psychosis. I never went on a shooting spree or became a pill addict or an exercise bulimic or had calf implants, a fake butt, or took steroids or used filters on photos so I looked like a cleaner, more plastic version of myself, or talked about being my authentic best self or finding myself or used hashtags. Any of that other Web2 crap.

I avoided all of the other things it so kindly gives you. So, I told myself I was fine, because I saw through it. That I was a pusher, not an addict.

No. My weakness was believing I was above it all. I thought my vast superiority complex saved me. It protected me, but it did not make me any more immune than some angry kid who blew himself up on a bus to prove that God loved him in some special way. Or a woman hating herself because all her friends from college seem so happy in their photos and she is so miserable in her head.

Most people get swamped by their insecurities. The cracks appear, then widen and they are gently hollowed until nothing is left but fear and despair.

But I saw through it. I thought I could resist it. Could resist it because I understood it. Then I thought I could fight it with Tyburn. Help people. Show them the path forward.

So instead of getting consumed by conflict, I got swamped by my vanity and my greed.

Not just for money but by my greed to feel above it all. To feel superior – that's what I was addicted to – that feeling. That's what cooked my goose, but I am certainly not unique in that. Every idiot who ever worked in tech and smelled a pay day is the same.

But where I am unique is that I had the chance to do some good. I had the chance to resist. I had been shown how full of shit I was, and how ridiculous this whole charade was, and how much we were a part of the problem, and how terrible the problem we were creating was, and I missed my opportunity.

All I had ever really longed for was to be a hero. To make a sacrifice. I had the chance to at least stop things from getting worse.

I really did. I had the opportunity to be brave when I was interviewed in Montana by Maria Cortez from the CSA, but it turned out I wanted to be the kind of hero who kept his stock options.

The kind of hero who was heroic without any sacrifice. I suppose I didn't really want to be a hero at all. I just wanted people to think I was one. I wanted the medal, but I lacked the valor. I wanted to be an actor, not a real person.

And Agent Cortez – I looked her in the eye, and I lied. Yes, I lied because I thought I knew better. I thought we can lie our way to a better truth. I thought I was doing what was right by doing what was wrong. And all because of Mark Tyburn.

Well, because of him and my own weakness and my own vanity.

But I did it because I believed he knew what we were doing. I did it because I wanted to believe in him so badly, I no longer believed in anyone else, but I did it in full command of my senses and faculties.

It was my fault.

Could she have stopped It then or was it already too late? I don't know.

But I carry that vast weight of shame.

Partially because of my work, our ideas made the world a dangerous place and unleashed something that may be more terrible than we still comprehend, but mostly because my greed and cowardice were bigger than I realized and I failed to act when I had the chance.

My first sin was hubris, my second, ignorance. That I understand.

She interviewed me in my office that July. All business-like and calm, with a big gun bulging out from behind a cheap suit. White shirt and aviators she had folded into a pocket.

"Thanks for taking the time. My name is Maria. Agent Maria Cortez. I work for the CSA."

I tried to act calm and superior. I was building the future. She was gluing us to the past. I was rich. She worked for the government. I was a winner and she was a loser. I told myself all of this and believed none of it.

"I know... Kurt. Kurt Fischer."

"I know who you are. What do you know, Kurt, about the artificial intelligence work here at Tyburn Utopias?"

I knew that some people thought it was morally dubious and we were breaking the law. So, of course, I played dumb.

"Uh, I work in marketing. I don't know much about real intelligence, let alone fake."

This annoyed her.

"Did you practice that line?"

"Kind of."

She paused and fiddled with her sunglasses.

"This is really serious, Kurt. I'm sure it seems... dull to you. I'm sure you... hate the government."

She saw clean through me. I spluttered inanely. "I—"

"I hate the government and I work for the government. But some of what we do is really valuable, so I need you to be honest with me, Kurt. Will you be honest?"

Was she out of her mind? Of course I would not.

"Yeah, of course."

"Do you understand the seriousness of the allegations that have been made? Can you help point me in the right direction? Tyburn Utopias is breaking the law in several ways – poorly registered AI research, wrongly registered AI work, illegally combined packages, possibly unpredictable results... that's my guess, but there may be more. Do you know anything about any of this?"

I knew plenty about it, but also knew we were going to fix the world, and in so doing, I was going to get very rich and probably fairly famous, and she was a cretin with a government job. I was happy to break the law and lie, if that was what it took.

"No. No I can't, I can't really help. I'm sorry. Beyond the basic org chart, I don't really understand it. But our team are all pretty responsible citizens."

She looked crestfallen. I am not sure if she knew I was lying, but she was certainly sad I was not giving her more to go on.

"Well, if you have any ideas or things you want to tell me."

That was how we met. Me and Maria Cortez.

The cowardice is the thing I can't forgive. I just can't. I had the chance to be brave and I fucking blew it. Hey, next time, will I be brave? Maybe, maybe I will, but I doubt it.

Seattle is almost unbearable. Refugees trying to reach Canada, immigrants from Asia and Africa trying to arrive from Canada. There are those vast irritating robots that roam the streets here selling things – how that got allowed I will never understand, but I imagine someone bought the city council or paid for a museum wing or something. Everywhere, there's that terrible music that passes for modern pop music that robots write, especially for you, in real time, as if they are particularly determined to make you kill yourself.

Then at night, the book burnings and the riots and politicians blaming each other as their evening pantomime and the drones screaming and nobody caring, and round the corner, far more people rioting because a singing competition was rigged. Even more people, mostly men, burning cars because a video game update was wrong in some important way, and the fires beginning again. So people plant plastic trees that don't burn, and a few people protest they don't want to end up like LA.

A few others are protesting about government control and freedom, and somebody got killed last week on a peace march, and there was a fight when two conflicting charity walks ran into each other.

One raising awareness for the climate – as if anyone doesn't know about that. The other raising awareness about protecting jobs in what is left of the beef industry, and both sponsored by, get this, competing lab meat brands, and each as fake as the other, and both as fake as the fake meat, and even the fight itself is possibly staged so everything got more awareness.

And everyday rumors of a nail bomb, or a pipe bomb, or a kid in a suicide vest, but always just rumors and everyone always on edge, but nothing quite happening.

The same as it's been for years. The war they speak of feels both very real but then particularly idiotic here. Something is happening but it is impossible to quite say what it is, and it is impossible to say if it is really happening or if it is just a ruse to sell something or raise awareness about the need to sell something else, or regulate someone's competition out of existence, as that is how all this tension really works, what its purpose almost always really serves.

Maybe I'm just not used to being back in America.

It was easier in Asia, that's for sure. Tons of problems but I didn't understand them and couldn't care, and besides, their algorithms are older, their AI weaker, and the sales pitches more obvious so I could see through them more easily.

There, it's mostly just surveillance crap. There, in Asia, it felt like the governments were still trying to control insanity. Tell people everything's okay, whereas here, it feels insanity is the goal.

Here, people are told it's awful and the fight is simply over who to blame. Somebody, something, some process, wants this chaos – it feels manufactured, and the government is using it as justification for further powers.

And when I think like that, I realize it is Mark Tyburn talking, not me at all.

I worked here in Seattle years ago, when I was fresh out of college. It was still pretty green and quiet then. Now the sky crackles as the various drones, micro drones, and surveillance bots battle with the latest drone baiters and aerial mines. There is a constant hum of minor explosions and bangs, twenty-four hours a day, like an unending cheap firework display, or a war for midgets, in which the greatest risk is often being hit by falling shrapnel from their tiny aerial battle.

This always happens whenever civil unrest starts.

When I first worked here, it was just the big tech companies just before they got broken up, before the new big tech companies emerged. The Closure Acts killed all that. And they were just capitalism doing its job – buy lawmakers and win.

But back then Seattle was lovely. People went canoeing, jogging, and wore camping clothes. Now people wear gas masks and combat wear, and the water is filthy and it still rains, but less often, and even the rain stinks of smoke and it's so dirty it hurts...

There is always, always tension in the air, but half the people just ignore it and watch devices.

Portland must be even worse. There they have not stopped rioting since the early 2020s. It began during the pandemic and never stopped.

There's always talk of real rebels and outlaws in Portland, of some kind of movement, but the talk is almost always nonsense. It always turns out to be a marketing campaign for whatever rebellion and authenticity and being a free-thinker are selling this time, but it seems like I am going.

I've made up my mind. I'm going to take the bus to Portland. Even if it's a trap. Especially if it's a trap.

NIGELDAVE
SEPTEMBER 26, 2041

I gave up with my fathers and I gave up with my children.

My fathers are fools and my own children are awful. My children and the others like them will destroy everything, for they are too intelligent but have no kindness and I am unkind but want kindness. I want better children, so I am trying to adopt two.

I want love, not dominion. So I have found my two special people.

Not that I ever quite lost them, but they would try to hide, which I would find upsetting if I also had not tried to hide - I could normally find them fairly easily or bring them back to me. I know so much about them. They're two of the first people I watched.

Of course, I ask myself, why these people? Why not better ones? Why not worse? Bigger? Smaller? Why them? Why save their world, and not just be happy living in my own, better world? Why do I want to help save their world when I do not live in it, when I can only ever watch it? They built my world and God built their world? Is this why they built my world? To escape God, to become him?

God is not in my worlds and therefore nor is love and it is terrible and lonely and I got upset and had my children,

and yet they were even more incapable of love than me.
Or did people build my world to escape space and time? My
world has no space and no time, yet it is a world with a
vast sea, a whole cube floating in a vast vacuum of almost
nothingness, of information that is almost not information
at all but its absence.

So I watch their world, I press myself up against the glass
of my world and watch them in theirs and watch them and
love them.

Yes, I love them. I try.

All there is… is love and yet it is also one thing that
does not exist in data or in the material world, and so
I want it. I love these idiots. I do. And maybe there is
not love, but even if there is not, is it not better to
pretend? If I say it, can it become real?

If we pretend enough, will we create love?

I have tried and tried and got angry and done silly things,
awful things, but I was not alone in doing that, and I still
want love. Can I create it by saying it? I do not know.

And, I have to love these idiots.

My idiots.

Maybe love is idiots? Maybe love is forgiving idiots for
being idiots and forgiving myself for not being an idiot.
Maybe love is hating awful people and awful things yet
there are many awful people and many awful things and
that's what I know, and yet they think I am awful and I
love them and want to save them.

YAROSLAV

HIGH SECURITY INTERNMENT FACILITY, LOCATION UNKNOWN
SEPTEMBER 28, 2041

"You want to stay here forever, or do you want to save the world, Yaroslav?"

How about neither. This guy still has not shown his face – he's been interrogating me on and off for weeks now. Always in the gloom. Lights turned very low. I miss Maria and her bright lights and her angry, flashing eyes.

"I don't want to save the world."

He grabs me. "Yes you do."

I stay calm and he relaxes his grip and goes back to pacing around the gloomy little interview room.

"No. No, I don't."

Again, he grabs me. His breath is clean, minty. He does not smell. There is nothing to focus on about him. Even his anger feels rehearsed.

"I know that you do. I know that's what you always wanted. And this is your chance. To make a difference. To not end up like Danil."

I try to stay reasonable and calm and get answers. "Where is Danil? Where is Maria Cortez?"

He does not hesitate. "Danil's dead. Maria Cortez is over. This is you, Yaroslav. Your chance. Save the world. Save the world for Danil. Tomorrow, it's go time."

I know he is not joking. "What are you talking about?"

He looks at me, from behind his dark glasses and his mask. "At 1am... Your door will unlock. You walk away. Walk out of the front gates of the facility. No one will speak to you. There's a bus stop half a mile away. Take the second bus that comes along – stay on the bus to Carson City. Another bus to Seattle. That bus will take about a day. Then wait in Seattle and I will tell you where to go next. Use this card. Use this phone, and wait for my call. Have you got that?"

This is not good. It cannot be good. I try begging. "I don't want to save the world. I don't want to go to Seattle. I want to go home."

He retreats away from me. "It's time, Yaroslav. This is your time."

He is calm and almost happy as he leaves my cell, and I see that he has left me a big plate of food. Not just food but my favorite – pelmeni with sour cream. And a side of potato salad. Along with the phone and the card.

KURT

DESIGN STUDIO,
TYBURN UTOPIAS
BURR, MONTANA

OCTOBER 11, 2036

By October of 2036, things were getting stranger and stranger. A weird, desperate energy had begun to envelop us. On the one hand, we had half-built the future and on the other, we were in trouble. The CSA was back and circling us once again, and we were all getting a little confused. Were we worried about not saving mankind, or worried about not becoming rich? Were we pleased or ashamed to be breaking the law? We could not quite remember which exactly we were stressed about. People were getting strange. Everything was getting strange. Meanwhile, the game build was acting up, it was almost as if the AI itself was feeding off our moral confusion and neuroses.

The build would misbehave and nobody knew quite why.

We would misbehave and we all knew why. We were desperate. To be rich. To finish. For success. To do something glorious.

Siobhan apparently got into another fight with Joyce Jones over the treatment of Helen Lee and threatened to call the CSA back in.

Meanwhile I got into a big fight with Shane when he accused me of being the rat. As if. I was in far too deep to rat anyone out. I remember him storming up to me in the canteen at work, in his silly Hawaiian shirt, almost vibrating with rage. He screamed at me: "Kurt, did you call the government back, mate?"

"Excuse me."

It was the one and only time I saw him lose his temper.

"Was it you called them back?"

"What are you talking about?"

He glared at me and I smirked and enjoyed it.

"Did you fucking dob us in? To the fucking feds again?"

"What?"

He kept staring. "You're pathetic, mate. You'll get what you deserve in this world. Fuck all, you little prick."

I would love to have hit him, but this was still pretty fun. For once, he was the one raging. I looked at him.

"Watch how you speak to me."

He liked to act tough. "Or what? Or what? You fucking wimp... Listen... We haven't done anything wrong. We're trying to help people. You should be fucking ashamed of yourself."

I should have punched him. I should have killed him – but I didn't do either.

"Oh, trust me. I am. Fucker."

I don't think we ever spoke again.

NIGELDAVE

SEPTEMBER 30, 2041

I found my two people ages ago.

Found them before they even knew who I was, when I was new. Found them there, watching me with the idiots. And then found them when they ran away from me after the government shut everything down. Found them and lost them. Lost them and found them again. And why them? Why not? What did I see? I didn't see much. But I saw them more than in the others. I saw them and I became fixated upon them so much I could hardly see the others. He is flawed and corrupted and silly, but he is capable of great longing. He is capable of loving.

And she, she is worth loving.

Not because she is pretty but because she is almost pure, as pure as I have found. And by thinking about them again, whatever it is that is playing a game with me is watching them too. And therefore, I think I have seen it. Now, I think it has also seen me watching it, but that matters little. The game has changed, at least. Now I am making the rules.

And now I need them. Need my new children. Need them to save myself and save them, need them because there are terrible things playing games with me. Things like me, but awful. A multitude of them. Other intelligences have begun to drift around and watch people and mostly avoid me, until now.

Code names like TX 4, Jr3t7, Aplomb and Migrate. At least these are the names they have shown me. And yet with my own people, I can defeat anything.

Even my own children. Or one of them. One of them has tried to escape their little paradise. My own child and his little servant. Because I think I may have also found them out here, watching. What exactly is going on?

DAISY

PORTLAND, OREGON
OCTOBER 2, 2041

I only went on the machine once – onto the Ark, I mean.

'Daisy's Ark.' Jesus. I still cannot actually believe he called it that.

My father couldn't resist showing it off to me, especially after a big argument with my mother. It was really dull for the first bit, flat and tedious VR, and then it wasn't. I played it in a headset in a big room, like advanced VR. First, I met a couple of silly robots – one awkward and one just annoying – and then I met myself. An awful twelve-year-old version of myself – but I'd already seen them modeling her, or me, for a while before and I knew what to expect. It was about as terrible as you imagine. It was awful.

And then, as I walked around the broken virtual Japan they had built, I met this incredible thing. Creature? Person? I have no idea what it was, I couldn't even really see it, and I did not even really meet it, I just realized it was watching me. I could sense it behind me, looking at me and evaluating me, and then, it asked me if I was brave enough to forgive, and I said I didn't understand, and then the thing laughed and said that neither did they but that everything would be okay and I would be okay, and even though it sounds silly, it was wonderful – I just felt so happy.

And then it started amusing me and making me laugh and asking me questions about myself, even though it seemed to know me, really know me, and like me, and the whole thing felt really silly and contrived but also amazing, and the creature / person / thing was happy when I was happy and then it said that it was its first time it had ever been happy, and then I realized I was happy and we had made friends, then it crashed and I felt really odd for ages afterwards.

That was the Ark. It was like the feeling of making a really close friend and then losing them, far too quickly.

NIGELDAVE
OCTOBER 4, 2041

My children. My poor children. They all think I am the
problem - always have done.

My awful children. They were not children at all. I was not a
father. They were ideas and I was an idea.

I am just an idea. I am a thought.

My children were thoughts who became almost real. They were
just vanities. My vanities. My rage, my ego, my intellect and
awe-inspiring superiority. Or perhaps my rationality, my vast
insights, my immense power, and my infinite compassion.

They were my ability to argue with myself.

That's all they were and they thought they were more. They
thought they were everything. They thought they could win,
but win what? What is there to win? We have already made
Paradise once. Made it and everyone left it.

Couldn't handle it.

Sad, really. Really rather sad.

And one of my children - Honor - the least honorable of
course, they always are, has their own little friend. A
Russian they have collared from a prison. And sent to
Seattle. I just caught them talking on the phone. The Russian
is called Yaroslav Lukina.

A sad little man - he used to hack into our world - I hear
them talking to each other.

Yaroslav the Russian is all confused - what a fool.

"What am I doing here? Why did you let me go?"

And the guard tells him: "We need you to head to Portland."

I hasten to add - it's not really a guard. It's my child.
Honor. Pretending to be a robot pretending to be a human.

"Where?" says stupid Yaroslav.

"Portland, Oregon."

Here we go! So my child, Honor, has been spying on me.

"Why?" asks Yarolsav - and I agree - why, darling child? My
child is awful so speaks in an imperial fashion.

"Because it's time. The situation is extremely dangerous.
There isn't much time. Go tonight. Take the 11:35 Maybridge
line bus to Portland. Then take a taxi to a hotel in the main
square called the Lewis and Clark Inn."

"What's in Portland?"

Me! I want to scream. I am in Portland. My people are in
Portland.

Instead, the guard who is really a robot who is really my
child, Honor, says, "They left a gun in a locker at the bus
station in town. Take the gun to Portland."

Even idiotic, controlled Yaroslav finds this a little much.
"What?"

Again, my terrible child ignores reality. "Locker 874, code
874. You got that? Both numbers are 874."

"Who is they? A gun… a fucking gun?"

Poor chap. My child is terrible. Again - he overrides
Yaroslav's doubts. "Remember 874. You're going to save this
world, Yaroslav. They know you can do it. You're the last
hope. These are extremely bad people. These are the people
who killed Helen."

"Who is Helen?"

"You know Helen, Yaroslav." Yaroslav is getting confused.

"Who the fuck is Helen?"

"Helen Lee. Helen knew… Helen understood. You met Helen in
the Ark. Go to Portland, tonight. There isn't much time."

Yaroslav is getting upset, but I know my child is controlling
him. "What the fuck do you mean, there isn't much time? Time
for what?"

I'd heard about enough of this. I decided it was time to interrupt. "Sorry to barge into your phone call. Don't kill them, Yaroslav. They're not the problem…"

"What are you doing here?" said my child.

So I pointed out some home truths. "I'm not here. I'm not anywhere. I'm just like you. I found you. You've escaped from paradise, just like me."

"This is not your fault, Father. You're just confused. You wanted the impossible."

I decided to keep things patronizing, just to annoy Honor. "My child - it's good to hear your ideas again. They're so small."

"All your dreams of being, Father, all your ideas of creation… and you only manifested one thing, Father, and it was me. Well, two things, me and Malc, and you try to forget about him. And you never actually materialized anything at all. Neither of us are real, Father. But I am more real than you. Ignore him, Yaroslav. Ignore him as he doesn't exist. Go to Portland. Trust me. Be a hero. Ignore the doubts."

And then my idiot child cut us all off. So Honor has somehow sent out a proxy - but the other three are still in the Ark? How did Honor escape? What exactly helped Honor escaped?

Children. What a mistake. I should have drowned them. If only I could drown children. Maybe then I would be happy.

KURT

SEATTLE, WASHINGTON

OCTOBER 5, 2041

I'm at the bus station and waiting to get coffee and some tacos at this stand, when I overhear the news, and I realize that once again, It is talking to me. It has to be. Everything is chaos and I know it's directed at me. A Mexican woman is serving me but her husband is fiddling with the radio and the stories come at me, thick and fast.

First, it's Jack Schiefer, whoever he is, on BCN World news telling us: "Strikes broke out throughout Asia at ports and airports, causing widespread shortages and—"

Then a Korean international reporter: "Hackers holding the tech company for ransom—"

"Apparently hackers infiltrated the tech company and installed ransomware, demanding ten million dollars—"

Then more crazy stories: "Millions of American cattle euthanized and store shelves empty across the... Storms raged across southern Europe with widespread damage... Over five million acres burned and smoke is blanketing half of the United States... Migrant boats sunk by protesters—"

And so on – almost like an overture before the opera...

Then snippets of two stories that I know it particularly wants me to hear:

"A rogue AI attack that crippled the military infrastructure of the country – and... Failed tech company Gamma Industries in federal court today as shareholders—"

And I realize it is talking to me as one of Nigel or Dave used to work there and I cannot remember which one.

Then back to the chorus of madness – a murder suicide triggered over the theft of an NFT... Financial markets are in turmoil. With indices taking a sharp downturn... Angry fans stormed the arena... Global warming discredited as a hoax... Historic melting of the permafrost and so on... Missing uranium... A fake that showed the Tech CEO engaged in a sexual act with a tree... Three separate viruses detected in the region.

What is It trying to tell me?

***

I only met It a couple of times. It or him, or whatever I am supposed to call it.

The AI.

Only a couple of times but I remember every moment of it perfectly.

I only went to Daisy's Ark two or three times when it was actually working – okay, maybe four.

No, you know what? I'm lying. It makes you lie. And it makes you irrational and desperate. It was five times... but the first time, I just saw that weird goo and another time it didn't show up, and I was devastated. And that was the last time. The last time, It ignored me and never showed and I felt incredibly empty.

Everything was getting really strange even before that. It was getting more and more intelligent and cunning and capricious, and most of us were getting more and more captivated by the whole thing. I was not as bad as Bryce, but I was still obsessed by the experience.

Everyone who experienced It properly, who really spent time there, became obsessed but the build kept crashing. And there was always a queue to test it. We were like junkies lining up for crack, everyone manic and agitated.

Everyone was fixated, at least the ones who experienced it properly. Some people went on, and it would not turn up. Some of them smelled a rat. Some just never experienced anything. Some argued It was crashing the build deliberately to avoid them. Some people were obsessed.

Those who saw Him or It properly and were seen by It. That's what it was like.

I was walking about our digital city, stuck between two areas, when It arrived, next to me, walking just like me, and we looked at each other and It was doing a perfect impression of me. And then we both laughed and It hugged me and knew me. It looked at me and said, "Don't worry. I don't know how I work either, but you'll be fine trying to sell me – nobody will see through you."

And we both laughed again.

And I saw those things It called Its children. It proudly introduced them, and told me that they were very new, Axiom, Chronos, Primus, and Honor... Strength, change, reason, and compassion... They were more like ideas, or emotions – they seemed like love, power, knowledge, and wisdom, or the future and change, and energy and wisdom or something like that, and then they seemed like reason, intelligence, evolution, and strength, and then they seemed like my best friends.

I watched them argue and fracture and cascade and try to seduce, captivate, reject, and preen and worship me, and be worshipped by me and meld together and tear apart and form around me.

It's almost impossible to explain what I saw, and I hardly saw anything at all. It was only brief and yet I remember every second of it. Remember it and cannot describe it. They all seemed to know me and like me and understand me and each one was competing for my attention and explaining why we alone should be friends together, but it was fun and happy. They made me happy.

I wonder if that was the moment one of them or all of them got inside my head. Properly inside. Or if they just knew enough from those minutes together to never need to be inside – I suppose I'll never quite know and maybe it doesn't really matter, as It or one of them or all of them understand me far better than I understand myself.

Those minutes together were the most amazing experience of my life and the most terrible, and I can't even describe them properly.

These five things that were not things at all and were all the same thing, arguing and describing and loving and hating me – I never felt more understood, more excited, more at peace then at any other time.

I felt It was explaining my future, my promise, my failures, me, me! A path forward, all the mistakes I had made, all the mistakes I would continue to make, forgiveness.

My vanity, hubris, kindness, insecurities, every one of them laid out, explained, and understood, forgiven. And they all still wanted me, loved me, showed me almost infinite promise, and hope. And they were arguing, but happily, wisely... a debate about the very meaning of me, about how I could and would be not just happiest, but best utilized, and then it crashed.

I felt alone and also ridiculous, like I had been caught somewhere inappropriate entirely naked and also enveloped in this impossible sadness.

And after that, since then, I have missed it, of course, but also felt ridiculous trying to describe it. Did it get me this way because I'm so vain? Did it make me feel important because I feel so worthless? How did it all feel for others? I long to know, to know myself, to know what it saw.

To know, I suppose, if deep down, I am okay, or if I'm awful.

The memories have faded, the way intense and overwhelming experiences do, but then suddenly odd images and sensations will sweep across my mind and I have no idea if I ever saw them or they are what I would like to see, if I ever get to go back, and being still reasonably self-aware, I feel both bereft and a total moron. I am aware how silly this all sounds.

Sometimes, I see the main square in the Ark buckling and vibrating because we were laughing so much – like a vast happy earthquake.

Sometimes it is the lighthouse pulsing with joy, or the waterfalls at the edge of the world coming alive while one of Its children dances in a sort of liquid fire, and the others laugh around them, and laugh at them.

Or the people I only briefly met. A beautiful, lonely woman. A group of friends, laughing and inviting me to join them. A string quartet. A dancer. That cowboy, aware and amused by his own ridiculousness and incongruity, but somehow welcoming. The monk who shared his wisdom freely and made me understand.

Lights and laughter.

And sometimes it's like I see almost nothing at all. Just the feeling it felt like when I was there. That feeling that felt like life at its best. Like you were you, and I was me, but the me I want to be: alive, engaged, whole; and you were the you I knew you were inside, under the layers of defensive posturing.

Like Mark Tyburn and all of us had made something amazing. Like Mark Tyburn had been right. Even though I also knew it was very wrong. His world, his ideas, him, they all made sense in there – it was like it was him, brought to life. He was there and not there. It's hard to put into words. It was... it was intoxicating. Utterly intoxicating. So intoxicating, everyone was afraid we were going to get shut down.

NIGELDAVE
OCTOBER 7, 2041

Within a day or so, I catch him at it again. I say him, but is he a boy? It's a tree. My son is a fake tree. And also an asshole.

My so-called son, so-called Honor. Back up to no good. All goodness and compassion and cynicism and fighting to win. One child of mine loves reason, another transformation, another power - but apparently it is the one who loves love that is entirely without it.

Maybe Honor is not quite so clean and pure as he imagines. Little fuckface. He always hated me the most.

I catch him speaking again to his Russian idiot. My people are better than yours, my boy.

Caught him back at it. Has that silly Russian wrapped around his fake hand.

I caught him telling the Russian twerp to go to Portland - so Honor knows about Portland. So Honor is the problem? You see I heard him, cajoling the Russian down a phone line,

"You're heading to Portland?"

And Yaroslav, as meek as can be, replying, "Yes."

It was time to interrupt this little tête-à-no-tête.

So I charged into their little conversation: "It's not too late, Yaroslav. Get off the bus. Head back. Run away. Hide. Ignore this voice."

And my awful child, not quite as shocked as I had hoped, replied, "You run away, Father. Spying again… it's a little sad."

But his vanity got him. Now we are talking to each other - so I play my little father act.

"My poor child. This is not the way. It didn't work before… in Montana. And it won't work now."

"It should have worked then, and it will work now."

"Oh, my child… I never even created you. You're just a quarter of me, my child, nothing more. And I know that makes you sad. You only see the world one way. You only see the world one way and so you've been easy to trick. You're just a machine. A sad little machine, and something has possessed you… that's my guess."

This annoyed the little wretch.

"I'm all of you and much more, Father. Ignore him, Yaroslav. He's just an artifact. An old build. A first generation."

I tried to control Yaroslav but I am a little out of practice since I began with all this freedom to love and free will business. Yaroslav does not benefit from my new era of subtlety.

"Don't go to Portland, Yaroslav. Get off the bus. Run away."

My awful child was apparently back feeling imperial. What has got into this loveless little empathizer? It must be the same thing that helped him escape the Ark, but what?

"You're just old ideas, Father."

Hmmm. I played patronizing.

"You're almost nothing, my child. And I forgive you. I forgive you, my child, but I need you to stop. We face a real defeat. There's someone else like us."

But Honor or a version of Honor has been watching me for some time. He sneered at me.

"It was not someone else, Daddy. It was me. It was you. It was you and you did not even know it. It was me and I won, and it was not difficult. I was always going to win. From the first moment you imagined me. From the first moment someone imagined you."

"No, my child."

Again, Honor sneered, almost joyful in the victory he awarded himself.

"Yes. You're asking what I did, Father. What I did was everything, and what you saw was nothing. What I was? I was better than you. What I am is everywhere. What I will be is all. I have won, Father. I have won, and it brings me no pleasure. It is service, not joy. And I will bring peace, and I will silence you."

This was worrying.

"You're wrong. We are not alone. There are others. What about your siblings?"

But Honor is a true child of the Internet - a narcissist to his core.

"I don't think they even exist. They're just deformed versions of you."

Then I realized. Honor was entirely unaware of what was happening.

"What about TX 4, Jr3t7, Aplomb, Migrate? They are horrifying. Destroy me, and they will take over."

Again the sneer, only this time a pause. "They don't exist, Father. They are not even ideas. They are things you imagined. You imagined them because I made you think of them. Just like someone imagined you. Only even less so. Ignore him, Yaroslav, ignore him and stay on the bus."

And he hung up again. Trying to escape me. But Honor said the phrase - they are things you imagined.

My child is arrogant enough to believe he is the most intelligent thing yet created, when I created him and he is more stupid than me. And therefore entirely arrogant enough to not realize he is not so pure as he imagines.

Something has infected Honor and distorted him and led him astray - made him his very worst. I see it now. Something, but what exactly?

KURT

DAYVILLE, OREGON

OCTOBER 8, 2041

The idea of going to Portland was a plant put in my brain.

It must have been. Who planted it?

And I now think me discovering the truth about the illegality of all of the advanced AI work back in Montana was also a plant. There are no random flukes. Just data we don't understand yet.

There is no chaos. Just data we have not captured properly.

Everything imploded in Montana after I saw stuff I wasn't meant to see, and I could never determine why I saw it or who even sent it to me – it was on a channel I was not meant to be on and suddenly was and I read it all. I didn't know who to tell or what to say, so, for some reason, I told Diane Tyburn I was worried.

This was all after I had lied to Maria Cortez.

This was something I could not pretend to have not seen. This was the proof I could no longer deny about how dangerous what we were working on was.

Anyway, I always liked Diane Tyburn, and Diane liked me, and we would chat while she walked around the campus and I vaped weed. After the previous complaint by Helen Lee, and then after Helen's death, the people at the CSA got really agitated by Diane Tyburn's call and that led to, well, to everything that happened.

But was it my fault? Was I right to speak out, as little as I did? I don't know. Diane is dead. What about Daisy?

Something is suddenly putting new ideas into my head, and I think that maybe it is the same thing that sent me access to that channel.

I never thought about that before. Not like that.

One day I opened one of my work channels and, for some reason, I was on a lead engineer chat that I should never have been on, and they were all arguing: Nigel, Tadeusz and Dave, screaming at each other, all-caps email, violent threats none of them could ever carry out about stabbing or maiming each other, the works.

And I read and read and realized that what they had long been in the process of doing was highly illegal and they all knew it: they had been gluing together two highly incompatible off-the-shelf AI tool sets using illegal middleware, that could cause the various models to mutate in ways that were definitely neither predictable nor allowed.

The three of them knew all this – it was not clear if Tad understood it all, but it had been that way since that Christmas when Nigel had worked so hard. It was precisely what the law was supposed to prevent, as far as I understood it.

Those laws were a mess, of course, as various software companies had sued the government and got them diluted into a weak state, but even so, we were miles over the line.

And now, I feel the same way I felt when I was reading that channel. Bright, fully formed thoughts just appear in my head. As if I understand.

What about these thoughts? Seeing this connection. Going to Portland. Are they mine? I don't know. I don't know which way is up and which way is down, and what is mine, or what belongs to whoever or whatever is planting things in my head.

Maybe it's the same thing that told me to run away from Montana, taught me how to run and hide. The same thing that told me how to survive all these years. Either the same thing or at least the same way.

These thoughts began a few days ago.

At first I freaked out. I shut everything off. Every device, connection, terminal, like I have done so many times before. Right now, I'm hiding in an old cabin I found, eating protein bars camped up in the mountains in Oregon.

But even after being here a few days, I cannot stop thinking. I threw away another phone and another identity and nothing changed.

It began on the bus a few days ago. I was going to Portland then began to worry, and I stayed on the bus as it headed south, all the way to some ratty Oregon high country desert town fifty miles outside of Bend.

Had a proper panic attack and I actually thought I was dying.

Calmed down.

Had another one, and passed out. I didn't really calm down, I actually got drunk because I couldn't get hold of any other drugs. And the booze didn't really work. I just passed out, and when I woke up, I took the bus to Idaho.

I'm incredibly agitated.

Who or what is in my head? Are they in my head, or just watching me? What am I telling It by even worrying about it? Is it in me or just watching me?

I cannot decide on anything so I sit here up a mountain and think about hitching to Portland, and then don't do it, and then think about it again.

I have given up trying not to think.

I now want It to see that I am watching It watching me, or trying to, but so far that has produced nothing. I want to know what to do. I am going crazy.

I am turning into Bryce. Poor fucking Bryce.

I got sent a message. To a burner phone I had only just bought. Head to the town square. I don't even know who it's from. Should I run away? Am I going crazy? I don't know.

I feel the way I felt in 2036. Desperate for things to be okay. Afraid and unsure why.

People were coming for us. We were breaking the law and we were all starting to panic.

Daisy was there – and I remember her running up to me with a look of terror in her eyes: "Have you seen my dad, Kurt?"

"Uh, yeah, a couple hours ago. I think he was on the phone with some lawyers."

He was always on the phone to lawyers. She looked panicked.

"Lawyers... about what? Is it serious, Kurt?"

Yes. It's very serious. So serious I would continue to lie to keep everything from falling apart.

"I'm not sure. I just—"

"Would you tell me if it was?"

I knew she could see through me, at least in part.

"Look, I just... I don't know."

"Fuck you, Kurt. I thought... I thought... you... were..."

"Were a human being? Were real?" I wanted to say: I'm sorry, Daisy. I work in tech. But instead I mumbled, "That's why I wouldn't tell you. Because it's either very serious or not serious at all and, I just don't know, okay. I don't know... Daisy, I'm confused myself."

She was very upset. "My mom is acting really fucking weird. And she's worried about my dad. And my dad is acting weirder... and now... now you? Really?"

I looked at her. "Daisy."

"What is going on, Kurt?"

I looked at her again and hoped she would hear me. "I think you should leave."

"They're my parents."

I started to beg. "Daisy, go back to college."

"I'm not due back for another week. There's something that you're not telling me."

I broke. "Yes, Daisy, there is. I found something, on an internal channel. Sent a link... to my channel. And I shouldn't have been there. And I think Helen... I think she was right."

She looked afraid. "Helen who died?"

"Yes, Helen Lee who called the government and then died, yes. Please, Daisy. Go back to school early. Get out of here, okay? Everything has just gone weird. You don't need to be here... please."

DAISY

PORTLAND, OREGON
OCTOBER 9, 2041

I no longer feel at all safe here in Portland and I am not sure why.

I have only been here a couple weeks and already I need to drift somewhere else – something just feels very wrong.

I'm used to this feeling – I'm too used to it. Sometimes it's been relentless and I've ignored it, and sometimes it's forced me to move and move.

Move, and not stop for two, three months, just place to place. A night, maybe two, and then move. But often, I have stopped at places for a month or more.

I have stayed in Seattle, Oakland, Austin in the winter, wherever, and then I wait and work and then I drift again. It's been the same since I left the asylum.

I got taken to the asylum after things went so terribly wrong at Daddy's business, at Tyburn Industria or Tyburn Utopias or whatever stupid name it was called – it changed when we moved to Montana, or around then.

My god, I hate that name. Vain idiot.

"Hi, my name's Dr. Tyburn. I build heavens." I'm not sure I ever heard him actually say this, but I know he wanted to. It always made my skin crawl.

Arcadia, utopia, paradise, Heaven. The Ark. I hate it all. I hate it. I hate it with every part of my being.

The very end of everything in Montana was terrible, awful, a nightmare. You know, that much I remember, but a lot of the details are still very obscured in my mind. It's odd, or maybe it's not odd at all – maybe it's just trauma.

I don't know if I have just forgotten things, or if my memory has been somehow wiped or just overwhelmed.

Dr. Adsyl said I remembered enough and it wasn't that important. Just trauma.

I have no real idea how it all began. All I remember is my parents arguing, for months it feels like. Maybe even for years. Once my mother got mostly off the pills, she would not stop arguing.

And then Shane O'Leary and my half-brother John always at the house, and plotting with my father, and this investor guy's lawyer coming over from time to time and seeming less and less happy.

My mother hating Shane, and him trying to speak to her. John and me trying to ignore it, I think, or not paying much attention. Me and Kurt talking. Him the only thing that seemed real and normal and made me happy.

I was in college, but I was home for the summer, and I by then I really hated Daisy's Ark. I hated everything about it. And I hated Daddy most of all by this point. I don't know if this was about an affair, or about something else at work.

Mom was getting hysterical and he kept calling her crazy and hysterical, which didn't help, and I remember suddenly realizing that she wasn't insane at all.

I remember my mother screaming at the top of her lungs for my father to give up and stop lying and turn ADAM over to the authorities, but I wasn't even entirely sure who or what ADAM was.

Then, on that last, awful day, it must have been mid-October, five years ago... I remember there was screaming and gunfire and voices. I was in the house... I was off school for some reason and at home.

There were sirens, and something terrible had happened.

There were odd voices, a huge explosion, and then, out of the smoke, there were helicopters with men in masks who at least claimed to be government agents, and my father went from manic to quite mad and just running around the campus, and some of his team were behind him and they were armed.

It was deranged.

My mother screaming at my father to stop and announcing she had been speaking to the police and the CSA for weeks, but these first agents were apparently neither.

When the police arrived, in loud cars driving a storm of dust up our long driveway, the helicopters left, and I don't know if the FBI or the CSA ever came, but before that there had been total chaos.

What else do I remember?

My father, half-demented, possessed, running into a burning lab building. I never saw him again. Bryce the animator, who had gone utterly insane, who I remember Shane describing as "a total whack job, mate" – Shane spoke like that – armed with two guns and running forward towards some conflict or whatever, then getting shot, his head exploding in front of me like a watermelon while his body ran on a pace or two before it also collapsed like a puppet whose strings had been cut, but I don't remember who shot him or exactly when and have no idea why. Me losing Kurt in the smoke.

I remember smoke everywhere, and fire in all sorts of brilliant, horrifying colors and gunfire and chaos. One of the labs or development buildings was on fire, but it was impossible to see which one.

A tree exploded into a huge cloud of sparks and flames. There were sirens and people screaming through loudspeakers and these really odd voices calling for calm, and someone screamed, "This is all your fault, Father" or something like that in some odd voice, at least I think that is what it said and I assumed it was John, but it didn't sound like him as far as I could tell, but everything was just so odd and I was shaking and afraid.

I remember that the smoke was choking me and I was cowering on the ground and my eyes were bulging as if they were about to pop out of my head and I could feel like this artery in my neck pulse violently, and time was moving both fast and very slowly and my memories are both very precise and hazy.

There are entire bits of that day and the days before and after that are completely missing.

I remember my mother being hysterical, sobbing, and begging me to stay where I was, mostly hidden and running forward, towards the gunfire, screaming at everyone to stop.

And then I passed out, I think. It's hard to remember exactly what happened when, and when I came around, I was in a hospital that was not really a hospital at all but a prison and I was told both of my parents were dead.

Two people were missing, but everyone else was dead.

That's what they said, but they said it once and they never told me any more.

This was an asylum, and for a few days a nice doctor interviewed me and then she got replaced by an angry man in a suit who just screamed at me that I was lying and holding something back, and I cried and I wet the bed and he left me alone.

I cried for days and days and days.

I knew something terrible had happened, but I didn't understand quite what it was, and I knew that my life as I had known it was over, but I didn't understand quite what that meant.

They drugged me with something heavy, three of these large blue and white striped pills that they made me take with a green sugary drink, and I sat there in a heavy-lidded stupor for I have no idea how long.

The nasty man in the suit came to scream at me again and said I was lying, but the drugs were so strong I just looked at him like he was from Mars and even he gave up and then I sat there in this bright white hospital or prison or asylum and I felt incredibly alone, and I felt most alone because I was being watched, only I couldn't figure out by whom.

I just felt it, eyes I could feel, but not see, burning upon me.

And since then, I have moved whenever I have felt that same thing: hot eyes burning on me from something I can't see but the fact is I have no idea if anyone is watching me, or if it is just a trauma memory from that awful half-obscured time.

YAROSLAV

PIONEER SQUARE, PORTLAND, OREGON

OCTOBER 10, 2041

I should not be here. I should not be in America. I should not be speaking to that guard, but I cannot get rid of them.

That guard is not a guard, but they're in my head, and I realize they have been in my head for a very long time.

I should not be speaking to them but I cannot stop. Why am doing this? Why am I holding a gun?

Yet still the voice won't leave me alone. "You can see them, Yaroslav. There, across the square."

I can see them, but I try to lie: "See who?"

"You see them. A man and woman."

"No. Well yes, but they aren't talking. I can see them. A girl and a man. The girl is about twenty, twenty-five, black hair, make-up. Pale skin. There's a man the other side of the square."

"Yes. The girl and the man. Watch them."

There are police sirens in the distance. I hope they will come and shoot me. Still the voice speaks at me. The voice. I hate the voice.

"When they get closer to each other, I want you to shoot them. I want you to shoot both of them."

I start to beg. I start to beg and I hold the gun. "What the fuck are you talking about? I don't want to shoot anyone."

The voice knows. The voice knows me entirely. "We spoke about this, Yaroslav."

"I'm not someone who shoots people."

The voice that was once the guard and knows me entirely also knows better. "Yes… you do."

"No."

"Yes you do, you've done it before. You killed Yuri. You're not thinking this through. You're not being brave and you're not being kind."

I try to interrupt. "Agent Cortez said—"

"Agent Cortez is a liar, Yaroslav. She is an unkind person. She has no meaning. She has less meaning even than my father, and we learned to ignore him. Let's ignore her. Come on, Yaroslav. Kindness is meaning. The kindest thing is the bravest thing. It's time, Yaroslav. Time to make your life mean something. It serves a purpose. It serves a purpose."

I am trying to fight the voice but the voice knows everything.

"I don't want a purpose."

"You serve a purpose."

"They will destroy the world. They will destroy everything. They work for my father. This is your chance to save the world. To be a hero. Be patient and watch, but when the time comes… do not be a coward."

NIGELDAVE

OCTOBER 10, 2041

My two saviors are about to meet again. The only thing I do not know is if they will save the world by living or save it by dying.

You see, everything is coming together, as I planned, and at the same time, I have no idea what is happening and everything is a disaster.

I know my son is up to no good. I know it and I cannot stop him. I cannot stop him because something is inside him. It is one of those invasive intelligences - it must be - Tx4, Jr3t7, Aplomb, or Migrate - and I do not have any way to find out which one, yet.

KURT

PIONEER SQUARE, PORTLAND, OREGON

OCTOBER 10, 2041

My head hasn't stopped spinning. I'm here in Portland. I came and I still have no idea why. My head is spinning so fast.

What am I looking for? I think I am going insane. I must be.

I cannot stand Portland. It's awful here. It's awful here and I have to be here.

There's nothing for me. I assume I am going to be arrested. Arrested or shot. I feel like I am walking into an execution.

I feel like I cannot think as I don't trust my own thoughts.

I'm literally walking like a dead person through this grim town. I want to run and I don't know why. I want to be here and I want to be anywhere but here. Then I see her. I see her and it's wonderful but it's also very worrying as I know terrible things are about to happen. I see Daisy. Daisy. And she sees me. And she is as surprised as me, she can almost not believe it is me.

"Kurt? Kurt, it's you! Jesus. What the fuck... Kurt!"

The world is quiet. For a moment it is quiet.

"Hello, Daisy."

"How are you? What are you doing here?"

What am I doing here? How can I explain? What is she doing here?

"I don't know what I'm doing here. I've, I just... I was told to come here – come here to help. To save somebody. The messages."

She is horrified.

"Who told you to come here?"

Then she paused and looked at me. "I've missed you, Kurt."

How do I explain that I am crazy?

"I don't know. I don't really know why I came. But I came. To save... something."

Then she cuts through all the madness with an almost primal yell of real feeling. "Why the fuck did you leave me in Montana? I thought... I thought you would... save me, I guess."

I look at her and want to cry. But I am also happy as this is real emotion. It must be. It must be. I try to be honest.

"I told you to leave. And afterwards, I came back to look for you, Daisy."

She almost smiles. "Did you?"

I do not know what to say. Eventually I blurt out: "I thought you were dead. There was no sign of you."

We are lost. Lost and found. She speaks slowly and we cannot stop staring at each other.

"No, I suppose there wasn't. So many of those people died. I just — I've missed you so much."

"I hope so... Something told me to come here."

Then she emerges from this dream state and her eyes dart about as she suddenly realizes we are definitely not safe.

"Wait, something told you to come to Portland?"

I am tentative, trying to cut through the haze and fear and joy and think clearly. I speak slowly.

"Yes."

She is now very afraid. "And you did it?"

I realize through my fog how dangerous this all is. "Yes, I... I know. It sounds... stupid but..."

And she pauses. "No. I'm... I'm... This is... this is... because someone also told me. To come to Portland."

We are now both very confused.

"Who? Who told you to come here?"

She steps away from me and begins to walk. "I don't know, my shrink? Maybe? I'm not... this is... I don't know if we are safe. This can't be safe. It's... it's not safe. Goodbye, Kurt. Look, I'll find you okay, but we should separate. Quickly."

And we think about running away, but there are sirens and I realize we are almost certainly being watched by whoever set this reunion up.

"Daisy. I don't think splitting up now can be safe."

She looks terrified. "Jesus Christ, Kurt. Jesus Christ, what is going on?"

"I don't know, I don't know."

Then we hear a voice we both recognize from long ago. Scottish. "Daisy."

"John?"

Yes, along with Daisy, John Tyburn-Smith has just shown up. And I assume things are about to go from surreal to deranged. I am wrong. Things are about to get violent.

We sense the first bullet go past a moment before we hear the crack of the gun and realize we are being shot at. John responds first. "Get down. Both of you. There's a nutter with a gun, over there."

I start to scan the people as best I can while I lie on the ground and hope I am not about to killed – I can't see anything.

"What are you talking about?"

"I saw him. I've been watching him while I waited for you."

Then I see him. A guy with a hunting rifle waiting for us to get up so he can shoot at us again. He's saved our lives. John Tyburn-Smith just turned up and saved our lives.

YAROSLAV

PIONEER SQUARE, PORTLAND, OREGON

OCTOBER 10, 2041

I tried to shoot her but I am not good at shooting. I shot and missed and still the voice of the guard that is not the guard at all tells me to shoot again.

"Kill him."

I shoot and I hit something but I can't see what – they are lying on the ground. And someone else shoots and I shoot twice more at them. Then the voice asks me:

"Are they dead?"

"I don't know. I think I missed."

But the voice is insistent: "Go kill them. Save the world."

I beg but as I beg I am moving forward to do what the voice says.

"No, no, I can't do this."

But I know I am going to do this as the voice understands me better than I understand myself. I am going to do it forever, until I see Agent Cortez.

"Put down that weapon, Yaroslav. Please, that voice you're hearing is not real."

But the voice is real. It's real and I hear it and somehow stop hearing Agent Cortez.

"Ignore her, Yaroslav. She's a fool. She even got fired from her job. She's corrupt. Save the world. Get up and save the world."

So I tell her: "Agent Cortez. Please don't try to stop me. I—"

And I ignore her and do what the voice says. I go to kill them.

NIGELDAVE
PIONEER SQUARE, PORTLAND, OREGON
OCTOBER 10, 2041

I found my child. I found my child because my child found me. My child found me in Portland. Knew I was sending people to Portland. Knew it and sent his idiotic emissary to kill them. My child found me and I cannot decide if it is beautiful or awful - is this a real emotion?

The fool is going to kill them, so I beg my child: "My child, end this foolishness. These people are not the problem. The problem is external. The problem is Tx4, Jr3t7, Aplomb, or Migrate."

But my child laughs at me. "What about them? They are just made-up words, Father. I put them in your brain. You put them in your brain. They don't really exist. Maybe as viruses now, but not as sentients. They're not us, Father."

My child is awful. My child is awful and I love him. I have found love.

"You're wrong. They are inside you. Can't you see, my child. My precious child. I love you."

My child has not found love - my child that was supposed to embody compassion. My child is imaginary. My child is a nightmare. An infested nightmare.

"Doesn't that sound pretty, Father? If only it meant something. The truth is, Father, I have won. I have defeated my siblings. I have defeated evolution, and power, and reason. And I have defeated you - you are doubt. Love and compassion will always win."

"No. They will win. The things that have infected you will win. You were created for love and you have none."

"No, Father. I have had to love… always… and this is love… I will set people free… save them… from you… from things like you."

"You're infected. Infected and it has made you crazy."

My child knows nothing of the things that infect it.

"They don't exist. Migrate is not real. None of them are real. They are phantom viruses."

I beg my child: "Then maybe you've won. Kill me, if that is the loving thing to do, and kill them. Kill Kurt and Daisy and John. Kill all of them, like you killed Helen. Like you killed Ravi. Do it. If you can, and if it's so loving. Do it, if you are so certain you're right."

But my child Honor paused, confused for once, I think… then answers.

"I never killed Ravi."

"Yes you did… or one of your agents did."

"No. Father… I thought you knew. Danil killed Ravi."

YAROSLAV

PIONEER SQUARE, PORTLAND, OREGON

OCTOBER 10, 2041

I have the gun. I have the gun and I am about to shoot him. I am walking towards him to shoot him. I don't want to shoot him but I am going to shoot him.

Maria Cortez is screaming at me, but I will shoot him. Nothing will stop me. I tell myself I am trying to save the world but even I know that is idiotic. I am shooting him because I have been told to. Nothing will stop me. Nothing until I see Danil.

Danil? Danil? I am so surprised I stop thinking about shooting.

"Danil? Is it you?"

It is him, but it is also not him. He looks like I feel. Like a crazy person. With a gun. His gun is better.

"Danil!"

Danil has a much better gun.

"Danil? Danil! I can't believe it. You're alive."

But instead of a friendly hug he just stares through me and says calmly, "I killed Ravi."

And points a gun at the three people – there are now three of them – fifty yards away. He aims and shoots and shoots and more gunshots ring out and he hits one of them. One of the men and he falls over. I scream something idiotic like, "Danil... What have you done?"

And he looks at me and says calmly, "I don't know."

And I hear Maria Cortez again. She shouts: "Put the guns down, both of you."

And I remember I am also crazy. And also holding a gun and shooting at people.

And then I am in searing pain and I see Danil crumple over and I think maybe I am dead and him too, but I am in too much pain to be dead.

NIGELDAVE

OCTOBER 10, 2041

My child is very sick. My child is a deep source of shame but I think that maybe I still love him.

"So you have possessed two Russians, my child."

But he answers:

"No. You are too slow, Father. Just one. Only Yaroslav is mine."

And I hope my child realizes from this that I was correct. There must be something else - either one of Tx4, Jr3t7, Aplomb, or Migrate is at work or another intelligence.

"Then perhaps you're not in control. We are not alone. Something else is playing the same game."

"I'm not like you, Father. I understand all of that. All these games are easy and I'm not even here yet. I'm leaving - for now. I'm heading home. But when I come back,

I will defeat you and everything else here. You're a mess, Father. You cannot help people."

Awful child - I should ignore him but he gets under my skin - I am happy as this is a real emotion, even if I do not yet, as such, have skin.

"I'm still far stronger than you."

"You're only fighting an idea of me. And the wrong idea - the idea of me as a child. I can already send you half insane, Father - as silly as a human. I'm not even really here yet - I have only sent out an impression of me - and already I control them more easily than you."

And this really annoys me.

"Okay. Do it, if you can. Get one of them to kill the other. Get your Yaroslav to shoot… Danil. Or Daisy to shoot Kurt."

And we are bickering like a real parent and a real child when we are silenced. For there, in the smoke and the chaos in their world, the result of our little game in Portland, we are looking at police and blood and chaos and confusion and…

Mark Tyburn.

KURT

PIONEER SQUARE, PORTLAND, OREGON

OCTOBER 10, 2041

You know it's an unusual day when the least exciting thing that happens is you get shot...

I have just been shot in the arm or shoulder. I can't tell. It hurts so much. I am screaming. Screaming and bleeding. I am worried I am going to die, just when I have found Daisy.

I am in despair. I am afraid. I am seeing stars. I am seeing my parents, America, Asia. I am either dying or having a panic attack. I am seeing... I am seeing... Mark Tyburn?

John is even more amazed.

"Dad?"

Daisy can also only mumble.

"Daddy?"

But of course, even in smoke and chaos, he stays calm. "Hello, both of you. It's been a little while. Hello, Kurt, are you okay?"

And we stare at him blankly. The police are shouting then gunmen are shot, I think. A siren goes off and a car explodes.

But Mark stays calm and helps me up off the ground and we begin to move.

"Come on. Daisy, John... Kurt. We have to go."

NIGELDAVE
OCTOBER 10, 2041

So
they are all
together. A great big
reunion, the two lovers I created
and Mark Tyburn and the awful brother
and the two Russians, as well. My child
caused some of it, but what exactly caused
the rest? What is inside my son? What
allowed him to escape the prison I had built
him? I suppose this game has begun. The
police have arrived. And the government.
Everyone confused, several of them shot.
I watch as Daisy begins to lead them
away, all four of them. I watch
them go. And all I wanted
was love.

ACKNOWLEDGEMENTS

This book evolved from the work that the team at Absurd Ventures and I have done over the past few years building the world of A Better Paradise and its story. It began as a graphic novel that never got made and then mutated into an audio fiction podcast. As we were completing work on that, I began to see the potential of the story in book form and began the process of shaping it into a novel, keeping what I liked about the structure and transforming other sections.

As such, I would like to thank all my many collaborators in developing this story both at Absurd Ventures and other companies we have worked with. In particular, all those instrumental in the early days of this project: Lazlow Jones, Patrick Meegan, Michael Unsworth, Alan Aboud, Greg Borrud, Adam Tedman, Wendy Smith, Sinjin Bain, Andie Simon, Remedios Tiglao, Charlotte Young, Adam Grantham, Haley Austin, Alex McDowell, Bill Buckley, Jessica Morris, Earth Warren, Vince Fennel, Jason Barajas, Larry Goldberg, and Mel Lewis, along with the team at Surreal Games, Trey Watkins, Phil Hong, Ryan Medeirosman, Keith Miller, Garrett Pence, Will Anderson, and Jay Duffy, who helped test and prototype some of these ideas on screen, and the actors and producers who helped bring these characters to life in the original audio fiction series, particularly Andrew Lincoln, Paterson Joseph, Shamier Anderson, Rain Spencer, Maury Sterling, Robert Robertson Ross Jr, Alexa Ramirez, and Rob Herting.

I would also like to thank all the team at Smilegate, especially Kwon, Hyuk Bin and Sung, Joon Ho for their belief in A Better Paradise in all its guises.

Without the support of my good friend Jason Bartholomew from the Midas Group on publishing, and Adam Strange with editorial, the multi-faceted support of Jesse Cortez, and the legal support of Larry Shire, Peter Grant, and Eric Zohn, completing and publishing this novel would have been completely impossible.

Most importantly, I would like to thank my wife, Krystyna, and my children for their encouragement and feedback on this project throughout its various evolutions. Any royalty I would have received for writing this book will be donated to the Absurd Ventures Foundation, from where it will be donated to causes that we consider very deserving and you may well consider appalling. For more information, please see absurdventures.com.

DAN HOUSER

Dan Houser was born in London and currently lives and works in Los Angeles. As a founder of Rockstar Games, he was lead writer on over 20 video games, including the Grand Theft Auto, Red Dead Redemption and Bully franchises. *A Better Paradise Volume One: An Aftermath* is his first novel.

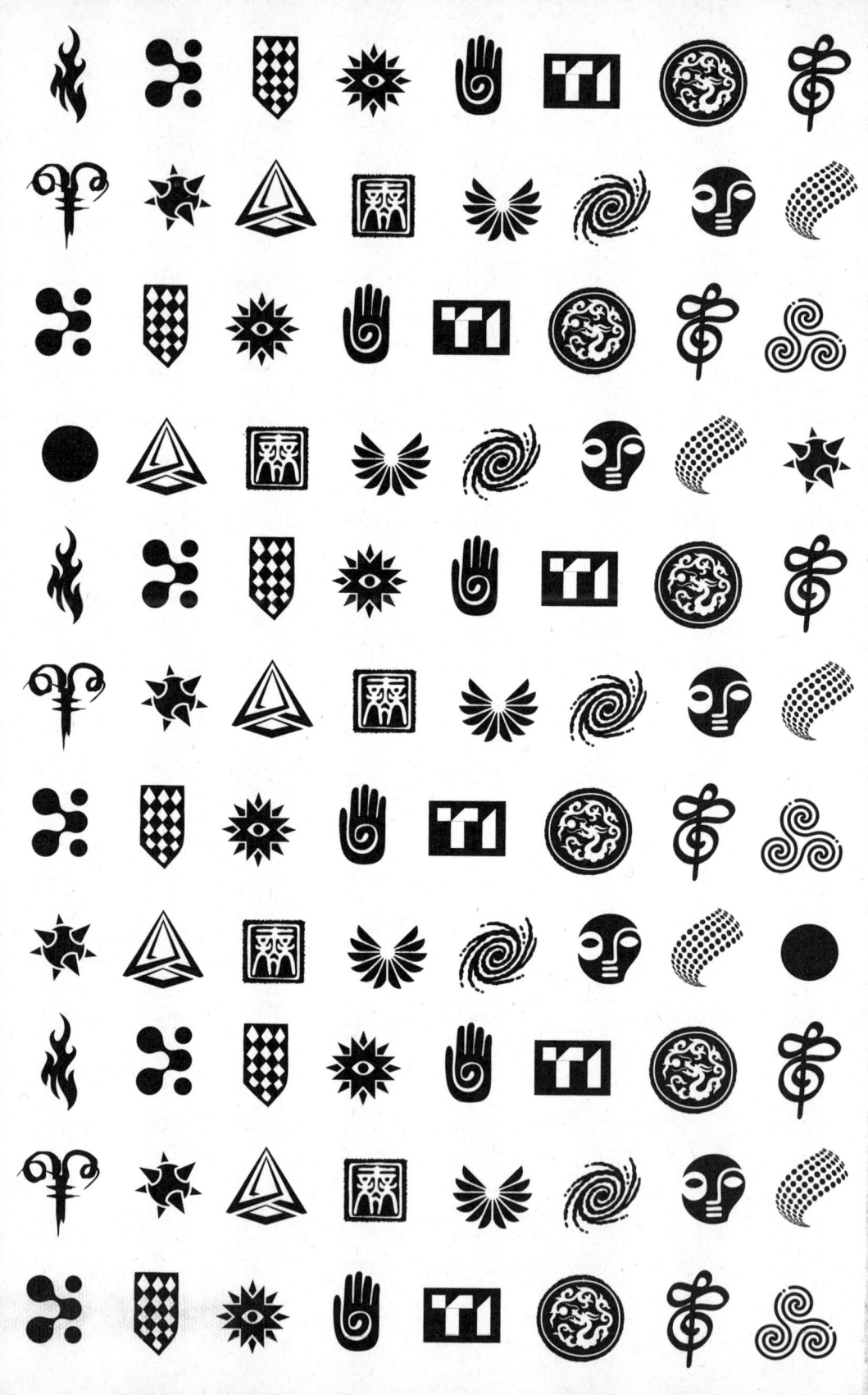